Big Book of American Ghost Stories

Jannette Quackenbush

Copyright © 2025 by Jannette Quackenbush
Dark Journeys with Jannette/21 Crows
ISBN-13: 978-1-940087-68-9

Jannette Quackenbush is an author of over 50 books, folklorist, naturalist, and paranormal researcher. She focuses on ghost stories, folklore, and hiking trails in the Appalachian and southern U.S. Known for her engaging storytelling, she has published many works on local legends and haunted places. Her project, "Dark Journeys with Jannette," features guided hikes where participants explore haunted sites and learn about the region's folklore, connecting them to the rich cultural history and stories of the area.

Alabama

A Ghost with a Coffin

Old Creek Road was once a primary route for locals connecting Marion Junction and Union Town in south central Alabama. However, it fell into disuse and was largely abandoned by the late 1800s in favor of a modern and more reliable turnpike. After so many years off the beaten path, it would have become entirely forgotten if not for roadwork on the turnpike in the early 1890s. During this construction, travelers were detoured to the old road to avoid the work being done.

If it weren't for the latter, a ghost haunting a specific area might have gone unnoticed. One late night, the local physician, Doctor Hardeman, was riding home on horseback after visiting a patient. It was dark, with no moonlight illuminating the night sky. However, he noticed a figure by the path: a man dressed in a dark suit and wearing a wide-brimmed straw hat, standing near a tall tree. He wore no coat or vest but coiled around his neck was a rope that trailed behind the figure for several feet. So tightly drawn was the rope that the man's face was gruesomely bloated and his neck swollen to three times the standard size.

Shocked, the doctor called out to the man several times. When the figure turned to look back at him, his bloated eyes seemed to glow, yet he did not respond. Doctor Hardeman tried to catch up with the man by urging his horse forward, but the horse reared, snorted, and refused to move further. Suddenly, the horse bucked without warning, throwing the doctor to the ground. The horse galloped away, leaving the doctor alone in the darkness. To make matters more bizarre, the ghostly figure had disappeared near the edge of the road. Disturbed, the doctor quickly left the scene, planning to return the following night, better prepared to investigate the strange mystery.

Doctor Hardeman returned the next night with a young man and a dog. Both men were armed with shotguns and revolvers, prepared to wait for the ghostly figure to reappear. Although no apparition materialized, a distinct moaning and groaning emanated from the same tree where the figure had stood the previous night. The dog leaped toward the tree repeatedly as if trying to attack an unseen presence, only to be thrown back each time. In a final charge, the dog was flung at the feet of its owners, dead from a broken neck. Fearing for their safety, the men left, vowing to return during the day.

The next morning, the doctor and his companion returned and caught sight of a ghostly figure floating near the tree. Behind him, he dragged a coffin. The doctor called out to the apparition, who turned to face him, his bloated features disconcerting. A ghastly grin spread across his face, causing the doctor's companion to flee in terror. The unnerved Doctor Hardeman followed closely behind.

Naturally, the townspeople dismissed their tale as mere ghost stories often are. However, several prominent residents decided to investigate the claims the following evening, armed with guns, to prove it was a hoax. As midnight approached, eerie moans began to fill the air, gradually escalating into loud bellows and wails that echoed through the forest.

Before long, the phantom appeared—its grotesquely shaped face framed by a rope twisted around its neck. This time, it carried a coffin on its shoulders. Among the group was Colonel Nugent, a man known for his level-headedness and bravery, who rushed forward and stepped on the trailing rope. Instantly, he was thrown violently to the ground, unconscious. The apparition vanished in a fog-like mist, accompanied by a loud, mocking laugh, and was not seen again that night. When Colonel Nugent regained consciousness hours later, he described the experience as feeling like an electric shock coursed through his body the moment he stepped on the rope.

In every community, there are always skeptics, and Judge Blackmore was the biggest doubter in Marion Junction. He mocked the locals about their ghost stories so much that he was ultimately challenged to confront the Old Road Phantom without fear. Accepting the wager, the judge, cocky and a bit egotistical about the whole matter, set out one night to call out the ghost, daring it to show itself and scare him.

A few moments later, his horse began to spook, its eyes wide with suspicion. The judge tightened his grip on the reins to steady the animal. Just as the horse became unsettled, a figure emerged before him. The judge was startled to see a man with swollen, bloated blue cheeks and a rope dangling around his neck grinning up at him. Startled, Judge Blackmore reined in his horse and took a few steps back. He raised his whip and struck at the ghostly figure, but the apparition kept pace with him. With another swipe of his whip, the judge hit the ghost, only for it to leap at him, wrapping its arms around his body and dragging him to the ground. The horse, startled, galloped away as the phantom's cold fingers tightened around the judge's neck, beginning to strangle him.

Suddenly, the judge regained his composure, fought off the ghost, and hurled it aside. Had the ghost not fallen across the coffin it dragged and lost, the judge might never have escaped. Seizing the moment, Judge Blackmore fled and found refuge in a nearby house. The ghost lingered outside all night, peering into the windows and knocking on the doors, only vanishing with the dawn.

It was only a matter of time before someone discovered the existence of the ghost. In 1889, an elderly woman named Nancy Pratt lived along the old creek road. She was found dead in the creek with wounds on her head, and most people believed her death was suspicious, as it seemed she had been killed before being dumped into the water. Shortly after her death, a tramp was found behaving strangely and had some of Miss Pratt's jewelry in his possession. He reported seeing the old lady rush out of her house, her head bleeding from wounds. Believing she had drowned after throwing herself into the creek, he took it upon himself to enter her home and steal her belongings, thinking she wouldn't need them anymore.

Nobody believed his outrageous story, and without any formal judicial proceedings, he was taken to a tree and lynched. This was the very tree where the ghost was later seen along the creek. After the hanging, some members of the community recalled that the old woman had threatened to kill herself many times, leading many to question whether the justice served was indeed faulty. As no one could determine how to make amends for the wrongs done to the tramp, nothing was done to rectify the situation. It gradually faded from memory, especially after the new turnpike was built. Although few traveled the road and the incident was nearly forgotten, the ghost returned to haunt the site of his tragic fate for many years, and he probably still does.

Alabama
Another Notch on Aunt Jenny's Hickory Stick

During the Civil War, the Confederacy implemented a draft due to a shortage of men willing to fight and a high number of casualties. Initially, it required all Southern white men aged 18 to 35 to serve for three years. Later, the age range was expanded to include men between 17 and 50. This move was met with resentment, particularly from those in the Appalachian Mountains, who believed that the wealthy were using the poor to fight their battles. They wanted nothing to do with a conflict they felt didn't affect their way of life.

The Confederate government had the authority to seize food, crops, enslaved individuals, fuel, and other supplies to support the armies in the field. Those who refused to comply faced the action of the Home Guard—men who, for various reasons such as age or disability, could not serve in combat.

The Home Guard was tasked with tracking down draft dodgers, also known as absentees without official leave, and Northern sympathizers. They were also responsible for confiscating property and crops to support the military, often taking resources from those who were already struggling to make ends meet and could not afford to lose their food supplies and livestock.

The government's strong arm significantly impacted many individuals, including a family who operated a hotel and tavern on Byler Road, not far from Kinlock Road. Although this section appears remote today, Byler Road was Alabama's first public road authorized in 1819. It was a 140-mile corridor for a stage route that transported cotton from the Tennessee River near Muscle Shoals in northern Alabama to the Black Warrior River near Tuscaloosa, a hub for transporting cotton to the Port of Mobile and ultimately to Europe. The inn was owned by "Aunt" Jenny and Willis Brooks, who lived there with their nine children.

This story is not primarily about the inn, the historic road, or the Confederate Army. Instead, these elements serve to connect Aunt Jenny to her life story—one that might never have been shared if not for a well-known vendetta arising from the war and the inn's connection to those who sought refuge within its walls. Moreover, some ghostly tales follow.

Aunt Jenny, born Jane Bates in 1826, was a half-Cherokee woman known locally for her midwife skills, spiritual healing through the laying on of hands, and herbal remedies. Like many pioneer women in the Appalachian Mountains and foothills, she lived a quiet life along Byler Road, where her family had a reputation for causing no trouble and being left undisturbed in return. However, everything changed for Aunt Jenny one fateful night in late 1863 or early 1864. Eight Confederate Home Guards arrived at her family's home.

Some say they were accusing Willis Brooks, her family member, of harboring war deserters hiding in the backwoods, both Union and Confederate. Others believe they might have come to draft John, her 18-year-old son. Regardless, at gunpoint, they captured Willis Brooks, bound him, then tortured him in front of Jenny and the young children-15-year-old Angeline, 13-year-old Mack, 11-year-old Amanda, 9-year-old Willis Jr., 7-year-old Donner, 3-year-old Gainum, and the infant Henry. Then they put a noose around Willis's neck and hanged him. John burst from the front door, and the Home Guard shot him dead. Legends said that Aunt Jenny laid her husband and son side by side and gathered the children around her. She placed each boy's hand into the blood on Willis's chest, swearing a "blood oath," a solemn promise that none of them would rest until all eight of the murderers were dead.

And so, the vendetta would begin. Following the murders of Aunt Jenny's husband and son, she trained her boys in marksmanship with the intent of avenging their deaths. Jenny and her son Mack shot the leader of the Home Guard off his horse. They dragged his body into the woods, cut off his head, and carried it home in an old burlap feed sack. She boiled that skull clean of the flesh, then used it to make a soap dish. Over time, some say forty years, several individuals implicated in the killings faced violent retribution, and seven of the eight men eventually met violent ends. Everyone knew how many because Aunt Jenny had a hickory walking stick with a notch for each act of retribution to the initial eight. And there were seven notches. When someone pointed out that the eighth was missing and most likely dead, she never claimed the last, although nobody knew the reason. And as Aunt Jenny was quoted to say later, "But seven uv 'em has been got."

Gainum Brooks was killed on April 12, 1884, during a gunfight with a neighboring family over a horse dispute. His death occurred at the feet of his mother, Aunt Jenny. As time passed, Mack found work as a cowboy in Texas around 1872. Still, he returned periodically to seek vengeance against those implicated in his father's death. Willis Brooks Jr. became involved in the ongoing vendetta against their father's killers. Although he married and settled down, he continued to be part of the family retribution efforts alongside his brothers until they eventually moved away from Alabama. Henry was shot dead in early 1920 by a large posse from nearby Winston County while he was making moonshine.

Aunt Jenny lived to be 98 years old and died on March 29, 1924, outliving all of her children. She once said proudly about her sons' quest for vengeance for their father and brother, "They all died like men, with their boots on!"

People who knew her well described her as kind. However, her kindness depended on how you treated her. But if you upset her, her demeanor could change dramatically, showing a fierce side. This mix of compassion and strength made her both loved and feared. Simply said, "Just don't get on Aunt Jenny's bad side, or you'll end up as another notch on her hickory stick!"

Aunt Jenny's legacy continues. Her grave has been reported to glow for those fortunate enough to see it, and her spirit has occasionally been sighted. Witnesses describe seeing the apparition of an older woman dressed in period clothing, accompanied by eerie sounds or lights. Her spirit lingers as Aunt Jenny watches over her descendants and the land she once inhabited.

Alabama
The Hole That Won't Go Away

On Alabama Highway 134 near Newton, a bridge spans the Choctawhatchee River. Like most bridges, it is designed to support a significant amount of vehicular weight. It is constructed with steel, guardrails, and concrete. However, this bridge has an unusual feature. There was once a hole beneath it that was consistently kept clear by the toes of a man hanged above. This man is William "Bill" Sketoe, a figure shrouded in mystery and legend. His tale unfolds in many versions, but they all share a chilling climax: a hanging and a haunting presence that refuses to be forgotten.

William Sketoe was a 46-year-old Methodist minister in December 1864. He had been serving in the Confederate Army since 1861. Still, when he learned that his wife was gravely ill, he returned home to care for her after a companion offered to take his place in the army temporarily. However, upon his return, word quickly reached the local Newton Home Guard, commanded by Joseph Breare. Breare was a lawyer who had been captured at Gettysburg and later exchanged.

After his return home, Breare took on the role of commander of the local Home Guard, whose duty was to track down and punish deserters. He was well-known for his harsh methods, having already hanged two men for desertion. He learned from sources that Sketoe's absence had not been approved, and the minister may have been aiding pro-Union traitors. On December 3rd, 1864, Breare set out to hunt down the man and found him crossing the wooden bridge over the Choctawhatchee River near Newton.

The Home Guards dragged Sketoe into the nearby woods, forcing him to crawl on the ground like a pig while they beat him about the head and back. Breare's men then dragged him into an old buggy. A man familiar with Bill Sketoe passed by and tried to talk the men out of killing him, but Breare would have none of it. Fearing for his own life, the man left for Newton to get help.

Now under pressure to perform the execution before help arrived, a name named Ardis jumped to action, slipped a rope around Sketoe's neck, and swung the rope over an oak limb. Sketoe was asked if he had any last words to say, and he answered. "I wish to pray." But instead of praying for his own soul, he implored God to forgive the men who were murdering him. The insinuation that they were the evil ones enraged the Home Guards. Breare whipped the horse pulling the buggy and sent it forward, leaving Sketoe hanging from the limb. But Bill Sketoe was a tall man, and along with his weight that bent the limb, his feet touched the ground erratically and frantically in a vain attempt to release the pressure of the rope. Quickly, one of the men who walked with a crutch swept in and gouged a hole in the dirt so that Sketoe slowly died from strangulation while his toes barely swept across the leaves and dirt.

Shortly thereafter, James Judah returned with men from Newton. They removed the corpse from the tree and placed it in a cotton house until the family could claim it. He was later buried at Mt. Carmel Cemetery.

The epitaph on his grave reads, "Our dear father, gone but not forgotten." How true those words would prove to be. For over 126 years, a hole approximately two and a half feet in diameter and eight inches deep, where Bill Sketoe's toes once swept across the leaves and dirt, remained. Whenever anyone attempted to fill it, the next day, it would reappear. In 1871, a bridge was built over the hole, but it was soon washed away. Workers and campers at the site noted that if they filled the hole each night, it would be empty again by morning. Rumors circulated that a friend of Bill Sketoe's, Wash Reynolds, secretly dug it out each night. However, he denied it; even after his death, the hole persisted.

As for the Home Guards, local legends tell of their terrible, mysterious deaths. One met his end while riding on a calm day when a large limb from an oak tree fell on him. Another was killed by a runaway mule. A third was struck by lightning, and a fourth was found dead in a swampy bog.

Today, the old hole is gone, buried beneath the rip-rap laid to support the bank. However, a monument has been placed at the site of Sketoe's murder, and people still come to visit it.

Haunting Shorts: Alabama

• Within Maple Hill Cemetery in Huntsville lies the Dead Children's Playground, an eerie spot that comes alive with the laughter and playful spirit of ghostly children. Visitors often report witnessing the swings swaying gently as if pushed by unseen hands.

• The Drish House in Tuscaloosa is haunted. In 1867, Doctor John Drish died in an accidental fall down a stairwell in his large, stuccoed brick mansion. After his death, his wife, Sarah, saved his funeral candles for her future use. However, when she passed away in 1884, the candles were nowhere to be found. Enraged, her ghostly hands lit the candles in her third-story tower, resulting in what appeared to be a fire. Even today, mysterious lights come from the building at night.

• Sloss Furnace in Birmingham operated from 1882 to 1971, transforming coal and ore into steel. It holds the key to the story of the ghost of James "Slag" Wormwood, who haunts the site. In 1906, Wormwood fell to his death into a blast furnace. Some believe he was dizzy from the gases and lost his footing, while others tell a more disturbing tale: that he pushed his workers too hard to impress his bosses, leading angry employees to toss him into the melted iron ore. After his death, workers reported seeing a badly burned man wandering through the furnace.

• Fort Morgan, located along the Gulf Shore at Mobile Point, has stood since 1834, providing ample time for stories of ghosts to emerge. The fort is most renowned for its pivotal role in the Civil War, where Union Rear Admiral David Farragut led a victorious campaign during the Battle of Mobile Bay. Within the old barracks, the spirit of a prisoner who hanged himself there in 1917 lingers, with his cries still heard to this day.

Additionally, some visitors report seeing the apparitions of dead soldiers walking the grounds or hearing the anguished screams of men who perished in an explosion. There are also accounts of a young woman who wanders the fort, a victim of an attack in the 19th century.

- At Huntingdon College in Montgomery, a young woman named Martha took her life on the fourth floor of Pratt Hall when it was still a dormitory. She became known as the "Red Lady" because she was often seen dressed in red. However, long before this Red Lady, another woman haunted the campus when the college was located in Tuskegee. This scarlet-dressed woman, who carried a red parasol and never spoke, was known to roam the residence halls, often appearing with a red glow.

- The PMC Prattville Manufacturing Company, established in 1846, was one of the earliest textile mills in the South. It operated as a spinning and weaving facility located on the east side of Autauga Creek, which is now part of Heritage Park. The building suffered a fire in 2002, and although little remains, the spinning rooms were once rumored to be haunted. On Friday, March 24, 1893, ten-year-old Willie Youngblood, a worker in the spinning room, stopped to talk to other workers near an elevator shaft. While peering down the shaft to see the workers below, he unfortunately lost his footing and fell 30 feet down, striking the elevator below. Willie survived for only one day after the accident, remaining unconscious due to severe head and neck injuries. Years later, his dead grieving mother, Lavenia, returned to stroll through the spinning area of the old mill, startling employees working there where she became known as the Lady in Black.

- Sweetwater Mansion, a large plantation house located in Florence, Alabama is a site rich in intriguing ghost stories.

Among the tales are sightings of a Confederate soldier patrolling the grounds, reports of a phantom casket believed to belong to a member of the Patton family, and the sound of children giggling echoing through the mansion. These stories contribute to the mansion's reputation as a haunted historic site.

- At the U.S. Army Corps of Engineers, Haines Island Park, along Nancy's Mountain Trail, lies the story of Nancy, a woman who walks with a lantern, as she did during the Civil War, waiting for her son to return. Her boy was killed in battle, and his body was never recovered. Nancy and her husband searched for him each day until, one day, her husband did not return. He was later found frozen to death against the grave of an unknown soldier. Shortly after, Nancy disappeared, but her ghost returns, continuing to walk the trail with her lantern in hand.

- The face of Henry Wells left a mark on the second-floor window of the Pickens County Courthouse in Carrollton. A free Black man, he was accused of burning down the courthouse in 1876, despite a lack of evidence to support the accusation. He was confined to the attic of the current building while a mob began to gather outside. As Wells peered out of the window at the mob below, lightning struck nearby, etching his image indelibly onto the pane before he was lynched.

An Alabama Cryptid
White Thang

The legendary White Thang first captured attention in the 1940s, and sightings emerged from the woodlands of Morgan, Jefferson, and Etowah counties. This elusive creature is known for astonishing speed and agility, darting effortlessly across the forest floor on all fours and leaping over fallen trees and boulders. While accounts of the White Thang vary, many describe it as seven to eight feet tall. Its body is cloaked in long, thick, shaggy white fur that shimmers in the moonlight, giving it an almost ghostly appearance. It has glowing red eyes, and some suggest that the head resembles a lion, characterized by a long mane. The most unsettling aspect of the White Thang is its spine-chilling cry. This high-pitched scream resonates through the night, resembling the anguished wail of a woman in excruciating pain.

Alaska
Ghost Phone in the Haunted Cabin

The Alaskan Railroad, built between 1903 and 1923, runs about 470 miles, connecting Seward and Fairbanks. Along its route at about Mile 412 in the interior of Alaska and roughly 55 miles southwest of Fairbanks is Nenana, initially established as a trading post and roadhouse for river travelers and trading. It is settled at the confluence of the Nenana and Tanana Rivers, a strategic location for hunting, trade, and fishing. With the discovery of gold in Fairbanks in 1902, settlers flocked to the region seeking their fortunes, and the town grew. However, outside its bounds, the area was an incredibly remote and deep wilderness inhabited mainly by a few hardy settlers, Native Alaskans, hunters, and trappers.

In the early to mid-1900s, not far from Nenana and around Mile 386 of the Alaskan Railroad, hunters, and trappers used an aged line cabin as a base camp. For many years, it offered shelter and a place to store supplies and equipment during the 7 to 8 months of the hunting/trapping season. It was also a place travelers refused to stay as something ominous existed there.

Within the building, there was an old phone. Those who took shelter there were almost always awakened by the jingle of the phone deep into the night and after falling asleep. When they wriggled out of their blankets and stumbled sleepily across the room to answer it, a soft-spoken woman would ask, "Is anyone home? Can I come over?" Of course, it baffled those who heard the voice, some even going outside to wait for the woman to appear. When she did not, they returned to the phone only to find no intact lines connecting it to the outside world.

A man named Tom Bagley took it upon himself to rid the cabin of the spirit. He burnt the building down after having enough of the shenanigans of the ghostly voice. Thus, the ghost phone in the haunted cabin came to an end. Of course, this is only until an unsuspecting hiker walks by the lonely spot and sets up camp. Perhaps the phone will ring out again in the dark of night, echoing from deep within the earth, frightening yet another traveler with a soft woman's voice asking if she might pay a visit.

Alaska
Phantom Ship

There were rumors of a ghost ship sailing the coast of Alaska, drifting through the icy waters as if manned by a phantom crew. It began its life as a Swedish steel-hulled cargo steamer built in 1914. In 1921, it was acquired by the Hudson's Bay Company and dubbed the SS Baychimo. This large vessel measured 230 feet in length and had a powerful engine that allowed it to reach speeds of up to 12 mph. The Baychimo primarily sailed along the northern coast of Canada in fur trading with the Inuit settlements.

The ship had completed nine successful voyages before encountering trouble on October 1, 1931. While on a trading run loaded with furs, it became trapped in pack ice off the coast of Alaska. The crew had no choice but to abandon the ship temporarily in search of shelter. When they returned, however, they found the vessel had broken free of the ice. Most of the cargo was retrieved, and it was initially believed that the boat had sunk because it completely vanished.

In reality, it had not sunk, and this is when legends began to emerge of the ghost ship. It would appear and disappear for miles as if ghostly hands were guiding the boat. In January of 1932, the Baychimo was spotted floating near a shoreline. Over the following years, hunters and explorers continued to witness the ship. In August of 1933, Isobel Hutchinson, a Scottish Arctic botanist collecting plants in the region, boarded the boat with a group of local Eskimo men from the community where she was staying. By this time, the ship had been stripped of its furs, leaving little more than typewriters, ledgers, and handcuffs near the hatch.

Not long after the encounter, the ship sailed past another vessel. "You'd think someone was steering her," remarked the captain of the Trader as he watched the Baychimo maneuver itself without anyone at the wheel. At the same time, his ship was trapped in the ice. "I guess she is haunted. She steers clear of the shoals like a master hand was at her wheel."

The last confirmed sighting of the phantom ship occurred in March 1969, 38 years after being abandoned, when a group of Inupiat found her frozen in an ice pack between Point Barrow and Icy Cape. Over the years, many others have searched for the ghost ship, but it seemed to have disappeared entirely, and no wreckage has ever been found.

Alaska
Hanged Man's Ghost

In the early 1900s, a man named Fred Hardy lived a life that would have faded into obscurity, his name merely etched on a weathered gravestone. Yet, his story took a dark twist that transformed him into both a murderer and a ghost, earning him a notorious reputation that reverberated through the ages. The eerie legacy he left behind—haunting those tied to his tale—truly captivates the imagination.

In early June of 1901, 26-year-old Fred Hardy was released after spending a year in Alcatraz prison for murdering a man during a knife fight while serving in the military. There is very little known of Hardy's childhood that might have alluded to his violent nature except for a strict stepfather who raised him after his father's death, who Hardy rebelled against because he was harsh and cruel. What traumatic events led up to that date, we do not know, although it is noted that Hardy frequently got drunk. We can only guess that something horrible happened that always compelled Hardy to want to escape reality.

Even while in prison, Fred Hardy gained the nickname "Diamond Dick," primarily due to his time spent reading popular dime novels. Diamond Dick was a serial novel with the main character well-known for taking matters into his own hands and always ending as the hero. Indeed, Hardy identified with the character's dark hair, mustache, handsomeness, and diamond-studded clothes. He must have craved being like this sensational heroic figure, often facing adventures loaded with crime, romance, escapism, and action that contrasted so differently from his life. Hardy, too, identified with the novel character himself as someone who takes risks and was often in dangerous situations.

It is no wonder he took the next step after his time in Alcatraz. Hardy learned about gold prospects on the secluded coastal islands of Alaska. Determined to escape his criminal past and distance himself from the law, he boarded a fishing boat, the F/V Aragon, shortly after leaving prison. The ship was headed to Unimak Island, the largest of the Aleutian Islands, located at the end of the Alaska Peninsula. He signed a contract to work on the boat in exchange for passage.

At the turn of the 20th century, Unimak Island had a small population, primarily due to the early interactions between native populations and Russian explorers and traders. Despite this, there was gold prospecting on the island, and its remoteness attracted individuals like Hardy, who were seeking fortune away from the hustle of civilization. However, after he was assigned to find fresh water as part of his work duties, Hardy escaped into the wilderness. He soon realized he was ill-prepared for survival in such an isolated environment. Desperation seized Hardy as he roamed the island, scavenging for resources. Eventually, he stumbled upon a gold prospector's camp with a treasure trove, including a cabin and survival gear.

He found camping equipment, tents, and firearms—a rifle and a pistol. The equipment belonged to four men: Con Sullivan, his brother Florence Sullivan, P.J. Rooney, and Oscar Jackson. The Sullivan brothers had relocated to the area from Montana just a month earlier for the prospecting expedition. They built a small cabin about a quarter mile from a small cove. The gold hunters took a rowboat across a small bay to their mine each day and returned at dusk.

Upon their return on the evening that Hardy had come upon their cabin, the men were bantering about. A small thicket lay between their camp and the boat, and it was here that Hardy hid, determined to take the items for himself. Knowing that being caught would mean a swift return to prison, Hardy, armed with their guns, shot and killed the two brothers and Rooney. After the brutal murders, Jackson managed to evade Hardy for two weeks and wandered across Unimak Island. Near death, he was eventually rescued by a ship and taken to Unalaska, where he reported the gruesome events to the authorities.

Following the incident, authorities tracked Hardy and another accomplice, George Aston, to a nearby fishing village. Although Hardy claimed innocence, he was put on trial and convicted of murder on September 7, 1901. He was subsequently sentenced to hang.

Mary E. Hart was a reporter for the Los Angeles Herald in Nome and served as a correspondent for several newspapers in Washington and California. In 1901, she was sent to cover the Nome gold rush. While there, she was assigned to interview Fred Hardy in his cell for the newspaper. During her time with him, she aimed to uncover the details of his case and his motivations and perhaps elicit a confession. Her reporting on the sensational case contributed enormously to the public interest.

Still, even to his death, Hardy maintained his innocence of the murders. During the conversations, Mary Hart stated in newspapers that Hardy bequeathed his earthly possessions to her. Then, before she left the final time, he asked of her, "Missus Hart, would you be frightened if I came back to you after I am hung? I want to return and bring further proof of my innocence." Mary Hart did not balk and humored him, stating that it would not bother her and that he was welcome to do so.

On September 19, 1902, over 150 people gathered in the small icehouse, which served as a makeshift execution area next to the jail, to witness the hanging of Hardy. The execution lasted nine minutes and 48 seconds before he died. Mary Hart captured about twelve photographs after the execution. While developing the glass plates, she noticed a shadowy figure of an old man appearing near the coffin. The image was printed in the April 9, 1905, edition of the St Louis Globe. "Immediately after the execution, I took at least a dozen photographs of the body of the convict, the gallows, the jail, the icehouse, and the grave," she stated in the newspaper. "When I developed my plates, I was astounded to find on one the ghostly figure of an aged, bald-headed man half in the room where the body lay and half through the wall. I swear that there was not another person in that room except myself and my tripod boy, who stood back from me when I snapped the lens." She revealed that a few nights later, she had a vivid dream in which Hardy appeared alongside the elderly man from the photograph. The man seemed eager to communicate something to her, but she could not understand him.

During her year-long stay in Nome, this same dream haunted her two to three times a week. If that was not enough, Mary Hart declared, "I was in my office writing the story of the hanging, which I had witnessed. It was quiet, and I was alone.

And then Fred Hardy, whom I had seen dashed into eternity, came back to haunt me for many hideous weeks. I sat rigid in my chair, unable to move or speak. It was as though I were being choked to death, as if I were undergoing what that 21-year-old youth must have experienced during his last moment. I am confident I would have died but for an interruption. A girl we know as 'Sunshine' in Nome knocked at the door, entered, touched me on the shoulder, shrieked, 'My God, Hardy is here!' and fell to the floor, alternately fainting and hysterical. She spoke in Hardy's voice describing death torments—'Sunshine' who had not witnessed the hanging, speaking in Hardy's low, peculiar voice! It was frightful beyond words." Hart went on, "That almost lethal paralysis left my body at the instant 'Sunshine' touched my shoulder, but from that day until I left, Nome was haunted, day and night, by that explicable presence. It was destroying my health. I had to come away—"

Hart would confide the haunting did not stop until a year after the execution when she took a trip to Seattle. During the journey, she noted a woman who often watched her intently. The woman approached Mary Hart and introduced herself as Missus Barker, a clairvoyant. Although Missus Barker could see spirits, she claimed she could not communicate with them. She told Hart that a young man appeared to be standing by her side each time she saw her. During dinner, he even attempted to help Hart pick up something she was reaching for. Curious, Hart asked Missus Barker to observe the figure and report what this shadowy ghost was doing. As the ship sailed farther away from Alaska, the figure grew dimmer and dimmer until Missus Barker said that once they reached the Bering Sea, it vanished. Mary E. Hart never returned; she died on March 25, 1939, her memories still clutching the horrible phantom of Fred Hardy that had haunted her.

Haunting Shorts of Alaska:

- The Alaskan Hotel in Juneau: According to local lore, a miner left his new bride at the hotel while he went off to work in a nearby mine. When he failed to return after three weeks, his wife resorted to prostitution to pay her hotel bill. Upon his return, enraged by her actions, he murdered her in one of the rooms. This story sets the stage for hauntings over the years. An especially gruesome incident involved a sailor who requested to stay in Room 315, which is known to be haunted. He jumped from the window of the room as if trying to escape from something terrifying. Although he survived the fall, there was mysterious blood on the walls when they were finally able to access the room.

- The Red Onion Saloon in Skagway operated as a fine bordello. It is haunted by Lydia, the spirit of one of the working girls. She has been seen as a translucent figure, followed by floral perfume and a cool waft of air.

- Fort Richardson, located near Anchorage, has phantom soldiers from various eras patrolling its grounds.

- Eklutna Cemetery near Anchorage has spirits lingering near the "Spirit Houses," traditional Dena'ina Athabascan structures built to honor deceased loved ones.

- The Fourth Avenue Theatre in Anchorage was once a movie theater and is haunted by the ghost of a woman who appears in mirrors between the restrooms.

- Along the Iditarod Route, a cabin marks the change from the inland race to the Bering Sea coastline. A woman who once lived there haunts the cabin. Race mushers are told to leave something for the Old Woman to avoid bad luck.

- Kennecott is a former copper mining town in Wrangell-St. Elias National Park and Preserve, surrounded by mountains and glaciers. Visitors report hearing footsteps at the Erie Mine Bunkhouse, which is situated on a cliffside.

Additionally, accounts of ghosts and vanishing tombstones have been shared by those who have explored the mines. People report seeing ghostly miners and railroad workers along the old railroad that once serviced the Kennecott copper mines in the Valdez and Chitina mining districts.

- Those fishing at Resurrection Bay, Seward have witnessed ghost ships.
- At Glacier Bay National Park in Gustavus, hikers have encountered the mysterious spirits of the native peoples who desperately try to guide them away in warning before vanishing as they are approached.
- The Birch Hill Cemetery in Fairbanks: A lady in white is seen within the cemetery.
- Castle Hill in Sitka is a National Historic Landmark and state park located in Sitka, Alaska. It was once home to a Russian castle. According to legend, a ghost known as the Lady in Black haunts the grounds. Adorned in jewels and a black veil, she was once a beautiful princess who took her life on her wedding night to escape an arranged marriage. Her ghost returns at the midnight hour.
- A father and five-year-old daughter haunt Badarka Road in Chugiak. The two were collecting firewood, and the father stopped to rest, his axe still stuck to the tree. Thinking she could help, the little girl tugged on the ax, and the tree fell upon her, killing her. Distraught, the father cradled the dead child in his arms for days until he froze to death in the snow. Those who take the road at 3:30 in the morning have seen the man holding the bloody child in his arms before they vanish.

An Alaska Cryptid
Qalupalik

The Qalupalik is an Inuit creature, often described as a sea monster or water spirit inhabiting the Arctic's icy shorelines and ice floes. This creature is typically depicted as having very long dark hair, slimy greenish skin, and long fingernails. It wears an amautik, a traditional parka worn by Inuit women; this parka features a hood and a built-in pouch for carrying a baby.

The Qalupalik has two flippers, and one of these can emit a shrill sound that paralyzes its victims. It can alter its appearance using a technique known as pilutitaminik. The Qalupalik lures children who wander too close to the water's edge by making an ethereal hum, enticing them into danger. In some stories, it devours the child; in others, the little one is kept to sustain the creature's youth.

Arizona

The Red Ghost

The Red Ghost first appeared around 1883, nearly trampling two gold prospectors while sleeping in their tent. The men would relate that the colossal creature was taller than two horses with what appeared to be a skeleton on its back. Upon investigation, the tracks around their camp were strange and unfamiliar. A thorough search was performed of the area, but it seemed to have vanished into the hills. Well, until it reappeared at a sheep ranch on Eagle Creek when herders were gone with their flock, leaving two women and their children at the ranch house. One of the women made her way to the spring to fetch water. Their dogs began to bay and howl, and the remaining woman inside the house rushed to the window, only to see something tear across the property in the same direction as the woman going to the spring. Screams tore out into the air, but the woman in the house, fearing for the safety of the children, locked the doors soundly.

That night, the men returned and quickly raced down with lanterns to the spring to find the woman, but she was dead.

Her corpse was crushed as if a herd of horses had trampled her. The coroner was quick to make a judgment, although not aloud, and sure, one of the women was angered at the other and beat her to death.

Word spread and others witnessed the strange creature. It was not until a hunter watched it come into view one day that he recognized the beast as a camel with a rider atop its back. However, whether the rider was human was unknown. Another time, two hunters shot at the creature, and it bucked and ran away. They noticed something falling from its back. When they rushed to the scene, they discovered a man's head dry and withered, but hair and mummified flesh were still upon it. Then, a cowboy, finding it in a corral, tried to lasso it and noted that it had what appeared to be a pack upon its back but was instead a partially decayed body. A cowboy finally shot it, and upon its back was the corpse of a dead man, minus the head. Nobody knows why the dead man was bound to the camel's back. But for years after it was killed, the ghostly figure was still seen roaming the area.

Arizona
Apache Death Cave

In 1878, Apache raiders attacked a Navajo encampment near the Little Colorado River, resulting in the deaths of nearly all the men, women, and children. Only three women were taken prisoner. As news of the massacre spread through the Navajo Nation, leaders dispatched men to seek revenge and rescue the captives. The Navajo tracked the Apache and their horses to an extensive underground cave system located beneath what is now Two Guns, a ghost town in Coconino County on the east rim of Canyon Diablo. The Navajo set fire to the cave entrance, trapping the Apache inside. One Apache managed to escape. When questioned about the whereabouts of the three women, he claimed they had been killed. Enraged, the Navajo intensified the fire until the death songs of the dying men ceased. After, they discovered over forty corpses inside the cave. From that moment on, the Apache considered the land cursed and refused to enter the caves. Later, settlers who built a town in the area reported hearing groans, moans, and voices within. Today, visitors hear footsteps and voices.

Haunting Shorts of Arizona:

- Along the North Rim of Grand Canyon National Park, specifically along the Transept Trail, a spirit known as the Wandering Woman has been spotted wearing a white dress adorned with blue flowers. Most believe she is connected to a fire in 1932 at the Grand Canyon Lodge, where some witnesses claim to have seen her apparition engulfed in flames. She is not the only spirit stuck there. Over 900 people have died within the borders of the Grand Canyon since the 1800s, including 128 victims of a plane crash in 1956.

- The Yuma Territorial Prison operated from 1876 to 1909, housing over 3,000 inmates. Today, it is a designated state historic site. During its operation, many deaths occurred, including suicides and murders connected to riots within the prison walls. Sightings of restless spirits are not uncommon, with ghostly screams and chilling cries echoing in the site's dim recesses. Visitors should exercise caution near Cell 14, which housed John Ryan, an inmate who was imprisoned for accosting women and ultimately committed suicide in his cell. This area is notorious for its cold spots and sense of dread.

- The Superstition Mountains, 40 miles southeast of Phoenix, are a rugged mountain range with steep cliffs, canyons, and desert landscapes. Within these mountains lies the legendary Lost Dutchman Gold Mine. In the 1840s, a Mexican family, the Peraltas, operated a mine in these mountains. During an expedition to transport the gold back in 1848, Apaches ambushed them. Most of the family members were killed, leaving only a few survivors. In the 1870s, Jacob Waltz, a German immigrant, allegedly discovered the gold mine with the help of a surviving Peralta family member. He hid the treasure and shared hints about its location with only a select few before he died in 1891.

Since then, many have searched for the mine and reported finding strange carvings and symbols on the rocks, which are believed to be clues. However, the treasure has never been located. Adding to the intrigue, some claim that Jacob Waltz's ghost guards the treasure, as hikers often report feeling a strong sense of being watched. The Superstition Mountains are infamous for unexplained disappearances of individuals searching for gold, which fuels even more bizarre tales surrounding the area.

- Window Rock is the capital of the Navajo Nation. Sightings and stories about Skinwalkers circulate among residents. The Skinwalker, called "Yee Naaldlooshii" in Navajo, is a shapeshifting witch often associated with malevolent acts and dark magic, a taboo subject many prefer not to discuss openly. It is believed that to become a Skinwalker, a person must commit a terrible act, such as harming a family member, which gives them the ability to shapeshift and grants them frightening powers. One story of a Skinwalker is The Laughing Ram. While working on an old ranch home near Tuba City, a contractor heard unsettling laughter from nearby sheep pens. Curious, he approached and found a flock of sheep cowering at one end while a lone ram stood upright on its hind legs at the other, crossing its front hooves over its chest. The ram laughed maniacally; its eyes eerily familiar. When the contractor looked dead into the eyes of the ram, he felt horrified. Still, just as quickly, the ram dropped to all fours and resumed normal behavior as if nothing had happened.

- The Mogollon Monster is seen along the Mogollon Rim, an escarpment stretching 200 miles across central Arizona into New Mexico. There have been sightings since 1903. It resembles Bigfoot, 7 to 10 feet tall with black or red-brown hair and red eyes. It is a night creature reeking of dead fish.

- El Tiradito is a shrine located in the Old Barrio area of Downtown Tucson dedicated not to a saint but to a sinner. It consists of the crumbling remains of a brick building and is steeped in local legends. One prominent legend tells the story of a ranch hand named Juan Oliveras, who had an affair with his mother-in-law. When his father-in-law discovered the romance, he killed Juan in a fit of rage. Due to the nature of his sin, Juan could not be buried in a Catholic cemetery and was instead laid to rest at the spot where he fell. Over time, women began leaving candles at the site to pray for Juan's forgiveness. This practice evolved into a wishing shrine, where visitors leave notes and candles for their heartaches and hopes.

- Initially opened for family entertainment, the Birdcage Theatre in Tombstone adapted as a saloon, brothel, and gambling hall to attract a different clientele, consisting of cowboys and miners, to survive. Owned by Lottie and William "Billy" Hutchinson, it enjoyed popularity from 1881 to 1892 until the mining industry's decline. During its years of operation, at least 26 people died in shootouts and bar brawls. Today, the ghosts of the women who worked in the brothel and the men who were killed in fights return to their former haunts.

- Eight miles southwest of Tombstone, there are ruins of an old home where at least twenty people were murdered within its confines. Frederick Brunckow, the German engineer who struck gold and built the house, was killed by his employees, who stabbed him with a rock drill and tossed him down the mineshaft. Nowadays, people who are camping nearby in cabins report seeing ghosts.

An Arizona Cryptid
Mogollon Monster

In 1903, newspapers reported the account of I.W. Stevens from Cedar, Colorado, who witnessed a strange "wild man" near the Grand Canyon. He described the creature as having matted gray hair covering its body and talon-like fingers and long claws. Its face appeared burned brown by the sun and had flaming green eyes. The creature carried a club in one hand. After Stevens fled the scene, he found the wild man feasting on a cougar he had killed. Compared to Bigfoot, this creature has been seen over the years. It is known as the Mogollon Monster, which inhabits the Mogollon Rim region of Arizona, characterized by dense forests and rugged terrain. Eyewitnesses describe it as being between 7 to 10 feet tall with a muscular build, covered in thick dark or reddish-brown hair, and having a hairless face with deep-set eyes. The monster produces an eerie scream and primarily forages at night.

Arkansas
The Crescent Hotel

The Crescent Hotel & Spa in Eureka Springs was built in 1886 and continued to operate as a hotel into the 20th century, catering primarily to visitors seeking the healing properties of the area's natural springs. In the early 1800s, most travelers camped in tents or wagons. However, by 1879, permanent structures were constructed, leading to the establishment of the hotel. Initially a hotel, the building transformed into a private school for young women.

It subsequently served as a clinic operated by Norman Baker, who falsely claimed to be able to cure cancer. After Baker's conviction for mail fraud, the property was sold and returned to its original function as a hotel. The hotel's history is marked by several hauntings from its past. Room 218, known as Michael's Room, is inhabited by the spirit of a stonemason who fell to his death during construction in the 1880s; his cries can be heard at night. Additionally, Room 419 is haunted by the lingering spirit of one of Norman Baker's patients who died while receiving treatment there.

Arkansas
The Gurdon Lights

A haunting mystery shrouded in time has captivated locals near Gurdon—an enigmatic light flickering along a desolate stretch of railroad tracks nestled deep within a murky swamp. Travelers passing through off Exit I-30 and Highway 53 can't help but be drawn to this eerie phenomenon, often called the "Gurdon Light." Skeptics dismiss the ethereal glow as mere swamp gas or the reflections of distant headlights. Yet, the more superstitious cannot shake the feeling that something far more sinister lingers in the air, especially when they learn that these spectral lights first appeared shortly after a chilling event—the disappearance of Will McClain.

On that fateful evening of December 4th, 1931, panic gripped the small town when McClain's wife, Cora, approached the city marshal, her voice trembling as she reported that her 63-year-old husband, a diligent section foreman for the Missouri Pacific Railroad, had failed to come home after his shift. The search for answers began immediately.

As the marshal questioned those who had interacted with McClain that night, he stumbled upon Louis McBride, a fellow crew member whose demeanor raised suspicion. Upon being taken into custody for questioning, McBride confessed to killing McClain over a dispute being denied seniority privileges during layoffs. The worker became enraged during a conversation, struck McClain on the head with a shovel, and then pummeled him with a railroad spike maul or a spike hammer.

He led the marshal to the body found on the train tracks, revealing that McClain had not died immediately. Instead, he had tried to escape by crawling into the woods. Legend has it that he was holding a lantern when he was attacked and that he still clutched it in his hands when the corpse was taken away for burial. McBride was later executed for his crime. To this day, McClain still walks the tracks, with the light from the lantern still swaying in his grasp.

Haunting Shorts of Arkansas:

- Along Highway 365 in Woodson, drivers stop abruptly to help when they see a little girl with bruises and cuts on the road. After she tells them she was injured in an accident, they offer her a ride home. However, they are shocked that she is no longer in the car when they arrive, and the little hitchhiker vanishes. When they knock on the door that the girl identified as her home, her father answers and informs them that she was killed in a wreck long ago.

- East Fayetteville has a wooded area known as Ghost Hollow, located near two old cemeteries: Confederate Cemetery and Walker-Sutton Cemetery. The haunting in this area began around 1853, linked to a tragic event involving a new bride. On her wedding night, a spark from the fire ignited her dress, and in her panic, she fled out the door, consumed by flames. Many times, before the Civil War, her ghost had been reported running through the hollow, witnessed by African American slaves living on the property who heard her desperate screams and saw her pale figure trying to escape the fire. Over the years, passersby have listened to her screams echoing through the hollow and have seen a white figure running through the woods.

- Between Crossett and Hamburg, people see spook lights much like the sway of an old lantern, believed to be a brakeman who got into a fight and had his head chopped off. It is called Crossett Light.

- The Cotter Bridge is a historic concrete arch bridge that spans the White River in Cotter. It was built to provide access to a part of the Ozarks previously unreachable by motorists. Apparently, it also opened the area for ghosts as witnesses have reported seeing a phantom woman being chased by baying hounds running across it and ghostly children playing below.

- The Fort Smith National Historic Site at Fort Smith had Judge Isaac Parker, known as "The Hanging Judge," who sentenced 160 people to death, and his victims haunt the grounds.
- Fort Chaffee, nestled near Fort Smith, carries a haunting legacy as a former military base. Its eerie barracks are frequented by the restless spirits of soldiers from days gone by, adding an air of mystery that draws thrill-seekers and ghost hunters alike.
- Mount Holly Cemetery in Little Rock has statues that some say move. Visitors have reported seeing ghosts dressed in period clothing.
- On Christmas Day in 1948, 54-year-old Ladell Allen ingested mercury cyanide in the master suite of the Allen House in Monticello. Her family rushed her to the hospital for treatment, but unfortunately, she passed away just a week later. Visitors to the house have reported hearing ghostly footsteps and moans, which are believed to be the restless spirit of Ladell.

An Arkansas Cryptid
Fouke (Boggy Creek) Monster

The area around Fouke was just a rural farming community of 394 residents when the colossal creature made its first known appearance at the home of Elizabeth and Bobby Ford on May 2nd, 1971. This creature, described as six feet tall and black, reached through a screen window around midnight while Elizabeth was sleeping on a couch. Elizabeth Ford said, "I saw the curtain moving on the front window and saw a hand sticking through the window," she declared. "At first, I thought it was a bear's paw, but it didn't look like that. It had heavy hair all over it and it had claws. I could see its eyes. They looked like coals of fire, real red."

Elizabeth's husband, Bobby, and her brother chased the creature away, firing several shots at it, but no blood was found. Afterward, scratch marks appeared on the porch, and three-toed footprints were discovered nearby. This creature, later dubbed the Fouke Monster or Boggy Creek Monster, returned to the area located along Boggy Creek.

During a subsequent encounter, Bobby was on the porch steps when the creature grabbed and pulled him down. Although he managed to escape, he was so rattled that he forgot to open the front door and ran through it instead. Bobby was so unnerved that he had to be taken to a hospital, nearly senseless.

Three witnesses reported seeing the creature along U.S. Highway 71 only a few weeks later. One described it as resembling a "giant monkey" that weighed more than 200 pounds. The driver of a vehicle feared hitting the creature, stating, "It was really moving fast across the highway, faster than a man. Its arms were swinging kind of like a monkey's, and it didn't seem to notice us or look at the car." Until that moment, like most people, the trio had assumed the monster was a hoax. Over the years, there has been a significant increase in reported sightings, which have fueled public interest and curiosity about the unknown.

California

The Whaley House

There's a place called Yankee Jims in the Sierra Nevada foothills. This place teeters on the edge of becoming a ghost town, yet a small group of resilient souls still call it home, keeping its spirit alive. Founded in 1849, Yankee Jims was once a bustling hub during the California Gold Rush, overflowing with life and energy. At its peak, over 5,000 miners, outlaws, and fortune-seekers filled the streets, living in tents and makeshift homes, all searching for gold. And really, the town means little to this ghost story except that its name comes from a disreputable character who searched for gold there. But here's where the story becomes intriguing: there were two figures known as Yankee Jim roaming the gold fields at that time! Both were less than savory characters, infamous for stealing horses and met the grim fate of being hanged. Yet, their stories became so intertwined that it led to one of the two haunting a famous building in San Diego.

In the 1840s, a seedy individual known as "Yankee Jim," or James Knowlton, emerged as a feared horse thief and robber. He led a gang of highwaymen along the isolated Yuba River north of North Fork. He left a notorious trail of destruction widely reported in newspapers. This reign of terror instilled significant fear in the miners who navigated the region. Ultimately, Yankee Jim Knowlton was captured and executed by hanging in March 1851. Still, the dark legacy of his actions would later contribute to another chilling tale.

At about the same time of Knowlton's notoriety, another Yankee Jim, James Robinson, had joined the California gold rush. His background is shrouded in mystery, as various individuals who encountered him offered differing accounts of his past. In June 1848, John Ross, a farmer from Oregon, led a group of men to the North Fork of the American River in California in search of fortune. Among the group, he would later write, was Robinson, whom Ross described as a rough sailor with a questionable reputation despite his ability to speak several languages. Ross suspected that Robinson had criminal connections to Sydney, Australia, a penal colony for Great Britain then. Many convicts from Australia, seeking wealth after discovering gold, had begun their journeys to California. Robinson was likely one of them, adding to his character's mystery.

In 1849, Ben Currier was part of a group looking for gold near Foresthill. They heard about gold discovered by a man named Yankee Jim Robinson. In November, Currier and his friends set out to find Yankee Jim's treasure. While camping at night and near where many believed the treasure was, they saw a light and followed it, later discovering a miner's camp. The men at this camp shared a tale about a disheveled miner living upstream. Ben Currier decided to investigate this lead and soon found Yankee Jim Robinson.

The only weapons Yankee Jim had were a knife and a Jaeger rifle. He mentioned that he needed more lead to make bullets. Currier complied, hiking back to his camp to retrieve some lead and returning to Yankee Jim. During their conversation, Currier learned that Yankee Jim was originally from Maine. He had also escaped from a ship, leading some to believe he might have been a prisoner on the Waban prison ship, a vessel converted to house criminals before San Quentin State Prison was built. When Currier returned to his camp, one of the men noted that skeletal remains of a man and horse had been found nearby, suggesting that this stranger named Yankee Jim might have been involved in a crime. Upon returning to the town, the men shared this information, and rumors began circulating about Yankee Jim's possibly shady reputation.

Around this time, Yankee Jim Robinson turned to rustling horses, finding it more profitable than seeking gold. However, he soon attracted attention and quickly fled the area. Heading toward San Diego, he encountered two more dubious characters, Jason Loring and William Harris. The three individuals were spotted stealing a rowboat, which they left behind on the shore. They were apprehended, with Yankee Jim Robinson receiving a blow to the back of the head from a shovel after being lassoed. The men claimed they had been rustling horses in Stockton and intended to take the schooner Plutus to lower California after selling the horses.

Loring and Harris were tried, convicted, and sentenced to a year in prison. Because of the stories that preceded him, Yankee Jim would get a more extensive punishment. During this time, and due to the high crime associated with the ships filled with convicts coming to the gold rush area, "lynching courts" were formed to quickly rid the town of offenders. These vigilante justice mobs took the law into their own hands, violently executing individuals without a proper trial.

It was in the hands of these self-appointed mediators and judges that Yankee Jim Robinson's destiny would fall, along with newspapers fed disinformation by those who wished to entwine the backgrounds of the two different Yankee Jims to make the acts more shocking. Wanting to send a clear message that this poor behavior would not be overlooked, he was given a guilty judgment and sentenced to hang in San Diego.

For a long time, Yankee Jim seemed to believe the whole process was just a ruse and that he would be released. It was hard to believe that his actions could warrant a hanging. It was only when he was placed on the wagon with the noose around his neck that he appeared stunned and asked, "Am I going to die?" As the whip went to the mules and the wagon began, he tip-toed along the back of the wagon until it slipped away from his feet. Because of his height of 6 feet 4 inches, he dangled too close to the ground, taking forty-five minutes to strangle to death. When life finally left his body, they discovered that his casket was too small. His legs had to be broken to fit within.

Both men should have been forgotten, as they left no positive legacy behind. Their bones would have been buried in a pauper's cemetery, destined to turn to dust, and with no one to care for the graves, a house or other structure would be built over them, consigning their lives to eternal oblivion. Their notorious actions would have likely been overlooked by uninterested historians sifting through old newspapers, passed over for more compelling news, and ultimately forgotten. Well, except for Trader Jim's return from the otherworld, maybe that age-old curse that follows those hung on a tree and the bad luck that follows those who intersect that path. And someone did. Thomas Whaley was an early settler of San Diego. In 1857, he built his brick home atop the spot of a public execution where Yankee Jim Robinson was hanged.

The Whaley House.

His wife Anna and six children (Anna Amelia, Violet Eloise, Corinne Lillian, Francis, Thomas Jr., and George) moved inside, not realizing that little plot of land just might be cursed. But it seemed as if bad things followed their move.

First, their young son Thomas, who was only a year old, died of scarlet fever in January 1858. On January 5, 1882, two of his daughters, Violet Eloise and Anna Amelia, married in Old San Diego. Violet married George T. Bertolacci, and Anna Amelia wed her first cousin, John T. Whaley. Violet would later discover that her new husband had deceived the family to obtain her dowry, leaving her just two weeks after the wedding while on their honeymoon trip.

Afterward, distraught over the public humiliation, she attempted to drown herself in the cistern and failed. Then, on August 19, 1885, at only age 22, at six in the morning, Violet shot herself with her father's .32 caliber pistol in the family outhouse.

The haunting message Violet left behind has profoundly impacted readers over the years, part of a poem by Thomas Hood:

Mad from life's history, Glad to death's mystery,

Swift to be hurl'd—Anywhere, anywhere

Out of the world! (Thomas Hood)

Not long after, Corinne Lillian's fiancé broke off their engagement due to the scandal of Violet's suicide. And then, the home was abandoned by the family for nearly 20 years.

The house, now a museum, is haunted. Many visitors have reported hearing the rustling of Violet's dress and the sounds of baby Thomas's cries and giggles. Even the elder Thomas Whaley returns, dressed in his frock, coat, and top hat, watching from the top of the stairs.

However, the most unsettling ghostly presence is that of a man who was hanged in the same spot where the house was built. During the family's time in the house, Thomas Whaley often heard heavy boots walking across the second floor, accompanied by the sound of a broken step—the awkward phantom tread of Trader Jim, whose legs were reportedly broken after death to fit into his coffin.

California
The Spook of Misery Hill

Pike City flourished as a boomtown during the California Gold Rush, reaching its peak around 1859. It was a place, for most, fraught with danger, misfortune or great fortune, and greed. The miners of this era were known as the Fifty-Niners. One such prospector was Tom Bowers, who owned a mine on Misery Hill. He chose to live as a recluse, avoiding social gatherings at local bars and the chatter around campfires.

One day, Bowers went missing. Other miners traced his footsteps through the snow from his dilapidated cabin. They looked over the edge of the slope where he had been prospecting, but he was nowhere to be found. A landslide had snuffed out his claim. They eventually dug his body out and gave him a proper burial. Yet, some people claimed to have seen Tom Bowers still wandering around his mine shaft. The other miners steered clear of the area, knowing bad luck and hoodoo could follow.

Jim Brandon had a devil-may-care attitude and was not afraid of such things as ghosts; in fact, he did not believe in them at all. He scoffed at the others and saw the abandoned mine going to waste. Knowing that Tom Bowers had found some gold while digging in the mine, Brandon hated letting the opportunity slip away. And for a while, Brandon made quite a bit on Bower's claim, paying off his debts and living a tiny bit of the good life as much as poor miners make. However, he soon noticed that someone else was working in the mine. The sluice had been tampered with, and the trespasser had left the water running. Brandon searched for the offender and warned the other miners—if it was them—that he was getting fed up with the situation and that it needed to stop. The mine was now rightfully his.

One night, Brandon prepared himself by loading his rifle and hiding in a suitable nook, peering out and waiting for the intruder. Only the distant sounds of the camp and the rustling trees filled the air. Something white against a tree caught his attention, so he tiptoed closer for a better look. He saw a note tacked to a tree that glowed with a peculiar phosphorescence: "Notice! I, Thomas Bowers, claim this ground for placer mining." Brandon sniffed in disregard and ripped the paper from the tree. Then he felt something tingle in his arm, which began to shake and then go numb. Still, Brandon smiled to himself, pleased that the notice on the tree was now gone. But shortly after, he could hear water flowing in the sluice again.

Angrily, Jim Brandon gripped his gun, but then he caught a glimmer in the corner of his eye—a moment later, the glowing notice had returned. He heard the noise coming from the mine, the clanking of pick and shovel. As his eyes turned to the mine, he saw old dead Tom Bowers there, his face pale, his hair white, his corpse skeletal, and his eyes glowing two bulging brilliant moons.

Brandon brought up his rifle and fired. Dead or not, the mine no longer belonged to Bowers as far as he could conceive. BOOM! A shriek erupted from the hole where Bowers had been, and the spectral figure came rushing right at Brandon with pick and took off on his heels. Up and down the hill, they went through the forest and over ditches and toward Pike City, where the miners were loudly celebrating in a saloon. Amidst the revelry, the sound of falling and a scream pierced the air, followed by an eerie silence. When the townsfolk emerged, they found Brandon's rifle and a pick and shovel with "T. B." etched into the handles. Jim Brandon came no more, but the sluice still runs every night on Misery Hill. It seems some ghosts are not meant to lie down easily to rest and never will.

California
Bodie: A Real Ghost Town

Bodie, a goldrush boomtown in 1876, was a thriving community with 2,000 structures and a bustling population. The town was named after Waterman Body, who discovered gold in the area. Once the gold boom ended, it became a ghost town. Today, Bodie is designated as Bodie State Historic Park. Visitors are welcome, but there is a curse associated with the site. Visitors taking anything from the old town will experience bad luck until the item is returned. Additionally, Bodie is haunted. At the Dechambeau House, a spirit is often seen peering from an upstairs window. In the Bodie Cemetery, there is an angel statue dedicated to 2-year-old Evelyin Myer, who was killed in April of 1897. She held her father's hand, swinging around and sliding on the ice. At the same time, a hired man was using a pick nearby to break the sheets of ice on the family's front porch and accidentally hit her. Her ghost plays with children who visit the cemetery.

Haunting Shorts of California:

- Point Sur Lighthouse, a light station at Point Sur south of Monterey, has a haunted history. More than a dozen shipwrecks have occurred nearby, each with a tragic story. The souls of those who perished in these wrecks have found supernatural solace within the walls of the lighthouse, making it a place of eerie tranquility.

- The Black Diamond's Mine Rose Hill Cemetery, managed by East Bay Regional Park District and Black Diamond Mines Regional Park, is a place of both historical significance and eerie tales. The cemetery dates back to the 19th century and is the final resting place of many early settlers and miners. However, it is also a site of reported paranormal activity. Cries of young women, ringing of bells, a cross levitating on its own, and bobbing lights were just a few warnings by the dead within this graveyard to leave them alone after vandals stole graves and plundered the cemetery.

- The Battery Point Light on the Crescent City coast was built in 1850. John H. Jeffrey served as a keeper from 1875 to 1914 and is believed to be the ghost associated with the sound of loud seaboots on the lighthouse stairway. He and his wife, Nellie, worked at the lighthouse for 39 years. Additionally, one caretaker reported hearing wet footsteps emerging from the rocks below the lighthouse. However, who or what made those sounds remains a mystery, as no one knows where they originated.

- Just west of Death Valley National Monument, in the Inyo Mountains, lies the ghost town of Cerro Gordo, a once bustling silver mining boomtown. At its peak, it had two brothels and no churches. The town is haunted by Alphonse Benoit, a murdered woodcutter at a nearby lumber camp.

Before the building burned down, he was seen in the kitchen window of the American Hotel, and he might still be nearby.

• Many people have reported seeing a woman dressed in white, weeping and walking along a windy road called Channel Road in eastern Fresno County, specifically in the farming community of Sanger. Some believe she is the ghost of a woman who lost control of her car, resulting in the deaths of her two small daughters. Now, she wanders in search of them.

• The infamous Cecil Hotel, built in 1920 in Los Angeles, has earned the nickname "Suicide Hotel" due to the alarming number of suicides that have occurred within its walls—at least 16 people. It gained notoriety in 2013 when Elisa Lam mysteriously disappeared and was later found dead in a rooftop water tank. Visitors to the hotel have reported experiencing strange noises, feelings of dread, and sightings of apparitions.

• Joshua Tree National Park, located in southeastern California, is known for its paranormal activity, previously home to nearly 300 mines. Visitors often report encounters with 19th-century Mormon apparitions, UFO sightings, and mysterious creatures like Bigfoot. One prominent haunted spot is the Lost Horse Mine Trail, a 4-mile round-trip hike leading to an old gold mine once owned by Johnny Lang. He discovered the mine in 1890 while searching for lost horses and faced threats from the McHaney Gang. Lang later partnered to mine the area but was forced out by a partner. After returning to the mine, he fell sick and passed away in 1925. His spirit lingers on the trail, with hikers reporting sightings of a shadowy figure and the sound of pickaxes hitting rock.

• Located on the west side of the forbidding Colorado Desert, Vallecito Stage Station, featured a natural spring.

It was a welcome stop for settlers and prospectors along the only road through the valley. But it wasn't just weary travelers stopping in; thieves also took the route. After two bandits quarreled, one riding a beautiful white horse, each shot the other, killing both. The horse ran off and, to this day, still returns in spirited form.

• The Carrizo Creek Station was once located in what is now Anza-Borrego Desert State Park along the bank of Carrizo Creek. It was an isolated outpost and a key stop on the Butterfield Overland Mail Line and the San Antonio–San Diego Mail Line. When a stagecoach driver was murdered along its route by bandits, the stage and the corpse of the driver continued on its way. Now it returns in ghostly form. When witnessed near the location of Carrizo Station and always after dark, four phantom mules pull the stagecoach with a hunched form at the reins. The following day, the stagecoach's tracks are seen in the sand.

• The Union Hotel in Benicia is known for its ghost story about Crying Mary, a woman of the night who fell in love with one of her customers. Unfortunately, her passion was unreturned, leading her to hang herself in one of the hotel rooms. Guests often report her sorrow and hearing weeping sounds attributed to her spirit.

• The Winchester Mystery House is a sprawling Victorian mansion in San Jose, California. It was owned by Sarah Winchester, the widow of firearms magnate William Winchester. After the deaths of her daughter and husband, Sarah began an extensive renovation of the house in 1886, which continued for 38 years until she died in 1922. The mansion is known for its architectural curiosities— staircases lead to nowhere, and doors open into walls. These odd features reflect Sarah's belief that she was haunted by the ghosts of those killed by Winchester rifles.

- Coloma Pioneer Cemetery in Coloma, established in 1848, is renowned for its rich history and numerous reported ghost sightings. The cemetery is the final resting place for over 600 pioneers and their families, who were drawn to the area for gold. One of the notable apparitions associated with this cemetery is a woman in a flowing burgundy skirt. She is unhappy because her grave is located far from her loved ones. Additionally, witnesses have also reported a tall, bearded gold miner dressed in ragged clothing wandering along the road near the cemetery

- At Golden Gate Park in San Francisco since the late 1800s, people have witnessed a frantic woman with eyes bulging and mouth open in a scream riding a ghostly black horse pell-mell through the park. In the late 1870s, a young woman wearing a straw hat had gotten drunk and had stumbled out from a pub bordering the park. A policeman was mounted on a beautiful black horse outside, and she challenged him to allow her to ride the horse a short way, to which the officer jokingly complied. Once upon the horse, it bolted, and the woman, screaming in panic, took off on a wild ride. When she did not return, the officer searched her out and found both the woman and horse dead at the bottom of the lake about a mile from the pub. Once a year, the horse and rider return in death to ride their last ride around midnight before vanishing.

A California Cryptid
Bluff Creek Bigfoot

Bigfoot is a legendary ape-like creature said to inhabit the forests of Northern California. A notable encounter was in August 1958, when Jerry Crew, a logging tractor operator, came across the beast while working in the remote wilderness of Six Rivers National Forest. Crew discovered giant footprints, measuring 16 inches long, that resembled a human's. This discovery occurred near Bluff Creek, located in Humboldt County. On October 20, 1967, Roger Patterson, who had developed an interest in Bigfoot, researched the areas of sightings near Bluff Creek in Northern California. While riding horses there, he encountered a hairy, bipedal figure. He took a short motion picture known as the Patterson–Gimlin film (PGF), which is often cited as one of the most compelling and controversial pieces of evidence for the existence of Bigfoot.

A California Cryptid
Lone Pine Mountain Devil

The Lone Pine Mountain Devil is a critter associated with the Sierra Nevada region of California, a large, winged, bat-like carnivore preying on various animals and even humans. The legend emerged in the mid-19th century, overlapping with the inflow of settlers during the California Gold Rush.

In 1878, 37 Spanish settlers vanished in the Sierra Nevada Mountains. Their disappearance was shrouded in mystery until their remains were discovered by miners. A priest among the party named Father Justus Martinez survived, divulging the settlers had been celebrating when they were attacked by "beasts damned by the good lord," referring to the Lone Pine Mountain Devil, characterized as having multiple wings, razor-like talons, and layers of venomous fangs. The Lone Pine Mountain Devil targets those who disturb its habitat.

Colorado
St Elmo Phantom Hollow

In the 1870s, prospectors living in little more than dugouts and tents began to settle in an area of Chalk Creek Canyon that later became known as St. Elmo. The little boomtown flourished in the 1880s, with mines throughout the area rich in silver, gold, copper, and iron. At its peak, the town featured multiple saloons and dance floors, smelting works, five hotels, a telegraph office, merchandise stores, a town hall, restaurants, sawmills, a schoolhouse, and a weekly newspaper called the St. Elmo Mountaineer. Passenger stagecoaches and freight wagons drove along the pioneer route to Aspen. Eventually, it was along the Denver, South Park, and Pacific Railroad routes.

The town faced challenges after fires and the Sherman Silver Purchase Act of 1890. This law required the U.S. government to buy a large amount of silver each month. Although the law aimed to increase the money supply and support silver interests, it harmed the economy.

The boomtown would have probably faded into history without the Stark family consisting of Anton Stark, his wife Anna, and their three children: Tony, Roy, and Annabelle. The Starks ran the town's general store (Stark Brothers Mercantile Company), the Home Comfort Hotel, and the telegraph/post office. They were the last residents of St. Elmo, staying behind to run their businesses and protect the town from vandalism as it transitioned into a ghost town in the early 20th century. Later, they rented cabins to tourists. By 1934, the family had faced significant loss when Roy passed away, followed shortly by the death of their mother, Anna. Only Tony and Annabelle lived in the isolated town, which lacked indoor plumbing and electricity.

Tony died at age 77 on June 7, 1958. Annabelle went to live in a nursing home in 1958, where she passed away at age 77 on April 25, 1960. St. Elmo is now a well-preserved ghost town in Chaffee County, Colorado, in the central part of the state, about 20 miles southwest of Buena Vista. It has become a popular destination for those wanting to glimpse Colorado's mining past and its ghosts.

It isn't surprising that Annabelle haunts the town; she must have pined for it, worried about its fate those last two years of her life living so far away. Known for her eccentric behavior, including walking around town in tattered clothing and carrying a gun in later years, she had a powerful attraction to the area. Both visitors and locals have heard muffled voices and seen Annabelle's ghost wandering the town, a shadowy figure mainly near the old hotel (Home Comfort Hotel) and the Stark Brothers Mercantile Company. Some feel cold spots on warm days, and doors are known to open and close independently. Those walking through the old town have seen a young woman in a white dress standing at the hotel window.

Some believe the spirits of miners who died in accidents or endured hardships haunt the town. Visitors have reported seeing ghostly figures dressed in mining clothing and gear, watching twinkling lantern lights appear and disappear, and hearing phantom pickaxes striking the rocks. A Denver, South Park & Pacific Railroad train never left the town. On some nights, those nearby hear the distant whistle of this ghost train echoing through the valley.

Colorado
Death of a Gunfighter and the Ghosts that Came After

Joseph "Jack" Slade was a legendary figure known for living a life filled with contrasts. On one side, he worked diligently as the superintendent of stagecoaches and the Pony Express, overseeing operations that ensured mail was delivered quickly and reliably across the rugged American West. By eliminating corrupt stagecoach drivers and managers, he helped to make these transportation systems run more smoothly. In contrast, Slade's approach to cleaning up operations resembled that of a classic Western gunslinger. He was fearless, a heavy drinker, and disliked due to his ability to make others perceive him as a ruthless adversary with a quick draw. Unafraid to confront danger with a heavy hand, he frequently dealt with outlaws and lawlessness. People both respected and feared him for his strong presence and rapid reflexes with a gun. As a result, stories about him became legendary. As a result of his violent past, he and others he encountered left behind a few ghosts.

Andrew Ferrin was a teamster for the J.M. Hockaday & Co. freight line along the Central Overland route. He was shot and killed by Jack Slade, the wagon master and Hockaday division agent, during an altercation that occurred when the teamsters broke into boxes of liquor supplies, helped themselves abundantly, and defied Slade's authority. Slade was drunk and verbally reprimanding the other man, who retorted hotly back at him. Slade drew his gun and shot Ferrin dead. Ferrin's teamsters dug a grave by the roadside, wrapped the corpse in his blankets, and buried him in the unmarked grave. The act spurred Slade's reputation as a gunfighter, and word spread of his violence throughout the country.

In 1859, Slade was assigned to a perilous stretch of stagecoach line. His orders were to "clean up the line," replacing a man named Jules Beni. Beni operated a trading post, saloon, hotel, and store in the town named after him, Julesburg, Colorado. With a population of around one hundred residents, it was likely one of the largest towns within a couple hundred-mile radius. Central Overland California was a stagecoach line that operated in the American West in the early 1860s, most well known as the parent company of the Pony Express. The town became part of the Pony Express, a fast mail service route from Missouri to California. Beni was appointed as the division superintendent for Central Overland, overseeing a large area around the town. However, he began stealing horses and hay and selling them back to the company and likely was organizing raids on wagons passing through using men disguised as Native Americans to take the blame. Beni was hiding the plunder from the raids in a cave outside of town on the property of Uberto Gabello. Gabello began charging tourists to view the cave, and Beni shot and killed the Italian miner reputed to have amassed a fortune in the gold fields at Cripple Creek.

Beni was unhappy about being removed from his position, nor did he like that Slade was tracking down and hanging many who had been working with him rustling horses. In March of 1860, Beni ambushed Slade when he entered a restaurant in Julesburg Station, firing nearly a dozen shots at Jack Slade. The station keeper, James Boner, stated, "I never saw a man so badly riddled. He was like a sieve."

Slade survived after being taken by stagecoach and rail to St. Louis surgeons. Beni had a reward posted on his head, but when he returned to pick up some stock in August of 1861, two of Slade's men wounded Beni in a gunfight. They captured him and bound him to a packhorse. Some say Beni died along the way, and the men ended up sitting him up on a chair for Slade to "kill." Other legends say that when Beni shot Slade, Jack Slade swore vengeance, "I'll live to get you yet, Jules, and when I do, I'll wear one of your ears on my watchchain." And he was alive when the men brought Beni to him. Slade followed through on his threat by tying him to a corral post, torturing him for days, and cutting off his ears. Jack Slade carried his trophies on a watch chain for the rest of his days.

In November of 1861, Slade was fired from the stage company; his drinking problem led to erratic behavior. He would have drunk himself to death if not that on March 10, 1864, while intoxicated in Virginia City, Montana, vigilantes lynched him for disturbing the peace. Slade is not gone; he haunts Julesburg. He is recognized by his two shrunken, blackened ears that dangle from his watch chain, leaving an overwhelming dread in those who glimpse his shadowy form. Jules Beni, the town's founder and outlaw, also haunts the vicinity of the original Julesburg site and the Italian Caves, where he may have hidden his loot after his raids. Beni's ghost is malevolent, and drivers have reported seeing his apparition along Highway 138 between Ovid and Julesburg.

Haunting Shorts of Colorado:

- Silver Cliff is in a high valley between Colorado's Sangre de Cristo Mountains. It originated as a silver mining town in the late 1870s. Eerie, pulsating blue lights, often referred to as ghostly orbs, can be seen bouncing around the old Silver Cliff Cemetery. These lights were first observed by miners who used the cemetery as a shortcut in the early 1880s. However, the phenomena gained widespread attention in the mid-1950s when a group of teenagers on a night ride passed by the cemetery and were terrified to see the lights dancing among the tombstones. This sighting drew crowds of visitors to the cemetery, many of whom attempted to catch the lights only to watch them vanish upon approach. These mysterious orbs are still occasionally observed today.

- Aspen is a town in the Rocky Mountains renowned for its skiing, arts, culture, and ghost stories. One notable haunting occurs at the Hotel Jerome, Aspen's original luxury hotel, built in the 1880s. Following the 1893 silver crash, the hotel became a boarding house as the town's economy suffered. The spirit of a long-deceased maid rearranges furniture and bedding. The ghost of a 10-year-old boy who drowned in the pool in 1936, known as the "Water Boy," wanders the hallways, leaving behind puddles and wet spots on the floor. He is also seen in room 310, overlooking the pool.

- Montrose is in the heart of the Uncompahgre Valley on Colorado's Western Slope. The town is known for the legend of the "River Witch." According to local lore, she was a woman who lost her baby in the river over a hundred years ago. On nights when the full moon shines, those walking along the river at Riverbottom Park can hear her sorrowful cries.

- Located 25 miles from downtown Durango in the San Juan Mountains, Purgatory Resort is a ski resort near the San Juan National Forest, where hikers hap upon abandoned mines. Hikers have reported hearing bells behind the resort and ghostly train whistles. The name Purgatory comes from a nearby tributary of the Rio de las Animas Perdidas, Purgatory Creek, named in conjunction with the Rio de Las Animas (River of Souls). Purgatory is the place, in Christian beliefs, where souls undergo purification to enter heaven.

- Durango, Hermosa, and Trimble are in the southwestern corner of Colorado along the Animas River. The Animas River, originally known as the Rio de las Animas Perdidas, which translates to "River of Lost Souls," received its name from a blend of historical legend and cultural influences. It begins high in the San Juan Mountains of Colorado and winds down to its junction with the San Juan River in New Mexico. Spanish explorers called it the Rio de Las Animas, the River of Souls. In the late 1890s, newspapers infused a sense of drama and mystique into their stories. The river had gained a reputation for being treacherous due to its swift currents, unpredictable conditions, and subsequent mishaps. As a result, numerous tragedies in its waters led to the popularization of the name "River of Lost Souls," which ultimately became widely recognized. According to local lore, a group of early Spanish travelers perished near the river under mysterious circumstances, leaving their souls to wander the area. Their ghostly cries still echo in the waters.

- Trinidad, located in Colorado's southeastern plains, is known for its abandoned ghost towns and a past closely tied to the Santa Fe Trail, a significant route during the westward expansion. The "Mountain Branch" of the Santa Fe Trail passed through Trinidad, linking the eastern plains to the Rocky Mountains. The 1907 built Tarabino Inn is haunted.

It includes stories of ghosts from its past, including a woman in a gown wandering at the bottom of the stairs. Visitors often report cigar smoke lingering in certain rooms.

• Steamboat Springs in the upper valley of the Yampa River, is a mountain town surrounded by national forests and wilderness areas. One of the most well-known hauntings in Steamboat Springs is associated with the Sequoia Building, located at the corner of Ninth Street and Oak. This haunting is linked to the spirit of Laura Monson, who lived there. Locals often share stories of her appearing in a rocking chair after suffering injuries from an automobile accident in 1930, which forced her to return to Steamboat Springs, where she spent the remainder of her life. After she died in 1949, her old rocking chair mysteriously continued to move on its own.

• Fort Collins is lodged against the foothills of the Rocky Mountains and alongside the banks of the Cache la Poudre River. The Walrus Ice Cream Shop is located within and haunted by Charlie Dinnebeck, who owned a cafe in the early 1900s. The shop is located near the city morgue, where horse-drawn hearses delivered bodies. This proximity may explain the strange occurrences, such as upturned furniture and broken windows.

• Gold Camp Road, located near Colorado Springs, Colorado, is famous for its scenic beauty and historical significance. It was initially constructed to support the Pike's Peak Gold Rush as a railway connecting Cripple Creek and Colorado Springs. Known as the "Short Line," it transported people, supplies, and minerals around 1901. In the 1920s, the railroad was converted into a toll road for cars and eventually became a public road. Nowadays, visitors can explore the first two accessible tunnels along Gold Camp Road. However, Tunnel #3 is closed due to an older collapse.

An urban legend persists about a bus crash in 1988 within the tunnel, often shared around campfires. There is no credible evidence to support this story. Despite this, adventurers continue to visit the site and report hearing the sounds of children laughing and screaming within the tunnel. Some have even claimed to find mysterious tiny handprints appearing on their car windows and windshields after parking near the tunnel.

• Horse Thief Canyon is located near Fruita, Colorado, in the western part of the state. It is within the McInnis Canyons National Conservation Area, renowned for its stunning red rock landscapes, rugged trails, and desert scenery. The area is popular for hiking and earned its name from horse thieves who roamed the remote region, using it as a hiding place for their stolen steeds. According to legend, a woman's ghost haunts the canyon, killed when horse-rustling cowboys stampeded their stolen horses through it.

• The Fort Morgan Nature Trails are within Riverside Park in Fort Morgan, Colorado. According to local lore, there was once a woman known as the "River Witch," who was tormented by her neighbors and ultimately took her own life. Those who walk the trail have reported feeling her presence. One notable incident occurred in the 1950s when two teenagers parked their cars nearby. They heard scratching sounds on the roof, which terrified them, and they quickly drove away. When the boy stopped at the girl's house to drop her off, they discovered river moss and deep scratches on the car's rooftop.

• The Stanley Hotel is on a hill overlooking Estes Park. It offers stunning views of the Continental Divide, Rocky Mountain National Park, and Longs Peak. It is most famously recognized as the inspiration for the fictional Overlook Hotel in Stephen King's 1980 horror novel and film, "The Shining."

The hotel has developed a reputation for paranormal activity, with reports of hearing the laughter of deceased children, sightings of apparitions, and the sound of a piano playing.

- In the foothills southwest of Loveland, Colorado, lies Carter Lake. A three-mile-long trail in the area is haunted by the ghost of Bennet, a settler involved in a heated land dispute. His life ended when he was shot and killed along one of the roads near the lake. Bennet often wears old-fashioned clothing and carries a bag while roaming the roads surrounding Carter Lake. When the specter is approached, he mysteriously vanishes.

- La Llorona, known as The Crying Woman, is a significant figure in Mexican folklore and has become a well-known story in the United States. A specific version of the tale is passed down in the Purgatoire River area of Colorado: La Llorona was a female soldier who fought alongside her husband during the war. After his death, she fell in love with another man, the son of a Spanish rancher, but he refused to marry her. Despite having children together, he eventually found another woman. Overwhelmed with sadness, she went to the river seeking guidance and believed the river told her to set her children free into its watery depths, as it would take care of them. One by one, she tossed her children into the river, and they drowned. Realizing her grave mistake, she jumped into the water, but they were already gone by then. Heartbroken, she lay down on the riverbank and died. The following day, the townspeople found her body, buried her in a shallow grave, and thought they could move on with their lives. However, during the night, she rose from her grave to search for her lost children, wailing and crying as she walked along the shore.

A Colorado Cryptid
Slide-Rock Bolter

Rico is a small town in southwestern Colorado, nestled within the San Juan Mountains, which originated in 1879 after miners uncovered oxidized silver ore in the Telescope and Dolores mountains. The rapid growth that followed made for an inpouring of miners and settlers eager to exploit the natural resources. By 1892 and the railroad's arrival, Rico's population exploded with 5000 people, 23 saloons, two churches, two newspapers, a boarding house, a mercantile, a brick county courthouse, a theater, and a three-block red-light district.

The boomtown attracted many tourists seeking adventure in the wilderness just outside the hotel doors. It was also home to a large lumber mill, where timbermen eagerly shared cautionary tales and exaggerations about life in the wild, often scaring one another and travelers. One of those stories was the Slide-Rock Bolter, a gruesome creature who preyed on tourists.

In 1910, the Legend of the Slide-Rock Bolter emerged when William Thomas Cox, a State Forester, wrote: "Fearsome Critters of the Lumberwoods, with a Few Desert and Mountain Beasts." This book contained tales he had collected from logging camps. In it was a creature, Slide-Rock Bolter, the timber men had passed along. Here is how Cox described the beast:

"In the mountains of Colorado, where in summer the woods are becoming infested with tourists, much uneasiness has been caused by the presence of the slide-rock bolter. This frightful animal lives only in the steepest mountain country where the slopes are greater than 45 degrees. It has an immense head, with small eyes, and a mouth somewhat on the order of a sculpin, running back beyond its ears. The tail consists of a divided flipper, with enormous grab-hooks, which it fastens over the crest of the mountain or ridge, often remaining there motionless for days at a time, watching the gulch for tourists or any other hapless creature that may enter it. At the right moment, after sighting a tourist, it will lift its tail, thus loosening its hold on the mountain, and with its small eyes riveted on the poor unfortunate, and drooling thin skid grease from the corners of its mouth, which greatly accelerates its speed, the bolter comes down like a toboggan, scooping in its victim as it goes, its own impetus carrying it up the next slope, where it again slaps its tail over the ridge and waits. Whole parties of tourists are reported to have been gulped at one scoop by taking parties far back into the hills. The animal is a menace not only to tourist but to the woods as well. Many a draw through spruce-covered slopes has been laid low, the trees being knocked out by the roots or mowed off as by a scythe where the bolter has crashed down through from the peaks above-"

Connecticut
The Lady in White

Union Cemetery is a historic burial ground in Easton, Connecticut, with headstones dating back to the mid-1700s. The cemetery is known for its serene landscape, which includes mature trees, rolling hills, and well-maintained pathways. Despite its attractive appearance, the cemetery is also noted for its reported hauntings.

The cemetery sits on a little over 5 acres at the intersections of Sport Hill and Stepney roads. It is here that numerous sightings and experiences have been reported by individuals encountering a Lady in White. She is described as a figure dressed in white bedclothes or a wedding gown standing among the tombstones or walking along the roadway.

In their book "Graveyard: True Hauntings from an Old New England Cemetery," Ed and Lorraine Warren (renowned American paranormal investigators) told of two small boys who noted a bright light in the cemetery. Central to the glow was a beautiful woman with four darker figures trailing close behind. As she floated past, the shadier forms appeared to be arguing with the woman. As the boys grew older, one saw her gliding through the cemetery alone several times. The boys were not alone in coming face to face with the ghost. There have even been those who have hit her with their car. When the driver stops and rushes out to help the victim, no one is around, and the vehicle has no dents.

Although there is no certainty, some associate the Lady in White with a shocking hometown story in Easton that occurred in 1923 when 37-year-old Robert Edwards, a farmer and lumberman, murdered his estranged 19-year-old wife, Ruby. Newly married, Robert and Ruby had been living a cramped life with Robert's elderly parents at their farm, greatly irritating the young woman. So caught up in caring for the aging farmstead, Robert had no time for a job so that they could move to their own house, and the farm was barely making enough money to feed the family. To make matters worse, Ruby was kept under the watchful eye of a very jealous Robert, who limited interactions with family and friends.

Less than a year after marriage, Ruby had enough and moved back in with her parents. Then, one night, after running an errand to a neighbor, she stayed a bit late. The family, including Alma Swenson and her two teen sons, Arthur and Albert, walked her home. As they turned onto one street, Robert called to Ruby from the shadows, pleading for her to return home. As she walked away, she firmly told him he would have to go to the house if he wished to speak to her.

When she turned back to continue along her way, Robert, consumed with anger and jealousy, reached beneath his jacket to expose a shotgun and fired it, striking Ruby between the shoulders. When she fell to the ground in great anguish, he shot her again in the chest before turning slowly and walking away.

Robert fled into the forest, and not twenty minutes later, there were more shots deep in the woods. A posse was formed, and they beat back the brush in search of the killer for two days. It was brought to their attention that a friend of Robert's was sure that the man was probably in an outcropping of rocks near the summit known as Fox Ledge. True to word, a trail of blood and pieces of Robert's skull were found wedged in one of the crevices. He had taken his life. Although there are no records, Ruby Wells Edwards and Robert Edwards are believed to be buried in separate graves in Union Cemetery or nearby Stepney Cemetery. Perhaps it is young Ruby who wears the white dress and is still floating around.

Connecticut
Midnight Mary

The grave of Midnight Mary in Evergreen Cemetery is indeed haunted, say those who have visited the massive block of pink granite gravestone with a gruesome epitaph etched on its surface:

The People Shall Be Troubled At Midnight

And Pass Away At High Noon

Just From, And About To Renew Her Daily Work In Her Full Strength Of Body And Mind

MARY E. HART

Having Fallen Prostrate Remained Unconscious Until She Died At Midnight

October 15 1872.

Born December 16 1824.

Forty-seven-year-old Mary was a seamstress living in a quiet neighborhood around Winthrop Street. As the story goes, Mary was simply going about her daily tasks when suddenly she fell into a swoon, a deathlike state that was thought to be a stroke. She did not regain consciousness.

Everyone assumed she had died. She was buried, and life would go on, except that her aunt had a vivid nightmare that poor Mary was calling for her from the grave, begging the woman to release her from her coffin prison. She was not dead! Of course, they scoffed at the aunt but finally relented, and the body was exhumed. Alas, Mary had been alive. But in the meantime, she had really perished. The coffin was nearly torn to shreds, her fingernails peeled back from the flesh, bloody and torn from trying to escape from the coffin, her body giving the appearance of struggle, and her face contorted with terror.

Who could deny that surely no good could come from such a tragedy? Early on, a ghostly hearse pulled by horses drove to the cemetery and sank into the earth, disappearing nearby. A young man, paying a midnight vigil to the grave, was found rigid in terror, his clothes muddied and torn by brush.

Connecticut
Hell Hollow: Maud's Grave

Before it became Pachaug State Forest, Connecticut's most prominent state forest, the area was once a rural landscape filled with farms. One section, Hell Hollow, is characterized by its rocky terrain and susceptibility to flooding. The name given by early settlers seems fitting for such a challenging place to cultivate land. With a name like that, urban legends began to emerge.

Local lore speaks of a malevolent witch who allegedly lived in Hell Hollow during its early days. Accused of practicing dark magic, she was ultimately executed by the townspeople.

Her grave was placed far from the cemetery as if to banish her spirit. According to the tales, her ghost haunted the area, tormenting passersby and seeking revenge on those who wronged her.

There was once a five-foot cement cross marking her grave, which was stolen more times than anyone could count. It was repeatedly replaced until it eventually had to be hidden away in a closet at a local church. This cross actually belonged to Maud, the daughter of Lucy and Gilbert Reynolds. Maud was a little girl who died of diphtheria just three months shy of her second birthday in 1890. She was buried closer to her home than to the cemetery, so her grieving parents could be nearer to her.

If screams are heard in those areas as they sometimes are— it is more likely that it is Maud's spirit haunting the site, upset that someone kept stealing her grave marker. One must consider that the terrible twos may affect not only the living but also the dead!

Connecticut
Hannah Cranna: Witch

Gregory's Four Corners Burial Ground at Spring Hill Road and Main in Trumbull holds the grave of Hannah Cranna Hovey. Hannah was married to Captain Joseph Hovey, and the couple lived in Monroe Village, at Cragley Hill near Bugg Hill Road and Cutler's Farm Road. The couple lived quietly, and little was noted about their presence in the community until her husband's suspicious death drew the townspeople's attention, leading them to label Hannah a witch.

It was then Hannah Cranna's legend began. Hannah must have gotten so annoyed with her husband Joseph, a heavy drinker, that she dragged him to the edge of a lofty cliff called Helvellyn Crag (the original name for Bugg Hill) and pushed him over the edge. Thereafter, the rumors began to fly. She cast curses on those who wronged her and gave good fortune to those she liked. Hannah threatened neighbors with curses should they not give her food and firewood. When a local farmer's wife denied Hannah a fresh pie, Hannah cursed the woman so she could never bake again.

After a man was caught fishing in a brook on Hannah's farm, she condemned him to never being able to catch a fish again. And he did not. She was known to live alone with her only companion and confidant, a rooster named Old Boreas, who only crowed at midnight (except when something ominous was about to occur), which everyone knew was strange indeed as only such an unordinary creature associated with witchcraft would do such an odd thing.

Hannah Cranna died in 1859 when she was around 75 years of age. She predicted her death and instructed that her coffin must be carried by hand to the burial ground after sundown. However, on the day of her burial, heavy snow covered the ground, and the men decided to transport her body not by hand but by sled and pulled by oxen. As they began their journey to the cemetery, the coffin slipped off the sled and right back to Hannah's front door. Fearing repercussions, the men started out again carrying the coffin by hand, which took them nearly the entire day, and much to their surprise, they arrived after sunset just as Hannah demanded. The coffin was even said to have slipped from the men's fingers and slid directly into the hole dug for it. Just after the burial, Hannah's house became engulfed in flames. The fire smoldered for many days afterward.

Her grave may still appear along the little hillside, but it does not mean Hannah Cranna is not around. Nowadays, we do not fear witches as much, and duly so, we just learn to respect those different from us. The story of Hannah Cranna serves as a reminder of the importance of empathy and understanding, even towards those with whom we may disagree. Sometimes, those driving past see her standing near the roadway. In at least one incident, she materialized one night during a full moon at a farmhouse window, asking a girl sleeping in the room if she could spare any pies for her.

Haunting Shorts of Connecticut:

• The Old State House in Hartford, a rectangular structure made of brownstone and brick, has a haunted past. It was here on Meeting House Square on May 26, 1647, that Alse Young of Windsor was the first person on record to be executed for witchcraft in the 13 colonies, a scapegoat for an influenza epidemic. This event marked a significant turning point in the history of witchcraft trials in the New World. The spirit of Joseph Steward, a painter and museum curator, roams the grounds. Staff have reported the distinct turn of a doorknob and ghostly footsteps.

• The Mark Twain House, owned by Samuel Clemens (Mark Twain) in Hartford, was the famous author's and his family's residences from 1874 to 1891. Visitors often report experiencing the phantom scent of cigars, a habit Twain was known for, hearing voices and noticing shuffling footsteps at this historical site. One of the notable apparitions is the Lady in White, believed by some to be the ghost of Twain's eldest daughter, Susy Clemens, who passed away on August 18, 1896, at 24, due to meningitis. The connection between these ghostly experiences and the life of Mark Twain adds a layer of intrigue to the site's history.

• On a scenic stretch of Connecticut coastline, the brick complex of Seaside Sanatorium in Waterford is a haunting reminder of its dark past. Built as a facility to treat children with tuberculosis, the buildings now stand off-limits, shrouded in rumors of hauntings. The property is haunted by the spirits of former inmates who were abused by some of the staff.

• The dark history of those mistreated at Norwich State Hospital, located in Preston, Connecticut, has led to many ghostly entities believed to be trapped within its ruins of buildings shielded from trespassers by chain-link fences.

- The Doctor Ticknor House in Salisbury became a sensation when the Fenn family moved in during 1873. The father, blinded in an accident at a smelting furnace, was eager to purchase the house because it was very affordable. Immediately, the family reported unsettling events. One notable incident involved a rattling door to 15-year-old Byron's room. Byron claimed to have seen a figure dressed in white standing in the doorway of his room, initially mistaking her for his mother in her nightclothes. A guest in the home heard a woman pacing back and forth. Intrigued by the reports of supernatural activity, reporters flocked to the home, and eventually, the family abandoned the house. The ghost was thought to be Doctor Ticknor's long-dead wife.

- The Enfield Demon House, a duplex over two hundred years old in Enfield, has many strange accidental deaths, suicides, and murders—possibly over 25—which are thought to be caused by a demon.

- A ghost known as "Ernie," who was a former lighthouse keeper at the New London Ledge Lighthouse at the mouth of the Thames River in Groton, haunts the lighthouse after he took his own life upon discovering his wife's unfaithfulness. Ernie is often seen wearing a slicker and a rain hat and is known for slamming doors and moving objects around the lighthouse.

- The Seventh Day Baptist Cemetery, located on Upson Road in Burlington, serves as a burial ground for members of the Seventh Day Baptist Church. The cemetery is haunted by a ghost known as the Green Lady, who is thought to be Elizabeth Palmiter. Her tragic story begins with her searching for her husband during a snowstorm. She drowned in a nearby swamp. Her husband later found her body, which was dressed in a green gown. Her restless spirit, clad in green, continues to search for her lost husband.

A Connecticut Cryptid
Glawackus of Glastonbury

The Glawackus is a creature originating in Glastonbury, Connecticut, first reported in 1939. This intriguing hybrid measures around four feet in length. It stands about two and a half feet tall, resembling a blend of a bear, panther, and lion. Typically, it is described as having black or tawny fur complemented by a long and bushy tail. One of its most distinctive traits is its fierce vocalizations, which include screeches and cackles reminiscent of a hyena. Notably, the Glawackus is believed to be blind but possesses enhanced senses of smell and hearing. A particularly unsettling aspect of its mythology is that gazing into its eyes can erase a person's memories. This creature is known for stealing small farm animals and pets, adding to its reputation in local lore.

Delaware

Cape Henlopen's Corpse Lights

Delaware Bay is an estuary between Delaware and New Jersey on the northeastern seaboard of the United States. Along its shoreline lies Cape Henlopen State Park, where the land extends into the Atlantic Ocean. This area has always been dangerous for ships, with over 2,400 recorded shipwrecks from the waters off the Delaware coast to those of Chesapeake Bay. Various factors have contributed to these disasters, including stormy weather, combat, treacherous shoals, and bloody rebellions. Recently, researchers discovered the wreck of the W.R. Grace, a three-masted sailing vessel that measured 215 feet in length. The ship ran aground in shallow waters near Cape Henlopen on September 12, 1889. It was ultimately destroyed by a hurricane over a century ago.

The Faithful Steward was an 18th-century merchant ship from Ireland headed for Philadelphia. It carried 249 passengers and crew members, copper coins, and rose gold guineas. As the boat approached the mouth of the Delaware Bay, the captain decided to celebrate and began drinking.

During the night, while he was incapacitated, a fierce storm struck, causing the ship to run aground on a shoal and capsize. Sadly, 181 passengers and crew members lost their lives in the disaster, including 93 women and children.

Many people believe that the shipwrecks in the area are caused not just by natural events but also by mysterious, supernatural forces. According to old legends, these accidents are linked to a curse. The story goes that British soldiers once disrupted a wedding ceremony of a local tribe. In the chaos, nearly all the tribe members were killed. The few who survived then put a curse on the land and its shores. As a result, unusual lights called Corpse Lights have been seen at the point, which seems to attract boats and ships into dangerously shallow waters, causing them to sink.

Delaware
Maggie's Bridge

A bridge is located on Woodland Church Road near Seaford, about one mile south of the Woodland Ferry. It is surrounded by woods, features a typical steel guardrail, and spans a quiet branch of the Nanticoke River. There are countless bridges like it, but this one is unique because it is haunted. It is known as Maggie's Bridge. According to local lore, Maggie Bloxom was a young woman in the late 1800s who was expecting a baby. While traveling by carriage, she crossed the bridge, and her horse became spooked, causing the carriage to tumble into the river and sending Maggie to her death. Her spirit lingers, longing for the baby she never had. Those who stand on the bridge and call out to her, "Maggie, I have your baby!" hear mewling and cries from the water and the surrounding brush, where she crouches in hiding.

Delaware
Headless Horseman of the Battle of Cooch's Bridge

The Old Baltimore Pike was constructed before 1720 and connected Elkton, Maryland, to Christiana. This rugged path was later improved and became known as the Elk and Christiana Turnpike. To fund its maintenance, tolls were collected at Cooch's Bridge. The road was one of the leading travel routes in its early years, especially during the American Revolution when George Washington and Thomas Jefferson frequently traversed its rough course. Along this route was the farm and grist/sawmill of Thomas Cooch, which featured a two-story stone house facing east towards the Christiana River. A bridge was built over the river for transportation, likely a simple wooden structure made of planks and logs.

While this humble bridge, Cooch's Bridge, may seem insignificant today, it played a crucial role in September 1777. British forces, aiming to capture Philadelphia—the capital of the Thirteen Colonies and the largest city at the time—were slowed down by American troops at this location. A group of Hessian soldiers fighting for the British advanced along the old dirt path from Elkton toward Philadelphia. They were ambushed by Continental soldiers hidden in the woods, facing a volley of fire that left many Hessians killed or wounded. Reinforcements were called in by the German soldiers, who eventually drove the Americans back across the bridge.

This skirmish became known as the Battle of Cooch's Bridge, Delaware's only Revolutionary War battle. The battle lasted nearly a day, with the Continental Army fighting until they ran out of ammunition and resorted to using swords and bayonets.

Just up the road from the battle site is the Welsh Tract Baptist Church, a simple rectangular brick building constructed by Welsh settlers in 1746, accompanied by a nearby cemetery. Stories passed down tell of a cannonball that entered through a shutter on the east side of the church and exited through a window on the west side. Fortunately, the cannonball caused minor damage to the building, and repairs were easily made. However, the same could not be said for a soldier riding his horse across the cemetery during the battle. He found himself in the path of the cannonball and lost his head. Legend has it that he is still searching for what he misplaced. Witnesses have reported seeing the headless horseman riding along the battlefield path, near I-95, and towards the site of Cooch's Bridge.

Haunting Shorts of Delaware:

- The Cape May-Lewes Ferry terminal and parking lot are haunted by the spirits of Colonial-era sailors buried beneath the pavement. These include both shipwreck victims and sailors who died during their voyages and were thrown overboard. Locals would often bury the sailor's corpses on the nearby beach when they washed up on shore.

- Lums Pond Swamp Trail near Bear is haunted by the Wailing Girl murdered in the 1870s. You may hear her lamenting her death from far in the woods. Ghostly workers have also been heard going about their daily tasks at the mill.

- The Rockwood Mansion, now a museum in Wilmington, is haunted. Built in the mid-1800s by retired banker Joseph Shipley, the mansion has become a site where the family's spirits are believed to linger. Visitors have reported seeing a woman in white in the gardens and feeling a presence in her bedroom. The faint scent of perfume wafts through the air, reminiscent of the long-deceased Mary Bringhurst, Shipley's great-niece, who passed away in the home at the age of 100 in 1965.

- Ghostly sightings have been reported since 1815 at Woodburn Governor's Mansion in Dover, only 25 years after being built. While entertaining a circuit-riding preacher, Lorenzo Dow, the owners, Doctor and Missus Martin Bates, were amid a morning meal prayer. The preacher hesitated to allow another guest to enter the room wearing a ruffled shirt, knee breeches, and powdered wig. No one was present, and when he described the figure, Missus Bates recognized it as her father and the builder of the home, Charles Hillyard III! Visiting spirits include a wine-loving male ghost in a white wig, a former governor's wife, and a girl in period clothing who floats around.

- Fort Delaware State Park, located on Pea Patch Island in the middle of the Delaware River between Delaware and New Jersey, is a 19th-century island fortress. It was built to protect the ports of Wilmington and Philadelphia and served as a prison camp for Confederate prisoners of war during the Civil War. Visitors to the park often report mysterious occurrences, such as doors opening on their own and ghostly footsteps following them. Additionally, strange shadows are frequently seen lurking about the area.

- A ghost known as the Catman haunts the old Long Cemetery in Frankford, Delaware, located down a private drive. He was an old groundskeeper with cat-like features, and for many years, he had been scaring off teenagers who ventured too close. The Catman is buried in the center of the graveyard. According to legend, anyone who knocks three times on the brick wall behind the cemetery will find their car fails to start.

- The Fence Rail Dog originates from folklore in Delaware, along a stretch of Highway 12, Midstate Road, running through the towns of Frederica and Felton. It resembles a dog, but 4-foot tall and 10 feet long from the tip of its nose to the end of its bushy tail. It has glowing red eyes and maintains remarkable speed, even passing vehicles. Some stories suggest it is a phantom of an outlaw who took his life or the spirit of a boy killed by the man who kept him as a slave, roaming the area in search of peace.

A Delaware Cryptid
Prime Hook Swamp Creature

The Prime Hook Swamp Creature is a cryptid that was reported to inhabit Delaware's Prime Hook National Wildlife Refuge. The first notable encounter occurred in July 2007, when a witness, Helen J., observed the creature while driving along Broadkill Road, which runs alongside the swamp. According to her description, the creature stood approximately 2.5 to 3 feet tall, featuring long legs, a tan body, and a long tail. Its face was said to resemble that of a pug. Other individuals have reported additional sightings, including a local shop owner who claimed to have seen the creature while biking.

Florida
St Augustine Lighthouse Pranksters

The St. Augustine Lighthouse sits on the northern end of Anastasia Island in St. Augustine, Florida. The original St. Augustine Lighthouse was built on the site of earlier Spanish and British watchtowers that date back to the late 16th century, which were used for trade and defense. Due to erosion at its base, the lighthouse was rebuilt between 1871 and 1874 to improve visibility and safety for sailors navigating the coast. Hezekiah Pittee, the Superintendent of Lighthouse Construction, oversaw the project and brought his family—his wife, Mary, and their children, Mary Adelaide, Eliza, Edward, and Carrie—with him during the construction.

The children came upon a railway cart used to move supplies from ships docked at Salt Run to the building site. They were often seen riding the cart down to the water like a rollercoaster that ended with a wooden board at the end to stop the cart before it plunged into the water.

However, on July 10, 1873, the three sisters- 15-year-old Mary Adelaide, 13-year-old Eliza, and 4-year-old Carrie with a 10-year-old worker's child were riding their makeshift coaster, and tragedy struck. The wooden board that would stop them was missing. The cart tumbled into the water, trapping the girls beneath. Before help arrived, all but Carrie had drowned.

As the years passed, visitors to the lighthouse often reported hearing the chatter and giggles of young girls. However, despite thorough searches, no sources for these sounds could ever be found. Lighthouse keepers experienced strange noises in the living quarters, including footsteps upstairs. This unsettling atmosphere caused one head keeper, James Pippin, to leave, as he could not spend another night in the house due to its hauntings.

Staff members have also been subjected to pranks by who they believe are the ghosts of the little girls, chasing giggles up and down the stairs only to find no one there. They are not the only lighthouse residents with a penchant for surprising visitors. Over a century ago, Joseph Andre, a lighthouse keeper, fell to his death while painting the exterior of the tower, and he chose to remain in ghostly form. Some claim to have seen him looking out from the top of the tower.

Florida
A Haunt at Bellamy Bridge

There is a haunted trail in Marianna, Florida, surrounded by thick woodlands and a floodplain swamp that is often prone to flooding and overwhelmed with mosquitoes. This area is part of the upper Chipola River region. The path leading to the haunted trail and an old rusted bridge was not always like this; it used to be a winding clay and sand road lined with massive live oaks and poplars.

It led to a two-story townhouse mansion featuring white columns and a veranda with wide steps filled with the most expensive furnishings from Europe. Inside were cut-glass chandeliers, tall white columns, marble mantles, and a grand front double door that opened into an expansive hallway that extended to the back of the house. The mansion, known as Fort Plantation, belonged to Doctor Edward Bellamy and his wife, Nancy Ann (Croom) Bellamy, a young couple who had relocated from North Carolina.

The mild climate, ample rainfall, and fertile swampy soils in the region allowed the couple to thrive in the cotton and sugar cane industries. However, the conditions that enabled good crop yields also led to significant challenges. The area served as a perfect breeding ground for mosquitoes that carried malaria and yellow fever.

Edward's brother, Samuel, married Nancy's younger sister, 18-year-old Elizabeth Jane. They, too, moved to the area and settled not far from the plantation, near the Bellamy Bridge. In May 1837, Samuel, Elizabeth, and their 18-month-old son, Alexander, all fell ill with remittent fever, either malaria or yellow fever. This sickness would seemingly disappear, only to return with greater intensity. During this time, Elizabeth's sister Nancy became the caregiver at her and Edward's home in Bellamy Bridge. Samuel eventually recovered, but both Elizabeth and baby Alexander passed away within a week of each other. They were laid to rest in the family cemetery on Nancy and Edward's plantation by the Chipola River, close to present-day Bellamy Bridge.

Samuel Bellamy never remarried; he lost all his money in the 1840s and would have drunk himself to death if he had not slit his throat with a straight razor three days after Christmas, on Dec. 28, 1853. He has not returned in any ghostly form, but Elizabeth has reappeared. For over a hundred and fifty years, she has been glimpsed among eerie white and blue lights at Bellamy Bridge and in the swampy waters, accompanied by misty shadows that dance around her. If you dare, take the trail—it might lead you to her ghostly presence.

Florida
The Devil Trees

Port St. Lucie has a park with trails and large trees called Oak Hammock Park. Beneath its charm lies a dark secret. It is here at one of two "Devil Trees" that serial killer Gerard John Schaefer, a sheriff's deputy, murdered two teen girls in 1973 and buried their bodies; one tree has a particular knot in its trunk shaped like the head of a goat with horns.

Schaefer was known to attract girls by flashing his badge. His targets were typically younger girls traveling in groups of two hitchhiking along the roadways. Schaefer took them to a secluded spot near an old, abandoned home with its tree out back. There, he would torture them, cut off their heads, and do all sorts of terrible things to their corpses. Schaefer was ultimately caught and sent to jail, but he was later stabbed to death on the floor of his cell. The tree endured the consequences of violent acts against it; however, anyone who attempted to harm it faced severe repercussions. It is now protected, and according to the legend, the negative aspects are part of its past, though its reputation still endures.

Haunting Shorts of Florida:

• Devil's Millhopper Geological State Park near Gainesville is famous for its fantastic sinkhole, which has inspired many intriguing stories and legends. This sinkhole was formed thousands of years ago through a natural process. Over time, rainwater, acidic from breaking down plants, slowly wore away the limestone beneath the ground. Eventually, the limestone couldn't hold up any longer, and it collapsed, creating the striking sinkhole visited today by a long set of steps. In earlier days, the curious found the bones of animals within and explained it as this: A woman from the Timucua people lived near a sinkhole. One day, the Devil kidnapped her, prompting her father to send his bravest warriors to rescue her. As the Devil fled with the woman, he created a massive hole in the ground—a sinkhole—and jumped in. The warriors pursued the Devil, battling against the quicksand that threatened to pull them in. Finally, unable to defeat him, the men retreated. As the Timucua men tried to climb out, the Devil ate some and spit out the bones; when he was complete, he turned the remainder to stone. Since, water has flowed from the springs, the tears of the men who weep for the woman forever lost to the Devil.

• Key West is the southernmost city in the contiguous United States. It is connected by a highway in the Florida Keys. It is known for its tropical island atmosphere and white-sand beaches. It is also recognized as the home of Robert the Doll, a cursed handmade 40-inch-tall doll stuffed with wood wool and donning a sailor suit. Robert Otto received it as a birthday gift after his grandfather returned from a trip to Germany. He named the doll after himself, created a room for it in his attic, and began to blame the doll for the misfortunes in his life. According to legends, the doll has supernatural forces, allowing it to move and giggle.

In 1994, new property owners of the Otto home donated the doll to the East Martello Museum in Key West, Florida, and it is on display. Visit at your own risk.

• Fort Pickens is a historic military fort in Pensacola Beach, Florida, constructed in the early 19th century. In October 1886, Chiricahua Apache warriors, including Geronimo, were held as prisoners at Fort Pickens after his surrender to the U.S. Army, following their resistance against U.S. military forces and their raids across New Mexico, Arizona, and northern Mexico. Visitors to the fort often report hearing voices and seeing apparitions believed to be Apache spirits. Additionally, Fort Pickens played a significant role in military actions during the Civil War and served as a prison facility for captured soldiers. Many visitors have shared experiences of seeing soldiers walking through the fort and near the prison cells.

• The Gulf Breeze UFO incident refers to a series of alleged UFO sightings that took place in Gulf Breeze, Florida, in November 1987. The central figure in this event was local contractor Ed Walters, who claimed to have photographed a UFO and communicated with extraterrestrial beings. Walters reported numerous encounters, including being immobilized by a beam of blue light and witnessing a UFO landing, from which he claimed extraterrestrial beings emerged.

• Capitol Theatre in Clearwater was a popular vaudeville theater and movie house. Bill Neville, a former manager, was found dead on the theatre's balcony after two men robbed and beat him to death. A worker there claimed that a ghost saved them from a fatal fall on that balcony.

• Arbuckle Creek in Central Florida is a 25-mile-long blackwater creek that flows through an ancient cypress forest and is renowned for its scenic paddling opportunities.

There is now a steel and concrete bridge near Lorida, but in the past, it was likely a ferry or a wooden bridge that crossed this wild waterway. Long ago, a witch was hired to concoct a potion for a lovesick man. When he discovered that his payment would be his firstborn child, he became enraged and threw her into the water. A Cyprus knee impaled the witch. In a panic, he hid her in the swamp. Although her body may be gone, she still returns in a wraithlike form, awaiting her chance at retribution.

A Florida Cryptid
Florida Muck Monster

The Florida Muck Monster is a mysterious cryptid inhabiting Lake Worth Lagoon in Palm Beach County, Florida. The lagoon stretches about 21 miles and has experienced significant ecological changes over the past 130 years, primarily due to dredging activities for inlets. Initially, it functioned as a freshwater lake, receiving water through ground seepage from the Everglades, which raises the possibility of a diverse range of undiscovered marine life residing within. The Muck Monster gained attention in August 2009 when Greg Reynolds and Dan Serrano from Lagoon Keepers encountered what they initially believed to be a floating log in the lagoon. Still, it submerged each time their boat approached within ten feet. A marine biologist analyzed video footage from this encounter. He concluded it appeared to be an animal moving silently through the water without disturbing the surface—a behavior atypical of common marine animals like dolphins or manatees, which typically break the surface while swimming.

Georgia
Ghosts of Railroad Bed Road

The Savannah and Statesboro Railway operated from 1897, covering about 33 miles of track between Cuyler and Statesboro, Georgia, until it was abandoned in the 1930s. As the railroad developed, towns began to emerge, including Brooklet. This small town has a remarkable ghost story.

Every railroad employed switchmen, the workers responsible for diverting trains from one track to another and connecting or disconnecting freight cars and locomotives. Their jobs were dangerous, as they often worked between moving railcars, making it difficult for engineers to see them.

One such switchman was working on the Savannah and Statesboro Railway, connecting a couple of cars when the train unexpectedly began to move. He quickly tried to escape but tripped on some large railroad ballast stones and fell beneath the wheels. Instantly, he was decapitated.

Unfortunately, the engineer was unaware he had run over the switchman, so he continued driving the train. It wasn't until much later that someone noticed the worker was missing. A search party was dispatched to find him, and they ultimately located his body. However, his head was never found.

Not long after, ghostly yellow and orange lights danced and glided along the forgotten rail path, captivating the imagination of anyone who dared to wander that way. When the railway fell into disrepair and was eventually abandoned, it was transformed into Railroad Bed Road. Curious travelers soon discovered the enchanting yet eerie phenomenon in this quiet stretch. Those who ventured along this route couldn't help but be drawn to the mysterious lights, following them with a mix of wonder and apprehension, their hearts racing as they watched the glowing orbs flicker and fade into the darkness, leaving behind more questions than answers.

As whispers of the lights spread, adventurous souls began to explore further down Robertson Road. Here, a chilling tale surfaced: sightings of a ghostly figure, the apparition of an African American, standing where an old cemetery once lay, remnants of a nearby plantation long since abandoned to time. Onlookers reported seeing him bent over, seemingly digging a grave with a somber intensity. In this place where history and the supernatural intertwine, the line between the living and the dead seems to blur, beckoning those brave enough to uncover its secrets.

Georgia
Lady of the Lake

Lake Lanier is a man-made reservoir located in the foothills of the northern Georgia mountains. It winds and weaves for an impressive 26 miles, twisting and turning like a graceful serpent gliding through its habitat. The waters are clear and cold, making it a popular destination for swimming and boating. While it is visually stunning, a dark history lies beneath the surface. It is not just the dreadful backstory of the people whose fertile farmland is now beneath its depths. It is what came after those who worked the land were spurned. Swimmers often report feeling unseen hands tugging at their legs as if trying to pull them under. Others claim to hear church bells from a long-gone church. Many believe that Lake Lanier is cursed by the spirits of those who once lived on the land it now covers and those who have perished in its depths.

There was a town once where the waters now lay. Oscarville was established in the 1800s during the Reconstruction era, after the Civil War, when the nation was rebuilding and integrating newly freed African Americans into society. It was a thriving Black agricultural community with blacksmiths, bricklayers, farmers, and carpenters. In the early 1900s, it had over 1100 residents, farmers, and artisans, with at least 58 owning lands. Some even worked as hands in the cotton fields or for white residents in the surrounding communities. Life was never easy, especially with the constant threat of racial conflicts after the Civil War always looming over the town. But it was good, better than in the past.

Everything changed in September of 1912 when Mae Crow, an 18-year-old white woman, was found in the woods near Oscarville in the Big Creek community of Forsyth County. She was discovered bloody and concealed under a pile of leaves. Her skull had been bludgeoned with a stone, and a small pocket mirror belonging to Ernest Knox, a 16-year-old Black boy from Cumming, Georgia, was found nearby. It was enough to make the nearby town of Oscarville a primary target of a mob dubbed the Night Riders who drove the community out.

In the following years, the lands formerly part of Oscarville and the surrounding communities were sold to the government forcibly to build the lake. Nobody ever wanted to leave their communities but seemed condemned to do so for some reason. The government demolished the old towns and removed some of the cemeteries and the corpses beneath to dig their huge snake-like hollow.

After the waters filled that void, people using the lake began to die in odd numbers. Some blamed the freak accidents, disappearances, and drownings on reckless boating or underwater ruins. Others talked of something ominous.

They remembered the African American town submerged beneath the water, taken from the hands of those who had worked tirelessly to build it. Perhaps it was the spirits of its former residents waiting to pull people from the surface and drag them down. It seemed only fair; wouldn't it be right to reclaim what had been taken from them?

But these are not the only vengeful ghosts who lie beneath. In November 1990, while crews dredged Lake Lanier to expand the Dawsonville bridge, they made a gruesome discovery. Deep underwater, at a depth of ninety feet, they found a green two-toned sedan with three inflated tires. The scene was chilling inside the car: human bones, women's jewelry, a dainty slip, and a red sweater told a haunting tale. A watch, frozen at 11:30, marked when the vehicle plunged 110 feet into the water.

The remains belonged to 37-year-old Susie Roberts, who had mysteriously disappeared after driving home from a dance with her friend, 22-year-old Delia Mae Parker Young, in April of 1958. Eyewitnesses noted the car's descent that fateful night. Although skid marks were on the road, initial searches yielded no bodies. In November 1959, a man fishing found a body floating near the bridge. Still, its identity remained unknown until that fateful day years later. It was Delia Mae Parker Young. Some have called one of the wreck's victims "The Lady of the Lake." For many years, her horrific death was thought to be the cause of her ghost dragging victims to the bottom, leading to various mysterious mishaps.

Georgia
Specters of the Big Top

In the early 1900s, circuses were a popular form of entertainment, and their arrival in a city was a significant event. People would gather to watch the circus parade roll in from the train station, eagerly anticipating the excitement of the big show. Just a few days before Thanksgiving in 1915, the Con. T. Kennedy Circus was traveling from a major event at the Atlanta Exposition to Alabama with a trainload of performers and animals in small railcars. They were about six miles from Columbus when a Central of Georgia train suddenly barreled onto the main tracks and collided head-on with the unsuspecting circus train. The impact caused the train to burst into flames, resulting in the tragic deaths of at least a dozen people and countless animals. The fire was so intense that it reduced everything to ashes, which were later buried in a mass grave at Riverdale Cemetery near Victory Drive in Columbus.

The entertainers may not have finished their performances. Carnival music is occasionally heard at the cemetery. During the local fair, some believe those from the wreck return to the festivities, appearing in period clothing and mingling with the crowd. There have even been reports of a flying torso near the turn at Bull Creek, the site of the tragic accident.

Haunting Shorts of Georgia:

• Dink Melvin was a fisherman and guide along the Muckalee and Kinchafoonee creeks near Albany in southwest Georgia during the late 1800s. He was quite a character and was well-known for sharing his stories about a headless horse he often saw by the fairgrounds at nightfall. Once, the horse even tried to climb into his boat! Legend had it that a curse was associated with the horse: anyone who shot at it would die.

• Kennesaw Mountain National Battlefield Park, about 20 miles northwest of Atlanta, Georgia, is known for its spooky atmosphere. Many visitors have claimed to see ghosts of Civil War soldiers and even hear sounds of battles from long ago.

• The Olde Pink House in Savannah, Georgia, is currently a restaurant and tavern, but it was initially built by James Habersham Jr. in 1771 and completed in 1789. Over the years, the property has changed hands many times, including ownership by members of the Habersham family. James Habersham died in the house and returns in spirit, often seen in his Colonial clothing. Additionally, several enslaved children who lived in the house met untimely deaths, commonly due to yellow fever. Their spirits are believed to linger, sometimes appearing to play games, like throwing dice against the wall in what is now the tavern, previously the basement.

• Chickamauga Battlefield is a park containing nearly the entire site of the bloody Battle of Chickamauga in September 1863. Phantom cries and whispers are heard there. Ghostly soldiers still roam through, not knowing they are dead. Then there is Green Eyes; some say it is a soldier whose head was blown off by a cannonball during battle.

He wanders looking for his body. Others say it is a half-man and half-creature standing on two legs with stringy hair and jaws with sharp fangs drawn by the bloody brutality of the war.

• The St. Simons Lighthouse, established in 1872, is situated on St. Simons Island. During the tenure of Frederick Osborne as the lighthouse keeper in 1880, he worked alongside an assistant named John Stephens. Their professional relationship took a dramatic turn when Osborne made an inappropriate remark about Stephens' wife, leading to a tragic incident in which Stephens shot Osborne. After Osborne's death from his injuries, reports of odd and unexplainable occurrences began to surface. Not only did his ghost still show up at the lighthouse, but his footsteps were often heard on the spiral staircase. One notable report involves a later keeper's wife who called out for help to him when she experienced mechanical issues with the lighthouse's light; Osborne's ghost came to her aid before she fainted from shock!

• Spook Bridge, located between Brooks County and Lowndes County, is an abandoned arch bridge spanning the Withlacoochee River on a closed section of Old Quitman Highway. Blue Springs Resort once owned the nearby land, a tourist attraction featuring a natural spring close to the bridge. According to local legend, a wife was pushed off the bridge by her husband. After, those standing near the bridge could hear her phantom screams.

• Alice Riley was the first woman to be executed in Georgia. She was hanged in 1734 for the murder of William Wise. Riley arrived in Savannah as an indentured servant from Ireland, under the charge of William Wise, a cattleman whose background was sketchy. She fell in love with Richard White, another indentured servant working for the man.

On March 1, 1734, Wise was found dead in his home, believed to have been strangled and drowned. They found the man with his neckerchief bound around his neck and his head submerged in a bucket of water. His death marked the first murder in the colony of Savannah. Both Riley and White were accused of his murder; White was executed immediately. However, because Riley was pregnant, she was granted a temporary stay of execution. After she gave birth, she was executed by hanging in Wright Square, which has led many to believe that her spirit haunts the area, wearing her raggedy clothing. She tends to migrate toward mamas and their babies.

A Georgia Cryptid
Altamaha-ha

The Altamaha River spans 137 miles, flowing from the Oconee and Ocmulgee Rivers to the Atlantic Ocean. Its banks are adorned with cypress, Ogeechee lime, and tupelo trees. Along this river, as well as its smaller streams and abandoned rice fields, the Muscogee tribe, along with later settlers, would sometimes encounter a creature known as the Altamaha-ha, typically near the river's mouth. This creature resembles an alligator but measures 30 to 70 feet long, has a serpentine shape, and features a gray or green body with front flippers but no hind limbs.

Hawaii
The White Lady of Hawaii

The White Lady of Hawaii is a spirit associated with the Hawaiian goddess Pele, the Goddess of Fire. She is dressed in white and has long white hair. She may appear youthful or elderly, roaming the island on a full moon night. Sometimes, she is accompanied by a small white dog or can be seen hitchhiking along the roads. Occasionally, she will ask for a favor, testing the kindness of those who pass by. Those who ignore her often face misfortune. Witnesses have reported sightings of her on Highway 30. One story tells of a man traveling to Wailuku who picked up a hitchhiking woman. He noticed a glow around her, initially thinking it was only the moonlight. When he asked her where she was heading, she did not respond. As they drove, he observed that she appeared nearly transparent when he glanced into the rearview mirror. He looked away and asked her again where she wanted to go, but by then, she had vanished!

Haunting Shorts of Hawaii:

- Queen Emma of Hawaii was born in 1836 and became queen as the wife of King Kamehameha IV, serving from 1856 until he died in 1863. Tragically, her son passed away at a young age, and her husband followed shortly after. Queen Emma died in 1885 at the age of 49 due to strokes. At her summer palace in Honolulu, visitors have reported experiencing doors opening and closing on their own, and some have felt gentle touches, leading many to believe that the queen still haunts her former home.

- The Night Marchers, known as huaka'i po, are powerful ghostly entities in Hawaii. They are a group of spirits of ancient Hawaiian warriors who march in death through specific areas at night in a haunted procession, often accompanied by eerie sounds of drums and chanting. Sightings typically occur during certain lunar phases. If encountered, visitors should show respect by removing their clothes or lying flat on the ground to avoid incurring the warriors' wrath.

- Morgan's Corner is named after Dr. James Morgan, who lived at a hairpin turn on Nu'uanu Pali Road. This site is known for its dark legend, which blends fact and fiction and has gained notoriety for ghostly encounters. The tale that emerged involves a young couple whose car broke down under a tree one night. The girl stayed in the car while the boyfriend left to seek help. She heard strange scraping sounds on the vehicle's roof as she waited. After a while, she decided to get out and investigate, only to discover that it was her boyfriend hanging above the car, dead, with his toes scraping along the roof. Although there is no evidence to substantiate this story, there was a tragic murder that occurred nearby.

In 1948, Therese Wilder, a 68-year-old widow, was murdered by two escaped prisoners who broke into her home, bound and gagged her and ultimately caused her death through suffocation.

• Strange lights and mechanical failures in vehicles have been reported at Koloa Tree Tunnel, a stretch of trees brought from Australia for a wealthy man's expansive estate. After realizing he had ordered too many trees, he donated the excess to the Koloa community, which then planted them along Maluhia Highway. One night, two young men were driving down this road in a new truck when the vehicle began to sputter and eventually stalled. Despite the driver's efforts, the truck would not restart. Suddenly, a light appeared on the road ahead, as if another car was approaching, but no vehicle was in sight. After some time, the mysterious lights vanished, and the truck started working again. Like many others who have experienced similar phenomena, the young men concluded that some supernatural force was preventing them from proceeding, possibly the Night Marchers or the goddess Pele.

• On Pali Highway, located between Honolulu and Kailua, about five miles northeast of downtown Honolulu, Nu'uanu Pali Lookout is a picturesque location and historical landmark that offers panoramic views from 1,000 feet above the Windward Coast and the Ko'olau cliffs. This site marks one of the bloodiest battles in Hawaii's history, a conflict led by King Kamehameha in 1795. Kamehameha's warriors forced the men of Maui chief Kalanikupule to their deaths off the cliffs. This tragic event would have lasting repercussions, as the spirits of those who perished linger, with reports of eerie sounds echoing from the cliffs.

A Hawaiian Cryptid
Menehune

One of the most famous cryptids in Hawaii is the Menehune. The Menehune are a race of small, dwarf-like people, typically standing between 2 to 3 feet tall. They inhabit the Hawaiian Islands' deep forests and hidden valleys and are renowned for their exceptional craftsmanship.

They are credited with constructing significant structures across the islands, including temples, fishponds, roads, and houses. The Menehune enjoy eating fish and bananas and are known for being elusive, often working under darkness. Additionally, they are quite mischievous and frequently play tricks on people.

A Hawaiian Cryptid
Green Lady

The Green Lady of Wahiawa is a significant figure in Hawaiian folklore. She is known for her strong ties to the island's verdant rainforests. She is often described as a woman who has transformed into a nature spirit, characterized by her green skin and adornment with leaves, moss, grass, and seaweed in her hair. The legend holds that she lost her children in the woods, and as a result, she now roams the forest in search of them during her afterlife. In her anguish, she will grab any child she encounters, regardless of whether they are hers or not.

Idaho
Water Babies at Massacre Rocks

Massacre Rocks, often ominously referred to as the "Gate of Death" or "Devil's Gate," is a striking, narrow passage of rugged rocks that line the banks of the Snake River within Massacre Rocks State Park. This foreboding name was bestowed upon the site by early settlers who felt an unmistakable dread as they navigated the confined passage, fearing ambush from Native American tribes.

The landscape here is steeped in rich local lore; persistent tales suggest that the waters of the Snake River harbor ethereal beings known as Water Babies. These spirits are the souls of infants who tragically perished in the river's perilous currents.

According to legend, the Water Babies engage in a whimsical dance along the riverbank, their tiny voices echoing mournful cries that seem to beckon to the living. Curious passersby, drawn by the haunting cries, are warned that they risk becoming entranced by the allure of these spectral figures. In their desire to discover the source of the sounds, many have unwittingly stepped into the water, lured to a watery fate where they might join the dance of the Water Babies forevermore.

Idaho
Spirit Lake

Spirit Lake, located near the city from which it takes its name, is a rare, sealed bottom lake. This type of lake has deeper water layers cut off from the air, preventing these lower layers from mixing with the warmer water at the surface due to temperature differences.

Local lore tells of a legend associated with the lake, revolving around forbidden love and the Kootenai Tribe, who were hunter-gatherers living along the Kootenai River in Idaho, Montana, and British Columbia. According to the story, Fearless Running Water, the daughter of Good Chieftain, fell in love with Shining Eagle. However, an ancient chief named Yellow Serpent demanded that Fearless Running Water marry him, threatening war against her tribe if she refused. To prevent any bloodshed, Good Chieftain reluctantly agreed to this union.

Heartbroken, the young couple vowed eternal love and bound themselves together in a "marriage chain of rushes." In despair, they jumped into the lake from Suicide Cliff. Their bodies were never found, and on moonlit nights, some claim to see their silhouettes gliding across the water in a phantom canoe, along with the eerie cries of the doomed lovers seeking to be released from the grave.

Haunting Shorts of Idaho:

• Rose Hill Cemetery is in the heart of Idaho Falls, one of the oldest cities in the state, with its first settlers, a group of Mormon pioneers led by Brigham Young. Within the cemetery is an enormous mausoleum belonging to the Rogers family. Interestingly, those who knock on its door often hear a knock in response. Additionally, an elderly man with oxygen tubes has been known to politely approach visitors before vanishing into thin air. There is also a hitchhiking spirit reported in the area. Visitors driving through the cemetery have claimed that a spirit enters their car, causing disturbances such as flickering lights or tapping on their heads before disappearing.

• Built in 1870, the Old Idaho Penitentiary in Boise operated for 101 years. It is haunted by former inmates, including one of the ten men executed at the site: Raymond Snowden, who was hanged on October 18, 1957. Snowden was convicted of the 1956 murder of 48-year-old Cora Lucyle Dean, whom he violently stabbed more than thirty times with a 2.25-inch pocketknife. His execution did not go smoothly; he struggled to breathe for 15 minutes as he hung by the noose. To this day, visitors at the old gallows report hearing ghostly sounds reminiscent of someone gasping for breath. The prison was home to many notorious individuals, and at least 129 inmates died there, primarily from diseases, suicides, murders, and escape attempts. It is certainly not unreasonable to suggest that more ghosts remain within its walls—those who may not have been deemed good enough for heaven yet are unwilling to go straight to hell, which is their only alternative.

• Gold was discovered in Boise Basin in 1862 in Idaho City, bringing in thousands of prospectors eager for wealth.

Not all of them made it out alive; the Boot Hill Cemetery, with thousands of graves is proof. The old miners sometimes float around the old graves among tall pines. In the Chinese section, a young girl faithfully hovers over a burial.

• The Shoshone Ice Cave is the state's largest known lava ice cave, formed by underground eruptions and part of the Black Butte Crater Lava Field. This lava tube stretches 1,000 feet long and features ice depths that range from 8 to 30 feet. Many staff members and guests have reported hearing voices and heavy footsteps from the cave, leading some to believe it is haunted.

• In the late 1800s in the Yankee Fork area of Challis, Idaho, a figure known as The Bulgarian Monk emerged, noted for his eccentric lifestyle and reclusive nature. He was a tall, young man who often wore a distinctive black cloak that reached his ankles and a red fez hat. The Monk was known for preaching the Gospel to anyone willing to listen. According to local lore, he drowned in 1891. However, accounts from travelers on the roads in subsequent years reported sightings of a figure resembling him walking with a lantern. When approached, this apparition vanished.

An Idaho Cryptid
Slimy Slim, AKA Sharrie

Payette Lake is a significant 5,330-acre body of water situated in McCall, Idaho, formed through glacial activity. The lake boasts noteworthy depths, with some areas reaching up to 392 feet. Historically, Native American tribes spoke of a powerful spirit inhabiting Payette Lake, expressing a sense of caution regarding a potentially malevolent entity believed to dwell beneath the surface.

Documented sightings of an unusual creature in the lake began in the 1920s, when railroad workers reported encountering a large, log-like object estimated to be around 30 to 35 feet long moving swiftly through the water. Initially referred to as Slimy Slim, the creature's name was later changed to Sharlie in the mid-1900s. Witnesses have described Sharlie as having a dinosaur-like head, humps along its body, and skin similar in texture to that of a shell.

Illinois
Haunted Murder Castle

H.H. Holmes, born Herman Webster Mudgett, was a notorious con artist and swindler who resorted to murder to achieve his fraudulent goals. His schemes often involved swindling insurance companies or disposing of lovers when he grew tired of them. He is believed to have killed at least nine people, including men, women, and children. He faced the consequences of his actions on Earth before the Devil dragged him down to his fiery realm. Although some believe he creeps out occasionally to lurk around the living still.

H.H. Holmes was known for his bright and charming demeanor, complemented by a distinctive handlebar mustache and fashionable attire. He arrived in Chicago in 1885 after completing his education in medical school, where he had already begun a life of morbid crimes. While in school, Holmes filched corpses from the school's medical laboratory.

He disfigured them after taking out insurance policies on the deceased to collect the policy money. When he got to Chicago, he identified himself as a pharmacist and a doctor, Dr. Henry Howard Holmes. He established his residence and drugstore at 610 W. 63rd Street.

On December 24, 1891, Holmes committed his first known murders, killing 31-year-old Julia Conner and her six-year-old daughter, Pearl. Julia was married to Ned Conner, who worked at Holmes's pharmacy jewelry counter. After starting an affair with Holmes, Julia left Ned, taking Pearl to live in Holmes's building. The exact motives behind these murders remain uncertain.

In the subsequent years, evidence surfaced indicating that Holmes may have been linked to more murders, including that of 23-year-old Emeline Cigrand, an employee at his establishment in December 1892, and 24-year-old Minnie Williams. Minnie was involved in various schemes with Holmes, along with her 18-year-old sister, Nannie.

In 1894, Holmes was also implicated in the murders of Ben Pitezel, a criminal and his associate in various illegal activities, along with Pitezel's three young children: Howard, Nellie, and Alice. Ultimately, Holmes was tried and convicted only for the murder of Ben Pitezel. He received the death sentence and was executed by hanging in 1896 at the age of 34.

His old drugstore and home became sensationalized as the Murder Castle in early newspapers. Nobody knows for sure who or how many were killed in that building. The structure was torn down in 1938, and the Englewood branch of the United States Postal Service was built on the site; only a tiny section of the basement remains, matching the old building of H.H. Holmes. Some of the workers have heard strange sounds. They have seen shadow figures in the basement. Nobody knows who haunts the place; whispers suggest it is Holmes.

He now rises from his sinister past in specter form, a ghoul of sorts. He wanders the shadowy corridors, chilling the air as he seeks the unsuspecting, lurking just out of sight. As night deepens, a sense of dread thickens the atmosphere, leaving those who linger with the feeling they are not alone—and that whatever is watching is more than just a ghost of the past.

Illinois
Ghosts of the Eastland Disaster

It was an overcast day, dismal and rainy. Still, it did not stop the 2,573 passengers and crew from crowding aboard the Great Lakes excursion steamer, a slender, passenger steamer docked near the Clark Street Bridge on the Chicago River on July 24, 1915. It was a much-anticipated social event for workers and families at Western Electric Company of Hawthorne (now Cicero) Works factory in Cicero, Illinois. It would be a day-long outing with fun-filled activities, including foot races and ice cream, swimming, picnicking, and boating in Michigan City, Indiana, at the company's annual picnic at Washington Park Beach. Families hurried to board with encouragement from their employers to arrive early, and the boat became increasingly crowded, many women with young children working their way to the lower deck and out of the inclement weather.

The Eastland, known as the "Speed Queen of the Great Lakes," was only one of five boats chartered for the excursion. It was the largest and would be the first to depart the dock at 7:30 a.m. More than 7,000 tickets had been sold for the day-long festivities across the five vessels. The boat had a history of instability and had nearly capsized on previous occasions. However, this would be overlooked as the passengers, including men, women, and children, eager to be the first to begin the festivities, boarded at nearly 50 per minute. Those rushing in felt safe. They had no clue that although the Eastland was complying with new regulations for safety, the vessel was carrying more lifeboats and life-saving equipment than it was initially designed, making it quite unstable due to the weight on the upper decks.

15-year-old Grace Straan, a worker, was aboard the ship. 22-year-old Anna Quinn, a clerk at Western Electric, was one of those aboard along with a friend, Caroline Homolka, a 17-year-old fellow clerk, both young and eager to get on the first boat. Foreman George Sindelar was aboard with his wife Josephine and their five children: Adella (15), Sylvia (13), George Jr. (9), Albert (7), and William (3). Josephine's sister Regina Dolezal had also joined along.

It appeared the boat had filled, and others began to take on passengers. Frank Butler, who had hopped on another steamer nearby, had been looking over the edge when he saw the Eastland slowly and steadily list to one side. So quickly, the decks tilted at an increasingly sharper angle, causing passengers to helplessly slide across the surface. Like hundreds of ants swished off a counter by an unseen hand, they tumbled into the water, creating a scene filled with flailing and sinking men, women, and children.

Tragedy had struck the ship as it rolled into the river at the wharf's edge. Within minutes, 844 people lost their lives.

Those dead included 22 entire families, that of George Sindelar's included. Grace Straan, Anna Quinn, and Caroline Homolka were also among the dead and lost forever to loving families. It took days to retrieve the cold bodies of those poor souls from the river. In the aftermath, nearby businesses served as makeshift morgues for those who perished. Apparitions have been witnessed near these buildings; some say ghost-like figures still reach from the water where the ship went down.

Illinois
Resurrection Mary

If you are driving near Resurrection Cemetery in Justice, you might come upon a woman in a fashionable 1930s ballgown, light-colored but yellowed from age, with hair worn just above shoulder with deeply set waves. She walks alone along the busy Archer Avenue, appearing to be looking for a ride. Some have offered her a ride, only for her to disappear along the way. Others have been startled to see the woman and drive past before turning around. She is gone when they return to where they had glimpsed her. In 1939, Jerry Palus danced with her at the city's southwest side Liberty Grove and Hall Ballroom, one of the popular dance halls. As she did not appear to know anyone, Palus danced with her and offered her a ride home. He told a reporter, "As we walked along to the street, she says, *'Well, you might as well take me down to Archer Road.'* And I said *'What for? You live up here. Here where you told me.'* And she says, *'No I want to go out to Archer Road.'*"

At the cemetery, Palus reluctantly left her at the entrance, and she said, "I must leave you now; you cannot follow me." She vanished at the gate.

While no one is sure who the ghost was in life, some believe that the ghost is 21-year-old Marie Bregovy, who died in a car accident on March 10, 1934, and was buried on March 14, 1934, in Resurrection Cemetery. She was in the car with three other occupants when it hit a nearly hidden elevated structure on Lake and Wacker streets. Others, however, believe it is 12-year-old Ona "Majira" Norkus killed when the car she was riding in overturned in a ditch in 1927 and also buried in the cemetery. Still, others agree that we may never know.

Haunting Shorts of Illinois:

• A ghost tugboat sailed along the Chicago River past Deering Bridge toward the river's South Branch. It would blow a whistle that tooted like a foghorn and reveal ghostly lights near midnight for bridges to open, but no smoke came from its stack. It was believed to be manned by the ghost of a canal boatman killed near the gas company.

• Bachelors Grove Cemetery, located twenty-four miles south of Chicago in Cook County, has a burial history dating back to 1834. The cemetery contains around 80 graves, although many headstones have been lost to time and vandalism. It is famously known for the "Woman in White," a ghostly figure who reportedly wanders the grounds and was captured in a photograph in 1991. Other spectral statistics observed in the area include a farmer and his horse, who drowned nearby.

• Devil's Backbone is a rocky ridge approximately half a mile long, located in southwestern Illinois on the outskirts of the Shawnee National Forest. It is situated next to Devil's Bake Oven, a more significant rock formation that stands about 100 feet tall near the muddy banks of the Mississippi River. One ghost rumored to haunt the area is the daughter of an ironworks superintendent. She fell in love with a man whom her father disapproved of and died in misery. Her ghost has been seen wandering around the site, even though her haunted home has been demolished, and only the weathered brick walls of the superintendent's house remain.

• In 1839, John Randolph Davis married Penelope Pike atop Devil's Tower. While returning to the shore, the boats were caught in a whirlpool, resulting in the drowning of all passengers except one slave, who was rescued by fishermen. That day, a young woman in the family gave birth to a baby.

In honor of the bride, the babe was given the name Penelope Davis. In 1859, when Penelope turned twenty, she held a birthday party on Tower Rock. Witnesses reported that on that day, the spirits of the deceased members of the wedding party emerged from the river, handed a scroll to the young woman, and returned to the muddy waters of the Mississippi. The scroll warned of a great war that would tear families apart, a prophecy that proved accurate with the onset of the Civil War soon after.

• The Old Joliet Prison operated from 1858 until 2002 and housed infamous criminals such as serial killer John Wayne Gacy. Its dark history includes riots, executions, and tragic events, including the murder of a warden's wife in 1915. The spirits of these criminals haunt the prison's unholy halls.

• The Crenshaw House was the residence of John Hart Crenshaw, who is believed to have been involved in the secret kidnapping of free Black individuals and runaway slaves, returning them to slavery or forcing them to work at his salt mines. Blood-curdling screams and wails have been heard coming from the third floor, where victims were kept.

• The Lincoln Home National Historic Site was the residence of Abraham Lincoln before he became president. Visitors report hearing mysterious footsteps, doors opening themselves, and even encountering Lincoln's spirit.

• Stangle's Bridge, between Lawrence County, Illinois, and Knox County, Indiana, spans the Wabash River and is known as the Purple Head Bridge or the Wabash Cannonball Bridge. This swing bridge was built in 1897 for the Big Four Railroad to allow tall ships to pass underneath. Travelers crossing the bridge have reported seeing a bluish-purple head floating in the water. It is believed that a man tried to hang himself there. When he jumped, it ripped his head off.

An Illinois Cryptid
Enfield Horror

Illinois is known for its array of cryptids, each with intriguing stories. One notable example is the Cole Hollow Road Monster, resembling a hybrid between an ape and a caveman. Another is the Wolfman of Chestnut Mountain, frequently seen on backroads near Galena.

The Enfield Horror, which first came to public attention in 1973, is described as having a short body, two arms, and grey skin with a slimy texture. It has three legs and distinctively deep red eyes. Notably, there was an incident where it reportedly followed a young boy home, and its presence was corroborated by a neighbor and a local news director. Witness accounts vary; some describe the creature as a deformed kangaroo, while others see similarities to an ape. Others have drawn connections between the Enfield Horror and UFO sightings in the area, suggesting a potential link to extraterrestrial activity during the same timeframe.

Indiana
Phantom Night Watchman
Of Big Tunnel

The Big Tunnel, also known as the Tunnelton Tunnel, is a 1,731-foot-long tunnel that was constructed in 1857 for the Ohio and Mississippi Railway. It was carved through solid rock and later lined with brick. The tunnel is located near the East Fork of the White River, between Fort Ritner and the town of Tunnelton, which was established a couple of years after the tunnel was built and named in its honor. Still in use today, the tunnel has a history filled with tragic incidents, including one that left behind a ghost.

On Thursday, July 23, 1908, the day watchman for the Big Tunnel began his shift and, as was his routine, stopped at the small watchman's shack on the eastern edge of the tunnel to relieve the night watchman, 27-year-old Henry Dixon.

When he found the shack deserted, the watchman felt uneasy and crept to the mouth of the tunnel to look inside. There, he noticed a flickering light. Following it, he discovered Henry Dixon lying near the rails, 200 feet inside the tunnel, dead and already cold. Dixon's cap was nearly forty feet away, and beside him were two lanterns—one extinguished and the other still burning. His pockets had been emptied of cash.

Henry Dixon had been working at the tunnel for some time. His responsibilities included traversing the tunnel before each train to clear any obstacles that might hinder movement along the tracks. He was also tasked with signaling to the train engineer that the track was clear. At four in the morning, the fast passenger train #12 from St. Louis to Cincinnati began to ease through the tunnel without the usual flag signal, as it had not been cleared. The engineer spotted a man with signal lights and assumed it was the watchman. The man then went to the side of the tunnel and the engineer noted he was still standing with the lanterns after the train passed.

Dixon's death was investigated. It was revealed that several days prior, two young women from Fort Ritner had wanted to pass through the tunnel but were frightened away by insults from a group of men. They stopped at the watchman's shack to borrow a lantern for their passage, and Dixon allowed them to take one, escorting them safely through. After the women left, Dixon had a heated exchange with the men, one of whom threatened that if he found Dixon alone inside the tunnel, only one of them would come out alive, sparking speculation about whether the threat was carried out. The circumstances of Henry Dixon's death remain a mystery. He had a wound on the left side of his head appearing to be caused by a deadly blow. He was buried in Proctor Cemetery in Fort Ritner, but some say that Henry Dixon still walks within the tunnel. He is seen at the tunnel, carrying a bobbing lantern, before disappearing.

Indiana
100 Steps Cemetery

At the 100 Steps Cemetery, located between Brazil and Terre Haute, the site features a staircase with 100 steps. Local lore suggests that if you ascend the steps while counting them, you will arrive at the top of the hill after counting precisely 100 steps. However, when you go back down and count the steps again, a supernatural force will cause the number of steps to appear different.

Consider yourself fortunate if you can ascend and descend without encountering any danger. At the summit, the ghost of a long-dead cemetery caretaker may appear and reveal your impending death in a dream. As you descend, if the number of steps you count matches the number you counted while climbing up, the foretold death will not pass. However, if the counts differ, you will meet the fate the caretaker predicted.

Haunting Shorts of Indiana:

- The Avon Bridge was constructed in 1906 over White Lick Creek for the Big Four Railroad in Avon, Indiana. Local legends tell the story of a mother crossing the trestle with her baby in her arms. Suddenly, an oncoming train came barreling down the tracks. Unable to reach the far side in time, the woman jumped off the bridge, and both she and her baby lost their lives. While you can hike under the bridge along the White Lick Creek Trail, driving on County Road 625 East is the preferred route. Residents of Avon have a secret: the sound of a car's blaring horn as you pass beneath the bridge drowns out the echoes of the woman's screams and the baby's cries.

- In the rural farmland of Clinton Falls is an old covered bridge that spans Little Walnut Creek, known as Collins Bridge. This bridge is haunted by the spirit of a little girl named Edna Collins. Built in 1922, this Burr Arch bridge has become notorious for the eerie experiences reported by those who cross it. According to local legends, Edna's spirit lingers near the bridge. Her parents would drop Edna off to swim in the creek while they went into town. When they returned, they would honk-honk-honk their horn three times inside the bridge to let her know it was time to dry off and head home. Unfortunately, one day, little Edna did not come out of the water; she had drowned in the creek below. Nowadays, those who drive into the covered bridge and honk-honk-honk their horn three times often report seeing the ghostly figure of a young girl trying to get into their car. Some drivers have even found tiny handprints on their windshield when they get home.

- Stepp Cemetery is a sleepy little cemetery in the backwoods of Morgan-Monroe State Forest near Martinsville.

A ghostly woman in a mourning dress roams the rear of the cemetery near the tiny grave of her child, at times digging up the dead baby to cradle the little corpse. She then floats to a stump and sits down, rocking the babe back and forth.

• Queen's Court is in Le Mans Hall at Saint Mary's College, the first women's college in the Great Lakes region in Notre Dame, Indiana. Le Mans Hall is the largest residence hall on campus and is organized into different sections. Saint Mary's College is directly across the street from the University of Notre Dame. The college is also known for its ghost stories. One of these stories involves a spirit named Mary, who took her own life in one of the rooms. Mary is known to steal items from students and hide them. Additionally, a benevolent nun haunts the chapel.

• Alice Mabel Gray left her city-dwelling life in Chicago for a more free-spirited existence. She settled in a shack along the wild shore of Lake Michigan in Indiana, defying the social norms of her time. Gray became known as "Diana of the Dunes" when Chicago reporters began to cover the mysterious woman spotted by fishermen bathing in the lake and running across the sand nude to dry off. As a result, she became a legendary figure and a tourist attraction, drawing visitors to the shorelines. Gray later raised public awareness about the encroachment of development on the dunes, which led to the eventual creation of the Indiana Dunes as a unit of the National Park Service. Even though she passed away in the 1920s, tourists visiting the shoreline have reported encountering a woman dressed in period clothing who mysteriously disappears. Diana of the Dunes is believed to still wander the shores she cherished so much.

• The Culbertson House was owned by wealthy William Culbertson. Dark legends about the carriage house, including tales of fires and ghosts, have persisted for years.

Those who work and volunteer at the carriage house have reported seeing mysterious figures lurking in the rooms and hearing strange sounds.

• Whispers Estate was built in 1894 as the home of Dr. John Gibbons and his wife, Jessie. The residence also served as a doctor's office while the family lived there. 61-year-old Jessie Gibbons died in the house from pneumonia, and those who sleep there often report being awakened by the sound of labored breathing.

• The old Randolph County Poor Farm is haunted. Some visitors have reported hearing children's chatter, giggles, and pained moans and groans coming from the old building.

• The Grey Lady of Evansville's Willard Library has been a part of local lore since 1937, when a custodian encountered her in the basement and subsequently quit his job. Over the years, there have been numerous sightings of the ghost, including reports from police officers who observed two figures peering from a window. Some believe the ghost is that of Louise Carpenter, the daughter of the library's original owner, who lost the building in a lawsuit after her father's death. Some people believe that she haunts the library to announce her presence as the owner and to seek revenge. Others suggest that the ghost is a former librarian who watches over visitors and is sometimes seen looking out from the south-facing windows on the second floor, gazing toward downtown.

An Indiana Cryptid
Pukwudgie

The Pukwudgie is a creature native to Indiana, originating from the legends of Indigenous peoples, notably the Lenape (Delaware) and Wampanoag tribes. In Indiana, these little beings are often described as tiny, goblin-like figures about 2 to 3 feet tall. They have large noses, long ears, and porcupine-like quills running down their backs, giving them a troll-like appearance. Known for their mischievous nature, Pukwudgies enjoy playing tricks on people. They possess various magical abilities, including shapeshifting and invisibility. Historically, Pukwudgies were social with humans but have become hostile due to grudges stemming from human actions. These elusive creatures are difficult to spot in their natural habitats, as they sometimes transform into animals to conceal themselves.

Paul Startzman was an avid hiker, author, and amateur archaeologist in Indiana with a keen interest in early civilizations. In 1927, when he was just 10 years old, Startzman encountered an elusive Pukwudgie while hiking.

He described it as a half-sized man with dull blonde hair and protruding ears. Others have also reported sightings of these creatures hiding in the woods. For example, a child playing alone in the park was approached by a group of Pukwudgies, who seemed curious about what she was doing.

Mounds State Park in Anderson is a notable hotspot for Pukwudgie sightings. The park's dense forests provide an ideal environment for these creatures to remain hidden while engaging in their trickster behavior.

Iowa
The Gruesome Villisca Axe Murders and the Ghosts Who Came After

Villisca was a small settlement established in the mid-1850s between the Middle and West Nodaway rivers. Over time, it grew and prospered, reaching about 2,500 people by the 1900s. The town featured charming Victorian homes and tree-lined streets. Its downtown area served as a hub for business and agriculture, boasting hotels, restaurants, stores, theaters, and manufacturing facilities. The railway ran through Villisca, accommodating both passenger and freight trains. It seemed like a place of innocence, a sleepy little town where the American dream could come true. That is, until June 10, 1912. That was when a gruesome discovery roused it harshly from its slumber, shattering its tranquility: a brutal massacre had taken place.

In 1912, 43-year-old Josiah "Joe" Moore and his family lived in a white three-bedroom farmhouse on Second Street.

The family had resided there for about nine years. The home featured a parlor, a downstairs sewing room, a kitchen, an outhouse, and an upstairs attic crawl space. There was no electricity or running water. Joe was married to 39-year-old Sara, and together they had four children: Herman (11), Katherine (10), Arthur (7), and Paul (5). Joe was part of a large extended family, many of whom lived in Villisca, including his parents and six siblings. He was a prominent citizen who had left his job at the local hardware and agricultural store working for another resident, Frank Jones, an Iowa State Senator. Joe then opened his own implement and vehicle store across the street, J.B. Moore Implement Company, that included a John Deere dealership creating significant competition for Jones.

On the late afternoon of June 9, 1912, after rehearsing for a special presentation at the local church, Sara and the children left around 4:00 p.m. to visit Joe's parents, as they typically did every Sunday. Afterward, they attended the evening program at the Presbyterian Church. Two friends of 10-year-old Katherine—8-year-old Ina May Stillinger and her 12-year-old sister Lena Gertrude—were invited to stay the night at the Moore's home as a special treat. Joe called the Stillinger home to get their permission to stay, as the girls were afraid to walk to their grandmother's house after dark. After the performance, the family and their two young friends arrived home at about 9:30 p.m.

Only the murderer knows what happened that night. On June 10, 1912, eight people in the home were murdered with an axe sometime between midnight and 2:00 a.m. The crime scene was not discovered until the following morning when Joe failed to respond to his clerk. Concerned neighbors broke into the locked house and stumbled upon the horrific massacre.

While there were no signs of struggle elsewhere in the home, in the sewing room, which had been converted into a bedroom for Katherine, the Stillinger girls were found dead together in a single twin bed. Katherine and her brothers were in one bedroom, while their parents were in another. They had been murdered, and then the killer had returned to beat the faces so savagely that there were marks on the ceiling and walls, and the faces were unidentifiable. The murderer concealed the victims with cloths and clothing, as well as covering the windows and mirrors. He left the axe in the downstairs bedroom. After cleansing his hands in a pail of water, he prepared a meal of beans and locked the door behind him when he left.

The unsolved crime became known as the Villisca Axe Murders, leaving behind shattered families and a dark stain on the community. The house has been forever marked by tragedy and hauntings. Many have visited the Villisca House for tours and overnight stays. Some visitors have reported seeing a figure moving from room to room, often connected to the sounds of the 2 a.m. train rolling through town with its whistle blowing. Others have witnessed children playing with an unseen entity under the bed in the parlor bedroom where the Stillinger girls died. From items disappearing and then reappearing elsewhere to the echo of ghostly footsteps, the house continues to offer its newer guests a chilling experience from its dreadful past.

Iowa
Wails at Mossy Glen Hollow

Twenty-seven-year-old Pearl Hines Shine was a red-haired bride of less than a week when she, along with her 18-year-old boyfriend, Maynard Lenox, a harmonica player, and Deke Cornwell, a junk dealer, murdered her 58-year-old husband, Dan Shine, who farmed his 80 acres of property in Mossy Glen.

Minnie Hines, a 54-year-old mother of 18 children, and her husband, Jim Hines, assisted in the matter. On the day of the murder, Lenox struck Shine, and soon after, Cornwell hit him over the head with a beer bottle, rendering him unconscious.

The two dragged him up the stairs of the home, placed him in the closet, and Lenox shot Shine, tearing off half his face. They trussed him up in a clothes basket and put a string in his hand linked to the trigger of a rifle to make it appear as if he had committed suicide. However, the local police were not fooled, especially after the sheriff sent his wife to fetch clean clothes for Pearl while she was in jail. As the woman rummaged through a bag, she discovered a romance magazine with a corner crimped on an article titled "Why I Killed My Husband." Dan Shine was buried, and the murderers were sent to jail. At age 44, the state parole board released Pearl Shine from the Rockwell City women's reformatory. At 35, Maynard Lenox was also released by the board from the Fort Madison State Penitentiary.

Strange, fleeting shadows have been reported in the area where Dan Shine's house in Mossy Glen Hollow once stood. Among those who have died since his passing, some believe Pearl's ghost haunts the area, a small preserve located on the outskirts of Strawberry Point. This region is known for its natural beauty, featuring a box canyon and springs. The terrain is rugged and forested, densely populated with vegetation — and her ghost.

In addition to Pearl's spirit, another ghost finds shelter within the forest. A traveling peddler would frequently pass through the area, selling goods and wares to the residents. During one particularly desperate year, a group of locals ambushed and robbed him in Mossy Glen Hollow. They concealed his body in a secluded cave. Over time, reports of sightings of the peddler's ghost wandering through the hollow began to emerge. Witnesses report that his spirit manifests with a mournful wail. It is generally believed that part of Pearl's punishment in Hell involves eternally listening to the noisy ghostly requiems of the peddler.

Iowa
Phantom of the Trestle

The Kate Shelly High Bridge in Boone is associated with the haunting of a ghost train and Kate Shelley, a 15-year-old girl who lived in the 19th century on a farm near Honey Creek. On July 6, 1881, thunderstorms caused a flash flood on Honey Creek, which washed out the supports of a railroad trestle. A pusher locomotive, checking the tracks with four workers, crossed the bridge but tumbled into the creek below.

Kate Shelley heard the commotion and, knowing that another train was approaching at midnight, managed to locate the two surviving workers from the accident. She then crawled across the trestle using lightning as her only source of illumination. After walking two miles, she warned the passenger train in time for it to stop safely. Kate lived many years longer, but since this heroic event, Kate's spirit has remained tied to the trestle. Witnesses have reported sightings attributed to her ghost, including phantom trains, suggesting that her spirit may still be watching over where she once performed her brave deed.

Haunting Shorts of Iowa:

- The Pottawattamie County Squirrel Cage Jail, built in Council Bluffs in 1885, is haunted due to the five deaths that occurred within the facility during its operation. These deaths include a prisoner who died of a heart attack, another who fell while trying to carve his name into the ceiling, a suicide by hanging, and an officer who was accidentally shot during training. The jail remained open until 1969 and is one of only 18 rotary jails known for its unique design. Its architecture features pie-shaped cells that revolve within a cage, allowing only one cell accessible at a time through a single door. Reports of ghostly footsteps, shadowy figures, and disembodied voices have been documented.

- At Fairview Cemetery in Council Bluffs, a black angel statue serves as a memorial to Ruth Ann Dodge. Some have seen it take flight. Before her death, Ruth Anna had visions of an angel. The statue's eyes follow those who stand beneath it, and it is believed to bless the sick if they gently touch it.

- Along the rural Stony Hollow Road near Burlington, Iowa, is a cliff that hangs perilously over the side of the road, where the ghost of a young bride named Lucinda haunts. When her husband did not arrive to meet her, she feared the worst—that he had left her for another woman. In her despair, she climbed the cliff and fell to her death. Shortly after, her husband finally arrived; he had been delayed because his wagon got stuck in a muddy rut. Legend says that Lucinda will appear if you call her name three times. If she lays a rose at your feet, it foretells that you will share the same tragic fate within the next day or two.

- In Columbus Junction, Lovers Leap swinging bridge is linked to a Native American who, after losing her lover in battle, jumped from the ravine. Her cries are heard at night.

An Iowa Cryptid
The Van Meter Visitor

The Van Meter Visitor is a cryptid that haunted the town of Van Meter, Iowa, several nights from September 29 to October 3, 1903. Descriptions of the creature depict it as a half-human, half-animal being with dragon-like features, characterized by large bat-like wings and a distinctive horn on its forehead that emitted a blinding light. Witnesses noted that it moved like a crow, hopping in its movements, accompanied by a powerful, unpleasant odor.

Several prominent townsfolk, including U.G. Griffith, a local implement dealer, made the initial sightings. Griffith and others observed the creature flying remarkably high above the town's buildings. In a state of fear, Griffith fired shots at the beast, but it appeared unaffected by the gunfire. Other notable witnesses included a local doctor and a bank cashier, Peter Dunn, who documented the creature's presence by taking plaster casts of its three-toed tracks.

The pursuit of the Van Meter Visitor led the witnesses to an old mine shaft, where they heard sounds from within. Upon investigation, they discovered a smaller version of the creature inside the mine. Despite their attempts to scare it off with noise and gunfire, the creatures retreated into the mine.

Kansas
Molly Hollow

In the early days of Atchison, a trapper and fur trader named Mallow lived along the edge of a ravine that extends from 6th Street, overlooking the Missouri River. Somewhat of a recluse, his cabin was located just east of where the wetland habitat in Jackson Park is today. At one time, a small creek ran through that area, which was later dammed for Jackson Lake, and it is now gone. In the 1850s, he operated a ferry service at Port Lamb, just below the larger George Million ferry service upstream. George Million was the man who initially staked a claim to what is now the site of Atchison.

Mallow's ferry business was smaller, carrying groups of ten to twelve wagons of homesteaders across the Missouri River as they headed to Oregon and California. His land also provided a place for the settlers to camp and rest their animals. This allowed them to gather as a larger group for safety traveling through areas occupied by Native Americans.

In the late 1850s, Mallow mysteriously vanished, and his ghost began to haunt the hollow area with peculiar sounds and strange sights. Because of the haunting, few dared to enter the hollow for many years. It became an isolated hideout for outlaws, and during the Civil War, raiders used it to hole up. By the 1880s, the name of the hollow evolved from "Mallow's Hollow" due to mispronunciation into "Molly's Hollow."

By the 1950s, locals would walk down the tracks from the depot on Third and Main streets and head up to Jackson Park along the old valley. They whispered of queer screams and strange shadows that flitted about. However, time had passed along with the knowledge of the old recluse ferryman who lived there. Within the hollow, there was also a swimming hole for children. Some would pass around stories of screams and spooky shadows—as the area became known as Molly's Hollow, a girl named Molly, who lived in a cabin in the remote woods, was said to have been murdered within, with her cries echoing into the night. It was rumored that an old man hanged himself by a strap in that hollow. When he was found and cut down, the strap was left hanging from the tree limb, where it remained for what seemed like an eternity. Generations of children heading to the swimming hole would look up at the tree and see the strap still hanging.

Now, curious visitors flock to Jackson Park to see where Molly was hanged, unaware that the screams they hear and shadows they see belong not to a woman but to a man who, over 170 years ago, ferried boats below.

Kansas
Thundering Hooves
of the Pony Express

The Hollenberg Pony Express Station, located in Hanover, Kansas, was built in 1858 by Gerat H. Hollenberg as a way station for travelers on the Oregon and California Trails. From 1860 to 1861, it served as a home station for the Pony Express, where riders received supplies, meals, and overnight lodging. They would also switch horses and take time to rest.

Today, the station is a well-preserved historical site, and visitors have reported experiencing hauntings, including the sounds of thundering horse hooves and the voices of young Pony Express riders calling out to their hardworking horses.

Haunting Shorts of Kansas:

- The Theorosa Bridge, also known as the 109th Street Bridge or Crybaby Bridge, is located in Valley Center, Kansas, about 12 miles north of Wichita. This bridge, rebuilt in 1974 and 1976 due to fires, spans Jester Creek and has gained notoriety for the ghost stories and urban legends associated with it. The most prevalent story involves a young Native American woman who bore an illegitimate child with a white man. Overwhelmed with shame and grief, she drowned her baby in Jester Creek. Shortly thereafter, she took her own life, consumed by her sorrow. Her spirit now roams the area, crying out for her lost child, to which the baby's cries respond in return.

- Hamburger Man roams the sand hills north of Hutchinson, appearing in a remote area after dark. Curious locals search for his shack in the woods, which has a stump in front of it. When he is home, his axe is resting on the stump; when he is gone, the axe disappears as well. He has a disfigured face resulting from a grain elevator explosion. He is rumored to prey on unsuspecting teenagers and other victims, turning them into hamburger meat with his axe.

- Rochester Cemetery is on a bluff in Topeka, not far from Soldier Creek. Here, the lonely Albino Lady haunts the area after enduring terrible taunts during her life. She is seen carrying her white poodle and steals little children from playgrounds and streets if they stay out too late.

- The Mock family lived near the Saline River in the northern part of Ellis County and had hired a farmhand to help them with their work. One evening, as he was returning home, the ghost of a Native American appeared before him. The ghost, who was of great stature and build, warned him not to plow the pasture as his ancestors were buried there.

Although the family had planned to plow the pasture the next day, they halted the work after hearing the farmhand's message. The ghost did not appear again.

• Elizabeth Polly became known as The Blue Lady. She served as a hospital matron at Fort Hays, Kansas, during the cholera outbreak in 1867, where she cared for sick soldiers. Unfortunately, Polly contracted cholera herself, which ultimately led to her death. Although she was buried near the fort, local legends suggest that her spirit still roams Sentinel Hill, an area she loved. Her spirit wanders Sentinel Hill, glowing like a blue light and looking for soldiers to comfort.

• The Old Cowtown Museum in Wichita is an open-air museum of living history on over 23 acres with many buildings that recreate life in the late 19th century. Visitors have reported weird occurrences, including unexplained noises and sightings of apparitions dressed in period clothing looking from windows, especially at the old Murdock home where the daughter of Wichita Eagle founder Marshall Murdock and his wife, Victoria, named Love'n Tangle, died February 25, 1883, at age 8. Her funeral was held in the parlor downstairs. People have seen and heard the daughter playing around the house, peering out the windows, and hearing footsteps.

• The Prairie Spirit Trail in Ottawa, Kansas, spans over 50 miles along a historic railroad route that once connected Iola and Ottawa. This multi-use trail accommodates various activities and showcases the scenic beauty of rural Kansas communities. As visitors explore, they might even hear tales of a ghost train echoing through the landscape, adding an intriguing element to their journey.

• St. Jacob's Well has been an essential landmark for prehistoric peoples, Native Americans, early settlers and drovers moving cattle from Texas to Kansas in the 1800s.

It was frequently visited by Northern Cheyenne tribes during their exodus in 1878. This water-filled sinkhole is located in the Little Basin area of the Big Basin Prairie Preserve in Clark County, Kansas. The well is approximately 58 feet deep and has a funnel-like shape. It was formed when surface water eroded certain underground materials, such as salt or gypsum, causing the ground above to collapse into the empty space created. According to local legend, St. Jacob's Well has never run dry, even in the driest seasons. It is haunted by the ghosts of its past, including the spirit of a cowboy who died there in the 1890s and has left his legacy in eerie sounds.

• The Sallie House is a haunted home in Atchison, dating back to the 1800s and surrounded by local lore. The story centers around a young girl named Sallie, who died during an emergency surgery performed by Dr. Charles Finney. However, Sallie's spirit may be a facade for a more sinister presence. Former residents and paranormal investigators have reported experiencing mischievous tricks and have sensed a darker tone within the house.

• The ghost story of White Woman Creek in Kansas revolves around Anna-Wee, a white woman captured by the Cheyenne. She fell in love with their chief but ultimately lost her life while defending her tribe during an attack by the army. Her spirit now wanders the creek bed, searching for her lost family.

A Kansas Cryptid
Sinkhole Sam

Sinkhole Sam is a worm-like creature residing in a portion of Inman Lake called "The Sinkhole." Before the 1920s, the region was noted for small freshwater lakes and wetlands. However, many of these lakes were drained over time, leaving behind a few low-lying areas known as sinkholes. The wetlands left behind in Inman are known as the Farland Lake Marshes, which comprise Little Sinkhole No. 1 and Little Sinkhole No. 2, and the largest, called "The Big Sinkhole," where witnesses have observed the creature. Sinkhole Sam measures between 15 and 30 feet in length and is as thick as a car tire. In 1952, two fishermen stood on a small bridge over Big Sinkhole. They reported a massive serpentine form breaking the surface of the water. Some believe that Sinkhole Sam is a prehistoric creature that emerged from a flooded underground cavern when an oil company drained and drilled the area in the 1920s.

Kentucky
Phantom Dog of Golden Pond

Along Elbow Creek, there once was a small town named Golden Pond. During the 1920s, it became notorious for its moonshine and rowdiness. Today, the town is gone; the Tennessee Valley Authority evicted the residents in the name of flood control and recreation, and it now lies beneath the Land Between the Lakes National Recreation Area. However, this doesn't mean the ghosts have vanished. Reports of a ghost dog's lonely howl can still be heard by passersby in the area.

The dog once belonged to a man named Paul Jackson, who always had his dog by his side. One day, Jackson fought with Ned Crawford over a card game in a cabin deep in the woods. During the altercation, Crawford murdered Jackson. As soon as his owner fell to the floor, the dog lunged at Crawford in an attempt to protect him but was quickly killed with a knife. Crawford dumped the corpse of both dog and man into a pond nearby and went on his way as if nothing at all had happened.

When Crawford walked up the steps to his cabin the following night, he was confronted by a ferocious dog with glowing eyes. It was Jackson's dog, and from that moment on, the spectral creature would not leave the murderer alone. Everywhere Crawford went, he was greeted by white teeth, glowing eyes, and the growling hound. Crawford's crime had slipped past the authorities, but he could not escape the haunting presence of that dog. The old hound appeared in the darkness, growling and baring his vicious teeth wherever the murderer went. As Crawford's health began to deteriorate, he felt he had no choice but to flee the state, yet the dog continued to follow him.

He returned in even worse condition, and a local farmer, feeling pity for him, decided to hire Crawford. One night, as the two men were walking along the road, a large black hound appeared near a nearby pond. Slowly, the beast crept forward and revealed something in its jaws—the yellowed bone of Jackson's leg. This drove Crawford into a frenzy, and he confessed to his crime before going to jail. To this day, the ghost dog howls in the ghost town of Golden Pond, heard on moonless nights by those who listen.

Kentucky
Ghosts of Mammoth Cave

In 1839, Louisville Doctor John Croghan acquired Mammoth Cave, along with enslaved individuals, including African American explorer Stephen Bishop. Bishop was a tour guide and made significant discoveries while mapping the cave. In the early 1840s, Croghan built cabins within the cave, hoping to treat tuberculosis patients with the cave's air. Sadly, the patients' conditions worsened, resulting in the deaths of five individuals. Their bodies were placed on Corpse Rock, a stone slab inside the cave, before being buried elsewhere. Croghan's venture ultimately failed. But some say the ghosts of those who died there remain; phantom coughing is heard within the cave.

Mammoth Cave has a long history of exploration prior to Croghan's ownership, with its first known tour taking place around 1816. According to legend, John Houchin discovered the cave in the late 1700s while escaping from a bear.

Enslaved guides helped show the cave to visitors, and one earned his freedom by proving the existence of a rumored second entrance, which mysteriously disappeared shortly after the discovery. After the guide's death, a new owner relocated the man's body near the cave's entrance and erected a monument for tourists to visit. In the 1890s, visitors reported seeing the ghost of the guide near the cave. As the story spread, crowds flocked to witness the apparition, prompting the owner to reinter the guide's remains in the cemetery.

Haunting Shorts of Kentucky:

- Waverly Hills Sanatorium is a former tuberculosis hospital in Louisville, Kentucky, opened in 1926. Initially built as a two-story wooden facility, a new five-story building was completed the same year. At that time, it offered advanced treatments, including fresh air and exposure to sunlight, during a severe outbreak of the disease known as the "white death." Unfortunately, many patients died due to the lack of adequate medical treatments available at that time. Estimates suggest that between 8,000 and 10,000 patients lost their lives there during its operation from 1910 until its closure in 1961. The sanatorium is also haunted. One notable ghost is that of a nurse named Mary Hillenburg, who hanged herself. Her spirit is reported to roam the halls, along with the apparitions of deceased doctors and nurses and mysterious, foggy patients drifting through the corridors late at night.

- At Pine Mountain State Resort Park, along the Clear Creek Hollow Trail, there is an abandoned Louisville and Nashville Railroad spur in an isolated hollow, once used in coal mining operations. It followed the path of a stream known as Clear Creek. Even before the railway was established, this route was used by Native Americans, and explorers, who traversed what was once called Buffalo Creek. Hikers can find a tunnel cut through the hillside and trestles that cross the creek along the old track. In the area around the tunnel, some hikers have reported encountering the ghostly appearance of an early 1800s frontiersman who appears and then vanishes among the dense woods.

- In the mid-1900s, a couple married at Cumberland Falls near Corbin. The groom wore a dark suit, and the bride wore a beautiful long white gown made of silk and lace.

They were very much in love and had saved every penny they could to have their wedding at the falls and honeymoon at a well-known lodge. This day was a dream come true for them. They walked hand in hand by the waterfall to hold on to the moment. The groom brought a camera and asked his bride to pose near the falls for a picture. She blushed but agreed and stood by the cliff edge. As a gust of wind blew, her dress fluttered. She bent down to catch the fabric but lost her balance and fell backward off the cliff. In an instant, she hit the rocks below and writhed in pain. The groom rushed to her, but he could not save her. She slipped off the ledge and was swept away by the fast-moving water and drowned. Since, those visiting the waterfall at Cumberland Falls State Park have seen a ghostly woman in a white wedding dress.

• In the early 1800s, tensions between settlers and the Cherokee were high. War Woman Cornblossum, daughter of Chief Doublehead, prepared to lead Cherokee children from Kentucky and Northern Tennessee to safety to a white-run school in Chattanooga. By the summer of 1810, many families gathered at Ywahoo Falls. They faced danger from Hiram Gregory and his violent group, who aimed to attack the mothers and children. Following the Revolutionary War, settlers in Tennessee became obsessed with seizing Cherokee land, believing that killing young Cherokee would prevent their survival. At Ywahoo Falls, they brutally killed over a hundred women and children. Today, visitors to Yahoo Falls report strange sounds like singing, drumming, and the soft cries of the children who never reached safety.

• X Cave at Carter's Caves has an old legend. In the mid-1700s, a young Cherokee named Huraken fell in love with the chief's daughter, Manuita. He discovered a rich vein of silver and planned to create bracelets for her. However, when Huraken left for a great battle, he did not return.

Manuita, consumed by horrible grief, jumped off a cliff. Unbeknownst to her, Huraken had been mining silver and returned just in time to find her lifeless body. Heartbroken, he carried her into X Cave. When Manuita's absence was noticed, a search party found them together, believing Huraken had killed her. He pleaded for a final chance to see her, which was granted. He entered the cave but never emerged, leaving his fate unknown. The Cherokee believed the cave to be cursed. Manuita's body was taken, but her spirit still haunts X Cave, with hikers often reporting sightings of her pale figure near the cliff.

• Liberty Hall Historic Site is a museum in Frankfort, Kentucky. It was the home of wealthy Senator John Brown and his family. The site is known for hosting a few ghosts. One notable ghost is Margaretta Varick, an aunt of the family who came to visit in 1817 and passed away shortly after her arrival. She is often seen wandering the grounds in a gray dress and dubbed the "Gray Lady."

• On August 19, 1782, settlers, including Daniel Boone, living near what is now Mt. Olivet, set out to pursue British, Canadian, Shawnee, and Wyandot forces attempting to attack their fort. As they approached a rise at present-day Blue Licks State Park, they launched an attack but were quickly met with gunfire from above. Realizing they were at a disadvantage and panicking, the men started to retreat. The enemy pursued them down the hillside toward the Licking River, which forms a U-shape in the valley. Only by crossing the river were some able to escape death; however, not everyone did. In total, 79 were killed during the battle, including Daniel Boone's 23-year-old son, Israel. At Blue Licks State Park, hikers have reported seeing ghostly figures of combatants appear and vanish. Others have witnessed apparitions of early settlers engaged in their daily tasks.

A Kentucky Cryptid
Pope Lick Monster

The structure, built in the late 1800s, rises ninety feet above the Pope Lick, a tributary in the Fisherville neighborhood of Louisville. Spanning 742 feet in length, it still accommodates trains from Norfolk Southern. A chain-link fence warns, "Keep Off. Danger. Private Property." At the same time, beneath it lurks the infamous Goat-Man—a grotesque half-goat, half-man creature known for luring victims to their deaths with a siren-like call. Various legends describe the Goat-Man's origin. Some say a drought-stricken farmer made a pact with the devil. In contrast, others claim he is the offspring of a twisted farmer or a circus child mistreated by a cruel ringmaster. Despite the many tales, all agree that he dwells under the trestle, waiting to hypnotize and attack.

Tragically, several individuals have attempted to cross the trestle and have met with fatal accidents, including a 15-year-old girl in 2019 and others drawn in by the legend. However, no evidence supports the claim that the Goat-Man actively lured them. He typically remains hidden in the shadows, waiting for unsuspecting prey. For those attracted to the thrill of the Goat-Man, remember that the train above poses a real danger. At the same time, historically, the legend itself actually lurks *below* and does not require anyone to walk the tracks.

Louisiana
Marie Laveau

Marie Catherine Laveau was born in New Orleans, Louisiana, on September 10, 1801. She became a prominent figure known for her practices in Voodoo, herbalism, and midwifery. As a free woman of color, she was deeply involved in her community, blending herbal remedies and prayers with Voodoo and Catholicism to heal the sick and provide spiritual guidance. Laveau also visited prisoners on death row, advocating for pardons for those she favored.

The spirit of Marie Laveau continues to linger in New Orleans, solidifying her status as an influential figure in the city's Voodoo culture. She is buried in St. Louis Cemetery No. 1, which dates back to 1789 and is known for its numerous ghostly sightings. Many visitors have seen her walking among the graves. In contrast, others have reported sightings of her strolling along the street outside the cemetery.

Louisiana
Madame Lalaurie

Soniat du Fossat began constructing a mansion at Royal and Hospital streets around 1831-32 in New Orleans, which was later purchased by 44-year-old Madame Marie Delphine Lalaurie. She lived there with two of her children and occasionally her estranged husband, Doctor Leonard Louis Nicholas Lalaurie. As a wealthy socialite, she hosted extravagant balls and employed many slaves for household tasks. Madame Lalaurie amassed her fortune through inheritances and marriages.

She married her first husband at fourteen, soon becoming a widow and giving birth to her first child shortly after. On her twentieth birthday, she wed a wealthy French widower, with whom she had four children. She inherited a sizable amount following her mother's death, but her second husband's debts depleted her wealth. She then married the much younger Doctor Lalaurie.

The family seemed to live a perfect, prosperous life from the outside. Yet, neighbors often whispered about Madame Lalaurie's haggard daughters and slaves, except for one loyal servant who drove her carriage. He was always well-dressed, alert, and immaculate. A neighbor suspected something was wrong with Madame Lalaurie. One day, while the neighbor was climbing the steps, she heard terrible shrieks from the courtyard. Peering over, she saw an eight-year-old Black girl, one of Lalaurie's slaves, fleeing as Madame Lalaurie pursued her, whip in hand. The child ran until she reached the roof, where, in a moment of desperation, she jumped, and the neighbor heard the awful thud of the tiny body hitting the ground. The little one's corpse was quickly recovered, teeny arms and legs dangling lifelessly. Under darkness, the slave was buried in a shallow hole dug in one corner of the yard.

A fire broke out on April 10, 1834, in the Lalaurie home. Bystanders rushed to evacuate those inside but were blocked from entering the slave quarters. Undeterred, they forced their way in and found the 70-year-old Black cook shackled and chained near the fireplace. More horrors met them as other enslaved in the home were chained in painful postures to the walls. When the authorities brought the slaves outside, a stunned mob quickly formed, shouting at Madame Lalaurie and her family as they shut the door. The coachman arrived with a carriage, whisking Madame Lalaurie away to a boat. She abandoned her family, who fled through the windows.

She never returned, eventually settling in Paris. The house was burned down, leaving only a shell behind.

Madame Lalaurie is long dead, as are those in her immediate family who lived there. Pierre Trastour purchased the property and built a new house over the old one. In this form, it had many faces over time—a school for girls, a boarding house, a conservatory for music and dance, and a private home. No one stayed long. It seemed cursed, plagued with misfortune and strange occurrences. Many believe those who resided at the Lalaurie mansion and are now long dead are still around in phantom form. Caretakers of the building would hear pots and pans banging in the kitchen. A servants' door to the kitchen opens and closes by unseen hands, the knob turning on its own. Most frightening is that passersby have seen a young girl staring down from the roof of the building. Some have even seen Madame Lalaurie peering out the windows.

Haunting Shorts of Louisiana:

- Near Thibodaux, a pothole-ridden gravel road known as Devil's Swamp Road leads to a dead-end railroad track surrounded by old swampland. This area is infamous for local lore, which suggests that cars may stall and windows fog up, revealing ghostly handprints. The haunting is linked to the Thibodaux Massacre in November 1887, when the descendants of enslaved people laboring under poor conditions on sugarcane plantations initiated a strike for better treatment. This resulted in a violent response from white vigilantes, who gunned down strikers, leading to the deaths of thirty to sixty individuals, including women and children. Many victims were disposed of in mass graves or swamps, and their remains are still unaccounted for. The spirits of those murdered may linger as a reminder of this dark history or may seek revenge. Such a tragic past commands respect and those who disregard it should be cautious, for they may encounter more than handprints on their windows.

- In the early 1900s, a wealthy man donated several statues to the city near Popp's Fountain at City Park in New Orleans, including one of his daughters, who drowned in a lagoon. This bronze statue depicted her as Venus, featuring a soft Mona Lisa smile. Legend has it that the girl fell in love with a sailor, but her father forbade their romance, leading her to take her own life in despair. Over time, the area became overgrown and became a lover's lane. One night, a speeding car knocked over her statue, which led to tales of her ghost appearing, moaning sadly with the same smile and scratching at car windows. Though the statue was eventually vandalized and removed, witnesses still report hearing her haunting calls throughout City Park.

• Bayou Sale Road in south Terrebonne is a black-topped stretch of roadway that snakes its way through marshes and swamps, connecting the towns of Dulac and Chauvin. A ghostly hitchhiker roams the road, bidding drivers to stop. When they do, he tries to coax those within to give up the soul of one of the passengers in exchange for treasure.

• In the St Louis Cathedral alleyway, you may catch the faint singing voice of long-dead Père Dagobert on foggy mornings. He walks along the cobbled path in sandaled feet and robe, in a ghostly procession performing what some believed was a miracle. The old Creoles would once tell the young to listen with faith in their hearts and wait at this very alley before dawn, and when it rained, the monk would surely come and sing— "Kyrie eleison, kyrie eleison—" (Lord, have mercy —)

• The Myrtles Plantation in St Francisville is known for its haunting history, featuring the ghosts of family members and a slave named Chloe. It boasts a 120-foot veranda, French furnishings, and a Creole cottage-style exterior. The plantation is situated on a hill in the former Spanish territory of Bayou Sara, which is now part of Louisiana.

• Frenier was once a thriving community known for its timber industry and cabbage farming. Its rapid growth was partly due to the arrival of the New Orleans, Jackson, and Great Northern Railroad in 1854. However, this prosperity abruptly ended with a devastating hurricane in 1915. The storm caused major destruction and led to the deaths of many people who sought refuge in a railroad depot, which ultimately collapsed. Julia Brown, a local healer, lived on the outskirts of town. She felt unappreciated by the townspeople and predicted her own death, ominously warning that she would take the whole city with her when she passed away.

She cursed the residents, declaring, "One day I'm gonna die, and I'm gonna take all of you with me." The old woman often sang eerie songs about the town's demise while rocking on her porch. On the day of her funeral, which coincided with the hurricane's landfall, many believe her curse manifested as disaster struck Frenier. Following her death, stories arose claiming that her spirit haunts the area.

• The Calcasieu Courthouse is situated in Lake Charles, an area with a large population. It is haunted by the ghost of Toni Jo Henry, who was convicted of murder and executed in the electric chair in November 1942. Reports from jail officers indicate that her spirit lingers around the courthouse, with accounts of electrical equipment turning on by itself, her perfume wafting through the air, and mysterious whispers and screams appearing from nowhere.

• Loyd Hall Plantation, in Cheneyville, is a plantation that offers overnight stays and tours. It is still a functioning farm, surrounded by fields of sugar cane, soybeans, and pastureland. Built in 1820, the plantation has a reputation for being haunted. Many have claimed to hear footsteps when no one else is around and to sense the phantom aroma of baked meals in the air. One of the most notorious spirits is believed to be William Lloyd, who was called a traitor during the Civil War. He was tarred, feathered, and hanged by Union soldiers. Since then, there have been various strange occurrences, such as ringing doorbells and moving objects within the house. Other spirits that visit the plantation include a niece of the Lloyd family, who fell to her death from a window, and a Union soldier, whose bloodstains are still visible on a wooden floor on the third story.

• *If you are intrigued by the ghost stories of New Orleans, read Jannette's book, "Ghost Stories and Folk Tales of New Orleans," which includes directions for visiting these locations.*

A Louisiana Cryptid
Rougarou

The Honey Island Swamp is in St. Tammany Parish, Louisiana, within the Pearl River Wildlife Management Area. This swamp is home to wildlife, including alligators, deer, and snakes. One of its most famous inhabitants is the Honey Island Swamp Monster, the Cajun Sasquatch (La Bête Noire), described as an ape-like humanoid creature. In the eastern part of New Orleans, there is an area called the Little Woods near Grunch Road. This location is inhabited by the Grunch, a leathery-skinned creature resembling a goat with horns and sharp spines, standing three to four feet tall.

The Rougarou's origins trace back to French settlers exiled to American Colonies sometime between 1765 and 1785.

As Cajuns, they influenced the cattle industry and introduced unique foods while sharing folklore, including the loup-garou, linked to werewolf legends from France. It has long been said that something lurks among the mossy cypress trees and murky waters of the swamps in eastern and central Louisiana and the bayous near New Orleans. For centuries, its bone-chilling howl has echoed in the dusky night air. Some describe it as having a man's body but the head of a wolf, with claw-like nails and ferocious teeth hidden behind grinning lips. This wolf-man originated from a human cursed for some wrongdoing. In turn, it seeks out others of equally lousy character to pass on its curse and free itself.

The Rougarou hunts Catholics who ignore Lent for seven years. If someone draws the creature's blood, it breaks the curse and reveals its secret, but the person becomes cursed for 101 days unless they keep it a secret. The Rougarou often targets children, with parents warning them to be home by dark to avoid the creature.

There is a way to protect oneself from these creatures. By placing 13 small objects, such as pennies, marbles, or beans, on a windowsill, you can keep the Rougarou at bay. Because the Rougarou is compulsive, it will obsessively try to count the items. However, since it can only count to 12, it will become so fixated on counting that it will forget about trying to enter the home. As a result, it will have no choice but to retreat back to the swamps when the sun rises. There have been sightings of the creature—one account describes a black dog chasing two men returning from a visit to their neighbors. In their desperation, the pair jumped a fence to evade the animal. When the dog did not follow, they paused long enough to see a man standing on the other side of the wall, but the dog had vanished.

Maine

The Divine Specter of Nelly Butler

In 1799, in the small coastal town of Sullivan, Maine, along the rocky shoreline of Taunton Bay, Captain Abner Blaisdell and his family began to hear indistinct chatter and knocking sounds coming from the dank cellar of their home. Lydia, his fifteen-year-old daughter, was the first to report the mysterious noises during the late summer. Still, the family initially dismissed them as a result of her high fever when she fell ill. However, as the year progressed, the sounds became more pronounced, and other family members also began noticing the peculiar disturbances. After serving as a soldier in the American Revolutionary War, Captain Abner Blaisdell was known for his fearlessness and strict religious principles. He decided to investigate the strange noises from his cellar.

On January 2, 1800, Blaisdell called out while listening to the sounds, asking who was there. He received a message indicating that the voice belonged to the deceased wife of Captain George Butler, who was born Nelly Hooper, and she wished to speak to her father. Captain Blaisdell was familiar with her; Eleanor "Nelly" Hooper Butler's father, Dennis Hooper, lived only six miles away. Nelly died on June 13, 1797, at the age of 21, shortly after giving birth to her newborn. Her husband, George Butler, was 29 years old at the time of her death, and they were neighbors.

Blaisdell sent for Nelly's father, who, despite his doubts, still mourned his daughter's untimely death. He braved a snowstorm to reach the house and witness this strange phenomenon for himself. When Nelly spoke that day, Dennis Hooper was convinced by her answers to questions that only his daughter would know, affirming the ghostly presence as that of his daughter.

Not long after the news spread about what some described as a hoax, while others called it a specter or a demon, curious onlookers began flocking to the home. These mysterious occurrences centered around young Lydia. The ghostly interactions raised suspicions among locals, who speculated that Lydia might be possessed or involved in witchcraft due to her close connection with Nelly's spirit. One day, a woman named Mary Gordon witnessed and listened to the entity, which reproached the group for their mistreatment, false accusations, and rumors about the Blaisdell family. Gordon recounted, "At first, the apparition was a mere mass of light, then grew into personal form, about as tall as myself. We stood in two ranks about four or five feet apart. Between these ranks she slowly passed and re-passed, so that any of us could have handled her. At least the personal form became shapeless — expanded every way and vanished in a moment."

Nelly's sister, Sally Wentworth, shared her skepticism about the supernatural occurrences and believed they were demonic. One day, while visiting the Blaisdell cellar with a group, she remarked: "Capt. Butler, Mr. Wentworth, and I went with them to that house. Capt. Butler and I examined the cellar with a candle, and in a few minutes after, Lydia and I went down there. Capt. S-----n and some others, went with us, but none of them stood before us. While I held Lydia by the arm, we heard the sound of knocking. Lydia spoke, and a voice answered, the sound of which brought fresh to my mind that of my sister's voice, in an instant, but I could not understand it at all; though it was within the compass of my embrace, and, had it been a creature which breathed, it would have breathed in my face, and I had no impediment of hearing-" Sally Wentworth had gone upstairs and when passing through the room by the cellar, heard words plainly and exclaimed, "From this time I cleared Lydia as to the voice, and accused the devil."

By August 8, after additional visits to the cellar, Sally Wentworth remarked in response to a sarcastic comment from Nelly: "I heard much conversation. Her voice was still hoarse and thick, like that of my sister on her death bed, but more hollow. Sometimes it was clear, and always pleasant. A certain person did, in my opinion very unwisely, ask her whether I was a true Christian. The reply was, "She thinks she is, she thinks she is. She is my sister."

In the following months, the ghost of Nelly Butler was reported to have appeared and spoken to over a hundred eyewitnesses. Reverend Abraham Cummings, a Harvard-educated pastor known for his skepticism, began documenting these accounts. He collected testimony from more than 35 locals who either interacted with the spirit or heard its voice. During this time, Nelly started to speak with Lydia, expressing her wish for Lydia to marry George.

This revelation caused significant concern within both families, primarily due to the age difference—George was nearly twice Lydia's age. Despite Lydia's protests against this union, insisting that she did not want to marry someone so much older, her father, Abner Blaisdell, insisted it was God's will for them to be together.

The situation escalated when Abner took Lydia to meet George's father, Moses Butler, to discuss Nelly's demands. After several encounters with Nelly's spirit, including public appearances where she answered questions from townsfolk, both families ultimately came to accept that marrying Lydia to George was not only Nelly's wish but also aligned with divine intention.

On the ominous day of May 28, 1800, the unsuspecting couple, Lydia and George, exchanged their vows, blissfully unaware of the dark fate that loomed over them. Shortly after their union, a chilling specter materialized—the ghostly figure of Nelly. With hollow eyes that pierced the soul, she foretold a grim prophecy: the death of Captain Blaisdell's wife, followed by the tragic demise of Lydia and her husband, George Butler.

As March 1801 arrived, the air grew heavy with foreboding, and the specter's sinister predictions began to take shape. In a haunting twist of fate, Lydia succumbed during childbirth, fulfilling the dreadful prophecy. The spectral wails of Nelly echoed in the hearts of those left behind, a reminder of the bitter truth of their doomed love. And just like that, Nelly vanished into the night, her ghostly presence never to be seen again, leaving a chilling silence that haunted the community.

Maine
Ghastly Leftovers of Murder on Wood Island

Wood Island is a 32-acre island situated at the mouth of the Saco River, just off the coast of Biddeford. Since the lighthouse's construction in 1807, the island has been an essential navigational point and a critical aid for mariners navigating the Saco River. The surrounding communities of Saco and Biddeford thrived during the 1890s, primarily due to the textile, fishing, and lumber industries.

Fred Milliken served as a game warden and part-time sheriff at Biddeford Pool in the mid-1890s. Known as the "gentle giant," Milliken lived on Wood Island with his wife and three children. He owned two buildings on the island: a small cottage and another building that was once a chicken coop, which he rented to two fishermen, Howard Hobbs and William Moses, both around 24 years old. The lighthouse also had its keeper, Thomas Orcutt, who lived on the island.

In June 1896, Hobbs and Moses consumed alcohol heavily for two days while on the mainland. On the second day's afternoon, they rowed back to the island. When they arrived, Milliken stopped them to discuss their overdue rent, which had not been paid for several months. Hobbs entered his shack, retrieved his .42 caliber repeating rifle, and confronted Milliken, who tried to take the gun away from him. During the struggle, the part-time sheriff was shot. Upon realizing his mistake, Hobbs rushed to seek help from Thomas Orcutt, the lighthouse keeper, but it was too late. Milliken died 45 minutes later from his wounds in front of his distraught wife and three children. Hobbs went into the shack and used the gun to take his own life.

That day left a traumatic mark on the island. Witnesses report hearing low sounds from the area of the old chicken coop shack where Hobbs lived and strange muffled shouts and voices echoing through the lighthouse grounds. Some visitors describe seeing a shadowy figure, which they believe represents Milliken, particularly near the lighthouse walkway and at the top of the tower. Others have observed a woman's shadowy figure, thought to be Milliken's wife, flitting about.

Maine
Maiden's Cliff

A rock outcropping rises 800 feet above Megunticook Lake, offering stunning views of Ragged Mountain and the surrounding landscape. This location is Maiden's Cliff, and a tall white cross stands atop it. The outcropping acquired its name from a dreadful event and is associated with a little spirit that haunts the area.

Elenora French, an 11-year-old girl from Lincolnville Beach, was eager to join her 18-year-old sister, Antilla, and their local schoolteacher, Miss Hartshorn, as they were visiting friends on the warm day of May 7, 1864. After some persuasion, their mother agreed, and the excited little girl happily tagged along. The three of them soon met up with a man named Randall Young, and the group decided to hike to the top of Mount Megunticook.

While Young climbed around looking for a rock to toss down the cliff, Antilla and Miss Hartshorn sat chatting. The wind was blowing fiercely, so Elenora sat on a rock to put on her silk-braid hairnet, a popular headwear for girls then. Suddenly, Antilla heard a piercing scream and quickly turned around, only to find the empty rock where Elenora had been sitting. A gust of wind had blown Elenora's hairnet from her fingers, and as she reached up to grab it from the air, she lost her balance and fell 300 feet down the cliff face.

Young quickly descended the cliff to where Elenora had landed. She lay there peacefully, still alive but severely bruised and broken. A rescue party from Camden Village lowered the child down in a makeshift litter made from branches. Unfortunately, she succumbed to internal injuries from the fall and died at 12:30 that night.

After the tragic event, a cross was placed up where Elenora fell, and the rock outcropping called Maiden's Cliff. And those who hike the popular Maiden's Cliff trail in Camden Hills State Park say that Elenora still walks there.

Maine
Pitcher Man

During the time when the American colonies were fighting for independence from British rule, the small community of Goose River, now Rockport, saw many able-bodied men leave to join the war. Like many towns, it was left vulnerable to attack, with mainly women, children, and the elderly remaining. One man who did not go to battle was William Richardson, who engaged in guerrilla tactics against the British. Those fighting these minor battles would often gather to celebrate victories with ale. In 1783, news broke that the Treaty of Paris was signed on September 3, officially ending the American Revolutionary War and establishing the United States as an independent nation.

With the war concluded, Richardson hosted a celebration at his home. At some point during the festivities, he ventured out into the town with a pitcher in one hand, inviting everyone to join him. While crossing the Goose River Bridge, he unexpectedly encountered three loyalist men who had sided with the British. They ambushed Richardson, striking him on the head and ultimately murdering him. After his death, stories began circulating about sightings of Richardson's spirit wandering along the bridge, holding a pitcher and offering drinks. A notable report emerged in the 1950s when teenagers parked near the bridge witnessed a translucent figure resembling a man in Revolutionary-era clothing approach them with a pitcher. These sightings contributed to his nickname, "The Pitcher Man." He is still reported to be sighted today.

Haunting Shorts of Maine:

- Marshall Point Road is a scenic route that leads to the historic Marshall Point Lighthouse in St. George, Maine. The road offers picturesque views of Penobscot Bay and the surrounding natural landscape. It is associated with a legend about a young man named Ben Bennett, who was walking along the road when he encountered rum runners transporting illegal cargo during Prohibition. He was ambushed and murdered, and his ghost can be seen running along the road before vanishing.

- The Old Parish Cemetery, located in the heart of York, is surrounded by a rugged stone wall. In the cemetery's southwest corner lies the grave of 29-year-old Mary Nasson, who died in August 1774. This grave features head and footstones, with a large flat rock between them. While some believe that the stone was placed on the grave to deter grave robbers and wandering animals from disturbing the corpse, there is an earlier belief that it was intended to prevent a witch from rising. Despite these efforts, it seems that the stone was not effective, as sightings of Mary Nasson have been reported near the neighboring playground.

- Ayers Island is a private 62-acre island in the Penobscot River in the Town of Orono. It has been used for a few industries, from a sawmill, a pulp and paper mill, and a textile mill. It is haunted. John Tanner, a foreman at the mill there, died mysteriously and is believed to have returned to walk the land.

- In the shadowy town of Sabattus, an unsettling urban legend lingers. It speaks of a haunting well-hidden behind an old cemetery. A group of curious teens, enticed by the promise of the supernatural, ventured out one fateful night to uncover its secrets.

With trembling hands, they prepared a makeshift rope, tying it securely around a tire, which they hoisted to lower one of their own into the gaping mouth of the well. As the boy descended into the pitch-black abyss, the air grew colder, and an unsettling silence enveloped them, deepening with each inch he fell. The others stood at the edge, hearts pounding, desperately listening for any sign of life. Minutes dragged on like hours, but no sound echoed back to them. Fear crawled into their minds as they exchanged anxious glances. Finally, they decided to pull him back up. What emerged from the darkness was a horror none could have anticipated. His hair had turned a shocking white as if drained of all color; his skin was an unnatural, ghostly pale, glistening with a sheen of cold sweat. His eyes, once bright with youth, now flickered with a madness that sent shivers down their spines. He trembled uncontrollably, his gaze fixated on something unseen and his mouth moving in a silent scream as if trying to relay a nightmare beyond comprehension. He had seen something insidious and ancient. It was not long before he was taken away to an asylum, his mind shattered, vanished into the darkness, never to return.

• Haynesville Woods, located in northern Maine, is infamous for the "Haynesville Hitchhiker," also known as the "Woman in White," who appears on this lonely, desolate, and dangerous road. With dense forest on either side and broken pavement underfoot, this once-bustling trucking route is notorious for numerous accidents. A woman has been spotted standing in the middle of the road for many years. When drivers stop to check on her, she gets into the vehicle, and at a certain point, a chill fills the interior. When they turned to see where she was sitting, she had mysteriously vanished. In the woods, there are also the spirits of two young girls who died in an accident in 1967.

They can be seen waiting by the roadside but disappear when approached.

- In the 1950s, near Millinocket, a couple was involved in a car accident. Although neither was hurt, the man left to get help. When he returned, his wife had vanished without a trace. A body was never found, and he never saw her again. However, locals in Millinocket have reported seeing her ghost. She appears near the bridge outside of town and is known as the White Lady of Millinocket.

- The ancient North Manchester Meeting House in the pretty countryside of Manchester was built in 1793, and nearby lies a cemetery surrounded by a wall. In one corner of this wall, there is a stone featuring three distinct imprints that are said to be the devil's footprints, one of which resembles a cloven hoof. According to legend, during the construction of the wall, a worker became frustrated with a boulder that could not be moved. In his desperation, he exclaimed that he would sell his soul to the devil if the rock could be shifted. The next day, the boulder was moved, and the worker mysteriously vanished. The footprint is believed to be a sign of the pact he made.

A Maine Cryptid
Tote Road Shagamaw

Maine is home to several intriguing cryptids, each with distinct characteristics. One notable creature is the Specter Moose, a massive entity reported to stand between 10 to 15 feet tall and weigh nearly 2,500 pounds. This extraordinary moose was first sighted in 1891 and is known for its eerie appearance. Another fascinating cryptid is Billdad, an unusual hybrid resembling a mix between a kangaroo and a platypus. While it is generally considered benign, it is worth noting that its flesh may be potentially poisonous if consumed.

Additionally, there is the Tote Road Shagamaw, a creature often described by lumberjacks. It possesses the front paws of a bear and the hindquarters of a moose, allowing it to navigate on its hind legs like a bipedal being while also having the option to walk on its front legs. The Tote Road Shagamaw is known for its stealth and cunning behavior, particularly its insatiable appetite for cloth—especially cotton—which leads it to raid laundry left outside by residents. Its unique ability to move on two different sets of limbs may serve as a cunning strategy to evade those tracking it, resulting in confusion among woodsmen who may misidentify its tracks as belonging to either moose or bear.

Maryland
The Curse of Moll Dyer

Like many towns, the small community of Leonardtown in St. Mary's County, Maryland, was deeply religious in its early days, with some townspeople being overly zealous and superstitious. After a difficult growing season and a harsh winter, those fanatics sought to find someone to blame for what they believed was a curse upon their land, attributing such misfortunes to witchcraft. Whispers circulated about an old woman named Moll Dyer, who lived a quiet life on the edge of town. It was said that she had called upon the Devil to unleash terror upon the community.

A mob formed, and Moll Dyer, sensing the danger, grabbed her shawl and fled into the night, running as far as she could. As the chill crept into her bones, she realized she would not survive much longer. She found a boulder where she placed her right palm, raised her left palm to the moon, and let out a shrill cry, cursing everyone in the town. Her handprint discolored the stone, which can sometimes still be seen where it rests within the town now. Small trinkets are left at the site to appease the curse. Legends say that Moll Dyer still roams the land, seeking out those who sought to harm her. A road named after her runs alongside Moll Dyer Run, paralleling the rugged street.

Maryland
Headless Man of Paw Paw Tunnel

The Chesapeake and Ohio Canal Project built the Paw Paw Tunnel in the 1830s to bypass the rugged terrain along the Potomac River, including its bends. Most laborers were Irish or German immigrants. They worked 12 to 15 hours daily in backbreaking conditions, cutting through mountains and steep rock walls using black powder blasts. Others stood in knee-deep water, wielding shovels and picks to dig the trench where the boats would travel.

Tensions ran high among the canal workers, who engaged in strikes and riots, often fighting with one another due to prejudices between the English, Dutch, Irish, and German laborers. The workers lived in shanties within makeshift camps that provided little relief from the sweltering summer heat and biting winter winds. Cholera, malaria and yellow fever spread through the camp, causing countless deaths. Victims were often buried in mass graves or individually.

Their corpses were marked by simple wooden or stone markers, many of which have since disappeared.

Upon its completion, the Paw Paw Tunnel was so narrow that it could fit only one boat at a time. The tunnel was part of the canal until 1924 and is now included in the Chesapeake & Ohio Canal National Historical Park. Over the years, local legends have emerged about a headless man haunting the tunnel. Visitors have reported seeing shadows in the dark when no one else is around and hearing voices with heavy accents reminiscent of the early immigrants who lived, worked, and died there.

Haunting Shorts of Maryland:

• For generations, locals have recounted a haunting tale of a ghostly figure with a lantern roaming the Monocacy Aqueduct on moonless nights. This specter is believed to be the restless spirit of a soldier from John Mosby's band, known for guerrilla warfare during the Civil War. Mosby's raiders notoriously pillaged, stealing gold, silver, and heirlooms from residents, often burying their treasure along their route, hoping to return for it after the war. Legend says that those who follow this eerie ghost light might discover the hidden riches left behind by a soldier who never reclaimed their fortune.

• In the 1800s, timbermen logged much of what is now Green Ridge Forest. The Mertens family then purchased 32,000 acres, cleared the land, and developed an apple orchard from 1870 to 1920. With the arrival of the Western Maryland Railroad, they were able to sell their apples outside the village, leading to investments in the local economy, including a bunkhouse and jelly factory. However, the orchard went bankrupt in 1917, leading to abandonment and forest reclamation. By the 1970s, the railroad tracks were removed, leaving behind an abandoned tunnel known as Stickpile Tunnel. According to legend, a hobo was killed inside the tunnel, and his body was carelessly covered with sticks. Since then, many travelers passing through or near the tunnel claim to have seen the hobo's ghost.

• During the Civil War, a soldier named McCleary discovered an old gold mine in the Great Falls area of the Chesapeake and Ohio Canal National Historical Park. The mine changed hands multiple times, and in the early 1900s, a second shaft was added for a more valuable vein. On June 15, 1906, miners took a needed break at the hoist house.

An accidental explosion occurred when one miner ignited a fuse. Charles Eglin, the hoist man, died in the blast. Afterward, nightwatchmen reported mysterious footsteps and doors knocking with no one there. A tame mare that had worked at the mine began to refuse to approach the gate, acting as if terrified. Hikers can explore the Gold Mine Trail to see remnants of the mining operation, and perhaps they might even glimpse shadowy figures of miners from its past, as some others have!

• A haunted waste weir exists between Lock 28 (Point of Rocks Lock) and Lock 29 (Catoctin Lock) at Lander and downstream from the CSX Catoctin Tunnel, a part of Chesapeake and Ohio Canal in Maryland, now a trail. Canal boatmen and locals traveling the path would see a ghostly woman walk across the towpath to the waste weir and follow it to the river before vanishing.

• On a peninsula between the Chesapeake Bay and the Potomac River in St. Mary's County, there was a camp that held as many as 52,264 Confederate soldiers during the Civil War. Visitors to the park report feeling the presence of the spirits of these soldiers, hearing disembodied voices, and seeing shadowy while exploring the grounds.

• At Point Lookout Lighthouse, eerie sounds and unusual smells have also been reported. Visitors have claimed to see the ghost of Ann Davis, Maryland's first female lightkeeper, who is often spotted wearing a white blouse and a long blue skirt at the top of the stairs. Ann Davis was the daughter of James Davis, who died about two months after being appointed to the position at Point Lookout. Ann took over the job in 1830 and served as a lightkeeper for 17 years until her death.

• In September 1862, during the Civil War, Confederate forces captured the Union garrison at Harpers Ferry.

They executed a coordinated attack from multiple directions, overwhelming the Union troops, who eventually surrendered. Hikers crossing the rugged and steep Maryland Heights trail near Harpers Ferry have reported ghostly soldiers along the path. They assume these figures are reenactors and are shocked when they disappear.

• The Battle of Antietam, fought on September 17, 1862, near Sharpsburg, is one of the Civil War's bloodiest battles, with over 3,675 men losing their lives. Soldiers clashed on northern soil, leading to intense fighting along an old sunken road. Today, the battlefield is known for ghostly sightings. During a class field trip, students from one Maryland school witnessed a ghostly riderless horse. Visitors often report the scent of gunpowder and unusual heavy energy in the air. Civil War reenactors once heard eerie moans while camping along Bloody Lane.

• The Old South Mountain Inn, located along the historic National Pike near Boonsboro, served as a welcoming tavern for various travelers, including waggoneers, stagecoach drivers, teamsters, and tourists. Additionally, local legend speaks of a huge, ghostly black dog that would reportedly waylay travelers in this area.

• The Cecil County Pig Woman haunts a lonely bridge along Russell Road, known as Pig Woman Lane. According to the legend, a farm nearby once caught fire with a woman trapped inside. In her attempt to escape the flames, she jumped from a window, suffering severe burns that left her face disfigured. Driven mad by her trauma, she fled into the woods. Some dare to visit a bridge on Russell Road, her lair, where eerie pig-like grunts and oinks echo from beneath. People who have encountered her report chilling experiences marked by unexplained scratches on their vehicles. Some have even fled their cars in panic, never to be seen again.

- A jet-black vehicle driven by a faceless entity roams Seven Hills Road in Prince George's County, chasing down unsuspecting drivers late at night who pass the seventh hill at the stroke of midnight. According to witnesses, the truck appeared out of nowhere. It aggressively pursued them until they managed to escape or crash.

- Pocomoke State Forest in Maryland is home to the Pocomoke River, which flows through it alongside its cypress swamps. Many tales suggest that wraiths haunt the forest, believed to be the souls of those who drowned in the river or in the swampy waters. Mysterious balls of light have been reported in the area, and some believe these lights act as guardians of the forest, watching for any evil trying to enter. In the 1920s, a preacher held a revival in the woods, successfully converting many local women. However, their husbands were not pleased. When the enraged men formed a mob and descended upon the makeshift church to confront the preacher, their leader found himself unable to open the door. As the others attempted to knock it down, a fire erupted from the roof, coursing down the sides of the building and scaring the mob away. Some witnesses have described seeing the ball of fire hovering above them as if examining them before vanishing. It is believed that those with pure intentions may enter the sacred space, while those with evil motives will be repelled.

A Maryland Cryptid
Goat Man of Prince George's County

Maryland is known for its legendary beasts. One of the most infamous is the snallygaster, a creature described as a half-bird, half-reptile. It originated among early German immigrants in Frederick County. It terrorized local communities, with reports of its blood-sucking behavior and terrifying screeches dating back to the 18th century.

Residents speak of Chessie, a snake-like sea monster in the Chesapeake Bay. Another notable creature is the Dwayo, a large, hairy being resembling a bipedal wolf or dog, primarily sighted in the Middletown Valley.

One of the most formidable creatures is the Goatman, found in Prince George's County. This beast resembles a hairy humanoid figure with a human upper body and goat-like lower limbs. Standing around six feet tall, it is known for its creepy squealing noise before it attacks its prey. Reports of the Goatman date back to the 1930s, when several dogs went missing and were later found dead under mysterious circumstances. The creature reappeared in the 1970s, coinciding with the strange disappearance of pets. The Goatman has been frequently spotted near Tucker Road in Clinton, Maryland, and Fletchertown Road in Bowie, Maryland.

Massachusetts
Lizzie Borden's House

Lizzie Andrew Borden was born in the summer of 1860 and grew up on Second Street in Fall River, Massachusetts, alongside her sister Emma Lenora Borden, who was nine years older. Their father, Andrew Borden, was a wealthy real estate and furniture manufacturing businessman. Despite his wealth, he preferred to live modestly and was known for his frugality. This thriftiness and his rude demeanor led to a strained household, business relationships, and enemies.

Lizzie's mother passed away when she was only three years old, and Andrew later remarried Abby Durfee Gray. Despite her family circumstances, Lizzie was a respected community member and actively participated in various organizations, including the Temperance Union and the Christian Endeavor. She also served on the board of the Fall River Hospital.

Lizzie loved animals, which sometimes created tensions within the household. In the spring of 1892, she built a pigeon roost in the barn. However, in May of that year, Andrew Borden killed many of the pigeons with a hatchet, claiming they attracted local children who would come to hunt them. By mid-summer, tensions in the home escalated, prompting the two sisters to take extended vacations in New Bedford. Upon their return, Lizzie stayed in a boarding house for several days before going back home. At the beginning of August, the family fell violently ill, and some speculated this was due to eating mutton that had been left out.

On August 4, 1892, the day began like any other. Lizzie's maternal uncle, John Morse, was visiting for a few days to discuss some business with Andrew. He met Andrew in the morning, then left to buy a pair of oxen and see other family members. Andrew went for his usual morning walk while Lizzie's stepmother, Abby, went upstairs to clean the guest room.

When Andrew returned from his walk, he found his key would not work in the door latch. The Borden's' 25-year-old live-in maid, Maggie Sullivan, heard him and rushed to open the door. She helped him take off his boots and coat, and after he laid down on the couch for a nap, she headed to the third floor to rest. It wasn't long before Maggie heard a cry from Lizzie: "Maggie, come quick! Father's dead. Somebody came in and killed him."

Andrew Borden was found slumped on a couch in the downstairs sitting room, having been struck ten or eleven times with a hatchet-like weapon. Abby was discovered upstairs with her head bashed in, having been beaten at least 17 to 20 times.

Lizzie Borden was arrested and charged with the murders of her parents after several pieces of circumstantial evidence emerged against her. However, she was later acquitted of all charges during her trial in June 1893 due to insufficient evidence linking her directly to the crimes. In the following years, she faced public criticism in newspapers and within the community.

After passing away from pneumonia at 66, around the same time as her sister, the air in this historic home became thick with unsettling energy as if the very walls were steeped in whispers of the past. Lizzie Borden's story doesn't end with her death; it lingers in the chilling legacy that haunts the Lizzie Borden House in Fall River, Massachusetts. Visitors enter with an eerie anticipation, often recounting spine-tingling tales of objects inexplicably moving as though guided by unseen hands. The soft sound of marbles rolling across the floor echoes through the dimly lit rooms, awakening a sense of dread. A solitary rocking chair sways back and forth, seemingly possessed by a restless spirit yearning for comfort. The house fills with ghostly murmurs and indistinct footsteps on quiet nights, a haunting reminder that Lizzie and her parents may still roam the halls. Shadows flit from room to room, creating an unsettling dance that captivates and terrifies. Those brave enough to tarry may sense the chilling brush of history against their skin, leaving them to wonder what secrets the house still guards.

Massachusetts
Lady in Black

Fort Warren is located on George's Island in Boston Harbor and was constructed between 1833 and 1861 as part of a defense system for Massachusetts. During the Civil War, it functioned both as a military training camp and as a prison for Confederate soldiers and sympathizers. The conditions were harsh, and Union soldiers reported seeing ghosts during the war, experiencing odd shadows and a feeling of being watched. One notable figure during this time was Missus Melanie Lanier, whose husband fought for the Confederacy and was captured during the Battle of Roanoke Island in early 1862.

Determined to free him, she devised a plan and secured passage on a schooner to Hull, Massachusetts, where she stayed with a Confederate sympathizer. Disguised as a man, Melanie rowed across the harbor to George's Island under darkness. Once inside the fort, she communicated with her husband and other prisoners. Melanie signaled her husband and the other inmates on a pre-arranged night by whistling a popular Confederate tune. The prisoners then lowered a rope for her to climb into the fort through a rifle slit. Reunited with her spouse, the couple attempted to dig a tunnel beneath the parade ground to access weapons from the arsenal. However, they dug too close to a wall and attracted a guard's attention. In the ensuing chaos, Melanie fired a pistol at one of the soldiers but missed.

Amid the turmoil, her husband was killed, and Melanie was captured and sentenced to death by hanging as a spy. She requested to be hanged in a dress rather than the men's clothing she wore, and her wish was granted; she was hanged in a makeshift black dress. Following her death, soldiers reported seeing her spirit wandering through the fort, and visitors later claimed to have encountered "The Lady in Black."

Haunting Shorts of Massachusetts:

• The Salem witch trials were a series of events in Massachusetts from June 1692 to May 1693. During this time, 19 people, primarily women, were put to death because they were accused of practicing witchcraft. These trials were driven by social conflicts, strong religious beliefs, and personal grudges among the people in the community. This led to a lot of fear and panic spreading throughout the area. The accusations began when several young girls claimed to be afflicted by witches, prompting investigations that quickly spiraled out of control. Ultimately, 25 people died as a result of the trials—19 were hanged, one was tortured, and five died in jail awaiting trial. The trials came to an end when public opinion turned against them, leading to the disbandment of the special court and a halt to witchcraft prosecutions. Proctor's Ledge, where the hangings occurred during the summer and fall of 1692, is believed to be haunted. Some have reported seeing a Lady in White, while others have heard a ghostly voice.

• The Hoosac Tunnel is a 5-mile railroad tunnel running through the Hoosac Range of the Berkshire Mountains. It connects the towns of North Adams and Florida. During its construction from 1851 to 1875, over 190 workers lost their lives due to various accidents, including explosions and drownings. In March 1865, Ringo Kelley accidentally detonated an explosive charge while using nitroglycerin for blasting. This explosion trapped Ned Brinkman and Billy Nash under tons of rock, and they died. Not long after, Kelley vanished, and his corpse was found near the location his coworkers were killed; he had been choked to death. Many believed that Brinkman and Nash had returned from the dead to murder the man who killed them. For years, cries of agony swept out from the tunnel.

• At Rutland State Park, there is an abandoned prison complex that housed minor offenders convicted of non-violent crimes, such as public intoxication and tax evasion. Inmates worked on the farm daily and returned to their minimum-security accommodations at night. The prison was abandoned in 1934 and included facilities like a farm, cell blocks, staff housing, a water tower, and a tuberculosis hospital. Today, the prison ruins are open to the public for hiking. Some visitors have reported feeling strange sensations as if they were being watched, and one person even claimed to have felt something eerie follow them home!

A Massachusetts Cryptid
Dover Demon

Massachusetts is home to a foul-smelling Bigfoot creature spotted throughout the state, particularly in the Berkshire Mountains and the Bridgewater Triangle. Another intriguing location is the Hockomock Swamp, a 200-square-mile murky wetland known for UFO sightings, encounters with cryptids, and ghostly apparitions.

However, the Dover Demon is particularly notable. This mysterious creature was reported by three teens: William "Bill" Bartlett, John Baxter, and Abby Brabham. They described the creature as about four feet tall, with glowing orange eyes, hairless, and rough flesh-colored skin that appeared either tan or chalky gray. The beast had a watermelon-shaped head, skinny arms, and legs and seemed to lack a nose or mouth. It was seen crawling along a stone wall on Farm Street, running into a gully, and near a roadway.

Michigan
One-legged Man of the Haunted Old Bell Building

The 1853 George and Sarah White House once stood at the corner of Fountain and Division Streets in Grand Rapids, where the large Michigan Bell Telephone Building now stands. By the early 1900s, this once beautiful mansion had fallen into neglect and had become a boarding house. In 1907, 21-year-old Warren and Vashti Perry Rowland were amongst the tenants who had settled happily into the house in a single bedroom. They had been married for four years, and Warren had secured a good job as a brakeman with the Grand Rapids and Indiana Railroad. But, in 1908, Warren suffered a dreadful accident on the railroad, resulting in the loss of his leg.

Although Warren was fitted with a wooden leg, his typically good-natured personality changed dramatically. He became irrational and distrustful, often accusing Vashti of infidelity. His behavior grew increasingly violent, leading to the police being called multiple times; on one occasion, he even chased Vashti through an alley with a straight razor. Eventually, Vashti left Warren. However, in 1910, after weeks of relentless pleading, he convinced her to take a carriage ride, which ultimately led them back to the boarding house.

At one point in the room, Warren removed his wooden leg and began striking Vashti on the head until she was stunned and unconscious. He then moved around the room, sealing the doors and windows by stuffing the crevices with rags and pieces of clothing. Shortly after, Warren tore a gas fixture from the wall, causing the fumes to fill the room. He took out his straight razor and slit his throat, not enough to kill him. But the gas killed them both.

It was the smell of gas and the stench of rotting corpses that prompted another tenant to call the police two weeks later. When the authorities arrived, they discovered the bodies of the dead couple. Shortly after this, residents began to report hearing the sound of Warren's wooden leg thumping against the floor. Muffled sounds of fighting, crying, and screaming echoed through the hallways.

In the early 1920s, the Michigan Bell Telephone Company bought the house. The old tenant's home was demolished, and a new Bell building was constructed in its place. Shortly afterward, residents in Grand Rapids began receiving prank calls from the building during the night. Naturally, people speculated that the prank calls were the work of the ghosts of the couple who had once lived in the old tenement home on the lot.

Michigan
Beckoning Minnie

A small town in the eastern region of Michigan, known as Forester, was once a thriving lumber town and a busy ship port for boats hauling lumber along the shorelines of Lake Huron. Minnie Quay was born in May 1861 to James and Mary Ann Quay. At 14, Minnie fell deeply in love with a young sailor whose ship had docked in Forester. Naturally, her parents disapproved of the relationship, and her mother even exclaimed one day, "I would rather see Minnie dead than be with that sailor!"

In the spring of 1876, Minnie heard news that the sailor's ship had sunk in Lake Huron during a storm, shattering her heart. On April 27, 1876, while tasked with watching her younger brother as their parents were away, Minnie strode to Smith's dock. She leaped into the freezing waters of Lake Huron, drowning in the process. She was buried on a bluff where her grave still stands today.

It wasn't long before passersby reported seeing her ghost pacing along the shoreline. Over the years, several young women reported that she beckoned them with a waving hand toward the cold waters as if leading them to their deaths. Visitors often go to her grave to leave tokens and pennies to appease her spirit, hoping she will not follow them home.

Michigan
Starving Charlie of Isle Royale

In 1845, a 17-year-old Anishinaabe woman named Angelique Mott and her husband Charlie, who was French-Canadian, were hired by a man named Cyrus Mendenhall to explore Isle Royale for copper deposits. They were also tasked with guarding a discovery that Angelique had found during a previous visit to the uninhabited island. Mendenhall was a disreputable character who organized mining companies on Isle Royale for the Lake Superior Copper Company. He promised the couple that provisions and support would arrive within three weeks. Instead, they found themselves stranded, abandoned with only an old derelict fisherman's cabin for shelter and very little food.

Initially, Charlie and Angelique had a half barrel of flour borrowed from a mission, six pounds of rancid butter, and a few beans. Their supplies dwindled rapidly, and during a storm, they lost their bark canoe and fishing net, making it impossible to find food. As harsh winter set in, they foraged for bark and bitter roots, suffering severely from starvation. Charlie's condition worsened over time. Angelique later reported, "Charlie suffered from it even worse than I did. As he grew weaker, he lost all heart and courage. Then, his fever rose higher and higher until Charlie finally went completely out of his head. One day, he sprang up, seized his butcher knife, and began sharpening it on a whetstone. 'He was tired of being hungry,' he said. 'He would kill a sheep; it was something to eat he must have.' He then glared at me as if he thought nobody could read his purpose but himself. At that moment, I realized I was the sheep he intended to kill and eat. I watched him all day and night, not daring to sleep, expecting him to pounce on me at any moment. Eventually, I managed to wrest the knife from him, and that danger was over."

The couple was stranded for months, and tragically, Charlie died from starvation one winter night before any rescue could take place. In the spring of 1846, the sound of gunfire signaled the return of Mendenhall and his men. The ship Algonquin returned to the island, bringing Angelique home to her mother. She passed away in 1874 in Sault Ste. Marie, Ontario.

Mott Island, named after Charlie and Angelique Mott, is one of the islands within Isle Royale National Park, located in Lake Superior, Michigan. This island is part of the more extensive park, which includes the park's headquarters and visitor services. Following the tragedy of Charlie's death, local legends emerged about his ghost haunting Isle Royale. His spirit wanders the island, searching for food as he did during his life.

Haunting Shorts of Michigan:

- The Pointe aux Barques Lighthouse is situated along the northeastern tip of the Thumb region on Lake Huron's shores. Catherine Shook haunts the Pointe aux Barques Lighthouse. After the tragic drowning of her husband, Peter Shook, who was the first lighthouse keeper there in 1849, Catherine took over his duties. Her ghost is often seen wearing a white dress, wandering through the corridors, and climbing the steps of the lighthouse tower as if she is still fulfilling her responsibilities.

- There is a mysterious manifestation of light between Paulding and Watersmeet, often appearing in yellow, white, or red depending on atmospheric conditions. The lights hover in the air, growing and shrinking as they dance. In 1966, four teen couples drove down Old Military Road to Dog Meadow and turned off the headlights. Suddenly, a bright light illuminated the car's interior, frightening them so much that they reported it to a local sheriff. Since then, many others have observed the light. Old Military Road was constructed using an old mail route during the Civil War, connecting Fort Howard in Green Bay, Wisconsin, and Fort Wilkins in Copper Harbor, Michigan. It was built to quickly transport military supplies. Later, it was primarily used to access resources like copper and iron from the Upper Peninsula. Over the years, many travelers have used this route, leading to various ghostly theories about the cause of the lights. The prevailing story dates back to the early days when dogsled along the rugged path delivered mail through the forest. It was not uncommon for these mailmen to encounter robbers. One day, in a remote section, a mailman was murdered along with his dogs, and the killer was never found. Some believe that the mysterious light is the spirit of this mail carrier.

• In the Grand Rapids suburb of Ada, at Findlay Cemetery, witnesses have reported seeing a misty apparition with arms waving accompanied by shrieking and weeping. This figure is believed to be connected to a 19th-century murder of a woman by her betrayed husband. However, she actually died from something much worse: typhoid fever. That said, dying from disease has never stopped anyone from returning from the grave to lament their early demise. After all, no one wants to die from either fate.

• Hell's Bridge is a metal footbridge in Algoma Township, Michigan, spanning the Rogue River. Legends passed down state that Elias Friske murdered several children and disposed of their bodies in the river, claiming he was influenced by a demon. After, the sounds of bodies being dumped into the water and the cries of children were heard there. Anyone tubing along the river with their toes wiggling in the water takes the chance of those water babies grabbing their feet and pulling them under.

• The SS Bannockburn was a Canadian-registered freighter that mysteriously vanished on Lake Superior during a severe winter storm on November 21, 1902. That day, the captain of the freighter Algonquin spotted the Bannockburn several times before it vanished into the fog. That night, heavy snow and winds prevailed, and crew aboard the passenger steamer Huronic reported seeing lights from a ship they believed to be the Bannockburn. However, the SS Bannockburn did not arrive at its destination the following day. It was officially declared lost by November 30 without sign of life. Despite searches over the years, no wreckage or bodies have been recovered from the ship. After its disappearance, sightings of a ghost ship resembling the Bannockburn were frequent on stormy nights, earning it the nickname "The Flying Dutchman of the Great Lakes."

• The abandoned Old Scio Cemetery is overgrown and hidden in a wooded area near Huron River Drive and Zeeb Road in Scio Township, Washtenaw County. Dating far back to the 1840s, it is rumored to be the final resting place of a warlock. The grave of Warlock Willie is particularly notable because it has become engulfed by old trees that have grown around it. The corpse is still believed to be buried beneath the roots of this tree. According to local lore, if one were to lie down in the hollow at the base of this tree where the gravestone once stood, sensations of entities or demons would pass through them. Some claim that cleaning up the cemetery can lead to increased supernatural activity as a form of gratitude from the spirits resting there.

A Michigan Cryptid
Dogman

Michigan is home to several intriguing cryptids, including a few notable ones. One such creature is the Nain Rouge, a little red demon dwarf associated with Detroit. According to legend, the Nain Rouge brings misfortune to those who encounter it. This legend dates back to the founding of Detroit in 1701 when it is said to have cursed explorer Antoine de La Mothe Cadillac. The Nain Rouge has been linked to significant disasters in Detroit's history, such as the Great Fire of 1805 and the riots of 1967.

Another well-known cryptid is Pressie, the Lake Superior Serpent, described as having a long neck, a horse-like head, and a body that exceeds 25 feet in length. Sightings of Pressie have been reported since the 1800s. Some believe it could be a surviving prehistoric creature like a plesiosaur. In contrast, others think it is an unusually large fish.

The Michigan Dogman is a creature first reported in 1887 in Wexford County, Michigan. It is characterized as a seven-foot tall, bipedal entity resembling a canine, featuring either blue or amber eyes. The creature has a humanoid torso. It is known for emitting a distinctive, shrieking howl. According to early legends, the Dogman appears to follow a ten-year cycle, and it is believed that clapping hands can help deter its presence.

Throughout the mid-1800s into the 1900s, lumberjacks commonly reported sightings of this mysterious being, often describing it as having a man's body and a dog's head. In a notable account from 1937, an individual named Robert Fortney claimed to have been attacked by a pack of five wild dogs, one of which was observed walking on two legs.

Minnesota
The Wrathful Wraith

In March of 1872, heavy snow fell along the St. Paul and Pacific Railroad, blanketing the tracks. A train departed toward Randall Station, carrying workers and consisting of three engines, a boxcar, two cabooses, and a snowplow. During the journey, one of the cars broke loose and went unnoticed in the blinding snowstorm. The train stopped at Randall Station to let some laborers off. Still, while it was stopped, the detached car caught up and collided with the train, causing the cars to telescope and crash into one another. Conductor Fitzgerald, a brakeman named Knudson, and a section foreman named Connelly were killed instantly.

Replacing Connelly, the section foreman who had died, proved to be challenging. He was a skilled and industrious worker who had formed a strong attachment to his position and Randall Station. He had chosen to stay despite being offered higher-paying positions in less isolated locations. A new section foreman was hired to fill Connelly's role. Still, soon after starting, he found that Connelly's angry ghost would not leave him alone. The restless spirit, determined not to let another man take his place, would visit both night and day. At night, Connelly's ghost became so aggressive that he physically threw the new foreman out of bed, leaving him with bruises and welts. During the day, the wraith would follow him along the tracks, waving his arms in a desperate attempt to get him to leave.

Despite being frightened, the new foreman kept his ordeal to himself, fearing mockery from the other men. Then, one evening, as the men sat down for supper, the door burst open seemingly on its own. In the doorway stood the wraith of Connelly, demonstrating his wrath and desire for revenge before suddenly melting away. The men were so stunned by the apparition that they remained frozen in their seats. The new foreman immediately shared his strange stories about ghostly visits following the unusual event. After that night, Connelly continued to haunt the crew, hiding their tools to hinder their work. Engineers reported the ghost on the tracks, using a crowbar to lift the rails and gesturing as if directing a group of workers. At times, Connelly could be seen standing on the tracks with his arms outstretched as if warning of an impending disaster. The tracks still exist, paralleling State Highway 9. If you head northeast out of Clontarf and keep an eye out for the next mile and a half where the old Randall Station once stood, you might catch a glimpse of the ghost of old Connelly working on the tracks.

Minnesota
Bobbing Blue Light on
Arcola High Bridge

The Arcola High Bridge is a steel arch railroad bridge that spans the St. Croix River, connecting Minnesota and Wisconsin. Visitors at the Arcola Bluffs Day Use Area, after hiking the trails to the shoreline, have reported seeing a mysterious blue light swaying and bobbing. This light is often accompanied by the dark silhouette of a phantom carrying it along the tracks of the bridge.

According to local legend, during World War I, trains used this bridge to transport ammunition from the Twin Cities Army Ammunition Plant. A night watchman was hired to guard the bridge and prevent enemies from sabotaging the trestle. One stormy night, while inspecting the bridge, the watchman could not escape a train that approached unexpectedly. Today, he still roams the area, carrying a lantern and forever watching over the bridge.

Haunting Shorts of Minnesota:

• Dead Man's Trail in Thief River Falls is haunted. Hikers who venture there at certain hours often report hearing screams and wails. According to local legend, many years ago, a Chippewa warrior was banished from his tribe after being accused of murder. He wandered the area around the river and eventually made it his home. One day, a Chippewa mother was traveling nearby when the man began to chase her. Unable to outrun him while carrying her infant, she crafted a small nest along the riverbank, placed the baby inside, and ran for help, knowing she would return for her child. After she successfully evaded the man, she returned to the river, only to find that the water had risen and swept her baby away. To this day, her anguished cries are still heard in the area.

• On a gravel road just off 270th Street outside the town of Henderson, there is a bridge over a creek next to a large tree. This bridge is called Crazy Annie's Bridge. Local stories say that Annie lived in a house by this bridge with her three children. After her husband died in World War I, she lost her mind and drowned her three children in the creek before hanging herself from the tree. Now, people say the children's handprints appear on cars, and the figure of Crazy Annie is seen lurking in the dark where she shrieks and wails.

• The Washington Street Bridge in Minneapolis, which spans the Mississippi River, seems to attract individuals contemplating suicide. After they jump, their spirits return as ghosts, haunting the living. Those who cross the bridge at night often report hearing ghostly footsteps and feeling an eerie sense of being watched.

• The Warden's House Museum in Stillwater was built in 1853 and served as the home for prison wardens. The last warden to live in the home was Henry Wolfer. When he took over the Stillwater Prison in 1892, he had a different approach to prison management, trying to reform the convicts by teaching them reading and writing. Wolfer lived there with his daughter, Trudy. Trudy moved away near Mankato, had a son, and died shortly after from appendicitis. The baby was sent to Henry Wolfer, who took the young boy in and raised him. Visitors to the museum report seeing a woman in the master bedroom, what they call a Woman in White. Many believe it is Trudy searching for her boy.

• Enger Park in Duluth is a scenic area that offers incredible views of Lake Superior and the city. It features the five-story Enger Memorial Tower, built from local stone in 1939 as a tribute to Norwegian immigrant Bert Enger. Visitors have reported seeing a mysterious man on the fifth level who disappears before they can reach him. It was rumored in 1948, a man allegedly committed suicide by jumping from the top floor of the tower.

• On February 5, 1924, a surface cave-in occurred at the Milford Mine near Wolford. The collapse happened when the mine tapped into mud directly connected to Foley Lake. 48 miners were finishing their shift about 170 feet underground when the shaft collapsed, rapidly flooding the mine with water and mud. Only seven of the men managed to reach the surface. After reopening, workers encountered the ghostly foreman, Clinton Harris, and heard the eerie echo of a phantom whistle. Harris, the electric hoist operator, stayed at his post and blew the warning whistle to alert others of danger. When his body was found, he had tied the whistle cord around his waist, ensuring he could guide others to safety even in death.

A Minnesota Cryptid
Wendigo

In the late 1960s, the Minnesota Iceman gained notoriety as a spectacle that attracted many visitors. This display featured a 6-foot creature resembling Bigfoot encased in ice. It was showcased at various fairs and carnivals throughout the United States.

In contrast, reports of encounters with Pepie, the lake monster from Lake Pepin, are far less common. Pepie is described as a serpent-like creature inhabiting the lake, but sightings remain rare.

More elusive is the Wendigo, a figure rooted in Algonquian legend representing insatiable hunger. The Wendigo is characterized as a malevolent spirit depicted as an emaciated, gaunt being with skeletal features that loom over humans.

It haunts northern forests, particularly during the bleak winter when food is scarce and starvation is prevalent. The creature's skin is ash-gray or yellowish, tightly stretched over its bones, with sunken eyes, elongated claws, and jagged teeth reminiscent of a shark's. Additionally, the Wendigo is known for a distinctive, foul odor that accompanies its presence.

Mississippi
The Betrothed's Mourning Chair

In the Chapel of the Cross Cemetery in Madison, Mississippi, there is an old wrought iron mourning chair at the foot of a grave. Legend has it that a ghostly woman has been seen sitting in that chair. Her story is as follows:

Henry Grey Vick was a 23-year-old man, bold and youthful, and he believed he would live forever. He came from a well-to-do family that was part of the upper class of Southern society in Vicksburg. In May of 1859, shortly before his wedding to Helen Johnstone, Vick traveled to New Orleans. While there, he stopped at a tavern and encountered James Stith, a former friend. An argument broke out between them, and Stith publicly insulted Vick by proclaiming that he would not drink in the same room as him. This was a grave affront among the Southern gentry of that time.

In the heat of the moment, Vick, believing he needed to restore his honor, recklessly challenged Stith to a duel. At this time, dueling had not yet been outlawed in New Orleans.

However, it was typically moved to the outskirts of town, with the location and time negotiated by mediators known as seconds. It was agreed that the duel would take place in Mobile, Alabama.

When the duel occurred in Mobile, Vick attempted to avoid violence by deliberately missing his shot at Stith. However, Stith did not share this sentiment; he fired his pistol and struck Vick directly in the forehead, killing him—just four days before Vick's wedding.

Vick's remains were transported back to the Chapel of the Cross Cemetery in Madison, where he was buried and a headstone with a cross placed atop. His funeral was attended by friends from Vicksburg and his fiancée, Helen Johnstone, who was dressed in mourning attire. After the funeral, as the days passed and the memories of the tragic event started to fade for others, Helen Johnstone, Henry Vick's betrothed, would often sit on a mourning bench at the foot of his grave. She spent countless hours grieving for him. Although she eventually married and was buried in a different location, her young soul remained intertwined with the trauma of that day and the loss of Henry Grey Vick. Even now, her ghost is occasionally seen sitting on the bench, mourning his death.

Mississippi
The Crossroads

Robert Johnson was a significant American blues musician and songwriter, born on May 8, 1911, in Hazlehurst, Mississippi. He died young, reportedly poisoned by the angry husband of a woman he was involved with. He is best known for his remarkable guitar skills and haunting vocal style, profoundly impacting the blues genre and inspiring countless musicians.

Johnson's talent gave rise to a legend associated with the intersection of Highways 61 and 49 in Greenwood, Mississippi. According to this legend, Johnson made a deal with the devil near Dockery Plantation. The devil is said to have tuned Johnson's guitar and granted him exceptional talent in exchange for his soul. His songs "Hell-Hound on My Trail" and "Me and the Devil Blues" helped to perpetuate the legend.

Haunting Shorts of Mississippi:

• Old rural streets wind through dense woodlands, transitioning from asphalt to gravel and eventually to Mississippi red dirt roads. These paths lead curious travelers to a location along the Chunky River, about 12 miles from Meridian, steeped in dark legend—Stuckey's Bridge. The old truss bridge is a historic landmark in Mississippi that spans the Chunky River. Local legends told that Old Man Stuckey was a partner of the infamous Dalton Gang, a group of outlaws active between 1890 and 1892, known for their bank and train robberies. The gang primarily consisted of four brothers: Bob, Grat, Emmett, and Bill Dalton. According to these tales, Old Man Stuckey killed and robbed guests at his inn, burying their bodies along the riverbank. The old man knew nobody would ever find the bodies in this deep pocket of nowhere where the river's current eventually swept the corpses away to the Pascagoula River, which flows into the Gulf of Mexico. His greed ultimately led to his downfall. After murdering more than twenty people, Stuckey was caught and hanged. After they cut the noose from the bridge, the specter of the old man carrying a lantern was spotted walking along the river's edge below. Loud splashes echoed the sound of Old Man Stuckey's lifeless body hitting the water when the noose was severed.

• Kosciusko Cemetery, located in Attala County, features a 20-foot grave marked by a gigantic statue of Laura Kelly. The statue, dressed in beautiful clothing with a cane at her side, honors Kelly, who passed away in 1890 at 38. The cemetery was once a popular destination for nighttime visits, mainly because of Missus Kelly's impressive statue, which was positioned so her grieving husband could see it from their home several blocks away. Legend has it that her statue is known to revolve on its pedestal at night and weep.

• The Natchez Drug Company, owned by John H. Chambliss, was located on the corner of Main and Union in Natchez, Mississippi. Chambliss had recently installed a gas-fired stove in the laboratory on the fourth floor. Among those who assisted with the piping installation was a 21-year-old plumber and volunteer fireman named Sam Burns. On the spring morning of March 14, 1908, workers noticed a strong odor of gas in the building. By early afternoon, Sam Burns arrived and started checking for a leak using a lighted candle, a common practice at the time. He began his inspection on the fourth floor. Next, he headed to the basement and apparently found the leak at 2:45 p.m. because that is when the explosion erupted, blasting the building, the young man, and those within to pieces. Workers picking through the wreckage found bodies and mixtures of torsos and pieces of a heart, liver, lungs, and charred bones. On that tragic day, 11 people, including both workers and pedestrians, lost their lives. Five employees trapped in the building, aged 12 to 21, all died. The owner of the Natchez Drug Company was heartbroken and commissioned a beautiful angel monument that overlooks five headstones of victims of the explosion at Natchez City Cemetery. This angel monument is known as the Turning Angel. Those who drive along Cemetery Road at night with their headlights on claim that it appears to turn as their car passes by.

• Waynesboro Shubuta Road is called "Devil Worshipper Road" after a farmer known as the Goat Man sold his soul to the devil and now chases cars, staring directly at those who stop. The cursed farmer resembles a satyr, standing seven feet tall with glowing eyes, furry legs, and horns while wielding a pitchfork. This road is surrounded by numerous little country churches, suggesting that revivals are often held in the area to keep the demon at bay.

- The Old Courthouse Museum in Vicksburg is haunted by spirits connected to its rich history during the Civil War era. Once serving as the Warren County courthouse, it is now home to one of the largest collections of Civil War memorabilia in the South. Staff members have reported mysterious occurrences, such as books flying off the shelves and an orb-like object appearing before them. The Siege of Vicksburg occurred from May 18 to July 4, 1863, during the American Civil War. This significant battle involved Union troops, led by Major General Ulysses S. Grant, surrounding and attacking the Confederate city of Vicksburg, a crucial stronghold for the Confederates. During the siege, men were stationed in the building as part of the Confederate Army's Signal Corps. The Union Army had 20 artillery batteries aimed at the structure, making it a prominent target. One night, the building was struck, resulting in the deaths of four soldiers inside. Whispers swirl around town that these soldiers come back not just as heroes, but as playful pranksters ready to unleash their mischievous side.

A Mississippi Cryptid
Pascagoula River Incident

Chatawa, a small community in Mississippi, is known for its local legend of the Chatawa Monster, often described as a large, ape-like creature similar to Bigfoot. According to regional folklore, this creature is believed to have escaped from a circus train that derailed near the Tangipahoa swamps in the early 20th century or may have originated from an exotic animal farm.

The Pascagoula River incident remains a notable event in UFO tradition. On October 11, 1973, Calvin Parker and Charles Hickson were fishing along the Pascagoula River when they encountered a peculiar bluish light and an egg-shaped craft.

It hovered above the water. They reported being approached by three humanoid beings who levitated them into their spacecraft for examination. The aliens were about six feet tall, had gray, elephant-like flesh, a bullet-shaped head, and crab-like pincers with slit lips. After the experience, Parker and Hickson were returned to the riverbank, reportedly traumatized by the encounter.

Missouri
Pickled Amanda's Ghost

The Hannibal Region in Missouri is famous for its caves, attracting many visitors. However, one haunting story from the area has become part of its history. In May 1967, three boys—brothers Billy and Joey Hoag, who were 11 and 13 years old, and their friend Craig Dowell, who was 14—went missing while exploring a cave called Murphy's Cave. This happened in a place where construction work was ongoing. The last time anyone saw them was around 5 p.m. on May 10, 1967. They had shovels and flashlights with them. Sadly, no one has ever found any trace of the boys.

Close by is Mark Twain Cave, a fascinating and eerie tourist attraction in the region, named after the famous author who spent part of his childhood in the community. The cave was formed through glacial activity and erosion over millions of years, with its discovery dating back to around 1819-1820. One of its notable early owners was Doctor Joseph McDowell, who acquired the cave in 1848. Although coming from a military family, he chose to pursue a medical career.

Doctor McDowell's medical practices were often controversial, and he attracted numerous dreadful rumors throughout his life. He was ahead of his time in understanding the importance of studying human anatomy through dissection to advance medical knowledge. However, his methods were not entirely appropriate even by today's standards. He resorted to grave robbing, a common practice in the medical field during his era. Doctors or the body snatchers they paid would slink in by night, scoop the dirt out of a fresh grave, and lug out a freshly deceased corpse that had yet to molder away (or just whittle out a finger, a thumb, or a brain, depending upon what parts were preferred.) But for those related to his victims, he was considered what they called these villains in the day, a ghoul. Fortunately for him, his reputation among the townspeople was merely that of an eccentric.

Doctor McDowell's daughter, Amanda, passed away at the age of 14 from pneumonia. Like many grieving parents of that time, Doctor McDowell sought to preserve his beloved child by using a casket filled with alcohol or other preservatives, often with a glass portion to display her face. These "pickling coffins" became a trend, and advertisements appeared in newspapers nationwide. After her death, he placed Amanda and her coffin in a cave, using it as a tomb. However, rumors began to spread that children were sneaking into the cave.

They would view the corpse, tell ghost stories about it, and even handle the dead girl. Disturbed parents eventually brought this to Doctor McDowell's attention. As a result, Amanda was buried in the family's conventional tomb.

In the shadowy recesses of the cave nowadays, an otherworldly hush envelops those who dare to enter on a guided tour. They say the ghost of Amanda, Doctor McDowell's young daughter, roams these dark corridors, her presence felt long before she is seen. Wisps of ethereal light sometimes dance in the gloom, revealing fleeting glimpses of her delicate figure, dressed in garments from a bygone era. Shadows flicker and shift, and her hand reaches out to latch on to something unseen, suggesting that Amanda may not be alone; her father's spirit is believed to linger nearby, forever watching, a guardian trapped between realms.

Haunting Shorts of Missouri:

• About a mile and a half from Levasy, Missouri, there is an old summit called Bone Hill, composed of slate and limestone. Locals pass down that Native Americans once used this site to stampede buffalo and slaughter them on the hill. Settlers who passed through the area discovered bleached buffalo bones and scraping tools to skin the hides from their kills. Before the Civil War, a family settled on the land with their many slaves. When the war broke out, the family buried their valuables, including gold, along a stone wall built by the slaves and then sold their land, believing they would return within seven years. However, they never came back. Since then, a strange light has appeared over Bone Hill every seven years, and it is the ghosts of the family returning to retrieve their treasures left behind.

• The Lemp Mansion, located in St. Louis, Missouri, was the home of the Lemp family, prominent figures in the brewing industry who lived a lavish lifestyle. The family's decline began with a series of personal tragedies, including the death of William Lemp in 1904, who shot himself in the right temple in his bedroom while mourning the loss of his 28-year-old son, Frederick, who had died of heart failure. Julia Lemp also died of disease in the same room in 1906. Today, unexplained noises are reported in the mansion, cold spots are felt throughout the house, and full-body apparitions of the former residents have been witnessed.

• In the Niangua arm of the Lake of the Ozarks, there is a park called Ha Ha Tonka. Within this park stands a castle, which is rumored to be haunted. The castle is surrounded by unique features typical of the park, including sinkholes, caves, sheer bluffs, and a spring. The castle was originally the extravagant home of the Robert McClure Snyder family.

54-year-old Robert died in a car accident in 1906; his driver was speeding when a child ran into the road. The driver braked suddenly, causing Robert to be thrown into an iron trolley pole. Despite this, his sons completed the castle's construction, designed to resemble a 16th-century European castle. Later, the building was converted into a hotel, but a fire destroyed it in 1942. By 1958, tourists could pay $1.50 to visit the castle's ruins. Today, visitors to Ha Ha Tonka can still explore these ruins. However, they might encounter ghostly apparitions from the castle's past. Numerous visitors have shared intriguing accounts of unexpected encounters with a diverse array of spirits, each seemingly hailing from different periods. These ethereal apparitions often embody distinct characteristics, attire, and behaviors reflective of their historical contexts. Yet, none of the spirits have been definitively identified.

• The Ozark Spook Light is attached to Hornet and Joplin, Missouri, and Quapaw, Oklahoma, where this strange anomaly is seen. The ball of light can vary from the size of a baseball to the size of a basketball flying down the road or hovering above treetops. Many legends are associated with it, but one prevails about a miner whose cabin was attacked while away. When he returned, his family had vanished. He searched for them for years, never finding them, and continues his pursuit after death.

A Missouri Cryptid
Momo

Missouri is known for being home to various cryptids that inhabit its remote and wooded areas. One of the notable creatures is the Ozark Howler, described as a large entity resembling a black feline or bear, complete with horns. The creature is known for its eerie call, which combines elements of a wolf's howl and an elk's distinctive bugle.

In Kansas City, there have been reports of a winged creature that resembles a demonic figure, standing taller than an average person and possessing an impressive wingspan of approximately 12 feet.

However, the cryptid that has garnered the most attention is Momo. This creature rose to prominence in the early 1970s when Louisiana and Missouri residents reported seeing a large, hairy being akin to Bigfoot. Witnesses, including local boys, claimed to have seen Momo near the woods, where it was allegedly observed carrying a dead dog. Momo is estimated to stand around seven feet tall. It is noted for its strong, unpleasant odor and its distinctive large, pumpkin-shaped head.

Montana
Grizzle-Bearded Ghost

Butte was initially established as a mining camp in the northern Rocky Mountains and became one of the most significant copper boomtowns in the West. It experienced rapid growth during its peak in the late 19th century, attracting many people seeking their fortune. However, not everyone who arrived had good intentions. On October 24, 1904, miner Henry Gallahan was found dead at a brickyard near McKinley School on Park Street in Butte, Montana. His body was riddled with bullets from a .44-caliber revolver.

His throat had been slashed. Witnesses reported seeing a man fleeing the scene shortly after the shooting occurred. Their description matched that of another miner, Miles Fuller, a grizzled-bearded, shady character in ragged clothing who always wore an old, tattered hat.

There was a well-known hostility between Fuller and Gallahan, rooted in personal animosity and exacerbated by disputes over mining claims. Both men were experienced miners in their 60s who had been involved in placer mining in the Butte area of Montana. Gallahan lived in a cabin near the west end of Silver Street, while Fuller's cabin was near the Bluebird Mine. Their rivalry intensified due to allegations of ore theft from each other's claims. Before the murder, Fuller had made multiple deadly threats against Gallahan's life. Over time, their deep-seated hatred grew, fueled by the competitive nature of mining, ultimately leading to an explosive confrontation.

Fuller was arrested for murder under Sheriff Quinn. He had previously fallen under suspicion due to a series of mysterious disappearances and deaths potentially linked to him in Texas and Montana. During the trial, Fuller adamantly claimed he was not guilty of the murder. However, witness accounts described seeing him flee the scene, and evidence indicated that he had been tracked to Gallahan's cabin by a distinctive footprint made by nails on the bottom of his shoe. Additionally, a wicked-looking knife, which the recluse was known to carry and was believed to have been used to slit the dying man's throat, contributed to the case against him, leading to his conviction.

As Fuller was escorted to the scaffold, he neither stumbled nor tottered. Still, he appeared startled when he saw the huge crowd of morbidly curious onlookers watching his final steps. The masked hangman emerged to carry out the execution.

The rope used was ¾ inch thick and made of hemp, purchased explicitly for this purpose from Chicago. Miles Fuller was hanged on May 18, 1906, at approximately 5:32 a.m. in the rear of the county courthouse. His body twitched slightly, with a few convulsive movements of his fingers and a slight trembling of his limbs. In eight minutes, he was dead. His last words were, "Don't put that cap over me, oh my God."

Strange occurrences began immediately after the hanging. It had been challenging to find pallbearers due to a superstition in the community about bearing the weight of a murderer to his grave. A few ministers, reporters, and city officials stepped up and volunteered for the task. As they lifted the coffin, a massive clap of thunder suddenly erupted in the sky, startling the pallbearers so much that they nearly dropped the corpse. Shortly after, in the jail yard where Fuller was hanged, witnesses clearly reported seeing his apparition, and this would continue for many years.

On the jailhouse's ground floor, a room was reserved for Sheriff O'Rourke and his deputies to use as lodging. This room opened into the courtyard, only 30 feet from where the hanging scaffold was positioned. Inside, Deputy Mulcahy kept some gruesome relics and memorabilia from past executions. These objects were collected by a former sheriff who had an obsession with macabre and morbid trinkets, much like a serial killer might collect items from victims to reflect on their crimes. Mulcahy continued this trend by adding more death relics to his collection.

Among these objects, the dead man Fuller seemed particularly attached to those kept in a bureau drawer by Mulcahy's bed. Night after night, he returned to visit the room until the officers using it eventually refused to stay. Mulcahy's collection included a piece of rope used to hang Fuller and the black cap placed over his face just before the trap was sprung.

He also had an execution invitation that included a photograph of Fuller along with this formal invitation to attend the hanging.

Fuller began to appear as thick fog, drifting in and out through the open window while Mulcahy and the other deputies slept. Two often admitted witnessing the phantom: Mulcahy and another deputy named Mike Friel. On one occasion, the ghost of Fuller rifled through a drawer where Mulcahy kept a scrapbook containing the hanging invitation and various items from his past, including the box of relics. When Mulcahy placed the scrapbook under his pillow for safekeeping, he felt something pulling on the book beneath it and under his head as the room darkened again. In a tragic turn of events, Deputy Friel died in a freak accident while duck hunting. This incident sparked rumors about hoodoo and supernatural occurrences, suggesting that Fuller's ghost could curse specific individuals.

In 1909, Henry Woodthorpe, a janitor at the courthouse, alerted the officers to someone prowling around the jail courtyard after he had exited the boiler room. The figure was described as an old man with whiskers. Fearing that a criminal had escaped, the deputies rushed outside, only to find no one there. Witnesses claimed to have seen the old man entering a window and disappearing. People who knew Miles Fuller agreed that the janitor's description perfectly matched the hanged man.

It should never have been a surprise that the old dead miner refused to lie down. Since Fuller's execution, travelers between Butte and Rocker reported seeing Miles Fuller's ghost. Described as a shadowy, phosphorescent figure, it would appear along the path, causing panic among coach drivers, horses, and pedestrians alike.

The first documented sighting occurred on a chilly December night in 1906, when a coach driver with a full wagon encountered the ghostly figure around midnight. The apparition startled the horses, causing them to refuse to move, pawing at the ground and snorting in fear. Suddenly, spooked, the team bolted through the darkness, and the carriage overturned along the roadside. Although the frightened passengers escaped unharmed, they fled to a nearby town. One person who had peered through the window during the horses' initial pause claimed to have seen two ghosts on the roadway: a woman shrouded in white riding a pale horse, leading a black horse upon which sat a dark figure of a bound man, with a black cap over his head.

Many others reported similar sightings, and the general consensus was that one of the apparitions was Miles Fuller. However, the woman's identity with her white horse remained a mystery, mainly because Fuller was known to have adamantly disliked women. Many claim he still walks the Silver Bow County courthouse floors and along the old roads leading from Butte to Rocker.

Haunting Shorts of Montana:

• Bannack, Montana, was founded in 1862 by Colorado miners who discovered a significant gold supply in Grasshopper Creek. Over the years, Bannack continued as a mining town, but its population declined, and the last residents left in the 1970s. Today, Bannack is a ghost town preserved within Bannack State Park. During its time as a mining community, in August of 1916, 16-year-old Dorothy Dunn, her friend Ruth Wornick, and her cousin Fern Dunn went to Grasshopper Creek on the outskirts of town to wade and swim. As they played, they accidentally stepped over a steep ledge into deep water; none of the three girls could swim. A 12-year-old boy managed to rescue Ruth and Fern, but unfortunately, Dorothy drowned, and her body was found several hours later. Shortly after this tragic incident, a friend of Dorothy's named Bertie Matthews, whose parents owned the Meade Hotel, reportedly saw Dorothy's ghost appear in a blue dress. Visitors to the old building, now part of the ghost town in Bannack State Park, have claimed to see a young girl wearing a blue dress at the window before she mysteriously vanishes.

• Garnet was a gold boomtown located at the head of First Chance Creek in the 1890s, home to over 50 mines in the area. However, it was abandoned twenty years later as the gold was depleted. At its peak, Garnet had over a thousand residents making their home in the town, including miners and settlers, seeking their fortunes. Today, Garnet is managed by the Bureau of Land Management and the Garnet Preservation Association. Many old buildings still stand as a testament to those who lived and died there. Laughter and singing are heard in the old Kelly Saloon, while ghostly footsteps are heeded as they walk down the floors of the Wells Hotel.

- Virginia City, Montana, was founded in 1863 following the discovery of gold in Alder Gulch. By 1865, it had rapidly developed into a boomtown. The population peaked at around 5,000 during the gold rush; however, as gold resources were exhausted, the population began to decline in the 1880s, leading to its preservation as a historic site today. During its peak, the Bonanza Inn building served as a hospital for the Sisters of Charity, active in Virginia City in the 1870s. One of the Sisters, Sister Irene, lived a long life and passed away at 87. She still returns to walk the streets and move through the rooms of the old hospital. Some visitors have reported seeing a dark-robed figure, hearing footsteps, and witnessing doorknobs move independently within the hospital's rooms.

- There was just a short notation in The Ravalli Republican on March 24, 1897: "Missus Edith Allen, the Marysville woman who killed her 11-year-old son and wounded her husband, has been adjudged insane and sent to the Warm Springs Asylum." Indeed, she was. On October 29, 1896, Edith arose from bed to make breakfast, hearing her husband reprimanding their son Wilmot in another room. Then, he used a lash to punish him, leaving her breathless with a sudden outrage. She snatched up the .32 caliber rifle and began to shoot, somewhat haphazardly, at her husband. She missed and shot her son, Wilmot, then turned the gun on her husband, who was able to wrestle the gun away and seek help, running out the door to shout to neighbors. Wilmot died soon after; the boy's last words were, "Mama shot me. I'll never forgive her." He must still hold a grudge and wishes for Mama to hear it all the way to wherever she has crossed over. Phantom gunshots can still be heard in the semi-ghost town of Marysville, a mining boomtown between Helena and Lincoln.

- Every town seems to have its hidden, off-the-beaten-path areas—places left behind by society where the poor live in shabby houses and scrape together a meager existence. Butte's Cabbage Patch neighborhood is known for its troubled history, filled with stories of drunken miners, deadly fights, and alcohol poisonings. One of the most tragic events in this area was the murder of 9-year-old Ethal Gill in 1898. Locals say her spirit lingers in the old buildings, where she is often felt playfully tugging at the hair of mothers.

- The Dumas Hotel in historic Uptown Butte is known for its intriguing ghostly sightings. Guests and visitors have reported seeing the apparition of a woman carrying a suitcase, quietly walking past doors and descending stairways. This ghost is believed to be Elinor Knott, who served as the madam of the Dumas Hotel from 1950 to 1955.

- People say that if you listen carefully at the Little Bighorn Battlefield, you can hear phantom sounds of horses and shouts. This place is known for a significant fight on June 25-26, 1876, between the U.S. Army's 7th Cavalry, led by Lt. Col. George Armstrong Custer, and a group of Lakota Sioux and Cheyenne fighters. The battle was fierce and resulted in many casualties on both sides. Custer's men lost 268 soldiers, while estimates indicate that between 50 and 100 Native American warriors also died in the fighting.

- Between 1913 and 1915, railroad workers and hunters reported sightings of a spectral figure near Fish Creek, about 40 miles west of Missoula. The first sighting occurred in August 1913 when a railroad crew saw "a radiant maiden" wandering the foothills. In 1915, investigators Ed Rendleman, W.E. Fuge, and F.J. Alberts spent time at an abandoned cabin near Rivulet, where Rendleman saw the apparition's tearful face at the doorway, dressed in a light silk bridal gown.

A Montana Cryptid
Flathead Lake Flessie

Flathead Lake, situated in Montana, holds the distinction of being the largest natural freshwater lake west of the Mississippi River, featuring over 185 miles of shoreline and covering roughly 200 square miles. Among its vast waters, the lake is home to a legendary creature known as the Flathead Lake Monster, often referred to as "Flessie." This creature is typically described as eel-like, with the potential to grow up to 40 feet in length. Its skin displays a range of colors from brown to deep blue, accompanied by grayish-black eyes.

The first documented sighting of Flessie occurred in 1889 when Captain James Kerr, while navigating the lake aboard the U.S. Grant steamboat, reported observing a sizable creature resembling a whale. His passengers also witnessed it.

This incident sparked significant interest and intrigue regarding the possibility of Flessie's existence in Flathead Lake. Additionally, local folklore recounts a story from the 1940s involving a 3-year-old boy who nearly drowned in the lake. When questioned by his mother about his escape from the water, he attributed his survival to the assistance of the Flathead monster, claiming that it "lifted me up."

Nebraska
Seven Sisters Road True Story May Be Far Scarier Than You've Been Told

There is a tale about Seven Sisters Road (Road L), a few miles from Nebraska City. The area around the road is rural, characterized by farmland, thick woods, and a few scattered homes. It has not changed much in the last century; the streets and surroundings remain the same, with only the people living there changing as they move away or pass on. As the lore goes, a family once lived nearby in a house with a father and seven daughters. One day, the father went crazy and took each girl to a hill along the road and hanged each one by one on separate hilltops until all were dead. Many travelers on the road report their lights dimming, engines stalling, and speedometers freezing. Bells, muffled whispers, and blood-curdling screams are heard nearby while red, demon-like eyes glow in the night.

However, there is no evidence to support this story's authenticity, except that one of the early pioneers of Otoe County, John Warden, and his family settled in the area along the property in the 1850s. He had seven daughters, and the name "Seven Sisters Road" is likely derived from these girls who lived along the route, none of whom were hanged. The family cemetery is located nearby on private property.

However, something wicked did occur in the vicinity, something so sinister that it became a national sensation. And that something could explain the screams, demon eyes, and whispers. In 1886, 35-year-old Lee Shellenberger lived on a farm just two miles away, as the crow flies, with his second wife, Marinda, his ten-year-old daughter, Maggie, and his fourteen-year-old son, Joe. Lee was quite the bully, notorious for mercilessly picking on the other children, especially young Maggie. He often resorted to using his whip on her with fervor. The children had attempted to run away several times, planning to escape to their grandparents' house in Missouri.

On one occasion, when they ran to a neighbor's house, Lee marched over and dragged them back home, punishing both children so harshly that they were left with painful red welts and bruises. He was overheard telling Maggie if she ever tried to run away again, he would cut her throat from ear to ear.

He would hold true to his words. On April 30, 1886, Maggie was found in a cellar beneath her home with severe injuries; her throat had been cut from ear to ear with a wooden-handled butcher knife. The circumstances surrounding her death were alarming. She was found lying in a dry goods bin, her body partially in and out of the box. Blood had covered the child, filled the container, and splattered the walls three feet away. Initial examinations revealed that she had sustained multiple cuts to her throat—five in total—indicating a violent struggle before her death.

The murder trial of Lee Shellenberger and his wife gained significant media attention across the U.S. Lee claimed that the girl attempted to cut her own throat. The doctor who examined her had a differing opinion. He stated that such wounds could not have been inflicted by the person whose neck was being slashed. As the investigation progressed, evidence and testimonies from various witnesses emerged. Eventually, both parents were arrested on charges of willful and malicious murder. Their motive appeared to be tied to financial gain, as Maggie was an heir to valuable property that would revert to her father upon her death.

The public was outraged, leading to threats of lynching against the accused. A mob of masked local farmers from the vicinity of the Shellenberger home marched to the jail, broke into the sheriff's office located directly above the prisoner's cell, and dragged Shellenberger into the street. He was hanged by a tree in front of the courthouse, and the mob dispersed as quickly as they could. On the day Maggie was murdered, she was one day shy of her 11th birthday.

Be cautious the next time you travel to Seven Sisters Road, known as Road L on maps. You might hear screams and cries from the woods—perhaps they are Maggie's last cries or a warning to stop as she tried so desperately to run to the neighbors again. If your car lights go out and the engine stalls, she may be trying to prevent you from going any further. Those large red eyes you see could belong to Lee Shellenberger, a murderer who, along with his wife, escaped from Hell to wreak havoc on the community that hanged him. Perhaps Maggie realizes that the two escaped demons are intent on revenge, believing that you are part of the mob of neighbors who lynched her father.

Nebraska
The Child Ghost of the Niobrara Valley

The Niobrara Valley in northern Nebraska is characterized by steep hills and bluffs that rise above the riverbanks. The river's path is lined with deep forests and grassy prairies. This region has a rich history of human habitation, with Native American tribes such as the Lakota, Pawnee, and Omaha having deep ancestral ties to the land. In the mid-1800s, homesteaders and ranchers began settling in the area and establishing communities.

Oldtimers said that the old immigrant trail, which once followed the Niobrara River during its early settlement, was often avoided by locals in a particular stretch above Long Pine. It was rumored to be haunted by a ghost. In 1893, three young men, including a man named Barker and another named Guildford, were hunting along the southern edge of a stream. As they rode, they spotted what they thought was a deer ahead, and one of the men aimed his gun and fired. However, as they got closer, they were horrified to realize it was not a deer but a five or six-year-old child.

Remarkably, the child did not seem to notice the gunfire. The small boy looked peculiar, with pale skin, dressed in a loose frock, and long, fair hair falling over his shoulders. His face was frozen in an expression that suggested he was trapped in the memory of some utter horror he had witnessed last. One hunter described the scene, "The little thing came on until it was within a foot or two of Barker, who had fired upon it, and who had been so afraid that the shot had struck it that he could not do anything but look at it; then when he was about to put out his hand and touch it the child was gone like a puff of wind." The men sat in shock on their mounts, then rode around the spot searching for the child, not believing what their eyes had seen. The child had vanished and could not be found.

Barker convinced the other two to return the following day to inspect the area again. As they approached, a wailing cry echoed from the thickets, and the pale boy glided toward Barker, his eyes still wide with terror. Barker's horse snorted and reared in panic, throwing the rider violently to the ground, leaving him unmoving. The other two men dismounted quickly, running to him and finding him taking his last dying breaths, Barker's neck broken from the fall.

Once, a farmer attempted to cultivate buckwheat on his land. Still, each time his laborers began to plow, despair overwhelmed them. A foul odor of putrid flesh filled the air, accompanied by an icy wind. When the workers refused to continue, the furious farmer grabbed the plowshare and tried to force his stubborn oxen to move. Suddenly, he was struck by a jolt of electricity that coursed through his body, causing the oxen to flee and drag the plow behind them. His men stood by, knowing that the same fate had befallen each of them in the past.

Leaving the field to be reclaimed by nature, the farmer forgot about it for several years. However, one day, a cow strayed into the area, and he followed its tracks to just a few feet from the cursed spot. As he started to search the grounds, he heard a low bawling that sounded like a newborn calf. His horse began to act strangely, trying to turn and flee. Suddenly, a small figure of a child appeared, and the farmer prepared to dismount, thinking it was a lost child who had wandered away from a nearby ranch. But something in the child's pained expression made him stop short. "Oh, I want my mama! Where has my mama gone?" the child cried out, and a wave of horror washed over the farmer as he realized he could see right through it. The ethereal figure darted toward the river and tumbled into its depths before the farmer could dismount. Strangely, the water remained perfectly still on the surface. That night, when the farmer returned home, he learned that his son had been kicked to death by a horse.

The old settlers traced the first sightings of the little phantom back to the 1840s, believing it brought misfortune to those who encountered it—a sign of impending death. Most thought the child was part of a family of immigrants passing through the area who were killed by Native Americans, except for the little boy who must have hidden in the grasses, watching in horror as they were murdered one by one. Although he survived that day, he likely succumbed to cold and hunger along the banks of the river. Despite the abundant game nearby, hunters returned empty-handed when camped by those sluggish, dark waters. Even the Native Americans avoided the spot, considering it taboo—a forbidden place.

Nebraska
Woman in White of
Prospect Hill Cemetery

On July 18, 1874, the Omaha Daily Bee reported on a ghostly figure, the Woman in White, terrified two brothers working at Stanwood's shop near Prospect Hill Cemetery in Omaha. The shop, owned by sculptor H. P. Stanwood, had a small house and a marble-cutting shop adjacent to the cemetery, where he employed several workers.

One evening, as a worker prepared for bed, he stepped outside briefly and glanced toward the cemetery. He saw a strange figure dressed in white: a woman who startled him intensely as she drifted toward him. Alarmed, he rushed back inside and found his brother, noting that the woman followed.

She entered through the front door and extinguished a lamp.

The brothers ran out the backdoor and reported the encounter to Stanwood, who dismissed their claims. However, Stanwood, feeling self-possessed, went outside to investigate. To his astonishment, the ghostly woman struck him on the back and asked where her children were buried before vanishing.

The following day, when the ghost reappeared, the two brothers fired shots at her, believing it was customary to defend themselves in such situations this way. They chased her into the cemetery, but she eventually disappeared once again.

Haunting Shorts of Nebraska:

- The Captain Bailey House is notable for its red-brick walls and seven pointed roofs. It was built by Captain Benson M. Bailey, who served in the Civil War after the tragic loss of his first wife during childbirth, along with their newborn. His life ended under mysterious circumstances; he and his second wife were both believed to have been poisoned, leading to speculation about their deaths. On December 27, 1880, Benson and his son returned home late at night after a lodge meeting. Upon entering, they discovered his 38-year-old wife cold and lifeless on the floor near the entrance. She had evidently gone to fetch her lamp to take upstairs, as one lamp was found standing upright on the third step, suggesting she had started to ascend the stairs before turning back. It was believed that she had been poisoned by ice cream, orchestrated by a widow who sought Benson's affection despite his lack of interest in her. Many believe that this same scorned widow was also responsible for Benson's sudden death on May 15, 1883. He was thought to have been poisoned by oyster soup that she had prepared for him. There is a haunting at the Captain Bailey House Museum. Some have heard a piano playing, while others say the ghosts will not allow the doors to be closed!

- The old Ball Cemetery near Springfield is often described as haunted. Visitors report hearing unexplained voices and laughter as they walk through the grounds. Additionally, there have been accounts of a tall ghostly figure seen by those who enter the cemetery. The identity of the specter is unknown.

- There is a one-lane bridge across the Platte River, just south of Grand Island, Nebraska. Local folklore advises that the bridge is haunted by a woman who practiced witchcraft.

She lived at one end of the bridge and cast curses on those who crossed it, leaving a lasting imprint. It is said that when a group of people, consisting of an odd number of individuals, stands on the bridge on an odd-numbered night and looks into the water below, they may see a reflection of themselves hanging. However, if they stare too long, the witch may appear in the water and drag them down.

• The Mormon Trail was a wagon route that connected Illinois to Salt Lake City, Utah. It ran along the north bank of the Platte River near Fremont, Nebraska. The original burial ground in Fremont, where Barnard Park is today, was Green Grove Cemetery. As the town expanded, a new cemetery was established, and many of the bodies from the old cemetery were relocated. However, not all of the remains seem to have been moved. At night, shadowy figures have been reported in the area. One story tells of a woman dressed in early 1830s clothing who is often seen weeping over a grave that no longer exists—a grave belonging to her daughter, who died along the Mormon Trail and was once buried there.

• The legend of the Salt Witch centers around a respected Native American chief whose violent temper could only be calmed by his wife. After her sudden death, he was no longer the man he once was, and many believed he should no longer be chief. One day, he left his lodge dressed for war and wandered alone. When he returned, he carried fresh scalps and prized lumps of salt. Everyone knew that the brave chief they remembered had come back. That night, while he slept, he was awakened by screaming. He saw an old woman with an axe struggling with a younger woman as if she were trying to kill her. As he rushed in to save the younger woman, he saw his wife's face in hers. Enraged, he killed the old woman. As he reached out to grab his wife, both women vanished into the earth, leaving only a pillar of salt.

The chief told his people about his dream, warning them to beat the ground with clubs while gathering salt to ward off the Salt Witch's evil. And so, they did.

• In the mid-19th century, Spring Ranch was a small community that thrived due to its proximity to the Oregon-California Trail. This location provided a lucrative business opportunity for its founder, who owned a store and inn, attracting many travelers. However, the town later declined due to floods and the loss of the railroad. Among its residents were 33-year-old Tom Jones and his widowed sister, 36-year-old Elizabeth Taylor. Their story begins with a conflict over cattle trespassing into neighboring crops, which prompted a local to threaten them, even going so far as to acquire a shotgun for protection. On March 15, 1885, tensions escalated when Elizabeth was involved in a violent confrontation over land disputes, resulting in the death of a man by gunshot. Many believed Elizabeth was responsible for the fatality. In response, a mob of 15 to 50 vigilantes formed and stormed the siblings' home in the early hours of the morning. They accused Tom and Elizabeth of cattle rustling and land grabbing, dragging them to a bridge over the Blue River, where they were lynched. Both were buried in Spring Ranch Cemetery, alongside their parents and Elizabeth's husband. Local lore suggests that if you visit the cemetery and the bridge at night, you can still hear their tortured screams. Tom and Elizabeth's spirits linger near the bridge over the Blue River, where they were executed, creating an unsettling presence and whispers that can be felt at those crossings.

A Nebraska Cryptid
Alkali Lake Monster

In 1921, J.A. Johnson reported a remarkable creature near Hay Springs, Nebraska. He identified it as an alligator-like entity measuring approximately 40 feet long, with dull gray and brown hues. This creature became known as the Alkali Lake Monster or the Walgren Lake Monster.

Various witnesses associated with this phenomenon described a large, horned beast that bore similarities to either an alligator or an enormous mudpuppy. They claimed that it preyed on local livestock and ducks. Observers further noted that the creature's size was so vast that the ground trembled as it moved and that it had the ability to create a dense fog that could disorient travelers in the vicinity.

Nevada
Haunting Howls at Gold Hill

Gold Hill and Virginia City were closely linked both geographically and economically, as they were part of the Comstock Lode mining district in Nevada. Founded during the silver and gold rush in the late 1850s, both towns experienced a rapid influx of miners and settlers that fueled their growth.

During its heyday, Gold Hill gained a reputation for being haunted. It started with thirty-four-year-old Alexander White, known as "Sandy" Baldwin. He was a partner in a law office in Virginia City and was appointed as a United States District Judge shortly thereafter. Baldwin owned a yellow and white mutt named Jack. The dog followed Baldwin everywhere, and when he was not with him, Jack would lazily wander between Virginia City and nearby Gold Hill.

Jack was a nervous dog prone to anxiety; he would react with great fear, howling and bolting at loud noises like gunfire or thunder. Tragically, Baldwin was among 17 people who were killed in a deadly collision of two passenger trains belonging to the Western Pacific Railroad out of San Francisco in November of 1869. This left Jack to fend for himself after wandering too far one day. The dog warden in Gold Hill found him and placed him in the pound, where he was condemned to die on his third day there.

Fortunately, a man named Jack Sheppard, who worked at the Crown Point Hoisting Works in Gold Hill, came to the pound on that final day. He paid the fine and took the dog home with him. Jack became Sheppard's loyal companion for years. Although the dog remained anxious, he stayed by Sheppard's side wherever he went.

One evening, the two entered a clothing store in town, and an engineer from the Yellow Jacket Mine thought it would be funny to blow up a brown paper bag and pop it over Jack's head. Jack let out a dreadful howl and collapsed onto the floor in a spasmodic fit. After some time, he managed to revive and stagger toward home with Sheppard until they reached Crown Point Ravine, near the old Kentuck Mine, where the dog collapsed and died.

Jack was an old dog who had lived a good life, so there's no need to feel sad for him. Besides, he isn't alone. At least 35 men lost their lives in the 1869 Yellow Jacket Mine fire, which spread to the Kentuck Mine in the same area the hound died. This area is haunted by the lost souls of the miners who perished there, as well as by Jack. If you find yourself in Gold Hill at midnight, you might hear the moans or groans of the dead miners. And if you hear a gunshot or the sound of a car backfiring, listen closely; you might just catch the haunting howl of the long-dead hound. In the old days, they did!

Nevada
Haunting of the Whole Dang Town

Bina Verrault was a notorious figure in the early 20th century. She was known for being involved in a swindling scheme targeting wealthy men across New York, Boston, and Philadelphia. Posing as a wealthy widow seeking love, she successfully charmed her victims and conned them out of nearly $3.4 million. Once her fraudulent activities were uncovered, she fled to the rugged mining town of Tonopah, Nevada, where she ultimately succumbed to alcoholism.

The whole dang town is haunted, and it appears they are more than happy to share that bit of information. They have it all mapped out in a guide at the visitor center, where you can see Bina. She has been spotted peering out the window. Several buildings appear to be home to spirits, including the cemetery established in the early 1900s. This cemetery is the final resting place for many miners who died in accidents, and it is known for frequent reports of full-body apparitions and whispers being heard within its grounds.

Haunting Shorts of Nevada:

• Julie Bulette arrived in Virginia City in 1859 when the town was booming due to the discovery of the Comstock Lode, which contained rich deposits of silver ore. In her late twenties and one of the few women in this male-dominated mining town, her beauty and charm quickly drew the attention of the miners, leading her to work as a prostitute. On January 20, 1867, Julie was discovered murdered in the bedroom of her small cottage. She had been strangled and bludgeoned. Within a year, John Millain, a French drifter, was arrested and charged with the crime. He was hanged despite maintaining his innocence, claiming he was only an accomplice in the theft of her home. Some residents have reported seeing a ghostly woman resembling Julie, dressed in period clothing, who appears and then vanishes around the town.

• Goldfield was a gold boomtown that emerged around 1902. The town flourished as thousands flocked there in search of wealth. The Goldfield Hotel, a plush establishment, was built in 1908 to accommodate guests. Today, visitors to the hotel report apparitions, strange noises, and unexplained cold spots. It is rumored that George Wingfield, a prominent figure in the town's history known for his success as a cattleman and financier, is responsible for these mysterious occurrences. Legends tell Wingfield's mistress, Elizabeth, became pregnant and was held captive in a room at the Goldfield Hotel until the child was born. After, she disappeared. Some say Elizabeth died during childbirth, while many suspect that Wingfield murdered her. Whispers circulated that someone had tossed the baby into a mine shaft. Visitors touring the Goldfield Hotel have witnessed Elizabeth's apparition; some even report hearing cries, presumably from Elizabeth, calling out for her child.

A Nevada Cryptid
Area 51 Aliens

Area 51 is a highly classified U.S. Air Force facility located in Nevada. It has been the focus of numerous stories and conspiracy theories about extraterrestrial life. The site became well-known after a former employee, Robert Lazar, claimed that the government was reverse-engineering alien spacecraft recovered from crashes. Since the late 1950s, there have been reports of Unidentified Flying Objects (UFOs) in the surrounding area, which coincided with secret military tests of high-altitude reconnaissance planes, such as the U-2.

The infamous Roswell incident in 1947 further fueled these theories; it is alleged that debris from a United States Army Air Forces balloon recovered near Roswell, New Mexico, was actually from a crashed extraterrestrial spacecraft. For years, Area 51 has been portrayed as a secretive hub for government experiments involving aliens and their technology, despite official denials that focus on military operations.

Over the years, many books, documentaries, and movies have shaped the idea that Area 51 is a place connected to aliens and advanced technology. This has created a strong belief that the base is not just a military site but also a hub for studying extraterrestrial life. This combination of accounts and popular culture has inspired intriguing ideas about what occurs at Area 51.

New Hampshire
Goody Cole, The Redeemed Witch of Hampton

Goodwife Eunice Cole, known as Goody Cole, was born around 1590 and died in 1680. She lived in Hampton, New Hampshire, in a small cabin at the end of Island Path. Goody and her husband William arrived from London after completing their service as indentured servants for a wealthy merchant. Eventually, they settled in Hampton, where they acquired a 40-acre parcel of land. William worked as a carpenter until his death on May 26, 1662.

Life in Hampton must have been very dreadful for Goody.

Like many close-knit towns of the time, it was a highly pious community, predisposed to fear and distrust anything that deviated from social norms. And Goody would have been far from the model, young Hampton good citizen born and bred in the vicinity. Goody was not a local; she was an outsider who moved there late in life. She was not only known for her mumbling habit and somewhat wild appearance—both considered sinister traits—but also conformed to the stereotypes of witches prevalent in the 17th century. She was elderly, with a wrinkled face, a crooked nose, and wild gray hair. The townspeople often treated her poorly, and she preferred to live in seclusion in her little cabin. Naughty little children would sometimes sneak to her cabin, peering into her windows and spreading wicked lies about seeing the devil at her kitchen table.

For lack of reason other than poor farming skills by a man who owned some cattle, she was accused of causing the deaths of two calves, which were attributed to alleged sorcery. It was believed that she summoned a cyclone that sent a group of four men, two women, and a couple of children to their watery graves off the Isles of Shoals. This tragedy occurred after the children in the boat made fun of her as they passed by. "You are brave today," Goody called out to them, "but I hear the little waves laughing and telling me that the broth waiting for you at home will be very, very cold." Soon after, the family ran into high winds and were never seen again.

Some also accused her of transforming into dogs, cats, and eagles. In one remarkable case, Anna Dalton claimed that her child had been swapped with an old and wrinkled "imp" by Goody Cole. "Tis no child of mine," she cried. "Tis an imp. Don't you see how old and shrewd it is? How wrinkled and ugly? It does not take my milk: it is sucking my blood and wearing me to skin and bone."

Shortly before her death, Goody was once again accused of witchcraft and confined to Ipswich jail. When she was released long after and died alone in her cabin, her body was buried in an unmarked grave, and twelve men drove a stake through her corpse to prevent her evil spirit from returning. This was done near the site of the first meeting house, where she had been convicted of having 'familiarity with the devil.'

In 1938, the residents of Hampton cleared Goody Cole's name. They turned all the manuscripts that had convicted her of witchcraft into ashes, which were then placed in an urn. Since then, a mysterious woman resembling Goody Cole has been seen occasionally in the fog around town. One night, a police officer encountered her while she was wandering in the cemetery. When he shined his flashlight on her, she disappeared. Occasionally, she is spotted along Island Path, making her way to and from home, perhaps now enjoying the company of those who accept her as one of their own.

New Hampshire
Getting the Willies at the Willeys

In the early years of 1825, Samuel Willey Junior, his wife Polly Lovejoy, and their five children—Eliza (12), Jeremiah (11), Martha (9), Elbridge (6), and Sally (4)—moved into the Old Notch House in Crawford Notch, New Hampshire. Although the area was desolate, they envisioned transforming it into a welcoming inn. Samuel went to work, ambitiously renovating the home into a two-story building and renamed it Willey House Inn and Tavern.

In June 1826, a horrible rainstorm caused a landslide near the Willey House Inn. To avert any danger, Samuel made a stone shelter above the home to protect it. Two months later, on August 28, 1826, another violent storm hit the area, followed by a prolonged drought, leaving soil loose and unstable. It was the perfect storm for catastrophic landslides on Crawford Notch, and debris cascaded down the mountain. The roar of the avalanche was heard twenty miles away.

Someone went up the hill to check on the family, but none of them could be found.

A search party was assembled and rushed to the Willey House Inn and Tavern. Still, no souls were inside, only what appeared to be a desperate departure of unmade beds, scattered clothing, ashes in the fire, and an open Bible on a table. The bodies of Samuel Willey Jr., Polly Willey, their two children, and two hired men were finally discovered dead nearby. Still, three of their children were never found. It was the belief that, most likely, the home's occupants abandoned the property as the avalanche approached and, unsure in the dark, placed themselves in the flow path.

The site of the house and the landslide is now an interpretive center within Crawford Notch State Park. Visitors often speak in hushed tones about the eerie presence that lingers where the old inn once stood. There is also a rugged and strenuous out-and-back hike to the summit of Mount Willie, which includes steep ladder climbs at certain points.

A child no older than seven wanders along the overgrown path. His pale skin glows faintly in the fading light, and he has a vacant expression. However, as quickly as he appears, he vanishes into thin air, leaving those who saw him with a sense of unease, that strange feeling gripping the soul right after sensing something horrifying. You know, it's that sensation people call "the willies," the feeling one gets when seeing a ghost. And that is what he is.

New Hampshire
Frozen Nancy

During the late 1770s, sixteen-year-old Nancy Barton was a servant for Colonel Joseph Whipple, who lived on a Jefferson, New Hampshire farm. She became infatuated with a farmhand named Jim Swindell and planned to marry him. The two made plans to settle in Portsmouth and start their life together, so Nancy entrusted Jim with her life savings.

However, Colonel Whipple supported the American Revolutionary War effort and persuaded Jim to join the army. With little money to his name, Jim used Nancy's funds to buy a uniform. Soon, Nancy heard whispers of Jim's betrayal and discovered he had abandoned her for the war. In her anger and determination to confront him, she recklessly set off on foot with only a meager bundle of clothing and no food. Ignoring the warnings of her neighbors, she headed through Crawford Notch in treacherous winter conditions.

Nancy hiked nearly twenty miles through the rugged terrain. Eventually, she stumbled upon the remnants of a fire that might have belonged to Jim. Exhausted and almost frozen, the young woman stopped to rest but ultimately succumbed to frostbite and hypothermia near a creek. When she failed to return, a search party was dispatched, and they found her frozen body sitting on a rock by the water. Nancy was buried at the site of her death, which can still be seen today, with her grave marked to commemorate her tragic fate.

Word of Nancy's death reached Jim Swindell, and he was so consumed by guilt that he descended into madness, dying in an asylum shortly thereafter. There are no memorials for Jim, but several locations are named after Nancy: the Nancy Brook Scenic Area, Nancy Cascades, Mount Nancy, and Nancy Pond. Legend says her ghost haunts those mountains as she searches for Jim Swindell. Hikers in the Nancy Brook Scenic Area of the White Mountain National Forest have reported hearing screams, cries, and eerie laughter echoing through the old mountains.

Haunting Shorts of New Hampshire:

• Edward Teach, known as Blackbeard, was an infamous English pirate who sailed the seas of the West Indies and the eastern coast of North America during the early 18th century. He was notorious for his fearsome appearance and brazen acts of piracy. Blackbeard often used the Isles of Shoals between Maine and New Hampshire to hide his treasure on the desolate and rocky uninhabited islands. Among these islands was White Island, where he spent time with a beautiful girl he had abducted from her home in Scotland. Despite his brutish behavior, she grew to love him. One day, while they were on White Island, one of Blackbeard's sailors rushed to warn him that a ship was approaching. The pirate quickly left, but before he did, he gave his mistress his white cloak and made her promise to guard the treasure with her life. A fierce battle erupted between the two ships, culminating in an explosion that shattered both vessels. Although some crew members from both ships managed to swim to shore, none survived the harsh winter. Tragically, Blackbeard's mistress also died of starvation. She continues to keep her watch. Her ghostly form, clad in the white cloak, with her golden hair blowing in the wind and her pale face turned toward the waters, waits for her pirate to return.

• Mount Chocorua is a bare, rocky summit in Albany, within the White Mountains of New Hampshire. It features rugged terrain and offers stunning views of the surrounding lakes and forests. The name "Chocorua" may have originated from the Algonquin language, meaning "Rocky Home of the Water Serpent," referencing the eroded rocks and the legend of a serpent guarding the area. Historians believe the peak became barren due to fires from the 19th to the early 20th centuries, destroying trees and brush on its summit.

According to local legends, a Native American named Chocorua was chased to the peak by settlers and ultimately murdered there. He cursed the land, resulting in its lifelessness and giving the peak his name.

• The Tilton Inn in Tilton is haunted. Some believe that the building is home to the spirit of a child who died when a rooming house was destroyed by fire at the exact location. The ghost has been spotted in various rooms and hallways throughout the inn.

• The Blair Covered Bridge over the Pemigewasset River in Campton was a critical connecting route for New Hampshire Route 175, U.S. Route 3, and Interstate 93. An arsonist, Lem Parker, burnt the first bridge down, claiming mysterious voices begged him to catch it afire and burn it to the ground. It took a bit to rebuild, and during that time, a doctor's horse oddly drowned where the bridge had been. When it was rebuilt, folks felt a peculiar and ominous presence when they crossed it. In 2011, the bridge was gored by a tree and rebuilt. Still, those weird feelings linger.

• Stark Road Graveyard, located just outside Conway, sits quietly among scrubby grass and trees, enclosed by a stone fence. Those who pass by at night often report seeing two large glowing eyes. The identity of the haunting spirit remains a mystery, but a video titled "Haunted New Hampshire: Stark Road Cemetery" by Ghosts of the White Mountains presents several theories. Some believe it could be the ghost of an angry Revolutionary War soldier named Stark. In contrast, others think spirits may be lingering from a smallpox epidemic in the 1790s. It could also be the ghost of a heartbroken woman who cursed the land after her lover was unfaithful.

A New Hampshire Cryptid
Woods Devil

New Hampshire is renowned for its legendary lake monsters, particularly in large bodies of water like Lake Winnipesaukee. These creatures are often described as huge, snake-like beings that appear to inhabit the depths of these waters. Characteristic features include elongated, sinuous bodies, dark skin, and large heads, with many reports mentioning humps or ridges along their backs. Sightings typically occur in the deeper regions of the lake, sparking intrigue and curiosity among locals and visitors alike.

In addition to lake monsters, New Hampshire is also home to the Woods Devil, often likened to Bigfoot. This creature is described as standing between 7 to 9 feet tall, with a slender physique and an approximate weight of 400 pounds. It is covered in shaggy gray or tan hair, with a distinctive horse-like face and large, expressive eyes.

Reports of the Woods Devil date back to early lumberjacks, with additional sightings surfacing during the 1940s and 1950s, particularly among hunters exploring the woods. One notable account comes from George Lavoie, who reported encountering a tall, hairy creature standing behind a tree near his hunting camp in 1948. These accounts contribute to the rich tapestry of New Hampshire's folklore and its mysterious wildlife.

New Jersey
Gully Road Creepers

Woodside was a township in Essex County, New Jersey, from 1869 to 1871. Within Woodside was Gully Road, a well-used path leading to the Passaic River, which had been traveled for many years by settlers, and the Lenni-Lenape, formed by an old gully created by rushing water.

In the township's early years, an elderly couple lived at the junction of Gully Road and Washington Avenue, where the town planned to build a road for wagons to access the river. They were told they must abandon their home, but the couple refused to leave. Their situation became increasingly difficult, and the stress took a considerable toll, ultimately leading to the wife's death. The old man was eventually forcefully removed from the property and disappeared. Following these events, the throughfare became known to be haunted. The spirits of the dead couple wander along the old road, creeping out to occasionally frighten passersby.

New Jersey
The Dead Man and the Golf Club

The borough of Mountainside in New Jersey is now characterized by suburbs and recreational areas. However, it was not always this way; its history dates back to the 18th century when it was primarily agricultural—

62-year-old Baltus Roll was a Dutch farmer who grew apples and raised livestock there. He lived with his wife, Susannah, and their son on the top of a ridge known as Baltusrol Mountain. On the night of February 22, 1831, their peaceful life was shattered when two men—one quite large and the other relatively small—came to their door and began pounding on it incessantly. When the family did not answer, the men forced their way into the home, dragged Baltus from the bedroom, and threw him from the bed before mercilessly beating him.

They pulled him to the front door, where the larger man warned Susannah not to follow. Ignoring him, she broke from the home and bolted into the wintry night, hiding nearby and watching as the men tied up her husband with a thick white rope. The larger man then jumped on Baltus and wrapped his hands around his neck, beginning to choke him.

Baltus called out to Susannah, but then she heard no more. In shock and fearing for her own life, she wandered into the woods, hiding for a while. From her vantage point, Susannah could see her husband lying in the snow, unmoving and stripped of his clothing. Believing he was dead, she made her way to a neighbor's house, where the neighbor thought she had gone insane. Nevertheless, she eventually returned to find Baltus dead in the snow.

Word of the murder spread quickly, and suspicion fell on Peter B. Davis, an opium addict, and Lycidas Baldwin, who had been desperately searching for a quick way to make money. It was rumored that Baltus kept a large sum of money in his home. Both men were eventually apprehended, but Baldwin committed suicide in a local tavern, overdosing on laudanum, a mixture of morphine and alcohol, before being caught. Davis confessed to the crime and died in prison.

The spirit of Baltus Roll haunts the area now known as Baltusrol Mountain, where the Baltusrol Golf Club was established in 1896 by Louis Keller on Roll's former farmland. According to those who golf there, Baltus Roll's spirit still wanders the grounds and fairways of his old farm.

New Jersey
Dead Shores at Absecon Light

The Absecon Lighthouse is located along the New Jersey coastline at the northern end of Atlantic City. It was built in 1854 in response to the high number of shipwrecks along the shores during the 19th century. A particularly notable tragedy that underscored the need for a lighthouse was the sinking of the wooden packet ship Powhatan in 1854. This disaster resulted in the deaths of over 200 passengers and crew members after the vessel encountered a snowstorm while en route to New York. The Powhatan ran aground on the shoals and broke apart, with bodies from the wreck washing ashore near Absecon. This led to speculation that spirits may linger around the lighthouse. Reports from visitors include hearing voices, phantom footsteps, and sightings of shadowy figures.

Haunting Shorts of New Jersey:

- There is reportedly a Devil Tree in a field on Mountain Road, believed to be cursed. Those who show disrespect or make negative remarks while standing before it will soon face harm.

- Shades of Death Road is a 7-mile-long, two-lane road in Warren County. This street was once home to a group of unruly squatters known for their frequent fights, which sometimes ended in fatalities. It also attracted highway robbers who would rather murder their victims than let them go empty-handed. A sudden fog, often called "The Great Meadows Fog," frequently appears in this area, rising from the old lake bed nearby. Some witnesses claim to see figures or shadows moving within the fog and hear strange noises that resemble feet trudging through rustling leaves.

- There is a bridge over Mossman Brook near Dead Man's Curve on Clinton Road in West Milford that is haunted by the ghost of a little boy who drowned there. His spirit lingers beneath the bridge, and people who toss a coin over it report that the coin is thrown back to them.

- In 1921, a mysterious light appeared in the belfry of St. Joseph's Catholic Church on Pavonia Avenue in Jersey City, prompting church sexton Matthew Guarino to investigate reports of unusual yellowish eyes in the steeple. When he didn't return home that night, his family searched for him and found his lifeless body in the choir loft. The strange light attracted thousands of visitors, and sightings of the yellowish eyes continued over the years, including a notable appearance on Good Friday in 1954. Local historian Bob Leach noted that many in the Cold War era saw the lights as a hopeful sign, adding to the tale's local significance.

A New Jersey Cryptid
Jersey Devil

The Pine Barrens is a vast expanse of dark landscape in southern New Jersey, shrouded in an unsettling stillness that echoes with whispers of its troubled past. The air is thick with an otherworldly silence, broken only by the occasional rustle of leaves or the distant call of a creature hidden among the shadows. The sandy, acidic soil is home to twisted trees and gnarled roots that seem to reach out like skeletal fingers grasping at ankles and feet. Scattered throughout the area are abandoned villages, with crumbling bricks and overgrown paths that seem better suited for ghosts and creatures best left undisturbed.

There is one particular creature that people should avoid—a being resembling a kangaroo or wyvern with hooves, bat-like wings, a goat-like head, and a forked tail. This creature is linked to Deborah Leeds, known as "Mother Leeds." She had twelve children, and upon discovering she was pregnant with a thirteenth, she cursed the child in anger, declaring it would be evil.

One stormy night in 1735, surrounded by friends, Mother Leeds gave birth to her thirteenth child. Initially, it looked like any other baby, but then it abruptly transformed into a gruesome, monstrous creature. Thus, the Jersey Devil was born. It growled and screeched before flying up the chimney, escaping into the dark forest of the Pine Barrens to feast upon the fears of those who travel there.

New Mexico
Billy the Kid Rides On

His name was Henry McCarty, but he is widely recognized as Billy the Kid, the legendary outlaw of the Old West. Many may be unaware that he haunts specific backroads in New Mexico. Still, it should not be surprising that he occasionally appears at the very site of his death. He was young when he died but had a lot of bad beneath his belt by the time he was killed. It was only a matter of time before his demons caught up with him. And they did. Or are they still chasing him?

At just 14 years old, he was a petty thief and an orphan after his mother died of tuberculosis in 1874. Billy was known to be slim and muscular, standing around 5 feet 9 inches tall and weighing about 140 pounds. His notoriety grew alongside the alias he adopted, William H. Bonney. In August 1877, he killed a blacksmith named Francis P. "Windy" Cahill during an argument, which made him a wanted man in Arizona, forcing him to flee to New Mexico.

In 1878, during the Lincoln County War in New Mexico, Billy joined a vigilante group called the Regulators, which was formed by cowboys and ranch owners to protect the interests of John Tunstall, a wealthy English landowner. Initially, the group was established to avenge Tunstall's death. However, the Regulators engaged in violent confrontations and ambushes against rival factions, leading to widespread bloodshed, numerous deaths, and escalating lawlessness in the region.

Billy's exploits were widely reported in newspapers, and he was often followed by bad luck. By December 1880, Sheriff Pat Garrett finally caught up with him after extensive manhunts due to his growing infamy. It seemed that Billy the Kid's fate was sealed in April 1881 when he was tried for murder and sentenced to hang. However, on April 28, 1881, he managed to escape from jail after killing two deputies.

Billy was attracted to Paulita, the sister of Pete Maxwell, who owned a ranch in Fort Sumner. He often visited her home, known for its hospitality and as a safe haven for outlaws. On the night of July 14, 1881, Billy was at the Maxwell home when Sheriff Pat Garrett came looking for him. Before reaching the house, one of Garrett's men recognized an old acquaintance at a camp and stopped to chat. As they spoke, they heard a voice that sounded like the outlaw's and spotted a man in a broad-brimmed hat passing nearby. Unbeknownst to them, Billy the Kid was sneaking through the darkness to grab a piece of beef for a midnight snack.

Garrett followed the direction of the voice and entered the Maxwell home. He found Maxwell in bed and quickly learned that Billy was nearby. Just then, Billy entered the room with a gun in one hand and a knife in the other, asking in Spanish who was inside. In moments, Garrett shot Billy, killing him. Billy the Kid was only 21 years old.

Billy The Kid's death site is behind the Bosque Redondo Memorial in Fort Sumner, where the Maxwell home once stood. Not long after the outlaw was killed, it fell into ruin, but a stone marks its place. The ghost of Billy the Kid still haunts this territory, a restless spirit bound by his faults or a desperate yearning to remain among the living—no one can say for sure. At twilight, his spectral figure rides the desolate plains, a chilling echo of gunfire lingering in the air, leaving an unsettling reminder of the violent past that refuses to fade. Those who wander too close can hear the thundering hooves and feel the icy breath of his presence, a haunting reminder that some souls are never truly at rest. His demons follow closely behind.

New Mexico
Death Waltz

Fort Union was established in 1851 as a military outpost to protect travelers on the Santa Fe Trail, which connected Missouri to Santa Fe, from potential attacks by Native American tribes. Additionally, the fort served as a central hub for supply distribution and coordinating of military operations. It also became the only place where soldiers could socialize with the few women who lived at the post or nearby.

One officer at the fort had a sister-in-law who was pretty and enjoyed the attention of the officers. She took advantage of the scarcity of women and often flirted with various men. Among them was a young lieutenant who was captivated by her charm. Naive in his feelings, he believed that her flirting was meant for him alone. He devoted much time to proving his worth to her, hoping to win her hand in marriage.

One day, a messenger rushed into the fort, breathless.

He brought news that Apache had attacked. The young lieutenant was put in charge of a detachment tasked with hunting the warring party down. Before he left, he took the woman aside and confessed his love for her. To his delight, she reciprocated his feelings, declaring that if he were to die on this mission, she would never marry anyone else. As he said farewell, he assured her, "That is well. Nobody else shall have you. I will return and make my claim."

The detachment returned a few days later, but the lieutenant was not with them. Many people noticed that the woman who had declared her love for him seemed utterly unfazed by his absence. It was no surprise when she announced that she would marry another man.

The wedding took place at the post, and the dining room was beautifully decorated for the dance. As the celebration began, the flickering candlelight started to dim. Suddenly, an eerie shriek pierced the air—a wraithlike cry that drew all eyes to the door from which it originated. The doors had burst open with a crash, and standing in the dimness was the dead man, his eyes protruding, his body bloated, and his uniform stained with blood. Upon his forehead was a gash from a hatchet, and the flesh of his scalp had been torn from the skull. His eyes burned with a glowing, eerie light.

He stumbled over to the bride, pulled her from her husband's arms, and began to dance the waltz. The musicians struck up a demonic melody, later confessing that they felt compelled to continue playing the macabre music against their will. The couple whirled and twirled around and around, the bride growing paler and paler until life slipped from her. Then, the dead lieutenant let her fall to the floor. He let out a scream and vanished through the doors. Only a few days later, troops who had been at the battle with the Apache returned with the body of the dead man.

Haunting Shorts of New Mexico:

• Thomas Edward Ketchum, known as Black Jack, was a notorious outlaw in the American West during the late 19th century, famous for his train robberies and other criminal activities. A canyon named Black Jack Canyon is associated with him, where he would often hide out with other outlaws. Although he was executed by hanging (the rope was too long, and he was decapitated instead of dying by a broken neck or strangulation) for train robbery in 1901, his legend continues to endure. His ghost still appears here once in a while at his old haunt.

• Giovanni Maria de Agostini was an Italian recluse who settled in the Organ Mountains of New Mexico in the mid-1800s. He built a nightly fire by his cave to signal safety, but in April 1869, the cave remained dark. A search party found it empty, and the next day, a sheep herder discovered Giovanni's bludgeoned body nearby. He was clutching a crucifix and wearing a cilice that had become embedded in his skin. Today, some hikers visit La Cueva to connect with his spirit, claiming to see his fire burning even when no one is around.

• La Llorona, known as "the Weeping Woman," was a woman who married a wealthy man and had two children with him. However, he grew distant after some time and left her for another woman. Upon discovering her husband's unfaithfulness, she was heartbroken and filled with rage. She drowned her little children in the river. Realizing the gravity of her actions and overwhelmed by guilt and sorrow, she chose to drown herself in the same river. As a result, she was denied entry into heaven and condemned to wander the earth for eternity. Now, she roams rivers and lakes at night, mourning for her lost children and searching for them.

A New Mexico Cryptid
Coco

The Coco is a well-known figure in folklore, often depicted in various unsettling ways that intrigue and frighten people. This creature embodies numerous forms, ranging from shadowy figures to frightening hairy monsters or even a sinister cloaked man. A notable characteristic of the Coco is its enormous ear, which is believed to be particularly adept at detecting the sounds of mischief made by children. The Coco is commonly thought to conceal itself in dark locations, such as under beds, in closets, or within the corners of rooms. It is often described as having bright, glowing red eyes that can pierce through darkness and sharp, jagged teeth that enhance its fearsome appearance. One of the more alarming attributes of the Coco is its shape-shifting ability, which allows it to manifest in different forms, contributing to the anxiety associated with potential encounters. Traditionally, the Coco is regarded as a creature that "snatches" children who misbehave or defy their parents' instructions, serving as a cautionary figure in various cultures.

New York
Old Fort Niagara Headless Man in the Well

Old Fort Niagara, located at the mouth of the Niagara River in New York, is a historic fortification initially constructed by the French in 1726 to protect their interests in North America. Over the years, the fort changed hands several times, becoming British in 1759 during the French and Indian War and later being transferred to American control in 1796.

In early 1759, during the French occupation, social gatherings were organized at the fort to build relationships between French officers and local Native American tribes. These alliances were essential during the colonial period. Additionally, these events helped alleviate some tensions among the men during those turbulent times of conflict.

Among those attending was a woman named Onita. Henri Le Clerc, an officer stationed at the fort, developed a fondness for her. At one gathering, another officer, Jean-Claude De Rochefort, whom Henri disliked, seated himself next to Onita.

He made great efforts to appear as if he was wooing the woman. As he drank heavily, his already crude behavior worsened throughout the night. Unable to tolerate it any longer, Henri challenged Jean-Claude to a duel.

The two men drew their swords, and the battle began down a twisting staircase. However, as Henri descended, he tripped and fell, striking his head on the stone floor. In a drunken rage, Jean-Claude stabbed the unconscious man on the floor, killing him. Realizing the seriousness of his actions, Jean-Claude knew he would face punishment for murder. He panicked, hacked the body to pieces, and began to toss them into Lake Ontario nearby, hoping that the other soldiers would think that hostile Native Americans had committed the dirty deed. But before he could finish, he heard voices coming down the stairwell. In his alarm, he spotted a well nearby and dumped the rest of Henri Le Clerc into its seemingly bottomless depths.

Henri's ghost can be seen from time to time emerging from the well. It seems that when Jean-Claude De Rochefort dumped the remains, the head went to the lake, and most of the body parts into the well. On certain nights, Henri Le Clerc climbs out of the well to search for his head.

New York
The Gruesome Remains of
Henry De Bosnys

Henry De Bosnys, also known as Henry Delactnack Debosnys, was a mysterious figure who garnered public attention following the curious deaths of two women. His actual background remains largely unknown, but it is believed he was born around 1836 in Portugal. Upon arriving in Essex in 1882, he claimed to be an educated and cultured individual who participated in the North Pole Expedition under McClure from February 1848 to October 1850. He also claimed to have served in several wars, including the Crimean War and the Franco-Prussian War. His descriptions depict a rather portly man with a round face, carefully shaved, and dark hair.

De Bosnys arrived as a farmhand in Essex County, New York, around 1881. Initially, he was accompanied by a woman named Eliza, whom he claimed was his wife. However, after they went away together, she disappeared shortly thereafter.

Not long after, De Bosnys began courting and eventually married a local widow, Elizabeth "Betsy" Wells, on June 8, 1882. Betsy had four daughters and owned a small farm. Early in their marriage, De Bosnys and Betsy began to argue as he pressured her to transfer ownership of her land to him, which she refused.

On the morning of August 1, 1882, Betsy went missing after going for a ride with De Bosnys to Port Henry. When he returned without her, her daughters became alarmed when she did not arrive home by the next day. Neighbors, after seeing De Bosnys acting oddly in the woods, searched the area and found Betsy dead with two bullet holes in her head and her throat cut. Her body had been covered with leaves. He was found later in the possession of a bloody knife and pistol.

The trial of Henry De Bosnys began on March 6, 1883, and lasted only two days. The jury deliberated for just eight minutes before finding him guilty of first-degree murder. On April 27, 1883, Henry De Bosnys was executed by hanging in Elizabethtown, New York, making him the last person to be hanged in Essex County. Today, his skull is preserved at the Adirondack History Center Museum in Elizabethtown, alongside the noose used in his execution. Legend has it that the enigmatic spirit of Henry De Bosnys continues to haunt the museum, hovering near his old head, leaving whispers of his presence in the air.

New York
Rapping Peddler

Katie and Maggie Fox were instrumental in the rise of spiritualism in the United States. They lived in a house located in Hydesville, New York, which gained a reputation for being haunted due to strange noises that often drove residents away. Along with their older sister Leah, the Fox sisters became well-known for their ability to communicate with spirits through "rappings."

On March 31, 1848, after the girls had gone to bed, they were kept awake all night by strange knocking sounds.

Curious, they began to clap and rap, asking the source of the noises to follow their cues. In this way, they communicated with the spirit of a peddler named Charles B. Rosna, who they claimed had been murdered in the house. They provided details about his death, suggesting that he was killed with a butcher knife and buried in the cellar.

When they dug in the cellar to find his body, it flooded, and no remains were discovered. Over the years, many concluded that the sounds simply resulted from the girls cracking their knuckles and toes. However, in 1904, long after the Fox sisters had passed away, the peddler's bones were uncovered within the crumbling walls of the home. This discovery reignited interest in the claims made by the sisters. Although the house eventually fell into ruins and was demolished, the original foundation remains, which can be visited, and some guests claim that the rapping sounds still echo within the area.

Haunting Shorts of New York:

• In 1835, a wealthy merchant named Seabury Tredwell purchased a home in New York with his wife, Eliza, and their eight children. The house was passed down through the family for nearly a hundred years before it was eventually converted into a museum. The youngest child, Gertrude, spent her entire life in the lavish environment of her childhood home. A story is told that Gertrude's parents were devout Protestants, and she fell in love with a Catholic doctor named Lewis Walton. However, her father forbade any thoughts of marriage to someone of a different faith. After her parents passed away, Gertrude vowed to honor her father's wishes. She never married and spent her later years alone in the family home. After her death, she seemed reluctant to leave. Not long after passing, the old woman's spirit was seen on the stoop, wearing a long brown dress.

• Fort Ticonderoga was an 18th-century fortress that was significant during both the French and Indian War and the American Revolutionary War. Initially built by the French and called Fort Carillon, it was positioned in a key area that overlooked the Champlain Valley, which includes parts of New York, Vermont, and Canada. The fort is also famous for ghost stories, one of which involves a woman named Nancy Coates, the mistress of General Anthony Wayne. According to legend, she drowned herself in Lake Champlain after he rejected her, and her ghost appears, floating face up in the water. The fort has been the scene of many fierce battles, especially in 1758, when one battle led to thousands of soldiers fighting. People say some of those soldiers can still be seen reenacting their deaths at the fort. Today, the fort has been restored and functions as a museum. Visitors often report seeing soldiers who appear and then vanish.

• A Lady in White visits the curvy stretch of roadway known as The Devil's Elbow on the secluded section of old NY-17C in Owego, New York. This thoroughfare has been an essential route for travel and trade for over 200 years. In 1932, near Glenmary Drive at the base of Devil's Elbow Hill, a steam shovel operator was clearing the area near a railroad crossing when he unearthed a skull. It was identified as that of a twenty-year-old woman who had lived at least a hundred years earlier. It appeared she had been killed by an axe or blow by a board to the head. The Broadhead Tavern, known for its rough reputation, had been situated nearby in earlier days.

• In the Hudson Valley in the Village of Leeds, a young servant named Anna Dorothea Swarts worked on the grounds of the Salisbury Manor in 1755. She tried to run away, but William Salisbury caught her and tied her to his horse. The horse bolted, and Anna Dorothea was dragged to her death. Residents in the community once claimed to see Anna Dorothea's ghost sitting on the wall outside of the privately owned manor and on the roads nearby.

• Captain Kidd was rumored to have buried treasure along the Hudson River. It is a location known as Kidd's Plug, which is a prominent knob along the rugged portion of the shoreline near West Point, referred to as the Crow's Nest. Allegedly, there is a concealed cavern hidden by a rock where the pirate stored some of his gold, and his ghostly form guards it.

• Split Rock Quarry, located near Syracuse, New York, has a haunted history. Originally a limestone quarry, it was transformed in 1917 into the Semet-Solvay Company to produce TNT for the war effort. On July 2, 1918, a catastrophic explosion occurred when a gear sparked a fire, igniting a hundred tons of dynamite, and 50 workers died.

There were speculations that the disaster might have been caused by sabotage from a German spy captured in a nearby town. Still, little evidence could be found to support this claim. Since the explosion, people have reported unexplained footsteps, strange lights, voices, and the sounds of machinery running.

• There is a road in Amsterdam, New York, called Widow Susan Road that has long been associated with a ghost. This ghost is believed to be that of Susan Thomas DeGraff, who was left a widow in 1848 when her husband, Hermanus DeGraff, died at 43. He is thought to be buried in the DeGraff family cemetery near the corner of Widow Susan Road and East Main Street. Following her husband's death, the community referred to her as Widow Susan. Susan passed away at 72 in 1892 and was buried in Green Hill Cemetery, as the DeGraff Cemetery had fallen into disrepair in the late 1800s. Shortly after her death, witnesses reported sightings of her spirit dressed in an old-fashioned white dress, appearing to cry as if she were searching for something lost. Most believe she is looking for her husband, as she may be uncertain about his burial location and why she was not interred in the family cemetery. Her spirit has also been spotted searching at Saint Casimir Cemetery and Saint Nicholas Cemetery.

• There is a ghostly reclining head on Matilda "Tilly" Bishop Gillette's grave in Lakeview Cemetery, Penn Yan. She died in 1936. Local lore suggests that she will be released to haunt the cemetery once her entire body is formed on this stone.

• Belhurst Castle is a historic hotel and resort located in the Finger Lakes region of New York, specifically in Geneva. The castle was built between 1885 and 1889 and has a history of untimely deaths and spooky apparitions.

One notable spirit is Isabella, a beautiful opera singer who roams the grounds in a white dress, mourning her lost lover. He died while attempting to escape through a hidden tunnel.

• The Starr Clark Tin Shop and Underground Railroad Museum in Mexico, New York, is haunted. During the mid-1800s, it served as a refuge for fugitive slaves. Visitors have reported experiencing remarkable phenomena, including shadowy figures swiftly moving throughout the building and disembodied voices echoing in the quiet spaces. Some individuals even claim to have felt ghostly fingers touching them.

• The Genesee County Poor House, founded in 1827 in East Bethany, New York, initially served as a working farm to support the needy, including orphans, widows, and the mentally ill. Residents, referred to as inmates regardless of their circumstances, were required to work on the farm, which involved raising livestock and crops to sustain themselves. Over the years, the poor house became the resting place for more than 1,700 documented deaths, with many other unrecorded individuals buried on-site. The location is haunted. One notable inmate named Roy suffered from gigantism, which resulted in his physical appearance being out of the norm—he had a protruding forehead and jaw, large hands and feet, and stood nearly seven feet tall. He was brought to the home at the age of 12 and remained there until his death at age 62. Despite his difficult life, Roy was known to be kind, and it is said that his shadow can still be seen lingering around the site.

A New York Cryptid
Hobgoblin of Fort Niagara

For years, people have reported sightings of a hobgoblin in the cemetery at Fort Niagara. This little, human-like creature is described as having pointed ears and wearing tattered dark clothing. The first recorded sighting was by a young man named John Carroll, who, after getting drunk, was thrown into a pit as a form of solitary confinement. While he was there, he was visited by the hobgoblin. In 1812, a soldier also reported seeing a creature resembling the hobgoblin in the graveyard.

North Carolina
The Ghostly Fiddler Plays

During the Civil War, small communities in Tennessee and North Carolina were divided in loyalties between the Union and the Confederacy, much like those in other states. The fighting, skirmishes, and raids by both sides seemed never-ending. However, an event in April 1864 stood out due to the haunting tune played before an execution—one that lingers in the air today.

Around 1860, a rough road called the Cataloochee Turnpike was carved out of the forest in the Great Smoky Mountains.

This narrow, winding road in North Carolina was intended to facilitate the quick transportation of livestock to eastern markets. Unfortunately, it also made it easier for Confederate Captain Albert Teague and his scouts to raid and harass Union sympathizers living nearby.

In late April 1864, 28-year-old Henry Grooms, along with his 30-year-old brother George Wiley Grooms—who was a private in the 11th Tennessee Cavalry of the U.S. Army—and his 21-year-old brother-in-law Mitchell Caldwell who had an intellectual disability, were captured while working in the fields by a Home Guard unit led by Teague. The three men were marched down that same road in Cataloochee Valley until they stopped by a small creek along an old Indian trail. There, the captors told Henry, who had been clutching his fiddle, that he must play a tune.

Understanding the gravity of the situation, Henry played his favorite tune, "Bonaparte's Retreat," but slowed it down to a mournful, haunting delivery. He then asked his captors if he could pray before the execution. George reportedly died cursing the Home Guards, while Mitchell's grinning at his captors unnerved them, leading them to make him cover his face with his hat before they shot him.

Afterward, Henry Grooms's wife took an ox sled to the site of the murders to retrieve their bodies and brought them back to Sutton Cemetery. The fiddle was found at Henry's feet. The men were buried in a common grave, marked simply with the word "MURDERED." For years, travelers along the Old Cataloochee Turnpike and hikers on the Little Cataloochee Trail have reported hearing the mournful sound of a fiddle playing. The song is "Bonaparte's Retreat."

North Carolina
Hitchhiking Annie, Lydia's Bridge

A pleasant walkway runs parallel to East Main Street in Jamestown, a quiet suburb between Greensboro and High Point. The path is relatively straight but takes a sharp curve before passing under an aging train trestle. It is here that the walkway takes on a dark history, as it marks the site where a young woman lost her life in the 1920s. Her ghost returns occasionally.

In June 1920, 35-year-old Annie Jackson, who worked at Vick's Chemical Company, was out with friends. While driving along the Greensboro-High Point Highway around 10 p.m., they hit a wet patch, causing the car to slide out of control and overturn. Tragically, Annie died in the accident.

She was thrown from the vehicle and struck her head on the concrete road. Shortly after this incident, drivers along the road began to report sightings of a lone phantom woman hitchhiking in the area.

Over time, the dangers of that curve were recognized, leading to the road being rerouted, and the old tunnel was eventually lost beneath overgrowth. Intrigued by the ghost story passed down by their elders, teens would visit the new tunnel, calling the phantom "Lydia" and scaring themselves at the site of the new bridge. Eventually, historians sifted through old newspapers and cleared away the brush to discover the true story behind the ghost. Today, that pleasant walkway invites visitors to explore the new path where the hitchhiking ghost of Annie roamed, and many believe she still does.

North Carolina
Bobbing Lantern of the Smokeys

Hidden beneath thickly forested hills, the old ghost town cemeteries and abandoned homesteads of Noland Creek Trail in the Smoky Mountains, about 8 miles from Bryson City, tell a haunting story steeped in eerie lore. There's even a dark settler's legend that accompanies this place.

One late afternoon, the daughter of an early settler vanished into the woods. When dusk fell, and she still hadn't returned, her father took a lantern and ventured into the growing darkness, calling her name. He searched along the creek shore for hours. Still, when he decided to extend his search beyond the familiar borders of Noland Creek, he wandered deeper into the forest.

His calls grew louder as he ventured farther, but she remained missing. As the night progressed, he became disoriented and struggled to retrace his steps. Despite his efforts, he realized too late that he was lost. He continued searching through the following day and into the next night, calling for his daughter until exhaustion took over. At last, he lay down to rest and seemingly disappeared into the depths of the forest, just like his daughter, never to be found.

Though no one ever located the man or his daughter, some hikers have reported seeing his lantern's glow moving through the Smoky Mountains' darkness. On several occasions, the old man has guided lost hikers back to the Noland Creek Trail, which was originally a Native American path and later transformed into a rugged roadway.

North Carolina
The Sordid Tale of Tom Dula

In the rugged heart of the Appalachians, where the tall pines sway with secrets of the past, Tom Dula emerged from a life of hardship in a tight-knit North Carolina community. He explored the hills as a boy, but he had his share of romantic interests as a young man. He was quite the ladies' man, as it was said. However, shy of his 18th birthday in 1862, the shadow of war loomed large. He joined the Confederate Army, enlisting as a private in Company K of the 42nd North Carolina Infantry Regiment.

After the war, Tom returned home, yearning for the familiar landscapes of his youth. Yet nothing was the same. He had lost three brothers in war. The girl he had loved, Ann Foster, had married James Melton, a local farmer and cobbler. He did not care. He rekindled his affair with her in secret, of course. But Tom's heart was restless, and in the spring of 1866, fate twisted its threads once more as he crossed paths with Ann's cousin, Laura Foster. He started wooing this young woman too.

Whispers filled the small town as rumors spread like wildfire—Laura was pregnant, and she and her secret lover, Tom Dula, were scheming to elope under the cover of darkness. Laura slipped away from her home on a fateful day, May 25, 1866. But as the sun set that evening, Laura vanished without a trace. Days turned into a haunting silence until the shocking discovery was made: her lifeless body was unearthed from a shallow grave, leaving the community in a chilling frenzy of questions and unease. It was reported that she was pregnant at the time of her death and had been stabbed in the chest. The young woman was last seen on May 25, riding a horse down Stony Fork Road.

Many stories have speculated that Ann murdered Laura Foster out of jealousy and that Tom took the blame for her. Ann's cousin, Pauline Foster, testified that Ann had taken her to the grave one night to ensure it was still well hidden. However, others tell a different story. Witnesses at the trial testified that Tom made an incriminating statement, saying he was going to "do in" the person who gave him "the pock," referring to the highly transferable disease of syphilis. Tom believed that Laura had given him syphilis, which he then passed on to Ann. However, a local doctor testified that Pauline Foster was the first to be treated for the disease.

Tom was arrested in Tennessee shortly after Laura's murder and was then returned to North Carolina for trial. Court records confirm that he confessed to the crime. He was convicted of murder and executed by hanging on May 1, 1868, despite Ann Melton being accused as an accomplice in the murder. While Tom was convicted, Ann was found not guilty and set free.

There are many legends surrounding the life and death of Tom Dula, the most notable being the claim that Ann Melton confessed to the murder on her deathbed in 1874. Laura Foster's ghost visits Tom's grave, marked by a chipped and worn stone in a field. In turn, he visits her headstone in a pasture surrounded by a white picket fence.

Haunting Shorts of North Carolina:

- The smaller Blue Ridge lies within the enormous Appalachian Mountain range that spans seven states. Brown Mountain lies within this range, and something strange happens here. Mysterious lights float on Brown Mountain in the Pisgah National Forest near Morganton, North Carolina. Witnesses report red, white, yellow, orange, and blue lights, varying in size from candlelight to firework rockets. These phenomena are said to have begun around 1200 after a battle between the Catawba and Cherokee tribes. Local legends suggest these lights represent the torches carried by women searching for fallen warriors. Another story tells of a pregnant woman murdered by her husband, with twinkling lights leading neighbors to her body. The townspeople hanged the husband, and the lights now serve as a reminder to wrongdoers that justice will prevail.

- In earlier years, Grandfather Mountain, named for the face of an old man seen on its cliffs, was a privately owned tourist attraction and a nature preserve with a rough road and trail leading to an incredible craggy view. In a deeply forested area there, a ghostly visitor appears. The cause of the hiker's appearance has never been fully explained. Still, people have been hunting, logging, and exploring its expanse for hundreds of years. Some say a man got lost on the mountain during a storm. He perished, and his body was never found. His ghost is still trying to find his way home.

- Roan Mountain, part of the Appalachian Mountains along the Tennessee-North Carolina border, features five summits, including Roan High Bluff and Roan High Knob, separated from Round Bald and others by Carver's Gap. Once, General John T. Wilder built the Cloudland Hotel, a lavish three-story lodge for wealthy guests, near Roan High Knob.

Known for the mist that often surrounded it, the hotel echoed with eerie sounds that led visitors to believe they heard a celestial choir or the lamentations of lost souls. Others speculated it was the cries of demons trying to lure the curious. One young man, drawn by the music, sought shelter in a cave during a storm and lost consciousness, experiencing a nightmare of demonically haunting songs. Abandoned in 1910, the hotel fell into ruins, but hikers near Toll House Gap still report hearing ghostly singing reminiscent of its past, inviting those who listen into its mysterious embrace.

• In the past, farmers drove their cattle to Roan Mountain, marking their livestock to signify ownership. Among them was a wealthy landowner with the largest herd, known for pushing his cattle further up the mountain to access the best grazing. His massive bull, adorned with a loud bell, often spooked other cattle, leading to stampedes. Townspeople complained that his greed left little for their herds, resulting in overgrazing. One spring, the landowner boasted of bringing the biggest herd yet. As he led his bull up to the lushest grass, a shot rang out from the fog, and the bull fell dead. Though gone, the bull never left Roan Mountain. Its bell can still be heard on foggy days, leading a ghostly herd to the richest grazing grounds.

• Chimney Rock is a granite outcropping in the Blue Ridge Mountains. On a July evening in 1806, 8-year-old Elizabeth Reaves saw what she believed to be a man on the rock, and soon her brother Morgan joined her, spotting thousands of flying figures. Their mother, Patsy, and another daughter witnessed the phenomenon for nearly an hour. In 1811, witnesses reported a ghostly battle atop Chimney Rock, featuring winged horses and clashing swords, lasting about ten minutes before one side vanished.

A North Carolina Cryptid
Spearfinger

North Carolina is undoubtedly home to a significant number of cryptids. Among these mysterious creatures are the Moon-Eyed People, described as pale-skinned and blue-eyed cave dwellers. Another notable figure is the bristle-haired Santer Cat, an elusive and predatory feline. The Beast of Bladenboro is a vampire-like cat, measuring 3 to 4 feet long and weighing around 150 pounds. It is infamous for its habit of attacking pets and emitting a cry that resembles that of a baby. Additionally, there is a 10-foot-tall Bigfoot frequently spotted at Carpenter's Knob, affectionately known as Knobby.

However, if one monster in North Carolina truly stands out, it may very well be Spearfinger. Many years ago, in the Smoky Mountains, there was a fearsome ogress the Cherokee called "U'tlun'ta," or Spearfinger. Her stone-like skin was impervious to weapons, and she could shape-shift into anything she desired.

Her right forefinger was long and sharp, and she preyed on young children. When she heard them playing outside, she would take the form of an old woman and follow their sweet scent, hobbling as if struggling to walk. "I am tired," she would say, sitting beside them. "Come sit on grandma's lap, and I will sing you a song." And one of them would come skipping and prancing over and plop their little head happily on her lap in anticipation of the special attention.

U'tlun'ta crooned and cooed over the child and slipped her fingers through its hair until the child fell into a blissful nap. Then, U'tlun'ta whipped her hand from its hidden pocket in her clothing, sinking the speared forefinger through the tender flesh of the back of the child's neck until the tip pierced its liver. She would drag out the liver and eat it as it dripped with blood, smacking her lips and sighing contentedly while the other children screeched and ran away.

North Dakota
The Gray Lady

Sims is an almost ghost town located in Morton County, North Dakota. While the area still has farms, the town was founded in 1883 primarily as a coal mining community along the railroad. It later included a brickyard. At its peak, Sims had a population of about 1,000 people. Still, by the early 20th century, the population began to decline sharply. Today, little remains of the town except for the Sims Scandinavian Lutheran Church, which was built shortly after the town's founding in 1884 and is still active, holding regular services.

In 1916, Reverend Lars Dordal, his wife Bertha, and their three children moved to Sims. They hoped the town's climate would help Bertha, who had contracted tuberculosis. Bertha became active in church activities and played the organ during services, but she passed away in 1917. Heartbroken over his wife's death, Lars struggled with his preaching and decided to visit his brother. While there, he fell in love with the young woman caring for his brother's sick wife, and within a year, they married. There was no drama surrounding her acceptance into the family; she was warm and endearing, winning the affection of the children.

However, many at the church in Sims, who had adored Bertha, found it difficult to accept this change. The situation became so awkward that Lars took a position in another part of the state and moved to preach for a different congregation. Not long after the family left, reports of Bertha's ghost appearing in the town began to surface. Witnesses claimed to see her wandering the rooms and playing the old organ. She opened and closed windows, and Olga Nelson, the pastor's wife during the 1930s, noted seeing "a gray shape upstairs," which is how the ghost came to be known as the Gray Lady.

A young woman who boarded in the upstairs rooms reported feeling a blanket placed on her during a cool night. When she mentioned this the following day, the pastor's wife was startled—no one *living* in the house had done it. There was even a moment when the pastor's wife was astonished to see the water pump moving up and down as if it were being operated by unseen hands.

The community has embraced Bertha's benevolent presence. She has been affectionately called the Gray Lady of Sims for many years. Bertha occasionally peers out of windows, and ghostly footsteps are heard within the home.

North Dakota
White Lady Lane

In 1921, Annie Storey was a 16-year-old girl living with her mother, Matilda, and two brothers, aged 8 and 11, in a small home by a railroad track near Leyden. A peddler named Sam Kalil was boarding on the ground floor of the Storey family's home. The rest of the family slept upstairs. One night, after discovering letters that the girl's suitor had sent, Kalil, consumed by jealousy over Annie's affections, sneaked upstairs while the mother and daughter were sleeping. He shot the daughter in the chest with a .33 caliber gun, killing her instantly. The mother quickly jumped up and rushed at him, and she was shot in the cheek. Kalil then fled down the stairs, but Matilda pursued him and managed to wrestle the gun from his hands before anyone else was harmed.

The peddler had grabbed a butcher knife and followed the woman upstairs, threatening to kill her. However, Matilda managed to take the knife from him and tossed it out of the window. Grabbing her son, Matilda rushed to Leyden, which was half a mile away, and brought authorities back to her home. Meanwhile, Kahill was sitting on the mattress of the bed next to Annie and had attempted to kill himself with the butcher knife but had failed. Sam Kalil was convicted of murder and sentenced to life in Bismarck State Prison. However, he was released after only ten years.

In contrast, Annie did not receive such liberty, as she was dead. She was buried in Walhalla Hillside Cemetery on November 19, 1921, up the road and across the Pembina River. Now, she wanders the roadways of White Lady Lane and the muddy bog areas near Eddie's Bridge in Leydon, still wearing her white nightgown and trying to make her way home.

Haunting Shorts of North Dakota:

• Harvey, North Dakota, is located along the banks of the Sheyenne River. It is typically a quiet place to live. However, in 1931, there was quite an uproar, followed by reports of a ghost. Sophia Eberlein Bentz, a 41-year-old wife of local plumber Jacob Bentz, was alive and well in Harvey, raising their two daughters until October 2, 1931. However, after she died mysteriously, the account given by her husband and the actual events that transpired are two very different stories. Jacob related his side to a judge when they found his wife dead with clawhammer marks on her head and burnt within their family car, "It all happened through an argument. I love her yet. I lost my head when we argued. I intended to kill myself, too. I felt so sorry. It wouldn't have happened if we hadn't quarreled." The judge did not believe Bentz. In reality, he struck her twice with a claw hammer, placed her in the car while she was still alive, and drove the vehicle into a ditch. Then Jacob set the car on fire. This was not merely a quarrel; Jacob called the insurance company after hitting her with the hammer to cash in on an insurance policy. A new library was constructed on the site of the old Bentz house that was relocated to another part of town. Sophia enjoys visiting the library from time to time to let the staff and patrons know she is present. Lights flicker on and off, and visitors often experience strange chills even when the room feels warm. Occasionally, the ghost even turns on computers.

• Fort Abraham Lincoln is a historic site near Mandan, North Dakota, along the Missouri River. It was established as a military post in the 1870s and served as a cavalry post during its operational years. The fort was the home of General George Custer, who commanded it before the Battle of Little Bighorn. Many believe the old site is haunted.

The buildings have been reconstructed after being torn down long ago, but the spirits of those who died there seem to linger. The area was known for its harsh conditions, and some soldiers reportedly froze to death in their beds. There were also fights among the soldiers and drownings in the river. Staff members have reported hearing footsteps and voices in the buildings, especially those once occupied by soldiers. Shadowy figures wander the grounds, and there are unsettling tales of soldiers who hanged themselves in the stables returning in phantom form, accompanied by the sounds of ghostly horses.

• Established in the 1870s, Riverside Cemetery is the largest cemetery in the Fargo-Moorhead area. Apparently, one of the mausoleums is haunted. If you knock on it, something will knock back. If you are lucky (or perhaps not so lucky depending on your perspective of ghosts returning to frighten the living), you might even hear someone calling out to you from within.

A North Dakota Cryptid

Miniwashitu

The Miniwashitu is an unsettling aquatic beast, striking fear into the hearts of all who dare to glimpse it. This creature boasts a wild mane of shaggy red hair that ripples in the water, giving it an almost otherworldly appearance. A single, unblinking eye that seems to pierce through the darkness sits at the center of its forehead. At the same time, a prominent horn juts ominously from above, adding to its sinister allure. It has human-like hands.

Its back is lined with a jagged, saw-like spine, each serrated edge reminiscent of a deadly weapon ready to strike. Folklore suggests that merely laying eyes on the Miniwashitu drives people to the brink of madness, with many succumbing to a chilling fate soon after. This fearsome entity lurks in the depths of the Missouri River, where it becomes especially active in the springtime, its massive, thrashing body powerful enough to break the frozen surface of the ice, leaving chaos in its wake.

Ohio
The Ghost of Moonville

A remote location near Zaleski, Ohio, was once so isolated that it was little more than a pathway connecting two points. It was not even marked with a dot on the map to indicate its existence. Initially, there were just a couple of farming families and a sawmill in the area. However, in the 1850s, the discovery of coal transformed the landscape. The Marietta & Cincinnati Railroad ran through the center of the community, establishing a depot and creating a tunnel in the hillside for trains to pass through. This led to the area being known as Moonville Station, with the tunnel referred to as Moonville Tunnel. Although the town did not grow significantly, small mining boomtowns emerged along the tracks. With limited roads, Moonville became a key hub for travelers using the tracks as a footpath.

Engineers dreaded the route through this part of Ohio due to its remoteness within deep pockets of untouched forest. Not only did eastbound and westbound trains share a single set of tracks, which led to several head-on collisions, but many also wanted to avoid a specific stretch a half-mile east of Moonville after dark. The dark path had long been reputed to be haunted.

Along the tracks, telegraph lines ran from train station to train station so that dispatchers could communicate with each other. Their interactions were critical as the railroad had only one set of tracks, and trains traveled in both an eastward and westward direction. The dispatcher's job was to monitor and control the signals so engineers knew when to pull off the tracks if there was a rockfall on the rails or to let an oncoming train pass. Most of the time, the system worked quite well. Sometimes, however, it failed. Theodore Lawhead was an engineer for the Marietta & Cincinnati Railroad. On a chilly November 4 in 1880, while Engineer Theodore Lawhead was heading through southern Ohio, the dispatch failed to notify the eastbound train of the westbound's route and time. The trains collided on a blind curve just a half mile from Moonville Tunnel, and Lawhead and his fireman, 25-year-old Charles Krick, died instantly.

After the wreck, many trainmen feared going along that stretch of the railroad. They said they would see the flicker of candlelight when they came along a particular section of the tracks near the tunnel in Moonville where Lawhead died. As they got closer and slowed, believing that someone was signaling an emergency ahead, a white-robed, translucent figure appeared carrying a lantern floating down the hillside with wide, bulging red eyes and a halo of tiny lights twinkling around its head. Then the ghost would vanish!

Ohio

Bloody Bridge

In the mid-1800s, passenger packets and cargo boats traveled the waterway connecting the Ohio River and Lake Erie, called the Miami & Erie Canal, from Toledo to Cincinnati. A driver guided a mule that walked the towpath along the shore and pulled the boat. During the canal years, between Spencerville and St. Marys, two boats were commonly seen along the waterway—the Daisy and the Minnie Warren.

Jack Billings was a big, softhearted man and a driver for the Daisy. A vile, temperamental man named William Jones led the mules for the Minnie Warren. The captain's daughter was on board this boat, and her name was given to the packet.

Minnie cooked for those on board and rode faithfully by her father's side on the canal route.

Minnie and Jack often flirted playfully with each other as their boats passed. After some time, they both realized they loved each other. Jack counted the hours between the time Minnie's boat disappeared after passing and when he would see it appear in the distance again. Minnie felt her heart pound wildly when she shyly caught the man's eyes in hers while they teased each other about whose boat was the better. This flirting made William Jones jealous as he loved Minnie, too. William would have mentioned his liking to the young woman. Still, the driver knew she only had eyes for Jack Billings, which would not have made a difference. So he just seethed over their fledgling relationship from sunup to sundown. He tossed and turned at night, dreaming up ways to get the girl all to himself.

It was not until one evening in the fall of 1854 that William's jealousy peaked after a social event both Minnie and Jack attended. They paused at the bridge late in the evening as they walked home along the canal. Little did they know William was waiting for them in the shadows with a sharp-edged ax. In one stroke, the bitter man cut Jack down. Minnie fell backward over the edge of the bridge and into the water below. She drowned in the murky waters of the canal. Some would say it was shock that sent her reeling to her death, but others believed the moment Jack died, she did not want to live at all and took the plunge to be with him.

Soon after, someone stumbled upon the ghastly scene of Jack's lifeless body and saw the girl floating dead in the water. They brought her body up and laid it next to the bloody corpse of her sweetheart. Gone, they were. But each of the young lovers left a mark of their dreadful doom after that awful day.

For nearly forty years after Jack's body was removed from the bridge, the bloodstains left from his body remained engraved in the wood. And hence, it received its name—Bloody Bridge. Those who looked over the edge of the bridge where Minnie died said they would see her face staring up at them from beneath the muddy canal water.

Haunting Shorts of Ohio:

- A ghostly worker walks above the old iron furnace, carrying a lantern at Lake Hope State Park's Hope Furnace. He fell to his death into its fiery depths during its early years.

- Before Hocking Hills State Park was established in southeastern Ohio, a nearby town called Cedar Grove was located near a sandstone gorge with Cedar Creek flowing below. Two boys from the village explored a recess cave and were startled by the ghost of an old man and a large white wolfhound, who vanished into the sandy floor. Curious townspeople began digging at the spot and uncovered the bones of the man and dog, an old flintlock rifle dated 1702, and some cooking pots. In the 1700s, one winter, a trapper named Retzler and his hound, Harper, went missing. Men camping nearby eventually discovered both of them dead in the cave. They buried them carefully in a shallow grave, giving rise to the legend of the ghostly dog. Over the years, travelers have visited the cave, often hearing the eerie baying of a hound.

- Dancing lights appear in the dark, mosquito-ridden forest of Goll Woods in Northwestern Ohio, a remnant of the Great Black Swamp. Some believe these lights are bioluminescence from insects or fungi. In contrast, others think they lure unsuspecting travelers into the murky depths of the swamp, never to return. In 1836, Peter and Catherine Goll brought their family from France to this area, where they lived for many years. Tiny lights have long been seen near their old family cemetery and homestead. This phenomenon is reminiscent of the French "feu-follet," or lights of unbaptized souls, which beckon travelers during Lent. Travelers once followed the lights, which often caused them to become lost in the shadowy bogs and perish.

Many locals believe these mysterious lights may be responsible for the peculiar number of disappearances in the region.

• The Ohio & Erie Canal, built in the 1820s and 1830s, connected the Ohio River to Lake Erie, greatly aiding farmers in transporting their goods. Along its route, various establishments like inns, taverns, and general stores emerged. One notable site is a building by Lock 38 in Valley View not far from Cleveland. It was initially constructed as a general store and home in 1827. It later became an inn and tavern known as Hell's Half Acre due to its rowdy clientele. Today, it serves as the Canal Exploration Center for the Cuyahoga Valley National Park, where visitors report ghostly voices and the scent of pipe smoke. The spirits of two young lovers from the Civil War era wander the towpath, forever seeking to reunite but are unable to cross the canal.

• In the early 1800s, the Hambleton brothers established Sprucevale, at what is now Beaver Creek State Park. The town thrived until the mid-1800s, during the decline of the canal boom. Today, the old grist mill remains, haunted by Esther Hale, a preacher from the Orthodox Friends. She worked with canal laborers, promoting temperance. Each year on St. Nicholas's Eve, Hale's ghost appears in white, scratching "Come" on the mill's wall before leading onlookers inside, where she vanishes.

• *If you're fascinated by the ghost stories of Ohio, consider reading Jannette's Haunted Ohio/Ohio Ghost Hunter Guides book series. This includes titles like "Haunted Hocking Hills," "Haunted Ohio," and "Ohio Ghost Stories and Spooky Legends: The Classics." These books feature a mix of both historic and contemporary hauntings, along with directions for visiting these intriguing locations.*

An Ohio Cryptid
Grassman

Ohio is known for the Loveland Frogman, a legendary humanoid frog said to be about 4 feet tall. Sightings of this creature have been reported in Loveland, Ohio, along the Miami River since the 1950s. On March 3, 1972, police officer Ray Shockey encountered an unidentified animal crossing Riverside Drive near the Totes boot factory. He described it as standing 3 to 4 feet tall with leathery skin, crouching like a frog before standing upright.

However, the creature most commonly associated with Ohio is the Hocking Hills Grassman, a regional variant of the Bigfoot legend linked explicitly to the Hocking Hills area. This creature is often described as a large, hairy, bipedal being, measuring between 7 and 10 feet tall, covered in shaggy brown fur adorned with greenish moss, which is how it got its name. Witnesses have reported a pronounced brow ridge and a sloped forehead. Sightings of the Hocking Hills Grassman have been documented by numerous witnesses over the years, notably around Moonville and Rose Lake at Old Man's Cave.

The Hocking Hills Bigfoot competes with the Bigfoot found at Salt Fork State Park, recognized as one of the "Squatchiest" places in the United States. This park has recorded over 36 reported sightings since the mid-1980s and hosts various Bigfoot-related events, including an annual conference. Notable locations within the park where sightings have occurred include Morgan's Knob, Parker Road (Buckeye Trail), and Bigfoot Ridge.

Oklahoma
Fort Washita Beckoning Ghost

For many years during the late 1800s and early 1900s, the curious would gather at Fort Washita to watch for a ghost that appeared each year on the anniversary of a death, accompanied by strange noises on the last nights of October and March. The apparition was that of a young, beautiful woman who beckoned to those watching, floating away toward a stream at the fort. Those who followed her also heard the pounding of hoofbeats from cavalry riding.

At the time, the Davis family occupied the officers' quarters at the fort. Each season, they would witness this ghost and her ill-fated story had been passed down to them. It began with a young lieutenant who was ordered to be stationed at Fort Washita. His fiancée was heartbroken, but they both understood that his official duty as a soldier came first.

They promised they would marry as soon as he was moved to another area or could set up living quarters for them both at the fort. For now, their marriage had to be postponed. However, only a week after the young man arrived at his new post, he fell ill and died. The name of his beloved was the last whisper from his lips. He was buried next to the stream. Soon after, the young woman fell ill as well and died. Ever since the ghost of the woman has been seen running toward the stream while the hoofbeats of the young soldier's troops echo across the ground.

Another chilling story is associated with an old spring at the fort, which involves a headless woman. In the early 1900s, a ghostly figure of a headless woman dressed in blue would appear day and night at this location. She encountered a young woman and, remarkably, spoke clearly despite lacking a head. The headless woman revealed that she and her sons had been murdered by two soldiers at the fort fifty years prior because she refused to disclose the location of her hidden money. The money was buried three feet below the surface in a nearby gully.

The ghost then offered to grant the young woman all of her tidy sum, except for a certain amount intended for a stone to honor her memory, if she would rebury her bones. The young woman fainted upon hearing this, and the vision of the headless woman haunted her mind thereafter. Eventually, this torment drove her to madness, and she died. Some people have seen this ghostly wraith of a woman beckoning to them, but fearing they might go mad, they do not follow, and she vanishes.

Oklahoma
Dead Woman Crossing

The sound of wagon wheels bumping and rattling over an old bridge on Dead Woman Road, accompanied by the mournful cries of a mother calling out for her baby, can be heard by those who truly listen. This story is true; just pay attention:

In 1905, Weatherford, Oklahoma, was an emerging agricultural and ranching community that had experienced rapid growth since its incorporation in 1898 and the arrival of the Choctaw, Oklahoma, and Gulf Railroad. The population had surged to approximately 1,500 residents. However, not all those who crossed the town's path had pure intentions; among them was a murderer who would leave behind a ghost.

Schoolteacher Katie DeWitt James found herself at a crossroads in life at the age of 29. Behind closed doors, her own life was anything but serene. Living with her husband, Martin Luther James, on a small homestead, their marriage was marked by turbulence and pain. Despite her love for their 14-month-old daughter, Lulu Blanche, the shadows of Martin's alleged physical abuse loomed large over their family. She decided to sue for a divorce from her husband and take custody of her child. According to the divorce documents filed by Katie, Martin Luther—"brandished a chair" and told Katie, "You ought to die; I have a notion to brain you with this chair." When her drunken husband returned home on July 1, 1905, an argument broke out, prompting Katie to flee to her father Henry Dewitt's homestead.

On July 7, 1905, Katie formally filed the divorce papers. Henry DeWitt went to Custer City to see his daughter off as she boarded a train to stay with her aunt and uncle in Ripley until things calmed down. She planned to travel to Weatherford first before continuing to Ripley. After several days without any word from his daughter, Henry became increasingly concerned when he found out she had not reached her aunt and uncle's home.

Henry first contacted the local sheriff for help locating Katie and Lula Blanche. However, the sheriff recommended that he hire Sam Bartell, a private investigator. Bartell soon discovered that on the train, Katie had made friends with Fannie Norton, a local laundress and ne'er-do-well with three children and a bad reputation. The two stayed overnight at a hotel operated by Fannie Norton's sister, America, and her husband, William Moore. The following day, Fannie and Katie arose early as Fannie had hired a buggy, and the two women were heading for Hydro and would be back in three hours.

Witnesses later reported seeing Katie, Fannie, and Lula Blanche leave the hotel in a buggy the following day. They were last seen at a field near Deer Creek. Upon learning this information, Bartell immediately began following the women's route. He came across a farmer named Peter Bierschied, who reported that a woman had driven her buggy past his home. She called out to a little boy and asked him to give a message to his mother, requesting her to watch over the child until she could return, as she needed to go to the city. The woman then drove off for a short distance and tossed out a bundle of baby clothing wrapped in a blanket. She never returned. The clothing was covered in blood, leading the family to conclude that something was terribly wrong.

Lula Blanche was returned to her family, and Fannie was located in Shawnee and brought in for questioning. While in jail, Fannie refused to admit to any crime. She took poison in a toilet room at the station and died. A desperate search was underway for Katie. She was not found until August 31, 1905, when G.W. Cornell stepped out of his buggy and noticed a skull beside his foot. He had discovered the skeletal remains of Katie DeWitt James along Deer Creek, and the skull had a bullet hole in it. A revolver was also found nearby. Henry DeWitt identified the remains as those of his daughter, Katie.

The coroner suggested that robbery was the motive behind the murder. However, the case was never solved, and although her husband had an alibi, some people questioned whether Luther James was involved. He received custody of the baby, and life continued on. Lula Blanche died at age 8 of spinal meningitis. The location where Katie's body was found, along the shores of Deer Creek, became known as Dead Woman Crossing. The spirit of the young, murdered woman lingers along the banks, calling for her baby. Fannie Norton's ghostly wagon wheels roll across. Then, all falls silent.

Haunting Shorts of Oklahoma:

- The Skirvin Hilton Hotel in Oklahoma City is famous for its ghost, Effie. According to legend, Effie was a maid and mistress of W.B. Skirvin. She became pregnant and tragically jumped from a window. This haunting has drawn significant attention, especially from NBA players, who have reported unsettling experiences during their stays at the hotel. They have described strange occurrences, such as eerie creaks and groans, and even claimed to have felt ghostly touches.

- There is a Cry Baby Bridge over Elm Creek, a small stream outside Oklahoma City, off East 134th Street and hidden among dense brush. This bridge was once the creek crossing for a house that has since deteriorated to just its foundation. On a hot June day in 1924, a storm struck while a woman and her baby crossed the bridge in a horse and buggy. Thunder crashed across the sky, causing the horses to panic and buck violently, overturning the carriage and sending the passengers tumbling out. The woman frantically searched for her baby; she could hear it crying, but the infant was never found. To this day, the baby's cries are still reported to be heard near the bridge.

- The Gilcrease Museum in Tulsa, founded in 1949 by oilman Thomas Gilcrease, houses art and artifacts from the American West. The original structure, built in 1913, was an orphanage for Native American children before becoming Gilcrease's home. Visitors have reported unusual occurrences, including sightings of Gilcrease as a full-body apparition and Native American children wandering the beautiful grounds.

- At Tucker Cemetery in Duncan, Oklahoma, on Tucker Road, the air hangs heavy with an unsettling stillness.

Many stones lie scattered, victims of vandalism and neglect, their carved letters fading into whispers of the past. But amid the desolation, an eerie phenomenon unfolds. Weathered and cracked, tombstones have been seen toppling over as if pushed by unseen hands, only to right themselves moments later!

• The Blue Belle Saloon was established during the April 22, 1889 land run, when John Sampsel claimed lot 9 and opened a tent restaurant that sold cigars. By 1892, F. M. Wyatt had leased the property, and between 1892 and 1894, a frame building was constructed, known as the Blue Belle Saloon. Eventually, a brick building was added, featuring gambling facilities on the second floor and rooms believed to be part of a bordello operated by a woman named Madame Miss Lizzie. Throughout its years of operation, especially in the late 19th and early 20th centuries, the Blue Belle Saloon gained notoriety due to its links with gambling and prostitution. It became known as a wild establishment that attracted infamous outlaws and gangs from the Old West era. Visitors have reported sightings of apparitions believed to be Madame Miss Lizzie and ghostly figures of women who worked at her bordello. Among them are Claudia and Estelle—two women thought to have been involved in tragic events during their lives at the saloon. Claudia's story is particularly haunting; she allegedly met a violent end and was buried on the premises.

An Oklahoma Cryptid

Oklahoma Octopus

The Oklahoma Octopus is one of the state's most popular and controversial cryptids. It inhabits three lakes: Lake Thunderbird, Lake Oologah, and Lake Tenkiller. This creature resembles an octopus but is much larger—approximately the size of a horse—with eight-foot tentacles, bulbous eyes, leathery red-brown skin, and a dome-shaped head. The Oklahoma Octopus has been blamed for numerous drownings in these lakes.

In Choctaw stories, "Ishkitini" is a malevolent giant horned owl believed to prowl at night, killing humans and animals; its screech is thought to foretell death.

There have also been sightings of a Bigfoot-like creature in Boggy Bottom Creek since June 1992, when three boys saw the creature walking along a country road near a watermelon patch in the dark of night. At first, they thought it was a large man standing against a tree, but then it growled deeply. A massive, red-brown, hairy beast stepped out and growled again, causing the boys to flee in fear. In 2006, an eight-foot monster scared two children playing in the water close to Caney, near the same creek. In recent years, tracks have been found along Boggy Creek, further adding to the local lore.

Oregon
Bloody Kerchief

A story was written about the Yaquina Bay Lighthouse that accounts for a mysterious face appearing there, often accompanied by screams at night. This tale has been shared for over a hundred years and has become a traditional story for visitors to the area. Murial Trevenard, a captain's daughter, stayed in Newport while her father traveled to Coos Bay in 1889. At that time, the lighthouse had already been abandoned. It had become a popular spot for teens, including Murial and her friends, to explore. During one visit, a group discovered a secret passage on an upper level that led to a deep shaft. Curious, the teens lit pieces of paper and dropped them into the darkness, but the shaft seemed bottomless. Unable to see what lay below, they grew bored and decided to leave.

Just as they were about to part ways at the lighthouse, Murial realized her kerchief was missing and rushed back to the passage to search for it. The others waited impatiently below and suddenly heard the shrillest screams from above. They ran into the lighthouse and hurried up to the passageway to the shaft. There, they found a pool of warm blood and Murial's handkerchief, but the girl herself was missing. The shaft was eventually sealed to prevent further accidents, but Murial was never found. On some nights, passersby claim to hear a high-pitched scream echoing from the lighthouse, accompanied by a girl weeping.

Oregon
Return of Joe Bush

The gold rush in Sumpter, Oregon, began in 1862 when gold was discovered in the Blue Mountains and Sumpter Valley. Prospectors flooded the area, establishing mining camps. Initially, the miners used panning and sluicing to extract gold from streambeds. As accessible gold became scarcer, they began large-scale excavations through dredging. This method involved using large buckets that scooped up earth from riverbeds or valleys without a water source.

The Sumpter Valley Gold Dredge was a significant piece of mining equipment that employed a series of buckets capable of processing more than seven yards of material every minute. It required a crew of 20 workers. Joe Bush was a miner who worked on the dredge and died under mysterious circumstances. After his death, the men operating the dredge reported hearing his footsteps and seeing strange wet footprints left behind on the decks.

Haunting Shorts of Oregon:

- In ancient times, a leader of the Multnomah people had a daughter who was set to marry a chief from the Clatsop tribe. During the wedding festivities, a plague struck the village, causing many to fall ill and die. A medicine man announced that the only way to stop the deaths was to sacrifice a young woman to appease the spirits. In a selfless act, the chief's daughter volunteered to be the one sacrificed after witnessing her fiancé succumb to the disease. She went to the top of the high cliff above Big River and threw herself upon the rocks below. After she died, the sickness vanished. Now, her spirit appears at Multnomah Falls, gazing up at the waterfall above.

- Along Highway 101, a stretch of road on Oregon's coast, a man wrapped in bandages resembling a mummy has been spotted on the side of the highway. Some witnesses claim they have seen him punch out car windows, while others report that as they pass by, they glance in the rearview mirrors and find him sitting in the backseat of their car!

- Near Hillsboro, Oregon, a large train trestle was constructed in the early 1900s. Initially operated by the Southern Pacific and Burlington Northern railroads, the Portland and Western now run it. The trestle spans Holcomb Creek and Dick Road. Shortly after its completion, it became a site associated with suicides, and eerie sounds of moans and groans were reported in the area.

- In Portland, Oregon, a picturesque park served as a campsite for the Lewis and Clark expedition in the 1800s. However, it also has a dark history due to a nearby murder. On August 15, 1949, Thelma Anne Taylor, a Roosevelt High School student, was waiting for a bus in St. Johns on her way to pick beans in Hillsboro when Morris Leland abducted her.

Leland took her to the Willamette River and murdered the girl that same night. Since then, locals have reported hearing Thelma's screams, especially when the wind blows strongly from the direction of the river.

- The North Portland Library has a rich history of being a community hub for over a century. Notably, some visitors have reported seeing a ghostly figure, described as an old man, particularly in a conference room on the second floor. In addition to these eyewitness accounts, security cameras have recorded a shadowy figure in the library, further contributing to the intriguing stories surrounding this historic location.

- Heceta Head Lighthouse is a historic lighthouse on the beautiful Oregon Coast, built in 1894. This lighthouse helps guide ships safely along the coast and has been home to lightkeepers and their families over the years. Local legends speak of a spirit often seen wearing a long gray skirt, but its identity remains uncertain due to the numerous souls who have died there. Shipwrecks have occurred off the coast there due to treacherous conditions, and crew members died. Some travelers walking near the rocky areas have been swept into the ocean by waves. Adding to this mystery is an unmarked grave on a hillside near the lighthouse.

- Lithia Park, located in Ashland, has a rich history that dates back to the late 19th century. The area was home to a flour mill established by Abel Helman and Eber Emery in 1852. However, as the town grew around the mill, the land and buildings fell into disrepair. They became an eyesore, linked to livestock and neglect. During this time, it is rumored that a little girl was murdered there. Today, visitors report seeing a blue light glowing above one of the park's ponds at night, which is thought to be the child's restless spirit.

• The Blanco was a two-masted schooner measuring 125 feet in length. Built for coastal trade, the vessel departed from San Francisco on November 6, 1864, heading for Coos Bay. It is believed that the Blanco ran aground near the mouth of Schooner Creek that same year after navigating through the narrow bar at Siletz Bay. Ben Simpson, an agent for the Siletz Indian Reservation, witnessed the wreckage shortly after it occurred. Not long after the incident, a phantom ship resembling the Blanco began to appear on foggy days along Siletz Bay, and sightings of this spectral vessel persist to this day.

An Oregon Cryptid

Batsquatch

Three of the most well-known cryptids in Oregon are Bigfoot, Colossal Claude, and Gumberoo. Bigfoot is described as a wild, hairy man who lives in the wilderness. Colossal Claude is a giant seahorse that is believed to be around 40 feet long and is said to inhabit the Columbia River. Gumberoo is a hairless, bear-like creature thought to make its den in the hollowed-out trunks of burned cedar trees.

However, Batsquatch could be considered the creepiest of them all. It was first reported after the eruption of Mount St. Helens in Washington State. Batsquatch is a large, flying beast that is a cross between a bat and Sasquatch with yellow eyes, blue fur, and leathery wings with a 50-foot wingspan.

Pennsylvania
Dead Man's Hollow

There is a dark valley along the Youghiogheny River, located south of McKeesport. It lies just under a mile from the Boston Ballfield Park along the Great Allegheny Passage Youghiogheny River Trail. This area is known as Dead Man's Hollow, and it has a rich history and a local legend.

Dead Man's Hollow received its grim name due to the corpses frequently found along the Youghiogheny River. This location serves as a perfect dumping ground because of the river's curves, where anything weighed down tends to wash ashore and settle in the still waters of Dead Man's Run.

Many bodies discovered here are victims of drowning, while others have mysterious origins. In the 1870s, a group of boys stumbled upon an unidentified decomposed body in the hollow, leading locals to shorten the name to Dead Man's Hollow. Over time, numerous lives have been lost in this area, and some believe that the spirits of these individuals linger.

On August 2, 1881, 35-year-old George McClure was a father of three and a co-owner of Hendrickson and McClure's hardware store. That day, a gang of thieves, including Ward McConkey, burglarized the store. McClure, dead set to locate the stolen goods, set out with two men—Joseph Lynch and George Flemming (the property owner who believed he knew where the robbers had hidden the loot). The three men searched the area all day but could not find anything. Around dusk, they stopped to rest when seven armed men surrounded them and opened fire. Flemming and Lynch managed to escape, but McClure was found dead around 9:30 p.m., riddled with bullet holes in the woods at Dead Man's Hollow.

A judge sentenced Ward McConkey to hang in May 1883 for McClure's murder. He maintained his innocence until his death. The 19-year-old declared just before his execution: "All I have to say, gentlemen, is that you are hanging me because you think I know something about the murder of George McClure and won't squeal, and the people of McKeesport want to see me hanged, but I'm innocent." Just before the trap was sprung, McConkey uttered, "Goodbye, murderers, goodbye."

There have been reports of shadowy figures lingering in the woods, accompanied by low voices despite no one else being around. One spirit is Ward McConkey, seeking revenge. Even on the scaffold, he insisted he was not the killer. So, if you find yourself standing in Dead Man's Hollow on a dark evening and hear a whisper in your ear saying, "Goodbye, murderers, goodbye," it is best to run.

Pennsylvania
Betty Knox

Betty Knox Road in Fayette County is named after Betty, who lived in the area during the Revolutionary War (1775-1783). She was raised by her father, who taught her to farm and take crops to the grist mill in Ferguson Hollow using an ox-drawn wagon. After her father's death, she managed the farm alone. At that time, Isaac Meason owned significant land in Western Pennsylvania and operated various mills. Betty frequently visited his stone grist mill to grind corn and wheat and sell her garden produce in Union Town.

Though she didn't socialize much, townspeople were intrigued by the solitary, independent woman and her ox. Tongues wagged when Betty arrived in town unescorted on her 28-mile round trip. Townspeople recalled how she had always come alone, nursing a wounded British deserter back to health and hiding him from the army. While he tended the farm, Betty drove the ox to town by herself. Then, one day, her trips ceased altogether. A search party was sent, but her home was empty, and her animals were nearly starving. They scoured the area, calling out, "Betty Knox, Betty Knox!" but found no trace of her.

Years later, when talk of Betty's disappearance had faded, two boys fishing found the bones of her ox tied to a tree. What happened to Betty remains a mystery. Some speculate she was taken by Native Americans, killed by a wild animal, or waylaid by thieves. If you visit the old road where Betty Knox Road crosses Tucker Creek, you might hear her ox's mournful cry in the misty air, along with someone calling, "Betty Knox, Betty Knox!"

Haunting Shorts of Pennsylvania:

• On the outskirts of Pittsburgh, the Pennsylvania Railroad's Peters Creek Branch served coal mines from Large to Snowden. Near Piney Fork, trains passed through Green Man Tunnel, named after 8-year-old Raymond Robinson. In 1919, he was severely injured by an electric shock while climbing a pole, leaving him with facial scars. Despite his injuries, Raymond maintained a kind spirit but became a recluse, hiking along Koppel-New Galilee Road. Local teens in the 1950s and 1960s nicknamed him Green Man or Charlie No-Face due to his appearance. Raymond passed away in 1984, but his legend lives on at Green Man Tunnel, a spot associated with his urban legend.

• Tunnels ran under the Jones & Laughlin Steel blast furnaces in Pittsburgh, allowing trains to bypass the mill. Workers often saw an old woman in the tunnel, known as Slag Pile Annie. When confronted about being in such a unsafe place, she replied, "I can't get killed. I'm already dead."

• On a warm Saturday, August 18, 1810, four children went to pick huckleberries near Georges Creek in the South Mountain Region. While exploring a ridge, they noticed something white in the brush under White Rocks outcropping. Curious, they climbed across the rocky terrain. There, they discovered something horrid—the lifeless body of a young woman with golden, blood-stained hair and a white dress lying at the foot of the rocks. A man from New Salem claimed 18-year-old Mary "Polly" Williams as his niece. She was doing light housework for her board while her parents searched for jobs. Engaged to Philip Rodgers, they had been on their way to their wedding in Woodbridge. A bloodstained trail along the cliff showed where her fingers had dragged against the stone as she tumbled from the ledge.

Rodgers was arrested, but acquitted, claiming he and Polly had argued and she accidentally fell off the edge. Years later, a stone was placed at Polly's grave reading: *Behold with pity you that pass by. Here does the bones of Polly Williams lie. Who was cut off in her tender bloom. By a vile wretch, her pretended groom.* Occasionally, Polly is seen atop the White Rocks, wringing her hands before vanishing.

- Twenty-year-old Jennie Wade lived in Gettysburg, Pennsylvania, during the Civil War. She was staying at her sister's home at Baltimore Street to help care for her sister and her newborn child in the downtown area during the Battle of Gettysburg. On July 3, 1863, while kneading dough to make bread for Union soldiers, she was struck by a stray bullet in the shoulder, which lodged in her heart. Jennie died instantly, and her body was later buried in Evergreen Cemetery in Gettysburg. Her ghost returns to the house, now a museum, and screams have been heard along the street.

- George and Elizabeth Spangler lived on a productive farm outside Gettysburg with their four children. During the Battle of Gettysburg, their home became a Union artillery staging area, a field hospital for the Eleventh Corps, and a burial ground for nearly 205 soldiers. About 1,800 wounded Union soldiers and 100 Confederate soldiers were treated there in barns, outbuildings, and some on bare ground. The conditions were grim, often compared to a "butcher shop" because of the numerous amputations performed. After the war, the Spanglers and their tenants reported seeing a figure dressed in white outside at night, carrying water buckets. Most believed it was the ghost of a servant still bringing water for the battle hospital.

- The abandoned Pennsylvania Turnpike features the haunted Sideling Hill Tunnel, 1.3 miles long. This tunnel was originally constructed as part of the Pennsylvania Turnpike.

The turnpike, opened in 1940, was designed to navigate several mountains. By the late 1950s, traffic congestion became a significant issue because of the bottleneck created by the two-lane tunnels, which led to their bypass and subsequent abandonment. The rough asphalt path was later converted into a rail-trail. Legend has it that the tunnel is haunted by the ghost of a little girl who died in a car accident within its confines. Visitors claim to see her apparition, and if you roll a ball into the darkness, she will roll it back to you.

• William Howe, a Union soldier, was executed by hanging on August 24, 1864, at the parade ground of Fort Mifflin. He had been suffering from severe and chronic stomach issues and was unable to receive hospital care, prompting him to return home to recover. While he was home, three officers arrived to arrest him, leading to an altercation in which Howe opened fire and struck one of the officers in the chest, resulting in the officer's death. Howe was subsequently captured, arrested, and sentenced to hang. Since his execution, visitors and staff at the fort have reported seeing a faceless ghost that many believe to be William Howe, as a bag was placed over his head before his execution.

• On October 11, 1926, around midnight, 32-year-old Margaret Gray, a mother of five, was involved in a fatal car accident on Wopsy Road in the mountains near Wopsononock, Pennsylvania. The accident may have been related to moonshine running from another county. The large touring car she was in skidded on wet pavement while attempting to pass another vehicle near a sharp curve known as Devil's Elbow. The car left the highway and rolled over several times. Just days after the crash, travelers along the route reported seeing a ghostly woman in a white dress walking along the roadway.

A Pennsylvania Cryptid

Presque Isle Storm Hag

Presque Isle State Park is a sandy peninsula extending into Lake Erie near Erie, Pennsylvania. Lake Erie is known for its unpredictable waves, shifting sandbars, and storms, leading to an estimated 500 to 3,000 shipwrecks along its coast. Early explorers used the eastern bay of Presque Isle as a refuge from storms, but many did not escape unscathed. The Lake Erie Quadrangle, where Presque Isle is located, is thought to hold more wrecks than the Bermuda Triangle.

According to legend, a fearsome Storm Hag resides at the bottom of Lake Erie. She has green skin, sharp nails, and a haunting song that lures unsuspecting sailors before summoning storms to sink their boats. One story recounts a ship caught in a storm in 1782. The captain sought shelter near Presque Isle but hesitated to navigate the dangerous shallows. Just as the storm seemed to relent, they heard the Storm Hag's enchanting song, and dark clouds returned. In a violent storm, she struck, dragging the ship and its crew to the depths. Walking along the beach, you might find tiny white crystals, said to be the tears of those left behind. It is believed that holding one during a storm may protect against the Storm Hag's wrath.

Rhode Island
Mercy Brown, A Vampire Laid to Rest So a Ghost May Rise

George and Mary Brown's family had been living a quiet life in the rural New England town of Exeter until they were confronted with a tragic series of deaths attributed to consumption, a disease caused by bacteria that attack the lungs. The victims suffered from labored breathing and cough and appeared pale and gaunt, with rosy cheeks and a feverish glow. For most, this illness ultimately led to death.

Mary died first in 1883, followed by her daughter Mary Olive in 1884, who lived as a 20-year-old dressmaker. By 1892, 19-year-old Mercy (Lena) and her 24-year-old brother Edwin had contracted the disease. Edwin was sent to Colorado's mineral springs, and while he was away, Mercy died on January 17, 1892. Upon returning from his trip with his wife, Hortense, he suffered a relapse.

As Edwin's health worsened, local superstition led neighbors to believe that one of the dead family members was a vampire responsible for his illness. It did not help that passersby declared seeing already-dead Mercy roaming about the cemetery and through fields. In delirium, Edwin announced that his sister was sitting on his chest, suffocating him. On March 17, 1892, George Brown, under pressure from the community, consented to exhume the corpses of his dead family members. The town marched to the graveyard, eager to find the truth. The exhumation was conducted by local villagers, a doctor, and a newspaper reporter. Both Mary and Mary Olive revealed typical signs of decomposition. Yet, when they examined Mercy's body—buried for two months—her corpse was well-preserved, and her hair and nails appeared to have grown. They were also shocked to find blood still present in her heart. This extraordinary state of decomposition, or lack of it, led the townspeople to conclude that Mercy was indeed a vampire. Her undead corpse was responsible for Edwin's illness.

The town fell into a vampire hysteria and performed a ritual in line with contemporary folklore. Mercy's heart and liver were removed, charred on a rock, and mixed the ashes with water to create a tonic for Edwin to ingest. Unfortunately, despite these efforts, Edwin succumbed to consumption just two months later. What remained of Mercy's body was buried again in Exeter's Baptist Church cemetery.

Apparently, digging up a grave and tearing the heart and liver from the corpse for a family member to dine upon is quite disturbing to the soul of the dead. After reburial, a glowing blue orb of light occasionally hovers above the headstone of Mercy Brown.

Rhode Island
The Mill Key Tucked in His Pocket

The Ram Tail Mill, established by William Potter along the Ponagansett River in partnership with his son-in-law, Peleg Walker, was used to clean and process wool into cloth. The mill is well-known for its industrial history and haunted reputation stemming from tragic events involving its former owner.

After the mill closed each evening, the 35-year-old Peleg Walker became a night watchman. He was known for his surly and disagreeable nature, patrolling the buildings at night with a lantern in one hand. In the mornings, he would awaken the workers by ringing a bell attached to a rope.

However, Walker knew how to get on people's nerves, including his in-laws. Following a disagreement, he famously declared, "You'll have to take the key to this mill from a dead man's pocket!" Strangely, no bell rang to wake the workers on May 19, 1822. When they eventually arrived for the day, they discovered Walker hanging from the bell rope, with the mill key tucked into his pocket.

The family buried him in their plot, but his ghost would not rest. The bell mysteriously began to ring at midnight, though its source could not be found. Soon after, the villagers were awakened by the sound of the mill operating with no workers present, and they noted that the waterwheel was turning in the opposite direction of the stream's flow. Witnesses claimed to have seen Peleg Walker wandering the mill at night, holding a lantern that lit his path. At the same time, the handle squeaked with every movement. He would meander from building to building, his lantern flickering in the wind.

The mill was ultimately destroyed by fire in 1873. However, the ruins still stand for those brave enough to hike the trail in search of Peleg Walker's ghost, who continues to fulfill his duties.

Haunting Shorts of Rhode Island:

• King Philip's War, which took place from 1675 to 1676, was a conflict between the Native American tribes of New England and English settlers. The war was named after Metacomet, who became known as King Philip, the chief sachem of the Wampanoag tribe. Tensions had escalated due to the encroachment on Native lands by English settlers. The conflict erupted when Native Americans attacked several settlements over land disputes and the expansion of the colony. Ultimately, the war ended in the defeat of King Philip's forces, marking a significant turning point in colonial-Native American relations. However, Captain Michael Pierce led a group of Plymouth Colony militia and Wampanoag allies during the battles in pursuit of the Narragansett tribe. They were ambushed near what is now Central Falls, Rhode Island, and ultimately defeated on March 26, 1676, with ten of the colonists taken prisoner. Of these, nine were tortured and executed. The remains of the slain men were buried by the colonists who discovered them, and a stone cairn was created as a memorial, which can still be seen today. They would probably still be lying in rest if not for curious New Englanders, especially one peculiar doctor, digging up the bodies repeatedly over the following years. A half-mile trail, Nine Men's Misery Trail, leads to the site. Those walking through the area have heard bloodcurdling screams and moans of the men riding along the wind.

• The Nine Men's Misery trail is in Cumberland Monastery Park, near the Cumberland Public Library. The library sits on the former site of the Monastery of Our Lady of the Valley, which was occupied by the monks of the Cistercian Order of the Strict Observance. The monastery's building burned down in the 1950s, but fortunately, no lives were lost, and the monastery was relocated elsewhere.

Visitors to the library sometimes report hearing ghostly voices and doors slamming shut, even when no one is around to have closed them.

• Rose Island is an 18.5-acre island with a lighthouse and a home once used for keepers and their families. It is located in Narragansett Bay, off the coast of Newport, Rhode Island. It has operated since 1868, when shipping traffic in Narragansett Bay flourished. Before, it was a lighthouse, and in the late 1700s, a fortification called Fort Hamilton was constructed on Rose Island with a barracks to house 300 soldiers. In the 1830s, there was a cholera epidemic in Newport, and the barracks were repurposed as a quarantine hospital for those afflicted with the disease. Many staying there succumbed to the disease, and they are still restless, it seems. Visitors to the lighthouse property, now a nature preserve for birds and wildlife only accessible by boat, hear footsteps, slamming doors, and other dins around the barracks. But those old ghosts may not be alone. Charles Curtis served as the lighthouse keeper from 1887 until his retirement in 1918, living on Rose Island with his wife Christina and their daughter Mabel. A dedicated worker, some believe that his ghost still roams the grounds checking on operations long after his term ended. To add to the mystery, a ghostly woman in white has been spotted, staring out to the ocean from the lighthouse tower.

• The General Nathanael Greene Homestead in Coventry holds historical significance from the American Revolutionary War as the residence of General Nathanael Greene, a prominent figure in the Continental Army. After Greene moved to Newport, he sold the property to his brother, Jacob Greene, who transformed it into a tenant house. The homestead is next to a cemetery where fallen troops were buried and later converted into a museum.

The old home is haunted. One intriguing phenomenon is the aroma of freshly baked bread that fills certain rooms despite no one cooking or living in the house. General Greene's grandniece, Elizabeth Warner, was the last family member to reside there until she died in 1899. She is buried in the family cemetery located behind the house. Elizabeth was deeply involved in the Temperance movement, which aimed to eliminate alcohol consumption. Those who sneak alcohol into the building, now managed by the Nathanael Greene Homestead Association, may hear a commotion as her ghostly shoes stomp along the stairs. However, for those who abstain from alcohol, there are also other spirits to enjoy. Revolutionary soldiers have been known to peek around corners or appear as shadowy figures nearby.

• The house where the wealthy and widowed poet Sarah Helen Whitman lived—famous for her brief romance with Edgar Allan Poe—is in Providence. This site features a rose garden believed to contain ancestral roses that Whitman tended herself. In this garden, Edgar Allan Poe first spotted Whitman nurturing her roses under a full moon in July 1845. The house overlooks St. John's Cathedral and its adjoining graveyard. Visitors have reported experiencing ghostly encounters, including sightings of Whitman's spirit, particularly in the garden where she and Poe shared many meaningful moments. Passersby have seen a glowing white figure outside on full moon nights around midnight.

• The 14-room Arnold House, also known as the Conjuring House, was constructed in 1736 and is situated in Harrisville, Rhode Island. In 1971, Carolyn and Roger Perron and their five daughters moved into the house. They soon began experiencing unexplained phenomena, including whispers, footsteps, and the apparition of a strange man in the kitchen. Items would go missing and weirdly reappear.

As the unusual events escalated, the family researched the history of the house and discovered that ten people had died either in or near the property. This includes two suicides by hanging inside the home, one death by poisoning, two drownings on the property, and four men who froze to death in the vicinity. The story gained notoriety when paranormal investigators Ed and Lorraine Warren were called in to assist the Perrons, claiming that malevolent spirits were present in the home.

• The Crescent Park Carousel, a park with views of the river, was constructed in 1895 by Charles Looff and features 62 hand-carved wooden figures and four chariots. This carousel is surrounded by local ghost stories that enhance its mystique, including tales of a phantom woman in Victorian clothing who has been seen walking nearby.

A Rhode Island Cryptid

Glocester Ghoul

In the 1830s, Albert Hicks, a notorious pirate, was searching for buried treasure in the woods near Glocester. While digging, he and his crew encountered a terrifying creature that resembled a mix between a ram and a bat. The beast was as large as a cow and covered in rattling scales. It had leathery wings that spanned several feet and fiery, glowing eyes. Twisted horns adorned its head. Called the Glocester Ghoul, one of the most chilling features of this creature was its ability to breathe fire. Witnesses reported seeing flames emitted from its mouth and experiencing a foul, sulfurous odor accompanying its presence.

South Carolina
A Ring for Dead Alice

The Grand Strand is a stretch of beach along the Atlantic Ocean in South Carolina. In this area lived a 15-year-old girl named Alice Flagg, who resided at The Hermitage with her mother and brother in Murrells Inlet during the 1840s. At that time, society pressured young women to marry into wealth and status. Despite this pressure, Alice fell deeply in love with John Braddock, a common lumberman, defying her family's expectations.

Alice's mother and brother were shocked by her choice and disapproved of the relationship. To maintain their love, Alice and John communicated secretly. Their engagement was symbolized by a simple gold ring attached to a blue ribbon that Alice wore around her neck and hid beneath her clothing. As tensions within the family escalated, Doctor Allard, Alice's guardian, sent her away to boarding school in Charleston to keep her away from John.

During her time at boarding school, Alice became despondent and frail, longing for her love. Tragically, she contracted malaria and slipped into a coma. Believing she would survive, Doctor Allard removed the blue ribbon and ring from her neck and tossed them into a creek. Sadly, Alice passed away and was buried at All Saints Waccamaw Episcopal Church Cemetery in Murrells Inlet.

At All Saints Cemetery, a stone marks the grave of Alice Flagg. According to local legend, those who walk backward around her grave 13 times and leave a ring will supposedly be rewarded with a visit from her spirit.

South Carolina
The Devil in Petticoats

Edgefield is in the western part of South Carolina, near the Georgia border. It is infamous for a woman whom newspapers called "The Devil in Petticoats." Her name, known for her notoriety, was Becky Cotton.

Becky Kennedy lost her mother at a young age, and her father, James, a cattleman known for his heavy drinking, indulged her wild behavior. She was quite a handful, and her father affectionately referred to her as his little "she-devil." As she grew older, she maintained her rebellious nature while being regarded as particularly beautiful. She married Erasmus Smith at a young age, and their relationship was tumultuous, as they fought like cats and dogs. It is said she stuck a needle through his heart, killing him soon on. She weighted his corpse down and tossed it into the pond of a beaver dam, marking the first time she became a widow. Less than a year later, Joshua Terry caught her eye, and the two got married. However, the marriage was short-lived; she grew tired of him and poisoned his tea with a deadly dose of nightshade.

His body followed his predecessor's fate and ended up in the pond, weighted down with bricks.

Becky, now a widow for the second time, married John Cotton, a local farmer, around 1784. Her father, James, was involved in a land dispute with neighbors who threatened his life. To escape the danger, he went to stay with Becky and John. Unfortunately, the neighbors managed to break through the front door and shot him in cold blood right in front of her. While this was happening, John took no action to intervene. This irked Beck to no end, so much that she buried an axe into his skull one night while he slept.

Becky Cotton was caught this time and taken to court. However, the all-male jury was enamored by her beauty and acquitted her despite her guilt. In fact, one juror, Major Eliss, was so taken with her that he ended up marrying her. A few years later, on May 5, 1807, Becky's brother, Stephen Kennedy, became enraged by his sister's apparent lack of remorse for her past actions. As she stood chatting on the steps of the Edgefield County Courthouse in the middle of the town square, he picked up a rock, rushed toward her, and struck her in the head, killing her.

Since then, she has haunted the area around the town square where the old courthouse once stood, wandering about in search of a new companion. So, gentlemen, please be cautious! If you're not careful, you may join the spirits of those men she killed, who haunt the area of Slade Lake, between Beaverdam Creek and the lake, howling and moaning in pain.

Haunting Shorts of South Carolina:

- A mysterious ghostly figure appeared before severe storms and hurricanes on Pawleys Island in South Carolina, known for its beaches and sand dunes. The legend of the Gray Man has been part of local folklore since at least 1822 when he was first reported to have been seen. His appearances serve as a warning to residents of impending danger. Locals who encounter him tend to be the lucky ones, as their homes are often spared from damage. This was the case for Clara and Jim Moore, who recounted their sighting of the Gray Man on television after Hurricane Hugo struck in 1989. The most widely acknowledged story about the Gray Man involves a young man traveling from Charleston to visit his fiancée in 1822. While on his journey, he drowned in quicksand-like pluff mud in the marshes near Pawleys Island. After his death, it is said that his spirit began to haunt the area, appearing on the beach as a harbinger, forewarning others about approaching storms. He has been described as wearing a long coat or gray clothing, and at times, he is seen without legs.

- The USS Yorktown, a famous aircraft carrier, was built for the United States Navy and launched in 1943. It played a crucial role during World War II and continued to serve in the Vietnam War. Today, the ship is part of the Patriots Point Naval and Maritime Museum in South Carolina. Visitors claim to experience strange happenings on board, including sightings of soldiers, mysterious shadows, and eerie voices echoing throughout the ship.

- The Old City Jail in Charleston has a notorious history, having housed some of the most infamous criminals from its opening in 1802 until its closure in 1939. One of these notorious figures associated with the jail is Lavinia Fisher.

Fisher and her husband, John, lived outside Charleston at the Six Mile Wayfarer's House. In February 1819, Lavinia and her husband were arrested for assault with intent to murder during a robbery. They were eventually apprehended, tried, and convicted of these crimes. Both were executed by hanging in 1820. Before her execution, Lavinia's last words to a preacher who wanted to comfort her were, "I will have none of it. Save your words for those who want them. But if you have a message you wish to send to Hell, give it to me; I'll carry it." Today, Lavinia haunts the Old City Jail, where she was imprisoned prior to her execution. Visitors have reported various supernatural occurrences, including unexplained cold spots and an unsettling feeling among those who enter the jail.

• Oakwood Cemetery in Spartanburg, often called Hell's Gate, was founded in the late 1800s and has a complex history, including the relocation of over 100 graves in 1914 for new developments. This has led to beliefs that the spirits are disturbed. Visitors report hearing children's laughter, seeing orbs among the graves, and experiencing equipment failures like cell phones dying while there.

• At Springwood Cemetery in Greenville, there is a notable ghost known as Fannie Heldman. Fannie was only 26 years old when she, overwhelmed by despair, attempted to take her own life just before her unwanted marriage to a local attorney. Initially, she was saved and confined to her room, but she managed to escape and ran to the Reedy River, where she drowned herself at a spot known as Ten Foot Hole. Despite local reports claiming the river was shallow enough for her to kneel and keep her head above water, she succumbed. Fannie is buried in the Heldman section of the cemetery, and visitors have reported seeing a white mist nearby, which is believed to be her spirit.

A South Carolina Cryptid

Lizard Man

In the swamplands of Lee County, a creature known as the Lizard Man has attracted attention since it was first reported in the 1980s. This phenomenon began with an account from Christopher Davis, a local resident who experienced a shocking encounter while changing a flat tire on his vehicle. Davis described the Lizard Man as a seven-foot-tall creature characterized by red eyes, three fingers on each hand, and green scales. According to his testimony, the creature jumped onto his car, prompting him to quickly retreat inside and drive away.

Following Davis's encounter, more residents stepped forward, sharing similar sightings and experiences, which fueled growing interest in the Lizard Man legend. Investigations conducted in the area uncovered footprints surrounding local homes, lending further credibility to these claims. The Lizard Man is noted for its aggressive behavior towards vehicles, with reports indicating instances of mirror removal and damage to car roofs. The combination of eyewitness accounts and physical evidence continues to captivate public interest in this mysterious creature.

South Dakota
Deadwood's Return of Calamity Jane

Deadwood, South Dakota, is a historic town in the Black Hills. It gained fame for its rich mining history. It began in 1876 when it became a bustling hub for miners and prospectors searching for fortune during the American Gold Rush. The town was notorious for its lawlessness, drawing various colorful characters, including outlaws, gamblers, and notable figures from the Wild West era. It was characterized by a rough-and-tumble atmosphere, with brothels, saloons, and gambling houses lining the streets.

During its early years, the lack of formal law enforcement resulted in significant crime and violence. One notable figure drawn to Deadwood during this tumultuous time was Martha Jane Canary, known as Calamity Jane. She was born on May 1, 1852, and arrived in Deadwood during the height of the gold rush. Calamity Jane was the eldest of six siblings, born to parents who had migrated from Missouri to the gold fields of Montana. After her parents passed away when she was just 14, she took on the responsibility of caring for her younger brother and sisters until she could find them suitable homes. Afterward, Martha made her way alone among the Union Pacific Railroad construction camps and military posts and finally to Deadwood at the height of the Black Hills gold rush.

This is when Martha gained notoriety for her adventurous spirit and larger-than-life persona known for her foul language, drinking, and donning men's clothing. She became known as Calamity Jane, a name some believe she earned because she would bring disaster to anyone who made her angry. Calamity Jane claimed to have participated in military campaigns against Native Americans around 1872-73. She said she earned her name after saving Captain Egan during an ambush. During this time, she boasted of heroic exploits, including riding alongside famous figures like Wild Bill Hickok.

Beginning in 1877, Edward Wheeler wrote about her daring exploits in at least 10 dime novels, which made her a household name, mainly through the series known as the 'Deadwood Dick' stories. These novels were a popular form of entertainment in the late 19th century; they were often serialized and sold at a low price, making them accessible to a broad audience. In Deadwood, she gained increasing fame and capitalized on it through storytelling and public appearances in Wild West shows and exhibitions.

As she got older and her fame began to die away, she struggled with alcoholism and financial instability, dying on August 1, 1903, near Deadwood, South Dakota. Her burial site is in Mount Moriah Cemetery.

Calamity Jane has been seen returning to her old haunts in ghostly form. She has been spotted walking the streets of Deadwood and near her grave. Alongside her in these spectral antics is Wild Bill Hickok, another legendary figure from the same era. Hickok was well-known for gambling and numerous shootouts, further enhancing his reputation through exaggerated tales of his adventures. He was shot and killed on August 2, 1876, while playing poker in Deadwood, famously holding what is now called the "dead man's hand"—two pairs of black aces and eights. His grave is located next to Calamity Jane's.

Haunting Shorts of South Dakota:

- Laura Ingalls Wilder was an author famous for her "Little House" series of children's books, based on her childhood experiences growing up in a pioneer family. In 1879, Laura and her family moved to the De Smet area in Dakota Territory, where they established a homestead that became central to her stories. During the winter, the family lived in the Surveyor House before moving to their homestead in 1880. Some visitors to this historic site have reported experiencing unusual phenomena, such as cold spots and mysterious shadows, leading to whispers that it might be a little haunted by Ma and Pa Ingalls.

- The Lewis and Clark Expedition began in 1804 to explore the newly acquired Louisiana Territory. During their journey, they visited Spirit Mound, located near present-day Vermillion. They had been informed that this mound was a "mountain of evil spirits," a "hill of little people," and a "place of devils." The Sioux, Omaha, and Otoe tribes conveyed stories about 18-inch-tall beings with "remarkably large heads" that inhabited the site. Legends tell of fierce spirits that, armed with sharp arrows, would launch their attacks on anyone daring enough to approach the hill. Their wrath was swift and unyielding, guarding the secrets of that sacred ground with an eerie intensity.

- Devil's Gulch, near Garretson, South Dakota, is tied to the legend of Nellie Harding and her fiancé, Dick Willowby. According to folklore, Nellie was kidnapped by outlaws and taken to the gulch. Dick traveled from Wisconsin to rescue her, confronting the kidnappers and managing to kill most of them but ultimately losing his life alongside Nellie. Since then, their spirits haunt the area, with eerie screams and reflections seen in the water.

• The Pactola Reservoir near Rapid City is the largest and deepest reservoir in the Black Hills National Forest. Many years ago, a fisherman fell through the ice during winter and lost his life. After his body was recovered and laid to rest, his ghost was reportedly seen fishing by the waters with a contented smile. Fishermen sometimes feel a strong tug on their lines, but when they reel in their catch, there is no fish on the hook!

• John Leary was born in 1849 in Newburgh, New York. At 16, he left home searching for gold and traveled to the Black Hills, specifically to the Old Grand Junction Mine in Custer City. While there, he was warming up frozen explosives with his hands when they exploded. After this accident, he became known for the special hooks he had made to replace the hands he lost. John had a unique way of moving, characterized by shuffling steps, and he would greet those he passed with cheerful "good mornings." He served as the night watchman in Rapid City for 41 years and earned the nickname "Hooky Jack." The citizens of Rapid City admired him greatly. One incident involving Hooky Jack occurred when some mischievous boys hung him up by his hooks one night. When he was discovered, the boys were spanked publicly in the street. Hooky Jack had an old terrier named Rags who was so blind that he kept his head against the cuff of Jack's pants to keep track of him. Hooky Jack died at the age of 77 on a chilly November day in 1926 after being run over by a motor car on Main Street near the fire station. However, Hooky Jack's spirit still returns. His ghostly apparition is reported to appear along his old route, accompanied by the footsteps and the click of him checking doorknobs to ensure they are safely locked for the night.

A Cryptid of South Dakota

Walking Sam

The unsettling legend of "Walking Sam" comes from the Pine Ridge Indian Reservation, where there has been a troubling increase in youth suicides. Walking Sam is a 7-foot-tall figure resembling a bogeyman who has no mouth and preys on vulnerable teens, telling them they are worthless. When he raises his arms, he shows them the bodies of previous victims hanging beneath so they do not feel alone. He convinces them that life is not worth living and collects their souls. Some believe he is the manifestation of the Lakota people slaughtered near Wounded Knee Creek during a massacre on December 29, 1890.

A Cryptid of South Dakota
Taku-He

The Taku-He resembles Bigfoot and is reported to inhabit Sica Hollow State Park and the Pine Ridge Reservation. According to various descriptions, Taku-He typically stands between 7 and 9 feet tall and has a robust body covered in dark brown or black fur. Its head is notably large, with a flat face, small ears, and a pronounced brow ridge. At night, its eyes glow red or yellow, contributing to its unsettling reputation.

Taku-He is characterized by long arms that extend down to its knees, comparatively short legs, and extremely large feet. It is known for its territorial aggression, often displaying this by mutilating animals and leaving their remains as markers. "Taku-He" translates to "big man" in the Lakota language. Sightings of this elusive creature peaked in the 1970s, prompting local authorities and tribal police to organize a large-scale hunt.

Tennessee
Pink Lizzie

Once, there was a mansion on Fifth Street in Memphis, built between 1855 and 1859 by Colonel Davie, who was the President of the Southern Bank of Tennessee. However, at the outbreak of the Civil War, he lost most of his money and sold the home. The mansion was then turned into Brinkley Female College, which opened in 1868. It was rumored to be haunted by Colonel Davie's spirit, who was believed to have gone insane after losing his fortune.

On February 21, 1871, a 13-year-old student named Clara Robertson was playing the piano alone in an upstairs room of the school when she encountered the ghostly figure of a gaunt little girl, about 8 years old. The apparition had dull, sunken eyes, scrawny arms that seemed like dried flesh over bones, and wore a dingy, tattered dress of faded pink, partly covered in a greenish slime and mold. She also had rusty shoes and mildewed stockings. The sight frightened Clara so much that she fled the room and jumped into the nearest bed. Although the ghostly girl floated toward her, she couldn't coax Clara to come out from beneath the covers.

Many were scared when Clara told her classmates and teachers about the ghostly girl. In contrast, others taunted her, raising concerns from her father regarding Clara's well-being and reputation at school. A few days later, while Clara was again in the music room with three other classmates, the ghostly girl appeared again. The ghost materialized as mere shadows to her classmates, but to Clara, she was as clear as any other child. On a third visit, while a teacher was present, the little apparition pointed a scrawny finger at Clara and told her that valuables were buried beneath a tree in the backyard and that she could have them if she found them. Although Clara heard the words clearly, they sounded like garbled nonsense to the teacher.

During the fourth encounter, the ghost revealed to Clara that the property was rightfully hers as she was an heir and the last to have died; the property was obtained illegally. The ghost wanted Clara to retrieve the papers for her, warning that nothing good would come to the school without them. Clara's father sought help from a spiritual medium named Missus Nourse, who conducted a séance at their home. During the séance, Clara's mind was overtaken, and they learned that the spirit was named Lizzie.

Lizzie began transmitting messages about treasures buried beneath a tree stump on the school grounds. Encouraged by these revelations and the media attention surrounding the ghost story—dubbed "Pink Lizzie"—it was decided to dig up the yard where Clara indicated the hidden treasures. A crowd gathered to watch as Clara and her father dug for Pink Lizzie's buried treasure, which they found sealed in a jar, precisely as the spirit had predicted. However, they were told by the ghost that they must wait sixty days to open it, so Clara went to stay with relatives during the wait. Then, just a few days before they were to open the mysterious jar, it was stolen.

The Brinkley Female College soon closed, and the building fell into disrepair. Over the years, it has served many different purposes. The original mansion that housed these events no longer exists in its original form; it was demolished in the mid-20th century, around the 1950s or 1960s. It was later discovered that in 1861, a child of that age named Lizzie Davie had died at the home. There were indeed questionable practices leading up to the exchange of the estate's title.

Tennessee
The Bell Witch

In the 19th century, John Bell and his family moved to the Red River area in northwest Robertson County, Tennessee. Between 1817 and 1821, the Bell family began experiencing disturbances caused by a supernatural entity. John Bell reported seeing strange creatures on their farm, including a dog with the head of a rabbit. Inside their home, unusual occurrences began to happen, such as unexplained knocking noises, gnawing sounds coming from the beds, the yowls and growls of dogs, and voices that seemed to mimic those of family members.

John's youngest daughter, Betsy, became a particular target of the entity, experiencing slapping and pinching. During one of these encounters, the spirit allegedly revealed its identity as "Kate," claiming to be the witch of a neighbor named Kate Batts. As word of the haunting spread, the entity intensified its actions, pulling sheets off beds while the children slept and assaulting Betsy so severely that she lost consciousness.

The spirit even predicted John Bell's death for December 20, 1820, and a vial containing a mysterious liquid was discovered beside his deathbed. After his passing, the intensity of the haunting decreased significantly and eventually ceased altogether. The house fell into ruin, but the story of the Bell family's experiences continues to be a part of American folklore.

Tennessee
Lost Lucy

On a chilly autumn night in the early 1900s, a young man named Foster traveled by horseback from Gatlinburg to his modest mountain cabin. The darkness was pierced only by the light of a full moon, which illuminated his path. He followed an old country road that wound alongside the Roaring Fork stream, passing through the quiet community of Spruce Flats.

A young girl suddenly appeared before him as he rode beside the stream. Startled, Foster gasped. He immediately noticed she was barefoot and wore a plain white muslin gown.

Foster kindly offered her a ride, and she accepted. As she sat upon the horse in front of him, he could not help but catch the scent of woodsmoke in her hair, so he knew she must have recently been by the fire. They rode together until the girl abruptly seized the reins, halted the horse, and jumped off the saddle, darting into the woods.

Deciding that the girl must be near home, Foster lingered for a moment before continuing on his way back to his own cabin. Curiosity eventually drew him back to the spot where he had seen the girl, and he followed the path along the Roaring Fork to a small cabin nestled in the woods.

Before he could knock, the door swung open. However, the young woman did not appear; instead, an elderly man and woman stood before him. Foster introduced himself and related his encounter with the mysterious girl. The man nodded in response. "That would be our daughter, Lucy," he said softly, and Foster's heart raced at the revelation, even as he noticed the sadness in the man's eyes.

"You are not the only one who has picked her up," the man continued. "But she has been dead for ten years. You see, she was killed when our cabin by the creek burned down. We could not bear to stay at the location where our only child lost her life, so we rebuilt further up the Roaring Creek. When she sees riders pass, she sometimes seeks them out, hoping to find us."

There have been others who have encountered the hitchhiking ghost of Lucy. Perhaps as you drive along the Roaring Fork Motor Nature Trail at the Great Smoky Mountains National Park in Tennessee, you will see a young woman waving for your attention. It will be your choice to pick her up or not!

Haunting Shorts of Tennessee:

• Elkmont, a one-time logging community and resort destination, can now be explored as the National Park Service continues restoring the buildings and maintaining outlying roads as trails. Those entering the almost abandoned town should know that some of those who once lived or vacationed here do not want to leave—even after death, including an old man who drowned in Jake's Creek in 1914.

• In 1825, Tink McCoy built a gristmill for grinding dried corn into meal along Lyons Spring Branch, now located within Big Ridge State Park. Later, he passed the business on to Lewis Norton and his sons. However, during the 1930s, with the creation of Norris Lake, the Civilian Conservation Corps moved the mill and used parts of it to construct a replica at Big Ridge State Park, not far from the entrance. Occasionally, a little girl is seen crying at the gristmill, but when approached, she vanishes. Even a park ranger tried to comfort her before she disappeared.

• Many years ago, farming families formed small communities that populated the area now known as Big Ridge State Park. In the early 1930s, when the Tennessee Valley Authority built Norris Dam on the Clinch River, the government forced about 99 nearby families to relocate. These families had to leave behind their homes, land, and towns. Maston and Martha Hutchinson settled in the area in the 1800s and established a farm there. Their grown daughter, Nancy, contracted tuberculosis and was cared for in the home before she passed away. During her wake, old-timers recalled that mourners heard a woman crying from the upstairs bedroom where Nancy died. Years later, after the home was vacated, travelers refused to ride past the old house due to the eerie sounds that emanated from within.

It became known as Ghost House, and even today, a sign marks the ruins of the home. Maston and Martha both died about a month apart in 1910 and are buried in Norton Cemetery along with some of their family and neighbors. Witnesses have reported seeing those buried in the graveyard rise and stand near their graves.

• In Petros, Tennessee, Brushy Mountain State Penitentiary was a high-security prison that housed notorious inmates like James Earl Ray, the assassin of Dr. Martin Luther King, Jr. It closed in 2009 but is open for tourists wishing to rub elbows with some incredibly evil dead people. Visitors often describe being watched or overwhelming dread inside the prison.

• The Bijou Theatre in Knoxville has a rich history dating back to 1817. Over the years, it has served various purposes, including that of a hotel and a Civil War hospital. General Sanders, a Union officer during the Civil War, died from his wounds in the bridal suite of what was then known as The Lamar Hotel. He appears, dressed in a Civil War uniform, on the balcony where the bridal suite used to be.

• The Grand Ole Opry, located in the historic Ryman Auditorium, is known for its intriguing history, including ghostly sightings. Notably, the spirit of its founder, Thomas Ryman, lingers within the venue, along with the ghost of legendary country musician Hank Williams, Sr., who is often associated with the area near the stage. Visitors to the Opry frequently share experiences of disembodied footsteps and unexpected cold spots, which many attribute to the presence of these spectral figures.

A Tennessee Cryptid

White Bluff Screamer

In the hollows of Trace Creek near White Bluff, a family lived in a remote cabin with the father, his wife, and their seven children. The children constantly complained about strange noises that resembled high-pitched screams, similar to those of a frightened young girl. Night after night, these noises grew louder, and soon, no one in the house could sleep. Frustrated, the father decided to rid the woods of whatever creature was causing the family such distress.

One night, he ventured deeper into the woods, following the sounds through the trees until, at last, they abruptly stopped. Frustrated, he returned home only to find his family had been torn to shreds within the cabin. Although the entity was never discovered, it was unmistakably branded as the White Bluff Screamer.

Texas
Servant Girl Annihilator

Between 1884 and 1885, a series of brutal murders occurred in Austin, Texas. Shocking and violent, a serial killer targeted young women, primarily those who were poor and worked as servants. This unknown assailant was given the name "Servant Girl Annihilator." Eight victims were claimed: seven women and one man, all attacked indoors while asleep and dragged outside. One of the victims was Eula Burditt, who married James Phillips at age 14. Their marriage was tumultuous, and they initially lived with James's family. Eula gave birth to a baby boy in 1884.

In 1885, James found a job on the farm of George McCutcheon, which brought the family a brief period of stability. However, Eula became pregnant with the farmer's child, and the pregnancy was terminated. At the end of the year, Eula and James returned to Austin, once again living with James' parents. By this time, James was unemployed and drinking heavily. During this period, Eula began an affair with a wealthy man named John Dickinson, the Secretary of the Capital Board. She would meet him discreetly at an assignation house, a rental place for romantic but forbidden encounters. However, after a short time, family members convinced Eula to move back in with James and his family, as he had found employment and stopped drinking.

On Christmas Eve, while everyone was asleep in the house, Eula snuck out to the boarding house where she had previously met her lover. None of the rooms were available when she arrived, so Eula left and returned home. Her body was found in the early hours of Christmas morning, 1885. She had been attacked while sleeping beside her 23-month-old son and husband in her in-law's home. James had been struck with an ax and was unconscious. The baby was sound asleep with an apple tucked into his arms. Eula's body was discovered outside; her face had been upturned and contorted in an expression of agony, her skull bashed in by an axe.

Eula's husband was initially found guilty of murdering her. He was later released when authorities determined that Eula was one of the victims involved in the serial killings. This string of murders came to an end on the night Eula was killed. The actual killer was never identified. But that was when Eula's ghost began to appear in Oakwood Cemetery in Austin, her face contorted as if she were still in the agonizing state of death, forever trying to escape from her killer, who was never brought to justice.

Texas
Weeping Woman of Galveston

Elize (Lizzie) Romer Alberti lived with her husband, Louis, and their eight children at the corner of 44th and Winnie Streets in Galveston. Their home was connected to a popular butcher shop, which Louis operated with his brother-in-law. Life seemed normal for the family until tragedy struck when their first-born child, Louis, died of lockjaw at the age of seven. Following this loss, the family noticed that Lizzie began to behave strangely. Less than a year later, she experienced the death of her 15-year-old sister, Dorothea, who succumbed to lung congestion. To compound the grief, their youngest daughter, Caroline, less than a year old, also died.

Lizzie's mental state deteriorated rapidly after these events, and she became increasingly unbalanced, sometimes exhibiting violent behavior. Overwhelmed by thoughts of death and mourning, she briefly stayed with her parents before returning home. On December 4, 1894, she called her young children into the dining room and offered them sips of wine. Louis joined in, unaware that Lizzie was using a different bottle for her drink than the one she had shared with the children. When one of the children commented that their mother had poisoned the beverage, Louis reassured her that it was okay and returned to work. It was late, so the children were sent to bed.

Seven-year-old Lizzie then carried out her 3-year-old sibling, who had fallen ill on the floor. She was also unwell and brought it to her father's attention. When Louis turned to his wife, who was sitting calmly in her chair, she smugly replied that she had put morphine in the wine. The doctor was called, but tragically, he could not save the children. 10-year-old Ella, 8-year-old Lizzie, 6-year-old Dora, and 4-year-old Willie all succumbed to the poison. Only 16-year-old Emma recovered, and 14-year-old Wilhelmina avoided drinking the tainted wine.

Just eight days later, a court declared Lizzie insane, and she was committed to an asylum in San Antonio. Years later, she died from a morphine overdose and is buried alongside her children at the Old City Cemetery. Even in death, her spirit roams; passersby have long been stunned to see a phantom woman wandering the grave, forever mourning the loss of what could have been.

Haunting Shorts of Texas:

• Ghost Road, also known as Bragg Road, is a dirt road near Saratoga, Texas, stretching approximately 7.8 miles. It was built around 1901 as a railroad spur for the Santa Fe Line, connecting Bragg Station to Saratoga during the East Texas oil boom. This line was used to transport local goods and workers. However, by 1934, the tracks were removed, and the area became a dirt road. Since the early 1900s, a mysterious light has been reported along this route. It is the spirit of a railroad worker who, while wandering the tracks with a lantern, was struck by a train.

• Caddo Lake, which spans the border between Texas and Louisiana, features a lake and a bayou with haunting, swamp-like characteristics. Eerie fog creeps around ancient cypress trees, and the air is thick with a mystical mist that envelops the winding bayous. At the edge of the water stands the slender Weeping Woman, her long, flowing hair concealing her face. Her tears fall into the lake, and soft cries fill the air. Local lore suggests that she is a woman who waited by the water daily for her lover to return from the Civil War, but he never did.

• In the desert of Marfa, Texas, mysterious glowing orbs known as "Ghost Lights" have been reported since 1883, when a cowhand named Robert Reed Ellison mistook them for Apache campfires. Eyewitnesses describe them as basketball-size orbs of light, appearing in colors such as white, yellow, blue, or red, dancing and floating across the landscape. The best location to view the Ghost Lights is along Highway 90, overlooking Mitchell Flat, 9 miles east of Marfa. Some speculate that these lights are caused by UFOs, the lost souls of Spanish conquistadors, an optical illusion, or even gases.

• A cruel Texas Ranger named Big Foot Wallace once beheaded an outlaw named Vidal and heartlessly tied his corpse to a wild Mustang, releasing it to the wild to warn other bandits. The unfortunate horse roamed the hills, instilling fear and impending doom in those who caught sight of it, its body bouncing atop it as it frightened travelers. Eventually, ranchers captured the Mustang in Ben Bolt, Texas, and removed its decayed body. Although the horse was freed, the headless ghost of the Vidal continued to haunt the hills.

• Lindsey Hollow Road, located in Waco, Texas, has ghosts in a pretty little park along the Brazos River adorned with rock-strewn hillocks and woods. During the 1870s and 1880s, the area was saturated with horse thieves and cattle rustlers. Law enforcement and vigilante groups were on constant watch for the robbers. According to legend, along the Brazos River, a rancher captured two notoriously thieving brothers with the last name of Lindsey. A fight occurred, and the brothers were shot; one of them was dragged from the road and buried quickly in a grave along the creek. The grave was too shallow, so the ghostly form of the man rose, haunting the hollow and the river shore nearby. Flickering lights and moans are heard along Lindsey Hollow Road near Cameron Park.

• The USS Lexington is an aircraft carrier that served during World War II. It played a significant role in naval operations, including numerous airstrikes against Japanese positions. Today, the ship is used as a museum at Corpus Christi Bay. Its long history includes many battles during which many sailors lost their lives, including one sailor in a white Navy uniform who was killed in a kamikaze attack in 1944. There have also been sightings of the spirit of a Japanese pilot associated with the ship.

- The Alamo, originally known as Mission San Antonio de Valero, was a Spanish mission established in the early 18th century. It later transformed into a military fort that is most famous for its role in the Texas Revolution. During the Battle of the Alamo, which took place from February 23 to March 6, 1836, a small group of Texan defenders, led by William Barret Travis, fought against a much larger Mexican army commanded by General Santa Anna. The battle ended in defeat for the Texan forces. Today, visitors often report hearing strange noises, feeling cold spots, and seeing shadowy figures of those who lost their lives during the battle, including one soldier seen running across the roof.

- The Lost Cemetery of Infants, also known as Berachah Cemetery, is a historic burial ground in Arlington, Texas. It was established by Reverend Upchurch alongside his rescue mission and orphanage for unwed mothers. Some children, including infants, passed away while living there and were never claimed by their families. At a time when unwed women faced significant stigma, the mission provided a safe refuge for both mothers and their children. This cemetery remains a poignant reminder of that mission, with as many as 80 graves marking the final resting places of those who died, numerous of whom were infants who had not even received names. The cemetery is haunted; visitors report hearing the soft sounds of a newborn crying, and a young woman's ghostly figure has been seen mourning over a grave.

A Texas Cryptid
Chupacabra

The Texas Chupacabra is a cryptid that gained fame from attacking livestock, typically goats or cows, and mutilating them, sometimes even sucking the blood entirely out of its prey. It is generally described as being about the size of a small bear with a pronounced backbone, hairless, with a row of spines or quills extending from its neck to its tail.

The Chupacabra is often depicted with long, sharp fangs and large red eyes, accompanied by a distinctive, screeching noise. It has sometimes been seen hopping like a kangaroo. This legend first emerged in Puerto Rico during the 1990s but has since expanded to various regions, including Texas, where numerous sightings have been documented over the past century.

Utah
A Utah Ghost Story

In September 1884, Jeremiah Reagan leased the Kennedy Saloon in Alta. In October 1884, after closing his saloon, Reagan went to bed in another part of the building. During the night, he was suddenly awakened by the feeling of being watched. When he slowly opened his eyes, he saw a ghost who introduced himself as Edward Crocket, with snow melting from his clothes. Crocket instructed Reagan to dig near a post in the cellar, claiming he would find a purse of money and some important letters. Then, he vanished.

Thinking someone was playing a prank on him, Reagan sprang up and lit a candle, but the form had disappeared. He spent the rest of the night unable to sleep, and the following day, he gathered enough courage to dig in the basement. However, after several hours of searching with a shovel, Reagan found nothing. Later that day, feeling more determined, he decided to dig again in the cellar. Sure enough, he discovered the purse, which contained 75 dollars and the letters and contact information, buried beneath the ground.

When Reagan contacted Crocket's associates, a chill ran down his spine. Snow slides, commonly known as avalanches, can be extremely dangerous in Utah, especially during the winter season and in the Wasatch Mountains. In the late 1800s, a man named Edward Crocket was killed in a snowslide near Alta, Utah, and his body was never found. He had left money and important papers in a secret location. Still, he failed to tell anyone where he had hidden them, and his friends could not find them. They confirmed that Reagan's description of the ghostly figure and his clothing matched what Crocket had been wearing on the day he died.

Haunting Shorts of Utah:

• Latuda, located seven miles west of Helper, was established in August 1917 by Francisco Latuda and Charles Picco to develop the Liberty Mine, part of the Liberty Fuel Company. The town flourished as a mining community at the turn of the century. However, in 1927, an avalanche swept through the area, resulting in the deaths of several residents. Although the land is privately owned, the vacant buildings can be seen from the road, and those passing by might glimpse a ghost. A woman in white, possibly the wife of a miner killed in the disaster, wanders among the buildings before vanishing.

• Mercur is located about 25 minutes west of Tooele and is the site of an abandoned mining town that once thrived until a fire in 1902 nearly destroyed it. The cemetery remains feature picket fences protecting the graves. Visitors have reported seeing a ghostly little girl and a phantom horseman who rides through the cemetery at night.

• There is a widely circulated story at Southern Utah University about Virginia Loomis, who was murdered by her boyfriend, Steven Farr, in a quarry near Cedar City in the late 1800s. Her body was found on a boulder with a huge amount of blood flowing on it. Farr fled the scene before he could be arrested. Years later, he returned and took a job as the janitor at the college. In 1948, while shoveling coal into the furnace in the cellar of Old Main, the furnace door suddenly slammed shut on his arm, igniting a fire. He burned to death beside the furnace. After investigations, it was discovered that the quarry stone from which Loomis had been murdered was used to build Old Main, with her blood mixed into the sandstone. Despite Virginia's payback, many report hearing ghostly footsteps and seeing a shadow near the belfry.

• Clarkston is a town in Cache County, Utah. Between Clarkston and Weston, Idaho, there is a desolate stretch of hills and farms known as The Washboards. Farmers began cultivating this land in the early 1900s. To obtain title to 160 acres, these settlers were required to live on the land for five years. The cabins they built were sparsely located and quite remote. One notable farm was situated along Birch Creek and was owned by the Seamons family. In 1872, the husband passed away, leaving his wife, Allie, alone. After a year of coping with loneliness and isolation, Allie took her life in August 1873. Since then, local farmers have reported seeing her ghost walking the fields north of Clarkston, often returning home before dusk to avoid encountering her spirit.

• Witnesses have reported sightings of a phantom steam locomotive at Golden Spike National Historical Park. This fascinating phenomenon has captured the attention of both visitors and historians, adding an element of mystery to the park's rich railroad history.

A Utah Cryptid
Skinwalker

Skinwalkers, referred to in Navajo culture as "yee naaldlooshii," which translates to "by means of it, it goes on all fours," are considered malevolent witches believed to possess the ability to transform into animals or control them. They are found typically in Texas and Arizona but also in Utah. These entities generally are seen as harmful and are shrouded in an air of fear and mystery. Individuals who claim to have encountered Skinwalkers often recount experiences involving shapeshifting and other supernatural abilities that these beings exhibit.

In Texas, the adaptation of Skinwalker lore incorporates indigenous beliefs along with local storytelling traditions. A notable account involves a Navajo family traveling home late one night along a remote road. They encountered what they first thought was an unusual coyote. However, as they drove past, the creature stood upright and shifted into a human-like form. Despite their desperate attempts to speed away, the figure kept pace with the vehicle, exhibiting glowing red eyes and a grin that seemed to mock their terror. Eventually, the family managed to turn onto another road, causing the entity to vanish, leaving them in a state of disbelief and fear.

Vermont
The Horrifying Bennington Triangle

The term "Bennington Triangle" was introduced by historian Joseph Citro, who noted a pattern of disappearances in the region and related it to the well-known Bermuda Triangle mystery. The Bennington Triangle and the Bermuda Triangle refer to geographic areas where many people have mysteriously vanished. This region encompasses parts of the towns of Bennington, Woodford, Shaftsbury, and Somerset, with a focus on Glastenbury Mountain. The area is well-known for its bizarre events and the unexplained vanishings of individuals who were familiar with the terrain.

From early on, strange lights, unusual odors, and untraceable sounds were reported in the region. Glastenbury, now a ghost town, was once a small community with a charcoal-making industry and a logging railroad in the 1800s, peaking at around 241 residents. It later struggled to become a resort but only lasted one season, as flooding destroyed the tracks, leading to the resort's closure. Many peculiar legends have emerged from this area and defy rational explanations.

During a drunken spree, 30-year-old William Conroy, also known as Henry McDowell, murdered fellow woodchopper John Crowley while working at a logging mill in Glastenbury. He struck Crowley violently with a rock or a stick. Afterward, he returned to his bunkhouse and mentioned that he had fought with Crowley and had "done him up." Later, Crowley was found with a crushed skull and succumbed to his injuries. Conroy confessed to the crime, explaining that he had been hearing strange voices. After fleeing the scene, he was eventually apprehended and sent to the Vermont State Asylum. While there, he was permitted to work around the property. At some point, while filling a coal car, he hid beneath a departing load and was never seen again.

While hunting in the woods of West Townshend in 1943, Carl Herrick did not return to the campsite he had used with his cousin, Forrest Hewitt. He was later found in a state that locals could only describe as being "squeezed to death by a bear." The man mysteriously had a punctured lung and was constricted to death. It was the only basis authorities could provide after noting the presence of bear tracks nearby.

On November 12, 1945, a 74-year-old outdoorsman named Middie Rivers was hunting in Bickford Hollow, about four miles from Bennington. He was seen leaving his hunting camp along the Long Trail but never returned. The only clue to his existence was a handkerchief found the following spring.

His disappearance was never solved.

Eighteen-year-old Paula Jean Weldon was a freshman at Bennington College when she left campus to hike on the Long Trail on December 1, 1946. She was last seen on Route 9 along the trail but never returned to campus. The FBI became involved in the search, but no trace of the woman was found.

On December 1, 1949, 68-year-old World War I veteran James Tedford vanished—three years to the day after Paula Welden's disappearance. After visiting relatives in St. Albans, he boarded a bus bound for Bennington. Witnesses believed they saw him get off the bus in Brandon, but he never returned home. Initially, his disappearance went unreported until administrators at the Vermont Soldiers' Home raised concerns about his absence.

On Columbus Day in 1950, 8-year-old Paul Jepson, a member of a local farming family in Bennington, was sitting in his family's pickup truck while his mother checked on some pigs. When she returned, he had disappeared. Legends suggest that search and rescue dogs last picked up his scent in the exact location where Paula Jean Weldon had vanished.

Frieda Langer, a 53-year-old woman, disappeared in 1950 while hiking near the Somerset Reservoir. After stepping into a stream, she decided to return to camp to change her clothes. She told her cousin to continue without her, assuring him she would catch up later. Unfortunately, her cousin never saw her again. Seven months later, her decomposed body was discovered along the Deerfield River, over 3.5 miles from the campsite.

Some believe that supernatural entities are responsible for the mysterious disappearances, whispering gibberish into people's ears until they drive them to madness. Even experienced hikers have reported getting lost in the area, overwhelmed by a dizzying confusion along the trail.

Others recount tales of the Man-Eating Rock of Glastenbury, which traps unsuspecting souls. Native Americans warned people to stay away, describing a massive rock large enough for someone to stand on. However, when a person does stand upon it, the rock becomes less solid and, like a living being, swallows the hapless victim. Whatever lures people in—rarely releasing and often keeping them to itself—remains unfound.

Adding to the mystery, strange stone cairns are atop Glastenbury Mountain. However, the reason for their existence remains unclear. Norman Muller and other specialists conducted extensive studies on these cairns. He proposed that they were created by Native Americans prior to the 18th century before white settlers arrived in the region. However, the purpose of these structures and the reason they were built at such a high altitude are still unknown.

Vermont
Looming Ghost

In the early 1900s, a ghostly figure began appearing in a cotton factory, working at a loom while emitting eerie groans and moans. Her story is as follows: In June 1900, a tragic accident occurred at the Lakeside Avenue railway crossing in Burlington, Vermont. Twenty-two-year-old Marie Blais was struck and killed by a train. She had previously worked at the nearby Queen City Cotton Mill. A train approached as she walked along the tracks, and she could not get out of the way. At that time, safety measures were minimal; there were no flashing lights or signals to warn pedestrians of approaching trains, and many people used the tracks for easier access between locations.

Not long after the accident, passersby were startled to see Marie's ghostly figure inside the cotton mill at night, working her loom under the flickering light of the train. With every movement, she emitted moans and groans. Even more disturbingly, many witnesses reported seeing her corpse illuminated in the headlights of trains on the old tracks, disappearing as the train passed. Her ghostly tale spread through the newspapers, and eventually, an underpass was constructed near the cotton mill to protect the nearly 500 workers who frequently crossed the tracks.

Haunting Shorts of Vermont:

• Emily's Bridge, officially known as Gold Brook Covered Bridge, is in Stowe and was built in 1840 near the site of an old sawmill. In the 1850s, a young woman named Emily was in love with a wealthy man, but his family forbade their union. The couple decided to elope and planned to meet at the bridge at midnight. However, while Emily waited for her love, he never showed up. She took her life on the bridge, and since then, her ghost has haunted it, unleashing her anger on those who cross.

• Green Mount Cemetery, in Montpelier, Vermont, was established in the 19th century. It is celebrated for its picturesque landscape and the notable figures buried within its grounds. One of its most famous features is the Black Agnes statue, which marks the grave of John E. Hubbard, who passed away in 1899. The statue was inspired by a work titled "Grief." Despite its name suggesting a female figure, Black Agnes represents Thanatos, the personification of death in Greek mythology. John Hubbard inherited a fortune from his aunt, which led to controversy, as he was reluctant to fully honor her wishes regarding charitable contributions. His adversary, a man named Burgess, was so enraged that on the night Hubbard died, July 17, 1899, he remarked that a tremendous hurricane-like storm burst from the sky, causing houses to tremble. The lightning was so bright it seemed like daylight, and the "incessant roar of thunder was like the discharge of a thousand cannon." By daybreak, the storm had ceased, and the "tragedy of that life was ended." As a result, the statue has gained a reputation for being cursed or haunted. According to legend, anyone who dares to sit on Black Agnes's lap at midnight during a full moon will face dire consequences—specifically, death within seven days and misfortune befalling seven of their friends.

• Cars traveling along Vermont Route 14, which runs parallel to the White River near West Hartford, will pass beneath a rusty railroad trestle that crosses over the river. Few would realize that this spot marks the site of a horrific train wreck that occurred at 2:10 a.m. on February 5, 1887, if it weren't for the plaque on the roadside commemorating the tragedy. On that fateful day, the last car of the Montreal Express derailed. Three cars plunged from the bridge and fell into the icy waters below. Embers from the coal stoves used to heat the cars ignited, engulfing the train in flames. Tragically, 25 passengers and 5 crew members lost their lives that night. The Hartford Railroad Disaster was so horrific that it garnered national attention. The disaster left lasting impacts on the community and a few haunting echoes. Locals sometimes catch the faint scent of burning in the air on certain nights, and a lonely figure in uniform has been seen wandering along the tracks in the evening. One notable survivor was Joseph Maigret, a thirteen-year-old French-Canadian boy who escaped through a window. Unfortunately, his father, Dieudonne, was not so lucky; he was pinned in the wreckage and lived long enough to attempt to retrieve his purse to give to his son while also conveying a tragic farewell to his wife as the flames closed in around him. Witnesses occasionally report seeing a solitary boy standing in the middle of the river, believed to be Joseph, reliving the horrifying memory of that night.

• Amid Evergreen Cemetery on Town Hill Road in New Haven, there is an unremarkable squarish concrete slab. However, what lies beneath is quite unusual: the tomb of Timothy Clark Smith, who died in 1893. Concerned about the possibility of being buried alive, Smith was interred in a specially designed tomb that features a plate glass window above a tube, allowing his face to be visible below.

Additionally, he was buried with a bell in his hand so he could signal for help if needed.

- The University of Vermont is haunted by several spirits. One of the notable apparitions is a female ghost dressed in 19th-century attire, known to appear randomly in Bittersweet House, which is part of the agriculture department.

- The Dutton House, built in 1782, is now located on the grounds of the Shelburne Museum. Over its long history, the house has witnessed at least 11 deaths and has served various purposes, including a store, inn, boarding house, and tavern. Staff members have reported sightings of an elderly man hiding under the roof slope and a young girl crying while wandering through the house during tours.

A Vermont Cryptid
Pigman

Vermont is known for its intriguing folklore, particularly surrounding legendary creatures that have captured the imagination of locals and visitors alike. One of the most famous is Champ, the Lake Monster of Lake Champlain. Described as a giant serpentine creature with a long neck and a humped back, Champ's legend has roots in the stories of indigenous tribes, including the Abenaki, who referred to it as "Gitaskog." Historical accounts date back to 1819 when a captain reported seeing a monstrous creature measuring an astonishing 187 feet in length.

Another notable creature is the Bennington Monster, first reported in the late 1940s and early 1950s in the Bennington area. This creature is described as a large, hairy figure reminiscent of an ape or a bear, and hikers have claimed to have been stalked by it in the woods.

Additionally, there is the Awful, a winged creature characterized by its gray skin, enormous claws, and a wingspan of around 20 feet. Sightings of this creature have been reported in the Berkshire and Richford regions.

Perhaps the most peculiar of these legends is the Pigman, a half-pig, half-human creature believed to inhabit rural areas near Northfield. Pigman is often described as having human-like features along with those of a pig, particularly a snout and ears. This unsettling appearance has led to numerous reported sightings, and the Pigman is frequently regarded as an omen of misfortune. These legends contribute to Vermont's rich tapestry of folklore and continue to intrigue those interested in the unusual and mysterious.

Virginia
Lost on Bluff Mountain

The Blue Ridge Parkway is a 469-mile National Parkway that winds through the Blue Ridge Mountains in Virginia and North Carolina, connecting Shenandoah National Park and Great Smoky Mountains National Park. Along its path is the ghost of a little boy who haunts a ridge along the trail in George Washington National Forest, Virginia. His story goes like this—

Edwin "Ed" Powell was a farmer and German Baptist Brethren preacher in the late 1800s near Pera, Virginia.

He and his wife, Emma Belle, had eight children, including their four-year-old son, Emmet. On a chilly morning, November 9, 1891, Emmet left for school with his siblings after asking to help his father, who was husking corn. Ed had a troubling dream the previous night, but he told Emmet to go to school.

Emmet attended a one-room schoolhouse with 25-year-old Nannie Ann Gilbert as the teacher. After a typical day of lessons, during a recess, Emmet wandered off to collect firewood and didn't return. Miss Gilbert quickly sent the boys to find him, but when they couldn't, the search spread throughout the community. Days passed, but all that was found was a trail where Emmet had dragged a chestnut branch. Nearly five months later, on April 3, four young men hiking Bluff Mountain discovered Emmet's lifeless body three and a half miles from where he went missing. The tragedy deeply affected the community and Ed Powell, who had searched relentlessly for his son.

A memorial was placed atop the mountain where Emmet's body was found. Later, the Appalachian Trail passed by it. Below is a shelter camp for hikers, Punchbowl Trail Shelter, built not far away so those taking the long trail could stop for respite for the night. It was then that more hikers came to the area, and whispers of a ghostly boy visiting the trail and shelter began to occur. He is witnessed standing near the camp, whimpering, before wandering away and trudging through the thick brush near the place where he laid down to rest and passed away.

Virginia
Killing Rock

Ira Mullins, a 35-year-old farmer and merchant, engaged in the illegal production and supply of alcohol in the mountains of eastern Kentucky and western Virginia. He often clashed with revenue agents, particularly Marshall Benton Taylor, who staunchly opposed liquor law violators and held grudges when wronged. Taylor lost his position as a U.S. Marshal after an altercation with Mullins, fueling his resentment toward the Mullins family. After a confrontation with revenue agents in which Mullins was shot, he was left paralyzed and unable to walk. Rumors began to circulate that Ira Mullins and other moonshiners were plotting to kill Taylor, placing a $300 bounty on his head, further agitating Taylor.

Fearing for his life, Ira Mullins and his family sought refuge with the Wilson Mullins family near Jenkins, Kentucky. After some time, they returned to Pound, Virginia, to gather their belongings. On the morning of May 14, 1892, the party set off across the mountain via the rugged Pound Gap, traveling along the Fincastle Trail. Ira lay in the back of a wagon on a hay pallet beside his wife, Louanza. She kept their thousand-dollar savings hidden in her clothing. 13-year-old John Chappel drove the two-horse wagon while Ira's sons—14-year-old John Harrison and Greenberry Harris—walked behind. Wilson and Jane Mullins accompanied them; Wilson walked ahead while Jane rode on horseback. The warm day brought budding leaves and birdsong. Still, gunfire erupted from nearby boulders where three masked men lay in ambush.

Within seconds, while the air filled with the reek of the gunshot, Ira Mullins lay dead with eight shots to his body. His wife was fired upon and died shortly after. Wilson ducked for cover, but the villains shot him dead. Two children, John Chappel and Greenberry Harris, were shot in the head and body. The massacre didn't last long; five people lay dead. Only two escaped: Jane and 14-year-old John Harrison Mullins.

Jane Mullins identified the killers as Marshall Benton Taylor, Calvin Fleming, and Samuel Fleming. Taylor was apprehended and sentenced to death, and on October 27, 1893, Marshall Benton Taylor was hanged. Calvin Flemings fled after the murders but was killed by bounty hunters in 1894. Samuel Fleming managed to escape.

Atop Pine Mountain, along a trail at Pound Gap, hikers can walk to a memorial near boulders marking the site where the family was massacred. This site is known as Killing Rock. The ghost of Marshall Benton Taylor, later called "Red Fox" due to his red hair and sly character, still lurks in the shadows of the mountains, waiting for someone to cross his path.

Haunting Shorts of Virginia:

• The Randolph-Peachy House is a historic house museum located in the heart of Colonial Williamsburg, at the northeast corner of Nicholson and North England Streets. This two-story structure has a reputation for being haunted. French General Marquis de Lafayette visited the house in 1824 and reported feeling a hand on his shoulder that nudged him away as if to prevent him from entering. When he turned around, no one was behind him. In the early 19th century, the Peachy family purchased the property. The ghost of Missus Peachy, depicted as a grieving, gaunt old woman, haunts the second floor, often seen wearing a flowing gown and a lace cap. The house was also utilized as a hospital for wounded soldiers during the Battle of Williamsburg in May 1862. Over time, numerous ghosts are believed to have made their presence known within the house, with at least 30 entities reported, including a child who fell from a window and another who fell from a tree. Visitors and staff have heard knocking and the giggles of children playing. In the 1970s, a security guard reported hearing moans from the cellar. When he went to investigate, the door slammed shut behind him and locked him inside.

• The Three Sisters are three rocky islands in the Potomac River in Washington, D.C., with a legend attached. Three Algonquian sisters crossed the river to win the release of their brothers abducted by another tribe. During their swim, they drowned and turned into stones.

• Edgewood Manor Plantation B & B is an 1849 plantation house built by Spencer Rowland. It is known for its tragic history, connected to a woman who carved her name into an upstairs window. The Rowland family moved to Virginia from New Jersey to run the old Harris Mill.

Their daughter, Lizzie, fell in love with the son of a neighboring plantation owner, who would ride his horse over to visit her. Lizzie could hear his horse's hooves as he approached, and she would stand by the window waiting. When the war broke out, he joined the Confederate Army and never returned. Heartbroken, Lizzie died within two years. In the days when people still rode horses along the road, the sound of hooves would bring her ghost to the window to look for her love. Even today, visitors to the old home occasionally report seeing her appear at the window, still waiting to see if her beloved soldier boy has returned.

• Explorer Tomas Walker led the first English expedition through Cumberland in 1750, noting key locations like Gap Cave. By 1819, the cave's spring powered sawmills and gristmills, contributing to the growth of Cumberland Gap. Workers later mined saltpeter within the cave. During the Civil War, Confederate and Union troops explored its depths, with King Solomon's Cave serving as a military area and Soldier's Cave as a hospital. After the war, some claimed a spirit stayed behind, described as a heavy-set man in a Confederate officer's attire, with a long gray beard and hollow eyes.

• Henry and Sarah Sarver built a two-story cabin around 1859 in a hollow beneath Sinking Creek Mountain, where they lived as mountain farmers for over seventy years. Today, only remnants of their old homestead remain. The Appalachian Trail runs nearby, and a camping shelter called Sarver Shelter is close to the old homestead. Hikers have reported hearing footsteps and voices, feeling someone shake them awake, and noticing rapping sounds on the shelter walls during the night while trying to sleep.

A Virginia Cryptid
Bunnyman

The infamous cryptids of Virginia would not be complete without an explanation of the Bunny Man. This urban legend emerged from two incidents in Fairfax County in 1970. This legend involves a man dressed in a rabbit costume who attacks people with an axe or hatchet, with incidents primarily occurring near the Colchester Overpass, a Southern Railway overpass. The Bunny Man is depicted as a life-sized figure wearing a white or light-colored bunny suit.

Another notable cryptid is Chessie, a serpent-like creature inhabiting Chesapeake Bay's waters. Reports of Chessie date back to the 1840s near what is now Virginia Beach.

Then there is the Snallygaster, described as a bird-reptile hybrid with enormous wings, a long-pointed bill, steel claws, and a single eye in the center of its forehead. First reported in 1909, the Snallygaster is believed to have flown to Virginia after being spotted in Maryland. It is often associated with the mountains and woods of the area, where it terrorizes the local population.

Washington
Ghoul of Grays Harbor, The Port of Missing Men

William "Billy" Gohl was an agent for the Sailors' Union of the Pacific, overseeing recruitment and union affairs in Aberdeen, Washington. Between 1908 and 1909, hollow-eyed, bloated bodies were discovered floating in Grays Harbor, leading to suspicions of his involvement in the deaths of numerous sailors in the area. Before tossing them into the waters weighted with an anchor, he was believed to also pilfered the money from their pockets.

Gohl was convicted of two murders in 1910, and newspapers accused him of being responsible for many more. However, some historians argue that Gohl was unjustly blamed for these deaths due to his strong advocacy for labor rights, along with the fact that the working conditions at Grays Harbor were perilous. The waterfront was notoriously dangerous, with numerous drownings resulting from drunkenness, falls from ships and log rafts, and a lack of regulations. Between 1905 and 1910, around 40 bodies were found floating near Aberdeen. As a result, Gohl became a notorious figure known as the "Ghoul of Grays Harbor," and the area was referred to as "The Port of Missing Men."

During Gohl's era, the riverfronts of the Chehalis and Wishkah Rivers were frequently occupied by lumber schooners and unfortunate sailors who met untimely deaths. It is believed that their ghosts continue to haunt the area. Today, the spirit of Billy Gohl, along with his murder victims, lingers in locations connected to his life and crimes, particularly around Aberdeen and its waterfront areas.

Washington
Lady of the Lake

Lake Crescent in Olympic National Park, Washington, is notorious for not releasing its dead from the chilly waters. However, at least two bodies have been retrieved from its cold, unyielding grasp. Both were in a unique state of decomposition. Due to the prolonged exposure to cold water, their body fat chemically converted flesh into a pulpy substance similar to soap called corpse wax. It tends to keep the body's shape while the tissues decompose.

One case involved the accidental death of a 23-year-old log truck driver who crashed into a lake west of Port Angeles. His soap-mummy body, preserved in an unusual condition, mysteriously reappeared six months later, around 1952.

Another tragic story is that of Hallie Illingworth, a 36-year-old waitress from Crescent Tavern who went missing after failing to show up for work on December 22, 1937. On July 6, 1940, nearly three years after her disappearance, two brothers fishing in Lake Crescent spotted a waxy gray body floating on the surface. Hallie's body was subsequently dubbed the "Lady of the Lake."

She was buried in an unmarked grave at Park Hill Cemetery. Her ex-husband, 36-year-old Monty Illingworth, was convicted of her strangulation, weighing her down, and dumping her into the water. Today, some visitors claim to catch glimpses of Hallie's ghostly figure floating in Lake Crescent. Still, she vanishes when they row across the water for a closer look.

Haunting Shorts of Washington:

- A stairway known as the Thousand Steps leads to Greenwood Cemetery in Spokane. This route is a dreary tunnel of brush that culminates at an old, dilapidated mausoleum. While walking up the steps, some visitors occasionally see ghostly figures just a few steps away, as if waiting to stop them from reaching the top. Once inside the cemetery, people have reported feeling touches from unseen spirits. The stairway, which is only about 60 steps long, has earned the nickname "Haunted Stairs."

- Hikers can explore a trail that leads to the ghost town of Monte Cristo, located at the headwaters of the South Fork Sauk River in the rugged mountains of eastern Snohomish County. This route follows the same path that gold and silver miners used during the mining boom of the 1890s. Those who hike to the ghost town often hear the voices of the long-gone miners, the sound of wood being chopped, and footsteps echoing within the cabins. Occasionally, full-body apparitions are even spotted.

- Pioneer Square was the heart of Seattle when the city was first settled. However, as the town grew, it became plagued by poverty and gangs. The Cadillac Hotel is located in this area. Originally opened as the Elliott House in 1890, the hotel was built after the Great Seattle Fire of 1889 and initially served as a lodging for laborers and transient workers. Over the years, it changed names several times and is now known for the ghostly activity of a single mother who, driven to despair, took her own life along with her child. This tragic history has led to reports of their crying spirits haunting the premises. Despite facing closure in the past, the Cadillac Hotel now serves as the permanent home for the Klondike Gold Rush National Historical Park.

• Northern State Hospital, located in Sedro-Woolley, Washington, opened in 1912 to address overcrowding in other mental health facilities. Although originally designed to provide therapeutic treatment, the hospital quickly became infamous for its harsh practices, including lobotomies and electroshock therapy. The Olmsted Brothers designed the facility with extensive grounds and various amenities. Today, the site is known as the Northern State Recreation Area, encompassing 1,086 acres of walking trails and recreational facilities. Remnants of the abandoned hospital still stand as haunting reminders of its past. Visitors to the area have reported strange occurrences, particularly at the cemetery that holds the remains of 1,487 individuals. Apparitions have been seen, and unexplained noises have been heard throughout the grounds. One visitor at the site saw the ghostly figure of an elderly man being pushed in a wheelchair by a nurse.

A Washington Cryptid
Sasquatch

The Tacoma Narrows Octopus is a notable marine creature weighing up to 600 pounds. It is linked to the legendary collapse of the Tacoma Narrows Bridge in 1940, which created underwater ruins that have become a habitat for various marine life. Many divers venture into these depths, hoping to encounter this elusive octopus.

Sasquatch is the most well-known figure in Washington State, boasting over 700 documented sightings in the realm of cryptids. Typically described as a massive, upright, ape-like being, Sasquatch is estimated to stand between 6 to 10 feet tall and weigh between 500 and 800 pounds.

This creature is usually covered in dark brown or reddish-brown fur. It is often associated with a strong, unpleasant odor. Reports of Sasquatch sightings frequently come from remote wilderness areas, particularly in the forests and mountains of the Olympic Peninsula and the Cascade Range.

In Skamania County, a law has been enacted that explicitly prohibits the killing of Sasquatch. Violators of this law may face fines of up to $10,000 and potential imprisonment. This legislation was put in place to ensure the creature's protection and prevent hunters from inadvertently harming others.

West Virginia
White Lady of Silver Run

The rural rails of the old Baltimore and Ohio track from Parkersburg to Clarksburg, West Virginia, fell silent when trains stopped running in 1985, and the tracks were removed. The sounds of horns and the vibrant life of old mining and rail towns have faded into ghostly echoes. Yet, history lingers with the North Bend Rail Trail and a ghost story passed down through the years—

There is a legend about a young woman who haunts the old Baltimore and Ohio tracks just outside Cairo. One night, a young engineer was driving the midnight westbound express along the tracks, starting in Grafton and heading toward Clarksburg, then Parkersburg.

As he approached a short stretch of railway near the entrance to Silver Run Tunnel #19, the moonlight and the train's headlights illuminated the scene, revealing a woman in a pale dress with raven-colored hair and golden slippers walking along the tracks. Horrified that he might hit her, the engineer desperately threw the brakes into emergency mode, but he could not come to a stop in time. He prayed that she would step off the rail.

Suddenly, she glided lazily along the track, away from the engine. Rattled, the engineer later reported to the watchmen at the Smithburg Tunnel, about 36 miles west, that he and the fireman had halted their run and jumped hurriedly from the train. However, fog blanketing the tracks seemed to swallow up the mysterious woman. The conductor ran up, wondering about the emergency stop, and joined the search. But the woman had vanished, so they decided to leave.

The engineer made this same run every other night, and he began to doubt himself, thinking the ghostly woman was nothing more than a wisp of fog. However, when his express train ran again, she appeared once more. The engineer was ready this time, taking in every feature of the mysterious pale woman in a white gown with a jeweled brooch pinned to the neckline, jet-black hair, and golden slippers. He slammed on the brakes, and the train came to a halt. The conductor, engineer, and fireman searched the tracks again. Still, once again, she faded into the fog, this time letting out a horrible, heart-wrenching moan that left them trembling.

As rumors about the ghostly woman spread through the railyards, another engineer named O'Flannery openly laughed at the tale. He swore that if he encountered the woman at Tunnel #19, he would drive right through her. Sure enough, she stood on the tracks one foggy night waiting for the skeptic.

O'Flannery confidently kept going and did not brake; he blew right through the wispy woman in white. O'Flannery felt quite smug until he arrived in Parkersburg. There, he received news that telegraphers, signalmen, and section men along the route reported a pale-faced young woman riding on his cowcatcher the entire trip. She had jet-black hair and wore a white gown with a jeweled brooch pinned to the neckline and golden slippers!

For years, railroad workers recalled seeing the ghostly woman on the tracks and her mournful moans as they passed through Tunnel #19. Sometime later, an aging engineer learned that workmen digging beside an ancient cellar of a house near the tracks had discovered the skeleton of a woman.

West Virginia
Greenbrier Ghost

Trout Shue was a charming, handsome man who came to work for James Crookshank's blacksmith shop at Livesay's Mill in October 1896. Soon after, he met Zona, the 21-year-old daughter of Mary Jane Heaster. They married on October 20, 1896, and moved into a tiny home. All seemed well for the newlyweds for two months until, on January 22, 1897, Trout Shue went to a neighbor's house to ask her son, 11-year-old Andy, to help with chores for Zona, who was recovering from an illness.

It was late afternoon before Andy could finally go to the Shue home. He let himself inside when no one answered, and found Zona's lifeless body at the bottom of the stairway. By the time the boy ran for the doctor, Trout had returned, moved Zona to an upstairs room, and dressed her in a high-necked collar and crepe veil. After a brief examination, the doctor declared, "It is an everlasting faint. Her heart has failed," and reported that Zona had died in childbirth.

After a brief funeral, Mary Jane Heaster reflected on her daughter's death, hoping for a sign from God regarding its cause, as the young woman seemed fine when they last met. One evening, while praying in her rocking chair, she saw a vision of Zona. As she reached out to embrace her, the ghostly figure vanished.

Mary Jane Heaster sensed something was wrong and prayed again, leading to a shocking revelation. The ghost of her daughter, Zona, returned in a flesh-and-blood form, disclosing the abuse inflicted by Trout Shue. On the night of her death, he had come home furious over the lack of meat on the table. Trout broke her neck. To show the savagery, the otherworldly Zona turned her head completely around!

Mary Jane compelled authorities to exhume the grave of her daughter. Two doctors and a surgeon performed the autopsy and found marks of fingers on her throat and her windpipe smashed. Trout had murdered her! Trout Shue was arrested and convicted of first-degree murder, primarily due to Mary Jane Heaster's bizarre account of her daughter's return, which led to an exhumation. He later died in Moundsville Prison. Zona's ghost still haunts the Soule United Methodist Church and Cemetery in Greenbrier County, known as the Greenbrier Ghost.

West Virginia
Screaming Jenny of Harpers Ferry

Harpers Ferry is located at the confluence of the Potomac and Shenandoah rivers in present-day West Virginia. It was originally settled in the 1730s by Peter Stephens, who established a ferry across the Potomac River. In 1799, the Harpers Ferry Arsenal, formally known as the United States Armory and Arsenal at Harpers Ferry, was established as a federal armory that manufactured firearms and served as a storehouse for military arms. This facility played a significant role in the development of interchangeable parts manufacturing and gained notoriety for its seizure in 1859.

During this event, the abolitionist John Brown led a raid on the Harpers Ferry Armory, intending to incite a slave rebellion across the South. Although the raid ultimately failed and Brown was captured, some claim to see his ghost walking along Shenandoah Street and near the building where he hid during the raid.

Not long after the arsenal was built, the B&O Railway began operating through Harpers Ferry, running close to the armory. As time went on, homeless individuals began to inhabit some of the older, abandoned outbuildings. One night, the dress of an elderly woman living in one of these shacks caught fire. In panic, she ran out of her shelter, screaming, and stepped in front of an oncoming train, dying instantly. For years, train crews reported seeing the ghost of the old woman as a ball of fire racing along the railway, accompanied by her screams. They named her "Screaming Jenny," and her cries can still be heard today.

Haunting Shorts of West Virginia:

• On a dark, foggy night, a couple drove along Hammonds Mill Road in Hedgesville. The mist was so thick that the driver had to slow down. Suddenly, the air inside the car turned frigid, and condensation formed on the windshield. When he swiped it away, a ghostly figure appeared in front of the vehicle. Panicked, he slammed on the brakes, causing the car to stall. A ragged soldier in a tattered Confederate uniform, about five feet four, with fiery red hair and a full beard, emerged from the fog. His blood-stained fingers rose in plea as he collapsed onto the hood, his eyes searching before he vanished. Terrified, the driver rushed out to help, only to find the soldier gone. When he returned to the car, he saw two bloody handprints on the hood, remnants of the ghostly encounter.

• In the early years of Benton's Ferry, three brothers lived on a knoll known as Vinegar Hill, where they made moonshine disguised as vinegar to sell to local taverns. One stormy night, while transporting a wagonload of their illegal barrels, lightning startled their mule, causing the barrels to shift. One barrel fell on the driver, pinning him to the muddy road, and despite the brothers' efforts to roll it off, he was crushed and killed. They buried him in a nearby cemetery. On stormy nights, locals report two glowing spots that resemble eyes and a fog rising from the road. This mist forms the figure of a flat man who dances and wails before vanishing into the graveyard at the top of Vinegar Hill.

• Driving along US-19 near Powell Mountain offers stunning views of the valleys, including Powell Creek Valley to the east. A short, dusty road off the highway, easy to miss, leads to a historic site. Before the September 1861 Battle of Carnifex Ferry, Union troops prepared for battle in this area.

On September 8, Henry Young and local militia members scouted the Union forces. Seeing them, Young fired a warning shot to his friends but was shot in the head and died on the mountain. His body was retrieved five days later for burial on that gravel road, which is now home to his cemetery. Locals tell of a headless ghost who rides a spectral horse from this spot, warning of his approach with clattering chains before vanishing where the road meets the highway.

• Booger Hole is a community in northern Clay County in the Rush Fork Valley with a reputation for mysterious occurrences and hauntings. In the early 1900s, Booger Hole experienced a series of murders and disappearances, with nearly a dozen individuals killed or missing during this time. One of the most mysterious cases involved Andy Hargis, a stonemason who disappeared in 1883 while traveling from Elana to Booger Hole. Another case was Joseph Clark, a watchmaker who disappeared in 1897 after spending the night at Booger Hole. A trail of blood was found leading to a nearby creek. In 1899, farmer Louis Cohen was murdered, and Lacy Ann Boggs, 74, was shot while peeling apples in an abandoned schoolhouse where she lived. A mob formed and dynamited five homes belonging to families connected to the murders. They posted handbills warning them to leave town, and they did. The area fell silent for a while—except for the ghosts. One of the most notable legends is that of the crying babies of Booger Hole. A woman lived in a cabin in the hollow. Whenever she gave birth, she would throw the screaming newborn into the fire. People walking near the home heard crying babies both day and night.

• *Intrigued by the ghost stories of West Virginia? Read Jannette's 3 books, "West Virginia Ghost Stories, Legends, and Haunts," which includes directions for visiting these locations.*

A West Virginia Cryptid
Mothman

The Mothman is a cryptid primarily reported in Point Pleasant, West Virginia, from November 15, 1966, to December 15, 1967. It is portrayed as an enormous humanoid figure with bird-like features, notable for its glowing red eyes and sizable wings. The initial significant encounter involved two young couples—Roger and Linda Scarberry and Steve and Mary Mallette—who reported that the creature pursued their vehicle at high speeds through a secluded area filled with abandoned TNT bunkers. They described the entity as "a large flying man with a 10-foot wingspan."

Following this encounter, additional sightings emerged, attracting considerable media attention and sparking public interest. The Mothman legend became even more prominent after the tragic collapse of the Silver Bridge in December 1967, which led to the deaths of 46 people. Some locals began linking the bridge disaster to the Mothman sightings, further intensifying the intrigue surrounding the phenomenon.

Wisconsin
The Ridgeway Ghost

The Ridgeway Ghost has been part of local legend since the early 1840s. This ghost haunts a stretch of U.S. Route 151 between Dodgeville and Blue Mounds, Wisconsin, an area distinguished by its rural farmland and historical significance related to lead mining. Between 1832 and 1845, lead mines were developed in southwestern Wisconsin. Thousands of immigrant miners arrived searching for fortune and settled in the area. As a result, towns emerged, providing travelers with places to water their teams and opportunities to find a room for the night.

There was a ghost that haunted this area, specifically along Old Military Road, which stretched from the early Pokerville settlement to near Dodgeville, a distance of about 25 miles.

The central focus of this haunting was the town of Ridgeway, which eventually became known as The Ridgeway Ghost. This location was bustling with activity as lead-laden oxen pulled wagons back and forth between settlements. Along this route were more than a dozen saloons filled with rowdy miners, gamblers, and downtrodden individuals. Robberies and murders were common occurrences in these establishments and along the nearby roadway.

The first person to see the ghost was a local doctor who was riding along the road well after dark and noticed, with dismay, a ghost riding on the back of his horse. Water pumps would move on their own, and one unfortunate man named Johnnie Owens was singing a song as he strolled along the road one night. As he approached a tree along the dark path, he noticed that something was hanging from the branches. Upon closer inspection, he realized that corpses were dangling from their necks! The following day, they were gone. This unsettling event caused at least one relationship to end: Jim Moore had a sweetheart living on a farm in Blue Mounds. One night, while returning from her house, he encountered a ghost walking alongside him to Pokerville. They didn't exchange a word, but Jim never revisited the girl.

One of the ghost's favorite tricks was to leap from the brush beside the road and land on the tongue of a buggy or wagon, causing the horses to panic and bolt, which often resulted in the wagon crashing. At times, the ghost would jump into the seat next to the driver, throw the driver out of the wagon, and send the horses galloping off in a runaway state. Occasionally, it would loosen wheels so the wagon would come crashing onto the roadway. A well-known local wrestler believed he could defeat the ghost in a fight and set off down the road. The next day, he was found dead within a fence, beaten by the ghost, with the roadway torn to pieces around him.

Two men from Pokerville were walking along the road one dark night, carrying wood on their shoulders. A white apparition suddenly leaped out at them as they passed a particularly lush thicket. Frightened, the men ran away, but the ghost followed, lashing at them with a stick as they fled. Eventually, they fell to the ground, exhausted and expecting the worst. When they stood up, the phantom had vanished.

Sometimes, the men driving the oxen wagons carrying lead would quickly stop at a tavern along their route. One night, John Riley decided to do just that. When he came out, he found his oxen unhitched and tied to the back of the wagon. To his astonishment, he saw an old ghost walking away down the road, carrying John's lantern and his oxen whip.

The frequency of oxen carts transporting lead and supplies along the roadway decreased when the Chicago and Northwestern Railroad arrived in the area. As a result, sightings of the ghost were also reported to have diminished. There were moments when the ghost would return to haunt a train track or frighten solitary travelers on the road. In the early 1930s, Louis Meuer, the sexton of the Catholic Church Cemetery, was found hanged in the cemetery shed. It was speculated that he had a disagreement with the ghost, leading more than a few to believe that the Ridgeway Ghost had the final say in the matter. There have been various explanations regarding the origins and identity of the ghost. A number of locals believe it to be the spirit of a man who was killed in a lead mining accident before the Civil War. Others think it could be a victim of a deadly bar brawl or a peddler who stopped at the saloon and never left. Additionally, there are accounts of two brothers who were murdered during a bar fight in the early 1840s. One brother was thrown into a fireplace while trying to escape, leading to speculation that their spirits merged into a single, twice-as-dreadful ghost.

Wisconsin
Green Bay Ghost

Much of downtown Green Bay is built over three former cemeteries, which has led to numerous reports of ghost sightings and unexplained phenomena in the area. Indigenous people initially used the site as a burial ground, followed by French traders and, later, settlers. However, this is not the only haunted location in the region. Fort Howard Park is located on the northeastern edge of Green Bay. It is home to remnants of the historic Fort Howard, established in 1816. The grounds are renowned for ghostly encounters, particularly related to its military past. Visitors report seeing phantom soldiers wandering the grounds, especially near the old fort structures.

Fort Howard Hospital has a grim history. Initially built in the 1830s by the U.S. Army for Fort Howard, the hospital was moved to Heritage Hill State Historical Park in 1975.

On a February night in 1832, Private Patrick Doyle got in trouble for drinking. He was placed in a jail at the Fort Howard military base. During the night, he requested a meeting with Lieutenant Amos Foster, who visited Doyle in his quarters. In a shocking turn of events, Doyle seized Foster's gun and shot him point-blank in the chest, killing him.

Private Doyle was subsequently tried and hanged on October 15, 1832. Lieutenant Foster was buried at Camp Smith, now part of Heritage Hill. At the Fort Howard Hospital building, strange footsteps and odd noises have been heard. Adding to the site's haunted reputation, Foster is reported to appear as a full-body apparition before disappearing.

Haunting Shorts of Wisconsin:

• The Driftless Area of Wisconsin is unique because it is entirely surrounded by glaciated land, providing a glimpse of Wisconsin's landscape before the Glacial Period. One notable feature in this area is Elephant Trunk Rock, which is made of Karst sandstone. This rock formation resembles an elephant's trunk in a valley carved by Willow Creek and its tributaries. In 1923, there were plans to blast the rock formation away. Still, it was preserved thanks to the opposition from residents and State Highway Commission. Since then, it has become a well-known landmark along Wisconsin Highway 58. Interestingly, Elephant Trunk Rock was not always known by this name. In earlier years, it was referred to as "Devil's Hitching Post." According to local legend, when a death occurred in the community, a mysterious figure known as the death angel would ride in on a black horse, tether his steed to the stone, and then walk to the bluffs above. Once, a man traveling along the road noticed the beautiful stallion and stopped to approach it. However, as he neared the horse, a dark figure appeared on the cliff above, and suddenly the horse struck the man, resulting in his death.

• Once a mining town, Mineral Point is now a travel spot with shops and hiking trails in the heart of Wisconsin's Driftless Region. It has a vampire. On the evening of March 14, 1981, there were reports of a strange man lurking in Graceland Cemetery in Mineral Point. Officer John Pepper approached a figure described as a 6-foot-five-inch tall man with a white face and black cape. When Officer Pepper called out to him, the man bolted, effortlessly clearing a 4-foot-tall barbed wire fence on the cemetery's edge and running into a field where Angus bulls were grazing. This mysterious figure is known by his extremely pale face and pitch black hair.

He is often seen wearing a black cape similar to the Victorian figure known as 'Spring-heeled Jack.' In 1837, Spring-heeled Jack was infamous for his terrifying appearance and extraordinary leaping abilities, resulting in numerous sightings across the UK. In Mineral Point, there were reports in 2004 of a man sitting in a tree outside an apartment complex. He leaped from the tree and fled when approached by the police. The most recent sighting occurred in 2008 when a couple fishing on a pier at Ludden Lake saw a pale-faced man with dark hair and a cape climbing out of the water and quickly ran to the police station to report it.

• Bloody Bride Bridge in Portage County, Wisconsin, is rich in local legend and ghostly tales. Officially known as the Highway 66 bridge, it is located near Jordan Park in the Stevens Point area. The bridge has gained notoriety due to the haunting story of a couple traveling to their wedding. During this journey, they were involved in a horrific car accident that resulted in the death of the bride. Those who travel the bridge at night, particularly during the winter months, have reported seeing the bride wandering back and forth along the bridge in a blood-stained wedding gown. One famous account involves a police officer who believed he had struck a woman with his vehicle. Upon exiting his car to investigate, he found nothing unusual. However, when he returned to his vehicle, he was startled to see the apparition of the bride sitting in the back seat. Additionally, anglers who frequent the waters below report strange occurrences connected to her ghostly presence and an unsettling atmosphere that seems more pronounced at night.

• Summerwind is the ruins of a mansion on the shores of West Bay Lake in Vilas County, Wisconsin, on private property. Built in the early 20th century as a fishing lodge, the manor was bought in 1916 as the Lamont family retreat.

After moving in, the family began to experience unsettling occurrences that led them to abandon the property shortly thereafter. The legends surrounding Summerwind are primarily credited to Raymond Bober, who claimed the mansion was haunted. Subsequent owners, notably Arnold and Ginger Hinshaw, reported disturbing events during their brief stay, including disembodied voices, chilly gusts of wind, and even discovering a corpse behind a hidden wall. Over time, the home fell into disrepair. In 1988, the building was struck by lightning during a storm and subsequently burned down, marking the end of an era for Summerwind. However, its story continues to linger on.

• According to the legends surrounding her in White Water, Mary Worth was accused of murdering her children with an axe. She is buried in an old crypt at Oak Grove Cemetery. Moments before her execution for these crimes, she cursed the town. Local lore suggests that her ghost wanders among the tombstones. On Halloween Eve, her spirit is seen moving through the graveyard. Witnesses have reported experiencing eerie sensations or sightings near her grave.

• The ghost of a former guest lingers in the Pfister Hotel in Milwaukee. This ghost roams the staircase, knocks, pounds, and scratches on walls, and turns electronics on and off. Built in 1893, the hotel hosted numerous baseball teams that visited to compete against the Milwaukee Brewers. Players have reported experiencing objects moving independently, apparitions appearing in hallways, and strange noises such as knocking and disembodied voices.

A Wisconsin Cryptid
Beast of Bray Road

The creature, often associated with the rural area near Elkhorn in Walworth County, has drawn comparisons to werewolves or Bigfoot. Sightings of this wolf-like entity date back to 1936. It garnered significant attention during the late 1980s and 1990s when numerous witnesses reported encounters along Bray Road. Eyewitness descriptions suggest the creature stands between 6 and 7 feet tall and possesses a human-like body covered in fur or hair. Its head resembles a wolf, depicted with large, glowing red or orange eyes.

This elusive being is noted for its stealth and ability to move upright on all fours, similar to a human. The first reported sighting occurred at St. Coletta School for Exceptional Children in Jefferson County in 1936. Throughout the 1980s, several individuals recounted their interactions with the creature, including instances where it allegedly came into contact with vehicles. One notable encounter involved witnesses Lori Endrizzi and Doris Gibson, who reported that the beast lunged at their car as they drove along Bray Road, leaving distinctive slash marks on the vehicle's exterior.

Wyoming
Ghost Dog of Fort Bridger

Fort Bridger was initially established in 1842 as a 19th-century fur trading outpost. It became a popular rest and resupply point for weary travelers journeying along the Oregon and Mormon Trails. The outpost had a mascot—a dog that survived a wagon train attack. The dog was named after Major Thornburgh, who was killed in a confrontation with Ute Indians near the White River Agency on September 29, 1879.

The dog grew up as a military camp follower and eventually went to Fort Bridger. He became quite the hero, saving a small boy from drowning, alerting others to impending attacks, and rescuing a soldier during a fight. At the fort, he formed a bond with Buck Buchanan, a muleskinner responsible for transporting supplies. Thornburgh was killed by a mule kick on September 27, 1888. Buchanan buried the dog nearby and had a tombstone carved for him. Thornburgh's spirit still wanders the area, locals say, protecting the cemetery.

Wyoming
The Murderess of Slaughterhouse Gulch

In the mid-1800s, the gold boomtown of South Pass attracted around 10,000 residents searching for fortune through gold mining. The thriving town had five hotels, seventeen saloons, and three general stores. It was well-laid out along the most straightforward passage over the Continental Divide to places like Green River Valley and Salt Lake Valley. It was a hub of through-travelers and used as a rest stop for wayfarers on the Oregon Trail. With so many people constantly coming and going, nobody kept track of their whereabouts, particularly solitary travelers like miners.

Even if they had family back east, survival in the West was uncertain due to risks such as attacks by Native Americans, illness, and robbery along the route. There was usually no way to track them down when someone went missing.

A family that arrived in South Pass took advantage of their surroundings. The Bartletts, consisting of Jim (whose name appears variably as John or Stephen in different accounts) and his daughter Polly, came from a rough neighborhood in Cincinnati where Jim had operated a saloon. After traveling west, they, along with a woman named Hattie, established a large log lodge three miles east of South Pass during the height of the mining boom in the late 1860s.

In just a year, they became skilled at attracting wealthy travelers to their inn under the guise of hospitality. However, their true intentions were sinister; they poisoned their guests with arsenic-laced food and drink. While Polly distracted victims by getting them drunk, her father was in the back corral digging their graves. The victims were typically solitary individuals who had come into possession of valuable items, such as gold, making them easy targets for robbery and murder. Polly's methods involved intoxicating her victims with whiskey before administering the poison.

In April that year, Edmund Ford visited the inn, where Polly flirted with him and tried to ply him with drinks. However, Ford was not a drinking man. When her father entered the room, expecting to find a dead body, he was surprised to discover that Ford was still alive. Discombobulated Polly could only react by kicking Ford out of the inn.

Unfortunately, Sam Ford, Edmund's brother and wealthy cattle broker, was not so fortunate. Polly served her usual fare and murdered him. Like many others, Edmund Ford assumed that his brother had been robbed and murdered on his way to South Pass, not suspecting the Bartletts of foul play.

Polly and her father were responsible for the deaths of approximately 22 men, whose bodies were buried on their property and later discovered. If not for one of her victims, Teddy Fountain, the son of wealthy mine owner Barney Fountain, going missing, she might never have been caught. When the 23-year-old failed to return home, it prompted an investigation led by Pinkerton detectives. Eventually, suspicions raised by Edmund Ford regarding his missing brother and his own strange incident at the inn led to Polly's capture following the death of her father at Ford's hands.

The bodies were found in a cow pasture, a place seemingly perfect for hiding corpses as they were constantly trampled by hooves. Teddy's belt was identified by his father. John Bartlett was killed while attempting to escape. Polly was apprehended while trying to flee to Oregon. While awaiting trial for her crimes, Polly was shot dead by Otto Kalkhorst, a foreman at one of Barney Fountain's mines, through the window of her jail cell on October 7, 1868. He was never tried for her murder.

Polly Bartlett, often called "The Murderess of Slaughterhouse Gulch," is a figure from 19th-century American folklore. She is reputed to be one of the earliest serial killers in Wyoming's history, allegedly committing her crimes around 1868 before Wyoming was officially designated as a state. Nowadays, it is a National Historic Landmark managed by the Bureau of Land Management, and folks can visit it. And it is always said that if anybody haunts the ghost town of South Pass, it must be Polly Bartlett.

Haunting Shorts of Wyoming:

- Winton, Wyoming, about five miles northeast of Rock Springs, was a mining boomtown established in the 1920s. At its peak, it had around 700 residents. The mines closed in 1952, and the town eventually fell into ruin. There are reports of a strange light that follows hikers in the area, but its source remains unknown.

- Fort Laramie was a 19th-century trading post and military structure located at the confluence of the Laramie and North Platte Rivers. It was initially established to support the overland fur trade. In 1849, the U.S. Army acquired the site to protect wagon trains traveling on the Oregon Trail and other routes for settlers. Today, Fort Laramie is managed by the National Park Service, which provides information about America's western migration. The grounds are haunted by spirits, with reports of a woman in a green dress seen wandering the area; some believe she was the daughter of an agent stationed at the fort.

- Ann Robbins, known as Prairie Rose for her bronc riding in rodeos, was born in the late 1800s. She lived with her husband on a homestead in the Green Mountains, about 50 miles northwest of Rawlins, Wyoming. However, her life took a tragic turn in 1933 when she disappeared during a snowstorm while trying to round up a lost pony. Her remains were not discovered until six years later, found only alongside a rope, strands of her red hair, and the silver belt buckle she had won as an award. According to cowboys who rode past the area where she was found, they reported hearing the ghostly voice of a woman calling for help on cold winter nights.

- Devil's Tower is a stunning natural landmark in northeastern Wyoming that catches nearly everyone's eye.

It was named the first national monument in the United States by President Theodore Roosevelt in 1906. This impressive site is mainly made up of a type of rock formed from molten lava and is famous for its unique, tall columns that rise from the earth. It's a great place to see the beauty of nature and learn about its geological history. In addition to its geological significance, Devil's Tower has become a prominent location for various legends and ghost stories, which add to its allure and cultural importance. Multiple tribes, including the Lakota Sioux and Cheyenne, have myths associated with Devil's Tower. One popular legend tells of a group of girls chased by bears. To escape, they prayed for help, and the Great Spirit raised the ground beneath them to create the tower, leaving the bears clawing at its sides.

- Lower Falls is one of the two significant waterfalls located within Yellowstone National Park. It is part of the Grand Canyon of Yellowstone. In April of 1870, a group of militia members encountered a band of Native Americans while pursuing stolen pack horses. The Native Americans crossed the river above Lower Falls on a makeshift raft constructed from driftwood. As they attempted to navigate the river's swift currents, it became evident that their raft was struggling against the strong flow, and they could not overcome the powerful current. One explorer urged his companions not to shoot at the Native Americans, as they were likely to go over the falls regardless of any intervention. The raft was swept over the brink of Lower Falls with its occupants aboard chanting a death song as they faced certain doom. Visitors have heard chanting in the canyon, particularly at night. These sounds are often attributed to the spirits of those who lost their lives in this area, creating an unsettling atmosphere for anyone who ventures nearby.

A Wyoming Cryptid
Shunka Warakin

One of the most famous cryptids in Wyoming is the jackalope, a hybrid of a jackrabbit and an antelope. The legend originated in Douglas, Wyoming, during the 1930s when two brothers created a taxidermy hoax by attaching deer antlers to a jackrabbit. Interestingly, there is a scientific basis for this legend; rabbits can occasionally develop horn-like growths due to an infection from the Shope papillomavirus.

The Shunka Warakin is a cryptid found in Wyoming, often described as a large, wolf-like creature that walks on two legs.

This being originates in Native American folklore and is reputed to have a predatory nature, with stories claiming it is known to "carry off dogs." Sightings of the Shunka Warakin have been reported consistently over the years, particularly in northeastern Wyoming and around Cheyenne. A significant encounter occurred in the 1880s when homesteaders claimed to have killed one of these creatures; however, evidence of this event has since vanished. In recent years, modern reports of upright canine sightings continue to emerge, suggesting that there may be more than mere legend associated with this enigmatic creature.

One of America's Favorite
Women in White

Frank Pritchard lives not far from Hocking Hills. During his younger years, he set off with friends to explore Old Man's Cave. Deep within the sandstone gorge, beneath a dense forest of towering hemlocks, there is a waterfall that cascades down the cliff walls with a stunning 50-foot drop. At one point, Frank climbed to the top of the falls to look down at the pool of water below. However, he slipped and fell, a tumble that should have cost him his life. But perhaps a guardian angel, or a few roots and scrubs, broke his fall.

When he came to, he found himself lying on his back, gazing up at an extraordinary sight. A woman in a flowing white dress looked down at him. She was there one moment and gone the next. Frank propped himself up on his elbow and blinked, trying to see where she had vanished. Quickly, he rose, as young people do, their bodies more resilient. His friends rushed over, and he exclaimed, "You're not going to believe what just happened! Did you see her?" They hadn't seen anything, and to this day, they do not believe that a Lady in White had come to him. But Frank knows better.

Across the country, stories of Lady in White are among the most frequently reported ghost tales I receive during my ghostly presentations, alongside accounts of ghostly hitchhikers and crybaby bridges. Each state has its version or or three of these phenomena, so I thought compiling a note from each would be fitting.

Alabama: In downtown Montgomery, people sense the Lady in White approaching before she arrives. She is dressed entirely in white and has long dark hair and fierce, animal-like teeth.

Alaska-West High School in Anchorage is haunted by a Lady in White who terrifies students and staff.

Arizona: A woman wearing a white gown is often seen wandering the halls of the San Carlos Hotel in Phoenix, Arizona, heartbroken because her lover did not return from war.

Arkansas: On December 24, 1863, a girl was murdered and pushed into Lorance Creek. In 1920, while drilling for oil near her grave at Cockman Cemetery, she reappeared in her white dress, crying out "Why?" before walking back to the creek and vanishing again.

California: At Stow Lake in Golden Gate Park, San Francisco, there is the ghost of a woman who lost her baby when she failed to notice her stroller rolling into the lake.

Colorado: A winding 11-mile stretch of Riverdale Road between Thornton and Brighton is home to a ghostly woman wearing white in an area known as the Gates of Hell.

Connecticut: A ghost known as the White Lady haunts Union Cemetery and Stepney Cemetery in Monroe, where she is seen wearing a white sheer nightgown or a wedding dress.

Delaware: The Bride of Rehoboth is a ghost rumored to haunt the Rehoboth Beach Boardwalk in Delaware. She is frequently seen on misty nights, wandering along the beach, and is believed to be a bride who drowned on her wedding day.

Florida: At St. Augustine's Tolomato Cemetery, a woman dressed in a flowing white gown is often spotted wandering among the tombstones.

Georgia: The ghostly figure of a woman donning a white dress wanders Chickamauga National Park in Georgia, searching for her husband's body from the battle.

Hawaii: The White Lady is the ghostly apparition of the goddess Pele, with long white hair, roaming the island.

Idaho: The Idaho Hotel in Silver City has a ghost named 'Screaming Alice' who vanished after her family died of measles. Some say she took her own life by falling down the steps.

Illinois: Bachelor Grove Cemetery is known for the Lady in White, a ghostly figure often seen roaming the grounds. She is believed to be a grieving mother searching for her lost child, and her image has been captured on camera.

Indiana: The Asher-Walton House, a Victorian mansion in Atlanta is haunted by a woman dressed in white, believed to be Julia Walton, the wife of the home's builder.

Iowa: In the Granger House Victorian Museum, a Lady in White is occasionally spotted staring out through the windows of the old home.

Kansas: Rochester Cemetery in Topeka is home to the Albino Woman, who wanders its grounds with flowing white hair, stark white skin, and glowing red eyes.

Kentucky: Cumberland Falls State Park features the ghost of a bride in a white wedding dress, who was swept away by the raging waters of the falls.

Louisiana: The Lady in White, known as Elsie, is a ghostly figure haunting the Rosa Heart Theater at the Lake Charles Civic Center believed to be the spirit of a jilted bride who ended her life by walking off a pier that once existed near the theater.

Maine: Near Haynesville Woods, there is a legend about the 'Haynesville Hitchhiker.' This figure, dressed in white, hitches rides from passing vehicles and mysteriously disappears.

Maryland: Ellicott City is a historic mill town in the Patapsco Valley, known for a Lady in White who wanders the halls of the historic B&O Railroad Station.

Massachusetts: At Proctor's Ledge in Salem, where the hangings took place in 1692, some have reported seeing a figure known as the Lady in White.

Michigan Catherine Shook, the lighthouse keeper, haunts Pointe aux Barques Lighthouse, where her ghost is often seen wearing a white dress.

Minnesota In Stillwater, at the Warden's House Museum, the daughter of a former warden returns in a white gown to search for her son after she died from appendicitis.

Mississippi: A woman dressed in white appears at King's Tavern in Natchez, Mississippi. She is the spirit of Madeline, the mistress of the tavern's original owner.

Missouri: A ghostly woman in white clothing in Marceline sought vengeance to railroad workers after being struck by a train while trying to retrieve her child.

Montana: In the early 1900s, railroad workers and hunters reported sightings of a spectral figure near Fish Creek, dressed in white and wandering the foothills: a tearful bride adorned in a light silk bridal gown.

Nebraska: At Prospect Hill Cemetery in Omaha, the Woman in White has been seen since she chased men at their workplace in July 1874 and asked one if her children were buried nearby before vanishing.

Nevada: There is a young girl in a white dress who haunts the Old Washoe Club in Virginia City, and she is rumored to be a victim of foul play.

New Hampshire: Carolyn Stickney was the wife of a wealthy hotel magnate who built the Mount Washington Hotel and who spent summers at the hotel in Room 314 until she died long ago. She returns dressed in white.

New Jersey: A Woman in White, believed to be a ghost of a young woman who died in a car accident on her way to her wedding, is seen at Branch Brook Park, where a tree once stood, wearing a white flowing gown.

New Mexico: La Llorona roams near bodies of water, mourning her children whom she drowned in a jealous rage.

New York· A Lady in White visits the curvy stretch of roadway known as The Devil's Elbow on the secluded section of old NY-17C in Owego believed to be a woman killed when a tavern was nearby.

North Carolina: A woman dressed in white, possibly a former resident from the 1900s, wanders through the halls of the Country Squire Restaurant, Inn & Winery, surrounded by the scent of lavender.

North Dakota: In a flowing white flannel nightgown, Anna Storey roams the byways outside Leyden, lamenting her murder at the hands of a peddler.

Ohio: At White Lady Point in Portsmouth, the ghost of Mary Fisk, who was murdered, still screams for help after boatmen along the Ohio River were unable to reach her in time due to fog.

Oklahoma: Rich Anna Ione Overholser returns dressed in white to the Overholser Mansion in Oklahoma City, floating through the front parlor to the music room.

Oregon: An apparition of a woman in a long white dress hurries quickly through the halls of Portland's Benson Hotel, carrying a purse.

Pennsylvania: A tragic car accident on a curve called Devil's Elbow in the Wopsononock Mountains left the ghost of Margaret Gray wandering the road dressed in white.

Rhode Island: Rose Island in Narragansett Bay, about a mile offshore from Newport, features a lighthouse and the old Fort Hamilton barracks, which were used during a cholera epidemic. Visitors have reported seeing a lady dressed in white in the lighthouse tower.

South Carolina: Anna Ravenel's ghost haunts the Unitarian Church graveyard in Charleston as she searches for her lost love, Edgar Allan Poe. Legend has it that after her untimely death, she remains near her unmarked grave, longing for the connection they once shared.

South Dakota: Hotel Alex Johnson has a young bride who reportedly committed suicide by leaping from the window of room 812 in the 1970s, She strolls the eighth floor in a white gown, searching for those responsible for her death.

Tennessee: A woman glides through the woods, around the Big South Tunnel train tracks and in nearby yards.

Texas: The Lady of White Rock Lake, located near Dallas, is the ghost of a young woman who drowned in the lake. She is often seen at night wearing a wet evening dress, appearing along the roadside of East Lawther Drive.

Utah: In Ogden Canyon, a woman dressed in white appears on the road and vanishes when cars stop to assist her, believed to be searching for a lost child in the canyon wash.

Vermont: Originally the site of the Evergreen Estate, Southern Vermont College has a haunting history. The spirit of a young woman who passed away on the grounds drifts across the campus as a figure dressed in a white gown.

Virginia: In Bedford, The White Lady of Avenel is a ghost believed to be Mary Frances 'Fran' Burwell, who waited on the front porch for her husband to return from the Civil War, but he never returned.

Washington: Olympic View Drive in Edmonds has a ghostly figure that appears in foggy conditions along the roadway. Drivers often report seeing her shape materialize unexpectedly.

West Virginia: A ghostly girl in a pale dress once rode the cowcatchers of trains along the rural routes of the old Baltimore and Ohio track from Parkersburg to Clarksburg.

Wisconsin: The William A. Irvin is docked along the waterfront of Lake Superior, near the Aerial Lift Bridge in Duluth, Minnesota, for tours where a woman dressed in white appears as a ghostly apparition wandering the ship.

Wyoming: The Atlas Theatre in Cheyenne is haunted by a 'Lady in White,' believed to have died with her child after succumbing to the cold while seeking shelter in the theatre.

Citations

Alabama:
A GHOST WITH A COFFIN IT TERRORIZES THE INHABITANTS OF AN ALABAMA TOWN. *The Philadelphia Times Philadelphia, Pennsylvania Sun, Sep 4, 1892 Page 24.*
(Bill Sketoe's Bridge Location: 31.343433, -85.610989)
William Sketoe: Bill Sketoe is Still Dying The Birmingham News Birmingham, Alabama Sun, Oct 10, 1954 Page 106.
Roughton, Randy. *Tall Tales. The Dothan Eagle Sun, Mar 27, 1994 ·Page 27.*
Rev William H. "Bill" Sketoe SR. (1818-1864)
Retrieved:findagrave.com/memorial/16248476/william-h-sketoe
(Aunt Jenny Location: 34.348000, -87.519000)
Mountain feuds of aunt Jenny Johnson and the brooks boys.
freestateofwinston.org/auntjenny2.htm
Aunt Jenny Johnson. auntjennyjohnson.blogspot.com/2009/03/aunt-jenny-johnson.html
Other Ghosts: Windham, K. T., & Figh, M. G. (2014). Thirteen Alabama ghosts and Jeffrey. University of Alabama Press.
BOONE, A. (2021, October 14). Ghost stories at Fort Morgan.
alabamascoastalconnection.com/2021/10/12/ghost-stories-at-fort-morgan/
A FATAL FALL. Little Willie Youngblood Falls Through the Elevator Opening in the Cotton Factory Dies from Injuries. The Prattville Progress Prattville, Alabama Fri, Mar 31, 1893 Page 3.
Nancy Mountain Trail: The legend of Nancy's mountain.
joecuhaj.blogspot.com/2017/10/the-legend-of-nancys-mountain.html
Alaska:
Haunted Cabin: Gale, George Jennings. Tuesday, January 08, 1963 The Ghost Phone in the Haunted Cabin Fairbanks Daily News-Miner.
ARR mileposts. (2017, July 25). Retrieved thealaskarailroad.wordpress.com/resources/arr-mileposts/
Ghost Ship: Tells About Ghost Ship of Arctic. The Nome Nugget Nome, Alaska Sat, Apr 21, 1934 Page 4.
Hanged Man's Ghost: Hanged Man's Ghost Keeps Writer from Nome. The Nome Nugget Friday June 02, 1916 Nome.
Fred hardy (1876-1902) - Find a grave memorial.
findagrave.com/memorial/177228619/fred-hardy
Williams, Jennifer Jun 10, 2024. APUS Research and Academic Excellence-The Trial of Fred Hardy: Mary E. Hart and Alaska's First Legal Execution. youtube.com/watch?v=c76dQ95dNrE
Occult feature of the execution of Fred Watkyns in Alaska. *St. Louis Globe-Democrat, Apr 09, 1905 ·Page 57.*
Terror of Hanged Man's Ghost Keeps Alaska's Leading Woman From Return to Nome Where She Saw Him Die. *Evansville Press Evansville, Indiana Fri, Aug 20, 1915 Page 3.*
Arizona:
Red Ghost: Mohave County Miner Sat, Feb 25, 1893 ·Page 3. The Phantom that Terrorized all Arizona for a Time [Mineral Park, Arizona].
Apache Death Cave: Apache death cave. (2013,). atlasobscura.com/places/apache-death-cave
(Apache Death Cave Location: 35.115447, -111.093630)
Brunckow: ghosttowns.com/states/az/brunckowscabin.html
El Tiradito:Arizona Daily Star Tucson, Arizona Sun, Dec 24, 1922 Page 16. Shrine's Origin Lost in Mists of Ancient Legends.
Tiradito. (1959, March 9). newspapers.com/article/tucson-daily-citizen-tiradito/5399305/
About the Navajo – Streams in the desert. streamsinthedesertaz.com/about-the-navajo/
Grand Canyon:
outsideonline.com/adventure-travel/national-parks/national-parks-ghost-stories/ - Google search. outsideonline.com/adventure-travel/national-parks/national-parks-ghost-stories/
Arkansas:
Baxter Bulletin Mountain Home, Arkansas · Fri, May 18, 2001 Page 16 A Few Facts About the Crescent Hotel.

Baxter Bulletin Mountain Home, Arkansas Mon, Oct 31, 2005 Page 3. *Stories about ghosts, monsters and unexplained phenomena haunt state.*
(Crescent Hotel and Spa Location: 36.408249, -93.737247)
Fouke Monster:
The Camden News Camden, Arkansas Fri, May 7, 1971 Page 1. *The Latest on the Paw in the Window Hairy Monster Creates Excitement in Fouke.*
Northwest Arkansas Times Fayetteville, Arkansas Tue, May 25, 1971 Page 2. *Fouke Monster Sited Again.*
The Gurdon light: (2020, February 11). thedeadhistory.com/2020/02/11/the-gurdon-light/
Gurdon, AR - Gurdon spook light. roadsideamerica.com/tip/2998 Road to tracks. Go West.
Gurdon Spook Lights
(Gurdon Light Location: 33.953113, -93.172184)
(Gurdon Light trail parking: 33.951044, -93.233080)
Specter of Ghost Hollow: Northwest Arkansas Times Thu, Oct 31, 1974 ·Page 1 Specter of Ghost Hollow.
California:
Whaley House: Hanging Yankee Jim Los Angeles, California Tue, Oct 7, 1873 Page 4.
The Very True Strange Tale of Yankee Jim. Stark, Michael :
youtube.com/watch?v=XgEETwbGeBU
Violet Eloise "VI" Whaley (1862-1885) - Find A...
findagrave.com/memorial/69942657/violet_eloise_whaley
Misery Hill: gutenberg.org/cache/epub/6615/pg6615.txt
Contra Costa Times Walnut Creek, California Wed, Mar 20, 1974 Page 34. *Psychics Probe Cemetery to Ease Miners' Souls.*
B, L. (2023, June 28). The haunting history of battery point lighthouse.
medium.com/@burrowslizzy/the-haunting-history-of-battery-point-lighthouse-151ca5e68243
The Desert Sun Palm Springs, California · Sunday, November 02, 1997 [Cerro Gordo's].
The legend of snake road. (2009, July 16). weirdfresno.com/2009/07/legend-of-snake-road.html
St Elmo: Historic American Buildings Survey, Creator, H C Bostwick, W W Maish, J H Garrison, Anna A Stark, Compiled After. Photograph. loc.gov/item/co0321/.
St. Elmo – The story of Annabelle. (2015, October 21).
olafphotoblog.com/2015/10/21/st-elmo-the-story-of-annabelle
St. Elmo. coloradoencyclopedia.org/article/st-elmo#:~:text=In%20the%201870s%20prospectors%20settled,only%20two%20full%2Dtime%20residents
(Location: 38.703421, -106.346246)
Carter Lake:Carter Lake is home to the most haunted hike in Colorado. (2023, July 2).
onlyinyourstate.com/experiences/colorado/haunted-hike-co
Kozma, M. (2021, July 12). 13 creepiest places to hike or camp in Colorado.
303magazine.com/2017/10/13-creepiest-places-to-hike-or-camp-in-colorado/
Gold camp road tunnels – Colorado springs-cripple Creek.
uncovercolorado.com/activities/gold-camp-road-tunnels/ (Location: (38.736273, -104.991718)
Old Glendale Stagecoach Station: 303magazine.com/2017/10/13-creepiest-places-to-hike-or-camp-in-colorado/ Location: (38.441350, -104.970396)].
Horsethief Canyon: Horse thief canyon, Mesa County, Colorado. (2021, April 18).
thedeadstillwalkamongus.com/2020/10/01/horse-thief-canyon-mesa-county-colorado/
Location: (39.146713, -108.758383)
Stanley Hotel: Location: (40.383200, -105.519089)
Fort Collins: Walrus Ice Cream k99.com/most-haunted-places-in-northern-colorado-we-saw-a-ghost-at-walrus-ice-cream/.
Location: (40.586840, -105.077796).
Steamboat Springs Sequoia House:
steamboatpilot.com/news/tales-from-the-tread-county-boasts-haunted-history/#:~:text=The%20Sequoia%20building%2C%20on%20the,until%20her%20death%20in%201949 Location: (40.487615, -106.834841).
Outlaw Slade: Chan, A. (2018, January 22). Jack Slade: Western Jekyll and Hyde.
historynet.com/jack-slade-western-jekyll-hyde/

Fort Collins Coloradoan Fort Collins, Colorado Tue, Mar 18, 1952 Page 8. Outlaw Slade Son of Prominent Family.

Nistel, K. The haunted and interesting history of Julesburg, Colorado. k99.com/the-haunted-and-interesting-history-of-julesburg-colorado/

The Oregon trail. freepages.rootsweb.com/~billie0w/books/oregon_trail/oregon_trail.htm Location: (40.984236, -102.268147)

Anamas River, Durango, and Vicinity:

Alltrails.com. alltrails.com/trail/us/colorado/purgatory-trail Purgatory Creek Trail follows the course of Purgatory Creek initially and then enters the Purgatory Flats area, where it traverses along Cascade Creek. (Location: 37.623613, -107.792272).

J, & The Durango Herald via Associated Press. (2018, April 7). Is the animas truly the 'River of lost souls'? gazette.com/news/is-the-animas-truly-the-river-of-lost-souls/article_3732d001-3aeb-5dd8-9553-a5e8f3c1ecf2.html (Location: 37.280940, -107.878221)

Slide Rock Bolter:

Fearsome creatures of the Lumberwoods,. google.com/books/edition/Fearsome_Creatures_of_the_Lumberwoods/cNgW5S102uMC?hl=en&gbpv=1

    The slide-rock bolter. (2017, October 12). wanderingwhaleroad.wordpress.com/2017/10/12/the-slide-rock-bolter/

River Witch: 1037theriver.com/paranormal-spirits-in-montrose-colorado/ (Location: 38.465318, -107.879117).

    Aspen hauntedrooms.com/colorado/haunted-places/haunted-hotels/hotel-jerome-aspen (Location:39.191216, -106.818837). :

        Silver Cliff Cemetery: atlasobscura.com/articles/silver-cliff-ghost-lights. Silver Cliff Cemtery: (Location: 38.122401, -105.442774).

        The legend of la Llorona:
        (Location: Purgatoire River 37.642425, -103.576811). (2024, October 25). The Legend of La Llorona As told by Adele Aguilar, southern Colorado actress, artist, and storyteller. (Location: 37.606047, -103.604478). historycolorado.org/story/2024/10/25/legend-la-llorona

        Gutierrez, B. E. Rhs Llorona story. smokesignalnews.net/13219/uncategorized/rhs-llorona-story/

        El Dorado:(Coloma Pioneer Cemetery in El Dorado: 38.796490, -120.889373)

Connecticut:

        Union Cemetery:Easton Slayer Evades Posse in Forest Flight Hartford Courant Hartford, Connecticut Fri, Jun 1, 1923 Page 1.

        Harry & the lady in white. (2022, October 28). historicalsocietyofeastonct.org/2022/10/28/harry-the-lady-in-white/

        Ruby, don't take your love to town. (2020, August 11). eastoncourier.news/2020/08/10/ruby-dont-take-your-love-to-town/

        Union cemetery in Easton, Connecticut - Find a grave cemetery. findagrave.com/cemetery/1124942/union-cemetery

        (Location: 41.272432, -73.296960).

        Midnight Mary: (Location: Evergreen Cemetery (41.299525, -72.948380 Plot 50, Grave 4).

        Midnight Mary May Join Others for Cemetery Stroll. The Bridgeport Post (Bridgeport, Connecticut) · Fri, Oct 31, 1975 · Page 21.

        Naugatuck Daily News (Naugatuck, Connecticut) · Fri, Oct 31, 1975 · Page 7. Legend of Midnight Mary Lives Again on Halloween.

        NHI 1: Midnight Mary (Evergreen cemetery) | New Haven - Yale inscriptions. (2024, November 10). campuspress.yale.edu/yaleinscriptions/2024/11/10/midnight-mary/

        Hell Hollow:The Day (New London, Connecticut) · Sat, Mar 15, 2008 · Page 9. Hell Hollow Road [(Trail Location: 41.648, -71.835 Off Cedar Swamp Road)].

        Ghost Story Firmly Planted in Local Lore. The Day (New London, Connecticut) · Sun, Oct 26, 2003 · Page 6 Downloaded on Dec 30, 2024.

        A Time of Tales and Hauntings in Hell Hollow. The Day (New London, Connecticut) · Sun, Oct 26, 2003 · Page 1 Downloaded on Dec 30, 2024.

        State House Hartford:

        trinitytripod.com/features/hartfords-haunted-past-unveiled-the-spirits-that-haunt-some-of-the-citys-historic-sites/. (Location: 41.767092, -72.701464).

Mark Twain House:Sylvia, A. (2021, November 24). Ghostly encounters at the mark Twain house. locationsoflore.com/2021/11/23/ghostly-encounters-at-the-mark-twain-house/

Norwich State Hospital:

Connecticut Historical Society ☐ Former Norwich State Hospital Grounds Preston, CT 06365 (Location: 41.490651, -72.072134).

Seaside Sanatorium Waterford, CT 06385 (Location: 41.301699, -72.129467).

Enfield Demon House:The Demon House in Enfield CT. The 1771 Enfield house CT. thedemonhouseinenfieldct.com/(Location: 41.996327, -72.601016).

Hannah Cranna: Connecticut Western News Salisbury, Connecticut • Fri, Jun 27, 1873

The Hannah Cranna legend: A transcription from 1900 versus the internet version. (2023, September 15). brombonesbooks.com/2023/06/25/the-hannah-cranna-legend-a-transcription-from-1900-versus-the-internet-version/

Hannah Cranna, or the witch's funeral: A story from Connecticut. (2013, September 8). newenglandfolklore.blogspot.com/2013/09/hannah-cranna-or-witchs-funeral-story.html

Hannah Tomlinson-Hovey (1763-1831). monroecthistory.org/hannah-tomlinson-hovey Hartford Courant Hartford, Connecticut Thu, Oct 1, 2015 Page U20 (Location:41.293487, -73.241532).

A haunting tale: The wicked witch of Monroe, CT. (2024, March 28). cemeteryinsightsandbeyond.wordpress.com/2020/10/14/a-haunting-tale-of-the-wicked-witch-of-monroe-ct/

New London Ledge Lighthouse:Connecticut Historical Society - A repository for historical documents related to Connecticut's past, providing insights into local legends and ghost stories tied to historical events. (Location:41.305876, -72.077448).

Delaware:

Cape Henlopen's Curse Lights: (Location: 38.800328, -75.101569).

Fine Line Websites & IT Consulting. Below the waves. delawarebeachlife.com/magazine/our-content/487-below-the-waves

Muras, C. (2022, November 28). Corpse lights in Delaware hide strange secrets in this state Park. onlyinyourstate.com/experiences/delaware/dangerous-nature-spot-de

Office of Communications and Marketing. UD research magazine Vol. 4 No. 1: Researchers solve shipwreck mystery. www1.udel.edu/researchmagazine/issue/vol4_no1/shipwreck_mystery.html

Maggie's Bridge: Maggie's Bridge (Location: 38.594116, -75.666192). wjbr.com/2023/10/16/the-8-most-haunted-places-in-delaware/

hangar1publishing.com/blogs/cryptids/delaware-cryptids?srsltid=AfmBOoogozPV7xfRDms1eL_pCQYNHes67JV78ZRWAE_eRGMXKGVtWJhH.

Battle of Cooch's Bridge:

Americanwarsus. (2017, November 19). Battle of Cooch's bridge | American Revolutionary War. revolutionarywar.us/year-1777/battle-coochs-bridge/

Cooch's Bridge Battlefield (Location: 39.641256, -75.732156).

Cooch's bridge. battlefields.org/visit/battlefields/coochs-bridge

George, P., & Livingston, S. (2024, October 10). These 12 haunted spots in Delaware have the spookiest histories. delawaretoday.com/things-to-do/haunted-places-delaware/

Josh Shannon jshannon@newarkpostonline.com. (2015, January 21). Colonial highway carried presidents, generals, Revolutionary War heroes. newarkpostonline.com/news/colonial-highway-carried-presidents-generals-revolutionary-war-heroes/article_585a9a09-0de6-5556-bcd3-07b41e8617b4.html

(Lums Mill Swamp Forest Trail trailhead: 39.558175, -75.715422). (Lums Mill Location: 39.551027, -75.713119).

(Rockwood Mansion Location: 39.772580, -75.520825).

wjbr.com/2023/03/23/frankford-delawares-urban-legend-of-catman-the-gravekeeper/ (Cat Man Cemetery Location: 38.509880, -75.245224).

woodburn.delaware.gov/ghosts-legends/woodburn-ghost/. (Location: 39.161534, -75.523073).

The News Journal Wilmington, Delaware Sat, Oct 31, 2015 Page A9.

Devil's MillHopper: Devil's Millhopper Geological State (Park Location: 29.707192, -82.395248).

Devil's Millhopper. Tampa Bay Times St. Petersburg, Florida Sun, May 13, 1984 Page 69.

Devil's Tree:The Devil's Tree (Location: 27.277714, -80.405146). bocamag.com/paranormal-historian-mark-muncy-talks-the-devils-tree/.

St Augustine Lighthouse: Ghost stories: The Pittee girls (Lighthouse and Museum Location: 29.885370, -81.288268). (2024, December 11). staugustinelighthouse.org/2020/03/02/ghost-stories-the-pittee-girls/

Bellamy Bridge: visitjacksoncountyfla.com/play/culture-heritage/bellamy-bridge-heritage-trail/. (Bellamy Bridge Trailhead Location: 30.871309, -85.257954) (Bellamy Bridge Location: 30.865999, -85.251389).

Cox, D. Photograph of the ghost of Bellamy bridge - Marianna, Florida. exploresouthernhistory.com/bellamybridge3.html

exploresouthernhistory.com/bellamybridge2.html

Elizabeth Jane Croom Bellamy (1819-1837) - Find A... findagrave.com/memorial/109675009/elizabeth-jane-bellamy

(Arbuckle Creek Bridge Location: 27.526751, -81.358885) trippingonlegends.com/2019/06/11/travel-log-witches-and-murderers-at-arbuckle-creek-in-lorida/.

(Fort Pickens Location: 30.329654, -87.290603).

(Gulf Breeze Location: 30.359891, -87.163852).

Cryptid: Muck monster | Wiki | Urban legends & Cryptids amino. (2020, March 13). aminoapps.com/c/urban-legends-cryptids/page/item/muck-monster/o4Gv_kquoI7a0Zgb4vvRR137oBgmgMRZLQ

Georgia:

(Railroad Bed And Old Ghost Road: 32.355874, -81.633919). Robertson road is one of America's creepiest roads. dangerousroads.org/north-america/usa/9308-old-ghost-road.html

Bulloch history by Roger Allen. statesboroherald.com/life/lifestyles-columnists/bulloch-history-by-roger-allen-17/

(Burial Location: 32.44911, -84.97960) Riverdale Cemetery Columbus, Plot 60 W 1/2 Section 1. Con T. Kennedy shows Carnival train accident... findagrave.com/memorial/15864281/con_t.-kennedy-shows_carnival_train_accident_memorial

Cox, D. (2014, October 22). Ghost of the headless horse - Albany, Georgia (Location: 31.559169, -84.144003). exploresouthernhistory.com/albanyhorse.html#google_vignette

historiccolumbus.com/post/from-the-circus-train-wreck-to-the-man-o-war-history-of-the-railroad-in-columbus-part-3-of-3.

Written By: John G. Clark Jr. Source: Jim Miles, Haunted Central Georgia. facebook.com/story.php?story_fbid=975588304565965&id=100063444147190 (Chickamauga Battlefield Location: 34.941202, -85.259971).

Bisbee daily review. [volume], June 11, 1903, Image 8. Grand Canyon Wild Man.

themoonlitroad.com/green-eyes-chickamauga-battlefield-georgia/ - Google search. themoonlitroad.com/green-eyes-chickamauga-battlefield-

The haunting of lake Lanier. oxfordamerican.org/magazine/issue-113-summer-2021/the-haunting-of-lake-lanier

exploresouthernhistory.com/gastsimons2.html. (St Simon's Lighthouse Location: 31.158220, -81.398132)

onlyinyourstate.com/experiences/georgia/creepy-bridge-to-nowhere-ga. (Spook Bridge Location: 30.7898, -83.4518).

Karimi, F. (2020, October 31). A Georgia lake's dark and deadly history has some people seeing ghosts. cnn.com/2020/10/31/us/lake-lanier-urban-legends-trnd/index.html

Morris, B. (2024, February 20). The haunting of lake Lanier and the Black city buried underneath. newsone.com/4185919/lake-lanier-black-city-oscarville/

Mystical legends of Georgia folklore. exploregeorgia.org/things-to-do/blog/mystical-legends-of-georgia

Rankin, Bill. 1950s mystery is laid to rest by forensic work Official identifies 'Lady of the Lake'. The Atlanta Constitution Atlanta, Georgia Sun, Nov 4, 1990

Relative of Oscarville resident shares history behind the city underneath lake Lanier. (2022, July 12). 11alive.com/article/news/community/voices-for-equality/oscarville-lanier-lake-black-town-riot-mae-crow-chattahoochee-beulah-rucker/85-8647e2be-a07b-4e80-91cc-61613d0ff472

Hawaii:

honolulumagazine.com/the-real-story-behind-honolulus-haunted-morgans-corner/ (Hairpin Turn: 21.347878, -157.823382).

mysteries-of-hawaii.com/hawaiis-most-haunted/koloa (Tree Tunnel Location: 21.949042, -159.466124).

Green lady of Wahiawa. obscurban-legend.fandom.com/wiki/Green_Lady_of_Wahiawa

Idaho:

Water Babies: Emerson. (2022, December 8). Legend of Idaho water babies at massacre rocks state Park. onlyinyourstate.com/nature/idaho/massacre-rocks-id

Idaho: The haunting of massacre rocks: The legend of the water babies. vocal.media/horror/idaho-the-haunting-of-massacre-rocks-the-legend-of-the-water-babies

Spirit Rocks:History. spiritlakeid.gov/history

facebook.com/groups/1047614935369200/posts/a-friend-and-i-were-recently-talking-about-folklore-and-he-mentioned-something-a/3395568377240499/?_rdr (Rose Hill Cemetery Idaho Falls Location: 43.477867, -112.040522)

Old Idaho Penitentiary (Location: 2445 Old Penitentiary Rd 43.602906, -116.162017). (2022, December 27). The story of Idaho's Raymond Snowden is scary beyond belief. onlyinyourstate.com/state-pride/idaho/idahos-jack-the-ripper-id

Sobottka, S. (2024, December 22). Pioneer Boot Hill cemetery (Location: 43.832373, -115.841365). hauntedhouses.com/idaho/pioneer-boot-hill-cemetery/

(Shoshone Ice Caves Location: 43.174820, -114.338398). thelittlehouseofhorrors.com/shoshone-ice-caves/.

Bulgarian monk of Yankee fork (Location: 44.475920, -114.216097). idahohauntedhouses.com/real-haunt/bulgarian-monk-yankee-fork.html

(Payette Lake Location: 44.934054, -116.105711), C. (2022, January 12). The legend of a Payette lake monster in Idaho may give you the chills. onlyinyourstate.com/nature/idaho/sharlie-payette-lake-monster-id

Illinois:

(The Location where H.H. Holmes Castle stood: 41.779315, -87.640141).

130 years later, was H.H. Holmes' englewood 'Murder castle' the house of horror legends claim? It wasn't even a hotel, experts say. (2023, May 16). chicagotribune.com/2023/05/16/130-years-later-was-hh-holmes-englewood-murder-castle-the-house-of-horror-legends-claim-it-wasnt-even-a-hotel-experts-say/

Did serial killer H.H. Holmes really build a 'Murder castle'? (2020, January 23). history.com/news/murder-castle-h-h-holmes-chicago

Research guides: H.H. Holmes and the murder castle: Topics in chronicling America: Introduction. (1035). guides.loc.gov/chronicling-america-h-h-holmes

Eastland Disaster:

(The site of the disaster at the corner of Wacker Drive and LaSalle Street Location: 41.887076, -87.632265). chicagobikeadventures.com/eastland-disaster-victims-map/

The Pantagraph Bloomington, Illinois · Monday, July 26, 1915.

People search. eastlanddisaster.org/people

Stranahan, S. Q. (2014, October 27). The Eastland disaster killed more passengers than the Titanic and the Lusitania. Why has it been forgotten? smithsonianmag.com/history/eastland-disaster-killed-more-passengers-titanic-and-lusitania-why-has-it-been-forgotten-180953146/

What happened. eastlanddisaster.org/history/what-happened

2017-10-29 A field guide to Illinois' fantastic beasts Chicago Tribune (Chicago, IL), p. 4-4.

Chicago Ghost Boat. The Chicago Chronicle Chicago, Illinois · Sunday, October 31, 1897.

Crenshaw House nps.gov/places/old-slave-house-crenshaw-house.htm. (Crenshaw House: 37.730278, -88.2925).

Eastland disaster: Stranahan. (2014, October 27). The Eastland disaster killed more passengers than the Titanic and the Lusitania. Why has it been forgotten? smithsonianmag.com/history/eastland-disaster-killed-more-passengers-titanic-and-lusitania-why-has-it-been-forgotten-180953146/

Eastland Disaster. (The site of the disaster at the corner of Wacker Drive and LaSalle Street Location: 41.887076, -87.632265). chicagobikeadventures.com/eastland-disaster-victims-map/

Eastland Disaster. People search. eastlanddisaster.org/people

Eastland Disaster. What happened. eastlanddisaster.org/history/what-happened

Ghost at Devil's Backbone. dailyegyptian.com/22847/archives/ghost-hunting-in-illinois-3/. (Location of Superintendent's house at Devil's Backbone: 37.635, -89.336944).

Old Joliet Prison. (Old Joliet Prison Location 41.545852, -88.072854). windycityghosts.com/most-haunted-places-in-illinois/

The Pantagraph Bloomington, Illinois · Monday, July 26, 1915.

Resurrection Mary: Chicago Tribune Chicago, Illinois Mon, Mar 12, 1934 Page 5. Killed in Car.

Resurrection Mary. findagrave.com/memorial/11851/mary-rozanc.

Resurrection Mary. findagrave.com/memorial/19720716/mary-bregovy Mary Bregovy Grave Section MM, Block II, Grave 9819.

Resurrection Mary. findagrave.com/memorial/39907931/ona-marija-norkus.

Wabash Cannonball Bridge. (Wabash Cannonball Bridge: 38.605212, -87.627148). wkdq.com/haunted-purple-head-bridge-legend/

Indiana:

(Location of Tunnelton Big Tunnel 38.769369, -86.306768) Murder of Henry Dixon at Big Tunnel. The Richmond palladium and sun-telegram. [volume], July 24, 1908, Page PAGE EIGHT, Image 8. Watchman May Have Been Murdered.

100 Step Cemetery (100 Step Cemetery Location: 39.49396, -87.23411). findagrave.com/cemetery/2238877/carpenter-cemetery visitindiana.com/blog/post/haunted-cemetery-in-indiana/

Big Tunnel: reddit.com/r/mrballen/comments/17u8fn3/the_headless_ghost_of_tunnelton_tunnel/

Avon Bridge (Avon Haunted Bridge Location: 39.757887, -86.414080). visithendrickscounty.com/blog/post/the-legend-of-the-avon-haunted-bridge-6286/.

Big Tunnel. The Bedford Weekly Mail Bedford, Indiana · Friday, July 24, 1908. Death Came Suddenly to Dixon Agency of Death is Mystery.

Collins Bridge. (2024, July 22). Edna Collins (Haunted?) covered bridge. goputnam.com/things-to-do/edna-collins-bridge/

Collins Covered Bridge (Location: 39.727372, -86.976306).

Cryptid: Pukwudgie (Mounds State Park Location: 40.096101, -85.620068). indianahistory.org/blog/pukwudgies-and-where-to-find-them/.

Culbertson House (Culbertson House Location: 38.286800, -85.812620). courier-journal.com/story/life/home-garden/home-of-the-week/2021/10/28/historic-culberston-mansion-southern-indiana-haunted/5835946001/.

Ghost stories on Halloween. (2011, October 31). bellerenee.wordpress.com/2011/10/31/ghost-stories-on-halloween/

Gray Lady of Willard Library (Library Location: 37.978333, -87.574167). Donald E. Baker, Director of the Willard Library Evansville. Two Publics: The Willard Library and the Evansville-Vanderburgh County Library, Indiana Libraries, Volume 6, Number 2 (1986).

Indiana Dunes. (Indiana Dunes Location: 41.668825, -87.027596) dailyyonder.com/visiting-dunes-on-a-dare-ghost-story-of-nature-loving-recluse-inspires-a-challenge-in-the-national-park/2021/10/01/.

(St Marys College Le Mans Hall Location: 41.707333, -86.256778).

Stepp Cemetery at Morgan Monroe State Forest

(Stepp Cemetery Location: 39.31360, -86.43000).

Stepp: A small rural cemetery that looms large in hoosier lore. indianapublicmedia.org/news/stepp-a-small-rural-cemetery-that-looms-large-in-hoosier-lore.php

Whispers Estate (Whispers Estate Location: 38.733621, -86.474538). southernindiana.org/2020/11/02/haunted-history-in-southern-indiana/.

Iowa:

Fairview Cemetery Black Angel Statue (Fairview Cemetery Black Angel Statue Location: 41.267855, -95.848566) onlyinyourstate.com/experiences/iowa/6-ghost-stories-in-ia.

(Mossy Glen State Nature Preserve: 42.706868, -91.427563)

Des Moines Tribune Des Moines, Iowa Thu, May 14, 1936 Page 14 historicmapworks.com/Overlay/?m=485828&c=US&lat=42.726282&lng=-91.427865 iagenweb.org/boards/clayton/documents/index.cgi?read=140971

(Kate Shelley High Bridge Boone, IA 42.059819, -93.969248)

The Des Moines Register Des Moines, Iowa Sat, Sep 8, 2007 Page 9

Pottawattamie County Squirrel Cage Jail (Pottawattamie County Squirrel Cage Jail Location: (41.257809, -95.851908)

onlyinyourstate.com/experiences/iowa/6-ghost-stories-in-ia.

Stony Hollow Road (Stony Hollow Road Location: (40.910902, -91.102009). onlyinyourstate.com/trip-ideas/iowa/stony-hollow-road-haunted-ia desmoinesregister.com/story/life/2016/10/25/these-10-creepy-iowa-ghost-stories-give-you-goosebumps/91465152/.

Van Meter Monster coffeehousewriters.com/iowas-van-meter-monster/ Des Moines Daily news, October 3, 1903.

Villisca Murders (Villisca Murders Location: (40.930871, -94.973338) findagrave.com/memorial/9484402/arthur_boyd_moore desmoinesregister.com/picture-gallery/life/2013/12/06/photos-inside-the-villisca-ax-murder-house/3898221/ docublogger.typepad.com/villiscamystery/history/ murderhouse.com/hauntings/.

Kansas:

Blue Lady (Blue Lady Sentinel Hill 38.863381, -99.343019). Fort Hays State University Archives. The Hays Daily News Sun, Oct 08, 2006 ·Page 23

Hamburger Man (Sand Dunes Location: Sand Dunes State Park 38.116464, -97.857193). Council Grover Republican Dec 12 1984.

Hollenberg Pony Express Station (Hollenberg Pony Express Station Location: 39.901614, -96.846647)

Molly's Hollow Location of Cabin, east of the old park lake dam: 39.543976, -95.114653 The Hollow extends about by the Guerrier Area: 39.540685, -95.111166 to about here: 39.544122, -95.112813 The Atchison Daily Globe Atchison, Kansas Thu, Feb 07, 1974 The Atchison Daily Globe (Atchison, Kansas) · Sat, Feb 8, 1947 · Page 8.

Old Cowtown Museum (Old Cowtown Museum Location: 37.694102, -97.359873). .kmuw.org/the-range/2021-10-29/boo-moo-haunted-attractions-draw-a-big-crowd-for-old-cowtown.

Prairie Spirit Trail Trailhead - Ottawa Trailhead, 1800 S Princeton Cir Dr, Ottawa, KS 66067

Rochester Cemetery Albino Woman (Rochester Cemetery Location: 39.102397, -95.679762). discover.hubpages.com/education/Rochester-Cemetery-More-Than-Just-the-Ghost-of-Albino-Woman.

Saline River Ghost. .jlangholz.com/saline_river_valley_indian_ghost.html.

Sinkhole Sam (Big Sinkhole Location: 38.202833, -97.737725). The Leavenworth Times Thu, Oct 15, 1953 ·Page 2 Seek Sight of Sinkhole Sam.

Theorosa Bridge (109 Street North Bridge) (Theorosa Bridge Location: 37.883157, -97.374091). Council Grove Republican Wed, Dec 12, 1984 ·Page 6 Plains Folk.

(White Woman Creek Scott Township, KS 38.426959, -100.904553)

mythcrafts.com/2018/10/11/white-woman-creek-a-kansas-ghost-story/

Kentucky:

Golden Pond (Golden Pond Location: 36.785556, -88.024167). kentuckynewera.com/article_ae3482ac-b358-539d-92f0-5fc283a9366f.html

Mammoth Cave: Mammoth Cave: Old Guide Cemetery: Trailhead/Small Parking Area: (37.186179, -86.104273)

Pine Mountain (Pine Mountain Spur Location: 36.728292, -83.727407)

Blue Licks Battlefield (Blue Licks Battlefield 40311 38.431982, -83.993116)

Cumberland Falls (Cumberland Falls Road Location: 36.836696, -84.342468)

Pope Lick Monster: (Pop Lick Monster Trestle along the Louisville Loop Bike Trail: 38.191965, -85.487397).

Quackenbush, J. (2019). Monsters, Cryptids, and mysterious wild beasts: West Virginia, Ohio, Maryland and beyond. and where to find them.

Quackenbush, J. (2022). Blue Licks Battlefield (38.431982, -83.993116) Haunted hikes of the Appalachian hills and hollers: Hiking trails with ghost stories, legends, and folktales.

Waverly Hills Sanitorium (Waverly Hills Sanitorium Location: 38.130325, -85.841529).

Louisiana:

(Marie Laveau's Tomb Location: 29.959104, -90.071251)

Ghost stories and folk tales of New Orleans (Ghost stories and haunted tales): Quackenbush, JANNETTE: 9781940087467: Amazon.com: Books. from amazon.com/Ghost-Stories-Folk-Tales-Orleans/dp/1940087465

Bayou Sale Road (Bayou Sale Road Location: 29.329983, -90.687744)

Calcasieu Courthouse (Calcasieu Courthouse Located in Lake Charles: 30.226515, -93.218768)

Marie Laveau Grave in Quackenbush, J. (2024).

Lost children of the Casquette girls: A story of the fille a la cassettes. 21 Crows Dusk to Dawn Publishing.

Loyd Hall Plantation (Loyd Hall Plantation Location: 31.034890, -92.354542) kolotv.com/video/2024/05/29/haunted-history-loyd-hall-plantation/.

Maine:

(Devil's Footprint at North Manchester Meeting House 143 Scribner Hill Rd Manchester, ME 44.357794, -69.861415)

newenglandhistoricalsociety.com/six-strange-rocks-new-england-eubrontes-man-eating-stone-glastonbery/ .

findagrave.com/memorial/248204534/eleanor_butler ancestors.familysearch.org/en/K2YM-7KB/pvt-abner-blaisdell-1753-1810 Works of Abraham Cummings: Immortality Proved by the Testament of Sense digitalmaine.com/cgi/viewcontent.cgi?article=1098&context=books wgme.com/news/local/is-maine-home-to-the-first-documented-haunting-in-the-us americanghostwalks.com/articles/nelly-butler-maine-ghost-story.

Marshall Point Lighthouse (Marshall Point Lighthouse Road Location:43.917984, -69.259972)

wcyy.com/theres-a-haunted-tale-behind-this-road-that-leads-to-a-maine-lighthouse/

Ayers Island (Ayers Island Location: 44.876355, -68.669738) gardinerpubliclibrary.org/the-spooky-side-of-maine-hauntings-urban-legends-from-the-pine-tree-state/

Sabattus onlyinyourstate.com/experiences/maine/urban-legends-me

Hayneville Woods (Hayneville Woods Hwy 2A Military Rd 45.826127, -67.991070)

Goosecreek Bridge (Goosecreek Bridge Location: 44.187477, -69.074029 maineghosthunters.org/2023/11/09/the-pitcherman-haunting-of-goose-river-bridge/

The Bangor Daily News Bangor, Maine · Saturday, July 04, 2009 Maiden Cliff

Elenora French: (Maiden Cliff Location: 44.256463, -69.093406)

The Bangor Daily News Bangor, Maine · Friday, July 23, 1915 Opening of Camden Turnpike Recalls Tragedy

findagrave.com/memorial/30108627/elenora-a-french Old Parish Cemetery (Old Parish Cemetery 23 Lindsay Rd, York, ME 03909 43.143913, -70.652440) The Ancient City of Gorgeana and Modern Town of York (Maine) from Its Earliest Settlement: Also Its Beaches and Summer Resorts (1894) by George Alexander Emery

gardinerpubliclibrary.org/the-spooky-side-of-maine-hauntings-urban-legends-from-the-pine-tree-state/ .

Wood Island (Wood Island Location: 43.457532, -70.332801) Biddeford-Saco Journal Wed, Jun 03, 1896 ·Page 3 (Murder-suicide) Murderer buried. Biddeford-Saco Journal Biddeford, Maine · Tuesday, June 02, 1896.

Maryland:

(Maryland Heights Trailhead: 39.329421, -77.731190).

(Paw Paw Tunnel: 39.544419, -78.460820).

(Stickpile Tunnel Location: 39.592859, -78.429268).

Burnside Bridge (Burnside Bridge: Overlook and Burnside Bridge 39.449957, -77.732583).

Cecil County Pig Woman The Cecil County Pig Woman Bridge: 39.650311, -76.107121 unchartedlancaster.com/2024/01/11/the-legend-of-cecil-countys-pig-woman/#:~:text=This%20tale%20centers%20on%20Cecil,particularly%20favoring%20the%20Eastern%20Shore.

Goldmine Trail (Hike: Goldmine Trail— Loop Location: 38.981935, -77.226427).

Moll Dyer (Moll Dyer Rock Leonardtown, MD 38.288716, -76.634156) (Moll Dyer Road: Leonardtown, MD 20650 38.262246, -76.591992) .somdnews.com/enterprise/community/columns/remembering-the-legend-of-moll-dyer/article_15414c58-08be-5046-8526-bf44cb9e3e67.html.

Pocomoke Forest (Pocomoke Forest 38.161544, -75.544851) chesapeakeghosts.com/haunted-pocomoke-forest-urban-legends/ .

Point Lookout State Park (Point Lookout State Park 38.063814, -76.338499) dnr.maryland.gov/publiclands/pages/southern/pointlookout.aspx .

Quackenbush, J. (2019). Monsters, Cryptids, and mysterious wild beasts: West Virginia, Ohio, Maryland and beyond. and where to find them.

Quackenbush, J. (2022). Haunted hikes of the Appalachian hills and hollers.

Quackenbush, J. (2023). Haunted hikes of the Appalachian hills & hollers 2: Hiking trails with legends, ghost stories, and abandoned places.

Massachusetts:

Fort Warren on Georges Island (Fort Warren on Georges Island Location: 42.320424, -70.927724 bostonghosts.com/bostons-lady-in-black/.

Hoosac Tunnel (Hoosac Tunnel East Portal 42.675463, -72.997865) This is an active train tunnel, do not go inside.

Lizzie Borden (Lizzie Borden House Location: 41.699025, -71.156226) findagrave.com/memorial/115/lizzie-borden Smithsonian Magazine .

Rutland Prison Camp (Rutland Prison Camp Rutland, Massachusetts 42.403184, -72.002304) atlasobscura.com/places/rutland-prison-camp.

Salem Witch Trials: (Proctor's Ledge Memorial Location: 42.517732, -70.909007) Who Was Killed In Salem Witch Trial?. whowhatwhendad.com/wiki/questions/who-was-killed-in-salem-witch-trial/ ghostcitytours.com/salem/haunted-places/proctors-ledge/?srsltid=AfmBOoqcdz-KEFWdFTQ_HxlSLBaMNzcszbY3po43gDzd32z6ZXlUa5NE.

Michigan:

(Findlay Cemetery Ada, MI 49301 43.001036, -85.492027) mysteriousmichigan.com/the-ada-witch-of-findlay-cemetery.

(Old Scio Cemetery: 42.32577, -83.84014) facebook.com/groups/205243586183665/posts/3582075718500418/.

Hell's Bridge: 43.148658, -85.598211 Detroit Free Press Detroit, Michigan • Sun, Apr 29, 2012 Page A14 .

Isle Royale: mikelbclassen.com/starvation-on-isle-royale-the-story-of-angelique-mott/ The Honorable Peter White, a biographical sketch of the Lake Superior iron country / by Ralph D. Williams (catalog.hathitrust.org/Record/003937089).

Michigan Bell Telephone Company building Grand Rapids: (Location:42.965496, -85.667984) The Alma Record July 15, 1909 Domestic Strife Leads to Crime 99wfmk.com/haunted-michigan-bell/ findagrave.com/memorial/194857682/virginia-randall associationofparanormalstudy.com/2020/04/17/the-michigan-bell/.

The Minden City Herald Thu, Oct 29, 2020 · (Pointe aux Barques lighthouse: 44.022776, -82.794921).

Minnie Quay (Forester Township Cemetery: 43.50370, -82.56950) findagrave.com/memorial/13580810/mary_jane-quay Detroit Free Press Detroit, Michigan Sun, Apr 29, 2012 Page A14 .

The Paulding Lights (The Paulding Lights Bruce Crossing 46.349683, -89.178493) The Grand Rapids Press Mar 19, 1978 Page 118 Mysterious Lights.

Minnesota:

(Randall Station about: 45.395324, -95.694422) Star Tribune Minneapolis, Minnesota • Sat, Oct 26, 1872 Page 4 Ghosts Star Tribune (Minneapolis, Minnesota) · Sat, Mar 23, 1872 · Page 4

Another Railroad Accident brombonesbooks.com/2023/08/20/railroad-hauntings-you-can-still-visit-around-a-station-house-in-clontarf-minnesota/.

(Wardens House Museum Location: 45.062328, -92.807797) startribune.com/minnesota-paranormal-group-describes-its-work-and-findings/229406561.

(Washington Avenue Bridge Minneapolis 44.973230, -93.239525) minnpost.com/max-about-town/2011/10/haunted-twin-cities-washington-avenue-bridge/.

Dead Man Trail: (Greenwood Trails Recreation Area Park 48.108231, -96.182323) mspmag.com/arts-and-culture/minnesota-scary-stories-to-tell-in-the-dark/

(Enger Park Tower: 1601 Enger Tower Dr, Duluth, MN 46.776148, -92.125018)

(Arcola Bridge: Access to view bridge along St Croix River shore Arcola Bluffs Day Use Area 11471-11871 Arcola Trail N, Stillwater 45.119359, -92.754529)

alltrails.com/trail/us/wisconsin/arcola-bluffs-trail--2

geocaching.com/geocache/GC47JH9_haunted-st-croix-2-the-arcola-high-bridge

(Milford Mine Milford Mine Memorial Park Crosby, MN 46.534973, -93.970805)

reddit.com/r/TwoSentenceHorror/comments/17iphr2/i_followed_the_tapping_sounds_through_the/

Mississippi:

(Blues Crossroads Location: 34.194966, -90.563898) Rock and Roll Hall of Fame - This source provides comprehensive information about influential musicians and their contributions to music history.

(Natchez City Cemetery 31.575812, -91.393713) newspapers.com/article/natchez-democrat-natchez-drug-company/43634376/ andspeakingofwhich.blogspot.com/2013/10/lost-in-flames-natchez-drug-company.html .

Chapel of the Cross Cemetery, Grave of Henry Vick (Chapel of the Cross Cemetery Location: 32.52249, -90.19138) findagrave.com/memorial/10745766/henry-grey-vick.

City Cemetery (City Cemetery Location: 33.053297, -89.587260) findagrave.com/memorial/10752221/laura-van-kelly.

Devil Worshipper Road (All along the road) (Devil Worshipper Road Waynesboro Shubuta Rd Waynesboro, MS 39367 31.770340, -88.720819) onlyinyourstate.com/experiences/mississippi/devil-worshipper-road-in-ms.

Old Court House Museum (Old Court House Museum Location: 32.352259, -90.878561) yahoo.com/news/old-courthouse-museum-vicksburg-haunted-163148871.html.

Stuckey Bridge (Stuckey Bridge Location:Stucky Bridge Rd Enterprise, 32.255880, -88.854707) Enterprise-Journal McComb, Mississippi Fri, May 27, 2016 Page A03.

Missouri:

(Bone Hill Levasy Location: 39.107392, -94.139593) cyclefish.com/forums/topic/73429/the-legend-of-bone-hill

(Ha Ha Tonka Castle Ruins Location:37.976210, -92.769805) martincitytelegraph.com/2022/06/05/before-it-was-the-lake-of-the-ozarks-it-was-ha-ha-tonka/.

(Ozark Spook Light Location: Hornet Spooklight Southeast 50th Avenue & Stateline Road, Oklahoma 74363 36.944282, -94.618878)

.joplinmo.org/575/The-Spook-Light.

Mark Twain Cave Location: 39.688390, -91.332946 horrorbound.net/blog/mark-twain-cave .

Momo. Retrieved from stateofhorror.com/momo.html

Montana:

(Butte Ghost of Miles Fuller Courthouse and grounds: 155 Granite Street. 46.014747, -112.538834)

Birmingham Post-Herald (Birmingham, Alabama) · Mon, Dec 24, 1906 · Page 4 The Butte Miner (Butte, Montana) · Sun, Oct 17, 1909 · Page 20.

Dorothy Dunn of Bannock: (Mead Hotel: 45.161975, -112.997065)

Dillon Tribune August 9, 1916

(Sister Irene of Virginia City: 46.825365, -113.338669)

southwestmt.com/ghosts/haunted-places/

southwestmt.com/ghosts/ghost-stories/dorothy-dunn/

Edith Allen (Marysville Location: 46.750503, -112.300605)

The Helena Independent including · Page 5 Thursday, December 10, 1896

Haunted Marysville, Montana (Haunted America)
Buttes Cabbage Patch Area The Independent-Record Wed, Dec 08, 1926 ·Page 7
(Little Bighorn Battlefield Location: 45.578519, -107.441697).
Nebraska:
(Brownville Bailey Museum 40.398110, -95.660291)
findagrave.com/memorial/68198167/bensen-mckendree-bailey.
(Seven Sisters Road is a road near Nebraska City, Nebraska. It's also known as Road L on maps. 40.624639, -95.815807)
Omaha World-Herald Omaha, Nebraska · Wednesday, October 25, 2017
Nebraska City News Fri, Dec 10, 1886 findagrave.com/memorial/62561458/john-warden
genealogytrails.com/neb/otoe/maggie_shellenberger.htm
findagrave.com/memorial/109962022/margaret_catherine_shellenberge.
(Witch's Bridge along 9 Bridge Road: 40.804703, -98.368352) Highsmith, Carol M, photographer. This looks like an ordinary one-lane bridge across the Platte River, just south of Grand Island, Nebraska and it is, on one level, but people hereabouts call it the "Witch's Bridge". Hall County Nebraska United States Grand Island, 2021. -12-21. Photograph.
loc.gov/item/2021758114/.
(Ball Cemetery: 41.021011, -96.192682)
nebraskahauntedhouses.com/real-haunt/ball-cemetery.html.
Devil's Canyon: 37.991882, -82.030717).
(Barnard Park Fremont, NE 68025 41.435038, -96.490163) phantasm-paranormal.com/barnard_park.html.
(Haunted Bridge over Blue River: 40.404886, -98.240752)
hastingstribune.com/news/memories-abide-in-ghost-town-by-little-blue/article_79277c3c-2ec1-11e7-9eb1-ab9c7f264342.html
(Spring Ranch Cemetery: 40.40651, -98.24841).
(Niobrara Valley above Long Pine: 42.732775, -99.745087)
The San Francisco Examiner San Francisco, California · Monday, January 23, 1893
(Prospect Hill Omaha, NE 41.278638, -95.960797)
history.nebraska.gov/publications_section/ghost-in-prospect-hill-cemetery/ .
folklore.usc.edu/the-salt-witch/.
Nevada:
(Virginia City/Gold Hill, NV 39.290965, -119.657358)
Gold Hill Daily News Gold Hill, Nevada · Wed, Nov 27, 1872 Page 3
(Tonopah Location: 38.068401, -117.230276)
tonopahnevada.com/old-tonopah-cemetery/
tonopahnevada.com/haunted-tonopah/
News and Record Greensboro, North Carolina Sun, May 10, 1908 Page 11
findagrave.com/memorial/14044119/bridget-verrault.
Historic Goldfield Hotel | Goldfield Nevada Hotel | Haunted.
travelnevada.com/hotels/historic-goldfield-hotel/.
New Hampshire:
(Blair Covered Bridge: 43.810390, -71.665683)
facebook.com/story.php?story_fbid=679333944196106&id=100063585190237&_rdr.
(Nancy's Grave: 44.11275, -71.35457 - The gravesite is at the end of a purple-blazed trail. It is marked by a large pile of stones at the top of a steep enbankment.)
findagrave.com/cemetery/2735893/nancy-barton-burial-site
Haunted Hikes of New Hampshire
outdoors.org/resources/amc-outdoors/history/the-haunting-tale-of-nancy-barton/.
(Stark Road Cemetery: 43.95806, -71.08556)
Ghosts of the White Mountains youtube.com/watch?v=yehslnU9vZs&t=427s .
(Tilton Inn 43.44243080, -71.5883785)
fosters.com/story/news/2007/10/28/restless-spirits-said-to-haunt/52527810007/.
(Willey House, now a park visitor center in its place: 44.182222, -71.399444)
New Hampshire Historical Society
twopeopleoneadventure.com/willey-range-trail
findagrave.com/memorial/231695617/sarah_willey .
Goody Cole Island Path: 42.910436, -70.825427

historicipswich.net/2021/04/15/goody-cole/
gutenberg.org/cache/epub/6615/pg6615.txt
nhtourguide.com/wp/places/hampton/goody-cole-2/.
Mt. Chocorua Liberty Trailhead and Parking, Chocorua Mountain Rd, Albany, NH
(43.917457, -71.293276)
newenglandfolklore.blogspot.com/2014/01/the-curse-of-chocorua-and-its-history.html.
Woods Devil northamericancryptids.com/wood-devils/
New Jersey:
(Baltusrol Golf Club/Old Roll Farm Top of the Summit Road Ridge: 40.692659, -74.352242)
help.18birdies.com/article/502-haunted-tales-from-the-golf-course-and-beyond
The Courier-News Bridgewater, New Jersey · Monday, December 01, 1975 Intrigue Popular
in Mountainside Tales
nytimes.com/2016/07/26/sports/golf/pga-championship-baltusrol-golf-club-new-
jersey.html
(Absecon Lighthouse Location: 39.366594, -74.414214)
rogerkreuz.com/gen/Powhatan.htm#:~:text=On%2016%20April%201854%2C%20the,hu
ge%20waves%20and%20fierce%20winds
(Clinton Road: 41.097314, -74.442028)
 northjersey.com/story/news/passaic/west-milford/2023/10/19/clinton-road-in-west-
milford-named-most-haunted-spot-in-nj/71239816007/.
(Devil Tree: 40.63, -74.5831)
(Gully Road: 40.765378, -74.164863)
losthistory.net/njhm/gullyroad.htm .
(Shades of Death Road: 40.917006, -74.896229) newjerseyhauntedhouses.com/real-
haunt/shades-death-road.html
(St Joseph Roman Catholic Church Pavonia Ave Jersey City, NJ 40.730679, -74.057117)
Courier-Post Camden, New Jersey · Thu, Jul 7, 1921Page 1
New Mexico:
(Billy The Kid's Death Site Tombe de Billy the Kid 34.404129, -104.199594 - located in front
of the fort foundations through a gate)
(Billy The Kid's Grave and Visitor Center 3501 Billy the Kid Road, Fort Sumner, NM
34.403830, -104.193538)
history.com/news/billy-the-kid-death-theories
newmexico.org/things-to-do/arts-culture/historical/billy-the-kid/.
(Ruins of Fort Union, New Mexico 35.907499, -105.011891)
THE DEATH WALTZ .gutenberg.org/cache/epub/6615/pg6615.txt.
The Chamberino Horror Albuquerque Journal Albuquerque, New Mexico · Tuesday, October
30, 1979.
Old New Mexico ghost stories The Albuquerque Tribune Albuquerque, New Mexico Thu, Oct
29, 1959 · Page 11.
Witch of Villagra's Hall Albuquerque Journal Albuquerque, New Mexico Tue, Oct 30, 1979
Page 54.
New York:
(Merchants House Museum: 40.727483, -73.992430)
merchantshouse.org/about/museum-history/.
(Old Fort Niagara: 43.262737, -79.063187) nytimes.com/2018/10/28/nyregion/halloween-
ghost-stories.html.
(Adirondack history center museum: 44.215253, -73.591254) The Post-Star Glens Falls,
New York Sat, Apr 28, 1883 Page 2 Murderers Nemesis .adkhistorycenter.org/exhibits.
(Devil's Elbow Lady in White near Glenmary Drive: 42.085748, -76.321970) Press and Sun-
Bulletin Binghamton, New York Wed, Oct 24, 2018 Page A5.
(Fort Ticonderoga: 43.841870, -73.3875290
ghostlogs.com/orb/fort-ticonderoga/ .
(Lake View Cemetery Pen Yan:42.661362, -77.065844)
.discoverupstateny.com/packages/3389/bishop-gillette-headstone/.
(Split Rock Quarry: 43.024539, -76.242194)
hauntedhistorytrail.com/explore?category=creepy-locations Syracuse Herald-Journal Syracuse,
New York · Monday, August 04, 1980.

(Starr Clark Tin Shop: 43.070542, -77.107873) hauntedhistorytrail.com/explore/starr-clark-tin-shop-and-underground-railroad-museum.

(The Fox Sisters Property 43.070923, -77.107701) hauntedhistorytrail.com/explore/the-fox-sisters-propertyhydesville-memorial-park.

(Widow Susan Road: 42.933703, -74.161459) .findagrave.com/memorial/195745515/susan-degraff .townofamsterdam.org/wp-content/uploads/2019/08/Widow-Susan-Legend.pdf.

Salisbury Manor Press and Sun-Bulletin Binghamton, New York Wed, Oct 24, 2018 Page A5.

North Carolina:

(Brown Mountain 35.903325, -81.907411) —

Warren, Joshua P. Brown Mountain Lights Morganton,

NC A Viewing Guide. Great Guide Offered by Discoverburkecounty.com -

(Haunted Bridge - Lydia's Bridge Jamestown, NC 35.996983, -79.925830) wral.com/story/solved-haunted-legend-of-lydias-bridge-ghostly-hitchhiker-has-roots-in-real-history/19918427/

findagrave.com/memorial/58464999/annie-lydia-jackson

(Grandfather Mountain: 36.11966, -81.79482) –

History of grandfather Mtn. (2022, October 20). grandfather.com/history/

(Roan Mountain/Cloudland Hotel: Roan Mountain, TN 37687 36.10636, -82.11115) - johnsoncitypress.com/living/features/a-stay-and-three-meals-at-the-cloudland-hotel-2-50-please/article_ff7b13c3-2880-51a5-ae46-fa1d00c67784.html

roanmountain.com/area-information/history/

The ghostly choir of roan mountain. (2018, May 12).

mountainlore.net/2018/05/12/the-ghostly-choir-of-roan-mountain/

(Noland Creek Trail: 35.457532, -83.526724) –

Bones Found In Swain May be J.C. Hunter's. Asheville Gazette-News (Asheville, North Carolina) · 10 Nov 1911, Fri · Pg 8. .

Quackenbush, J. (2023). Haunted hikes of the Appalachian hills & hollers 2: Hiking trails with legends, ghost stories, and abandoned places.

North Dakota:

(Fort Abraham Lincoln Park Custer House: 46.759883, -100.847225) National Park Service (NPS): North Dakota State Historical Society (NDSHS):.

(Harvey Public Library: 47.768185, -99.935475) newspapers.com/article/the-bismarck-tribune-front-page-sophia/4637176/ Harvey Man Sent To Prison After Confessing Crime ndtourism.com/articles/north-dakota-ghost-stories#shawna.

(Sim Ghost Town: 46.772746, -101.498837) inforum.com/news/north-dakota/the-real-story-behind-north-dakotas-most-famous-ghost-the-gray-lady-of-sims The Bismarck Tribune. 7 Nov 1927

facebook.com/photo/?fbid=8392815187411560&set=gm.7925797700772720&idorvanity=11 4006071951961.

Pembina Peddler Kills Girl: Leydon:

(White Lady Lane 48.929310, -97.818368)

The Ward County Independent Minot, North Dakota Thu, Nov 10, 1921 Page 1 Riverside Cemetery Fargo: onlyinyourstate.com/experiences/north-dakota/notorious-riverside-cemetery-

Ohio:

(Bloody Bridge: 40.61780, -84.35281)

Quackenbush, Jannette Haunted Ohio Hiking Trails With Ghost Stories ISBN-978-1-940087-60-3 .

(Canal Museum and Towpath Trail Valley View 41.372642, -81.614174).

(Goll Woods: 41.554640, -84.361394) .

(Lake Hope Furnace Location: 39.331907, -82.340194).

(Moonville: 39.308608, -82.324522).

(Old Man's Cave Location: 39.433661, -82.542202) .

Quackenbush, J. (2017). Moonville. Its past. Its ghosts. Its legends. 21 Crows Dusk to Dawn Publishing.

Quackenbush, J. (2017). Haunted Hocking hills.

Quackenbush, Jannette 2024 Moonville Ghost Stories and Haunts Along the Railway 21 Crows Dusk to Dawn Publishing.

Oklahoma:
(Crybaby Bridge: 35.334183, -97.405917).
geocaching.com/geocache/GC3CN5Y.
(Dead Woman Crossing 35.568442, -98.650669)
The Guthrie Daily Leader Guthrie, Oklahoma Tue, Sep 19, 1905 Page 1 The Taloga
Times August 10, 1905 The Mystery is Deepening Oklahoma
Today Magazine Haunted Bridge Living Mystery
wikitree.com/wiki/Dewitt-407
mystorical.blogspot.com/2010/02/search-for-truth-katie-dewitt-james.html.
(Fort Washita Historic Site Durant, OK 34.102652, -96.546993)
The El Reno Daily American El Reno, Oklahoma, Oct 27, 1908 Page 1 Will Watch for Ghost
New-State Tribune Muskogee, Oklahoma · Thu, May 2, 1907 Page 11.
(The Skirvin Hilton Oklahoma City: 35.469745, -97.513762)
sportskeeda.com/basketball/news-the-skirvin-hotel-nba-inside-dark-history.
(Thomas Gilcrease House Museum: 36.174899, -96.021322)
usghostadventures.com/haunted-stories/americas-most-haunted-middle/the-thomas-gilcrease-house-and-its-haunts/.
(Tucker Cemetery Duncan, OK 34.413918, -97.915939)
okcemeteries.net/stephens/tucker/tucker.htm.
Boggy Creek Monster rothline.com/Boggy_Bottom_Bigfoot.html.
Oregon:
(Bandage Man: Highway 101 Cannon Beach 45.887132, -123.958523) Statesman Journal Salem, Oregon Sun, Nov 27, 1983 Page 34.
(Cathedral Park in Portland 45.587397, -122.758699)
findagrave.com/memorial/13089920/thelma-anne-taylor.
(Haceta Head Lighthouse: 44.137360, -124.127897) portlandmonthlymag.com/travel-and-outdoors/tripster/articles/5-most-haunted-destinations-in-oregon-october-2013.
(Holcomb Creek Trestle on Dick Road: 45.597310, -122.898203)
thatoregonlife.com/2015/10/this-old-oregon-train-trestle-on-dick-road-is-said-to-be-haunted/.
(Multnomah County Library - North Portland 45.562558, -122.671516)
portlandghosts.com/the-haunted-north-portland-library/.
(Multnomah Falls Oregon 45.576353, -122.115811)
smithsonianmag.com/photocontest/detail/a-ghost-of-an-native-american-maiden-is-supposed-to-be-seen-in-the-mist-at-/.
(Newport Yaquina Bay Lighthouse 44.626236, -124.062574) The World Coos Bay, Oregon Fri, Oct 31, 1975 Page 16 Fair haired Girl Haunts Lighthouse.
(Sumpter Valley Dredge 44.742670, -118.206038) National Park Service.
Pennsylvania:
(Betty Knox Park: 39.944499, -79.581229).
(Dead Man's Hollow Conservation Area McKeesport, PA 40.314319, -79.846335).
(Fort Mifflin: 39.875402, -75.213143) phillyvoice.com/fort-mifflin-haunted-philadelphia-ghost-faceless-man-william-howe/.
(White Rocks: 39.880736, -77.520871).
Quackenbush, J. (2020). Little book of Gettysburg ghosts.
Quackenbush, J. Pennsylvania Ghosts and Haunts: West Pennsylvania. 21 Crows Dusk to
(Wopsy Rd Dysart, PA 40.557122, -78.455082)
jaredfrederick.blogspot.com/2016/10/the-white-lady-of-wopsy.html
Rhode Island:
(Crescent Park Carousel 41.757306, -71.359680).
(Nathanael Greene Homestead Coventry Rhode Island 41.694328, -71.543645)
rimonthly.com/haunted-places-rhode-island/.
(Nine Mens Misery Monument Cumberland, RI 41.940016, -71.406668)
rimonthly.com/haunted-places-rhode-island/
bucklinsociety.net/bucklin-family-history/william-bucklin/nine-mens-misery/
(Old Arnold Estate Conjuring House: 42.009177, -71.709251)
The Black Book of Burrillville frightfind.com/true-story-conjuring-house
(Ramtail Factor Ruins: Hopkins Property - Foster Land Trust 11-45 Rams Tail Rd Foster, RI 41.820140, -71.703898) at intersection of Old Danielson Pike and Ram Tail Road)

preservation.ri.gov/sites/g/files/xkgbur406/files/pdfs_zips_downloads/national_pdfs/fost
er/fost_hopkins-mill_hd.pdf
(Peleg Burial in Potters Lot: 41.82519, -71.70774)
familysearch.org/ark:/61903/1:1:QK9L-JDDF
newenglandfolklore.blogspot.com/2015/04/the-ghost-of-ram-tail-mill.html.
(Rose Island Newport 41.496641, -71.340629)
newportlifemagazine.com/featured/rose-island-is-rich-in-history-preservation-and-a-new-
generation-of-community/
fun107.com/newport-haunted-lighthouse-rose-island/.
(Whitman Rental and Garden: 41.831111, -71.409194)
edgarallanpoeri.com/home-of-sarah-helen-whitman/ Rhode Island Historical Society
Providence Preservation Society.
Mercy Lena Brown (Mercy Lena Brown Headstone 467 Ten Rod Rd, Exeter 41.581532, -
71.558353)
Providence Journal, March 19, 1892, Exhumed the Bodies
findagrave.com/memorial/6628164/mercy_lena-brown
rimonthly.com/haunted-places-rhode-island/.
South Carolina:
(Alice Flagg Grave: All Saints Episcopal Church Cemetery 33.467692, -79.140131)
Anderson Independent-Mail Anderson, South Carolina · May 22, 2011
findagrave.com/memorial/7421/alice-flagg.
(Becky Cotton Death Place Edgefield Courthouse Square:33.789487, -81.929645)
wjbf.com/news/hometown-history-bloody-edgefield/
historicedgefield.com/walking-tour-of-downtown The Bamberg herald. [volume],
September 28, 1916 Beautiful Betty Cotton.
(Fannie's Ghost Springwood Cemetery 34.855437, -82.394714)
findagrave.com/memorial/9353430/fannie-heldman .
(Oakwood Cemetery 184 Oakwood Ave, Spartanburg 34.958547, -81.914812).
(Old City Jail: 32.778767, -79.937262)
abcnews4.com/news/local/creepy-carolina-the-legend-of-lavinia-fisher-and-the-old-
charleston-jail-sc-paranormal-investigation-first-female-serial-killer-bulldog-tours-six-mile-
wayfarers-house-wciv.
(Slade Lake Edgefield, SC 33.779166, -81.912258)
exploreedgefield.com/murders-and-mayhem/becky-cotton-the-devil-in-petticoats
(Patriots Point Naval and Maritime Museum 32.790531, -79.908585)
patriotspoint.org/ .
(Pawleys Island:33.433049, -79.122087)
gardenandgun.com/articles/who-is-the-gray-man-get-to-know-hurricane-seasons-
friendliest-ghost/.
South Dakota:
(Deadwood Calamity Jane: Mount Moriah Cemetery Deadwood 44.375330, -103.723898)
theradiovagabond.com/261-south-dakota/
blackhillshikingbikingandmore.com/mount-moriah-cemetary
theradiovagabond.com/261-south-dakota/.
(Hooky Jack in Rapid City 44.081815, -103.230174)
Lead Daily Call Lead, South Dakota Mon, Nov 8, 1926 Page 1
Rapid City Journal Rapid City, South Dakota March 16, 1986
findagrave.com/memorial/31301234/john_henry-leary.
(Pactola Lake West Pennington 44.071076, -103.492635)
hauntedrooms.com/south-dakota/haunted-places.
(Spirit Mound 42.884858, -96.961411)
nps.gov/lecl/learn/historyculture/spirit-mound.htm.
(Walking Sam Pine Ridge Reservation 43.267647, -102.718732)
puzzleboxhorror.com/walking-sam-urban-legend/.
Taku-he northamericancryptids.com/taku-he/.
Tennessee:
Pink Lizzy. The Manitowoc tribune. [volume], March 30, 1871, Image 2 An Exciting Story
Brinkley Female College Haunted .

(Bell Witch 36.590091, -87.056695)
"A Bell Witch". Hopkinsville Kentuckian. July 3, 1894. p. 2
(Jakes Creek Trail 35.651897, -83.581144)
(Grist Mill Big Ridge Park Road Maynardville, TN 37807 36.245895, -83.922365)
(Ghost House Big Ridge Park Road Maynardville, TN 36.253959, -83.924229)
(Roaring Fork near Gatlinburg: 35.694280, -83.466592)
Texas:
(Corpus Christi Naval Museum USS Lexington: 27.815244, -97.388735).
(Eula Phillips Oakwood Cemetery Section 1, old grounds 30.27665, -97.72653)
servantgirlmurders.com/about-the-victims/
findagrave.com/memorial/7309443/eula-phillips
The Odessa American (Odessa, Texas) · Wed, Oct 30, 2024 · Page 4 Whispers in Texas Wind.
(Ghost Rd Scenic Drive Saratoga, TX 30.360746, -94.552441).
Hardin County Parks Department.
(Goatman Bridge (Old Alton Bridge) 33.129315, -97.104150)
dentoncountyhistoryandculture.wordpress.com/2017/10/27/
a-historic-haunt-old-alton-bridge/
findagrave.com/cemetery/900448/old-alton-cemetery .
(Lindsey Hollow Rd Waco, TX 31.574053, -97.151590)
hmdb.org/m.asp?m=203602
wacoghosts.com/texas-ghost-stories?lightbox=dataItem-igvjh4fp.
(Lost Cemetery of Infants, Berachah Cemetery 32.728992, -97.117151)
ghosttexas.com/berachah-cemetery-hauntings-infants-spirits-linger/
tuisnider.com/arlington-lost-cemetery-of-infants-a-surprisingly-cheery-tale/.
(Parking Zone Marfa Lights Viewing Area Marfa, TX 30.275539, -103.882852)
frankbures.com/2020/10/21/the-marfa-mystery-lights/
(Trinity Episcopal Cemetery 29.29365, -94.81173)
findagrave.com/memorial/33377220/willie_alberti
The Rocky Mountain News (Daily), Volume 35, Number 340, December 6, 1894.
Headless Horseman Ripley's Believe It or Not!
Utah:
(Clarkston: 41.922975, -112.049610) The Herald-Journal (Logan, Utah) · Fri, Oct 29, 1976 ·
(Mercur Cedar Valley Utah 40.321331, -112.211997).
(Old Main Southern Utah University 37.676181, -113.068534)
The Thunderbird Cedar City, Utah Tue, Oct 28, 1986 Page 7.
(Phantom Train: Golden Pike National Historical Park: 41.617440, -112.551506).
A Utah Ghost Story Morning appeal. [volume], October 05, 1884, Image 3.
Vermont:
(Black Agnes Green Mt Cemetery, Montpelier, VT 44.257943, -72.596637)
vermonthistory.org/journal/68/vt681_203.pdf
vermonter.com/ghosts-and-legends-black-agnes/.
(Emily's Bridge 44.440402, -72.679870)
stowehistoricalsociety.org/.
(Glastenbury Bennington Triangle: 42.9780894,-73.1158165)
Rutland Daily Herald Rutland, Vermont October 27, 1996
happyvermont.com/2014/10/23/glastenbury-ghost-town/
Vermont Phoenix Brattleboro, Vermont Fri, Dec 22, 1893 Page 2
Bennington Banner Bennington, Vermont Fri, Jul 28, 2000 Page 16
neara.org/pages/Glastenbury%20Mountain%20Cairn%20Site.html.
(Grave of Timothy Clark Smith 44.11610, -73.16000)
findagrave.com/memorial/19739131/timothy_clark-smith
vermonter.com/scary-locations-vermont/.
(Hartford Train Disaster: 43.681667, -72.393889)
vermonthistory.org/journal/81/VHS8101TheWrongRail.pdf
obscurevermont.com/fire-and-ice-the-hartford-railroad-disaster/
hmdb.org/m.asp?m=64891.
(Lakeside Railway Crossing Burlington Vermont Ghost of Marie Blais 44.461243, -
73.218759)

Burlington Daily News.
(Shelburne Museum Shelburne, VT 44.377321, -73.230186).
Virginia:
(Edgewood Plantation Charles City, VA 37.330510, -77.186626)
timscullion.wordpress.com/2018/07/25/blog-4-going-behind-the-paranormal-television-shows-edgewood-plantation-in-charles-city-county-virginia/
hauntedhouses.com/virginia/edgewood-plantation-bed-and-breakfast/.
(Peyton Randolph House 37.272463, -76.699688)
hauntedhouses.com/virginia/the-peyton-randolph-house/.
(Three Sisters Stones: 38.9039, -77.0806).
Gap Cave at Daniel Boone Visitor Center Along Old Wilderness Trail Ewing, Virginia
(36.601725, -83.660273).
Quackenbush, J. (2022). (Ottie Powell Bluff Mountain Appalachian National Scenic Trail
37.660277, -79.346345)
Haunted hikes of the Appalachian hills and hollers: Hiking trails with ghost stories, legends,
and folktales.
Quackenbush, J. (2023). Haunted hikes of the Appalachian hills & hollers 2: Hiking trails
with legends, ghost stories, and abandoned places
(Hike to Killing Rock—Pound Gap Massacre Site 37.149994, -82.625720).
Washington:
(Billy Gohl Grays Harbor WishKah River Washington 46.975526, -123.810987)
graysharbortalk.com/2016/10/13/5-haunted-hikes-grays-harbor/
The Tacoma Daily Ledger Tacoma, Washington Fri, Feb 4, 1910 Page 1
.thedailyworld.com/news/theres-more-to-the-bill-gohl-story-than-you-know/.
(Crescent Lake Washington 48.093198, -123.802112)
graysharbortalk.com/2016/10/13/5-haunted-hikes-grays-harbor/5/
The Seattle Star Seattle, Washington Wed, Oct 29, 1941 Page 3
Peninsula Daily News Port Angeles, Washington · Wednesday, June 13, 1990
findagrave.com/memorial/20841050/hallie_brooks-illingworth.
(Monte Cristo Monte Cristo Trail, Washington 47.985891, -121.393613 Trailhead:
45.926555, -121.582606)
(Northern State Hospital/Northern State Recreation Area Sedro-Woolley 48.528486, -
122.194754)
seattleterrors.com/top-10-most-haunted-places-in-washington/
(Thousand Steps Haunted Staircase, Greenwood Cemetery Spokane 47.661652, -
117.468040)
spokanehistorical.org/items/show/77.
West Virginia:
(Bloody Hands: Hedgesville, WV 39.544122, -77.905896 to 39.556903, -77.990288)
(Henry Young Grave: Gravesite: Young Cemetery Birch River, WV 38.44765, -80.79120)
(Mothman view of bridge Point Pleasant Point Pleasant, WV 38.842969, -82.139680)
Quackenbush, Jannette Monsters cryptids and mysterious wild beasts.
(Silver Run Tunnel: 39.20768, -81.19665).
(Vinegar Hill Vinegar Hill Road Fairmont, WV 39.424814, -80.162839).
Quackenbush, J. (2017). West Virginia ghost stories, legends, and haunts II.
Wisconsin:
(Elephant Trunk Rock WI-58 Trunk Richland Center, WI 43.365428, -90.265775)
richlandcenterwi.gov/sites/default/files/fileattachments/tourism/page/2886/elephant_tr
unk_rock.pdf.
Wisconsin:
(Bloody Bridge Bridge WI-66 Stevens Point, WI 44.576234, -89.501271)
dangerousroads.org/north-america/usa/11974-bloody-bride-bridge-is-one-of-the-most-haunted-places-in-wisconsin.html.
(Elephant Trunk Rock WI-58 Trunk Richland Center, WI 43.365428, -90.265775)
richlandcenterwi.gov/sites/default/files/fileattachments/tourism/page/2886/elephant_trunk_
rock.pdf.
(Fort Howard Hospital and Heritage Hill State Historical Park 44.474195, -88.033256)
heritagehillgb.org/discover/fort-howard nbc26.com/allouez/one-of-brown-countys-first-

murders-spurs-ghost-stories-nearly-200-years-later.

(Graceland Cemetery Mineral Point 42.85750, -90.19440) wisconsinology.com/the-weird/the-mineral-point-vampire.

(Mary Worth Oak Grove Cemetery Whitewater Wisconsin 42.834816, -88.723229) wisconsinfrights.com/whitewater-legends/.

(Ridgeway Ghost: Dodgeville 42.965665, -90.103987 to Blue Mounds 43.009772, -89.843142)

Wisconsin State Journal Madison, Wisconsin · Friday, October 13, 2006

content.wisconsinhistory.org/digital/collection/tp/id/39038

content.wisconsinhistory.org/digital/collection/tp/id/39057

timesmachine.nytimes.com/timesmachine/1902/12/07/117984825.pdf.

(Summerwind. Private. Helen Creek Land O' Lakes, WI 46.198543, -89.420663)

wisconsinfrights.com/most-famous-ghosts/

Life Magazine: Terrifying Tales of Nine Haunted Houses.

Wyoming:

(Fort Laramie 42.206250, -104.559669)

(Winton Wyoming 41.760567, -109.167320)

travelwyoming.com/article/haunted-places-to-visit-in-wyoming/

(South Pass: 42.474821, -108.801677)

findagrave.com/memorial/262527573/polly-bartlett

buckrail.com/wp-content/uploads/2017/12/PollyBartlettWyomingsAmazingPoisoner.pdf

(Thornburgh Gravesite US, Interstate-80, Fort Bridger, WY 41.318994, -110.390611)

hmdb.org/m.asp?m=90637. (n.d.).

Munn, D. D. (2023). Wyoming ghost stories. Rowman & Littlefield.

www.ingramcontent.com/pod-product-compliance
Lightning Source LLC
Chambersburg PA
CBHW051935020726
47501CB00001B/135